DEATH IN BLACK AND WHITE

FR. MICHAEL BRISSON, L.C.

Death in Black and White

A Novel

IGNATIUS PRESS   SAN FRANCISCO

The characters and events in this book are fictional, and any resemblance to actual persons or events is coincidental.

Original cover art montage and design
by Paweł Cetlinski
Using © Adobe Images

© 2024 by Ignatius Press, San Francisco
All rights reserved
ISBN 978-1-62164-680-8 (PB)
ISBN 978-1-64229-297-8 (eBook)
Library of Congress Control Number 2023945033
Printed in the United States of America ∞

To priests, especially those who are broken,
disheartened, or wondering whether
what they do even matters

CONTENTS

Part I: The Usual Suspects

1 Dominic   11

2 Andrew   22

3 Allison   32

4 Numbers   50

5 Maria   66

6 Lupita   77

7 Ashley   91

8 Sal   108

9 Connie   119

Part II: Suburban Noir

10 The Third Man   143

11 Shadow of a Doubt   151

12 I Confess   163

13 Rear Window   174

14 The Man Who Knew Too Much   180

15 Strangers on a Train   188

16 The Wrong Man   195

17 Trouble along the Way   210

18 The Harder They Fall   219

Part III: Femme Fatale

19 Sentimental Journey   233

20 Beyond the Sea   243

21 Bewitched, Bothered, and Bewildered   251

22 The Girl from Ipanema   264

23 Stormy Weather   276

24 House of the Rising Sun   297

25 Can't We Be Friends?   307

26 Fifty Ways to Leave Your Lover   317

27 With a Little Help from My Friends   332

28 Sinnerman   341

29 As Time Goes By   355

Acknowledgments   365

Part I

The Usual Suspects

Dominic

Sometimes I feel as if I'm in a black-and-white movie, a film noir to be exact. I keep waiting for Humphrey Bogart to step out of some dark corner and ask me to light his cigarette. But in the beginning, when I had been at St. Dominic's only six months, there was nothing noir about it. Life played in full Technicolor vibrancy, a feel-good film fit for the Hallmark Channel.

I still remember the first time I made it back to the rectory without using GPS. I was proud of myself. I had relied on it for months, but that morning I took a chance. I had been visiting my parish's homebound, one each day. Tuesday it was Mrs. Esposito, a sixty-nine-year-old paraplegic who spent most of her time knitting mittens and scarves for her daughter's Etsy shop. Wednesday was Mrs. O'Brien, a spry-minded, feeble-bodied eighty-six-year-old who had lost her husband three years back. Early in their marriage her husband had been diagnosed with paranoid schizophrenia.

"It was hard," she said. "I'd go shopping, and I'd tell him to wait for me in the car. But he couldn't just sit there, you know. He would think people were in the other cars, watching him. So I'd come back, and I'd think he was gone. I'd think, *Now I've done it. I've lost him, and who knows what he's gonna do.* But he wasn't gone. He'd just be all scrunched up in the back seat."

They had been married sixty-two years and had four kids. All Mrs. O'Brien wanted from me, her parish priest, was to reminisce with her about the good ol' days. And for her, they were all good days.

I never saw Mrs. Esposito again. She ended up moving to North Carolina to live with her daughter. And Mrs. O'Brien—well, we'll get to her.

As I pulled up Ash Avenue—the side street where the rectory's detached garage sat—it was as if I were slipping on a favorite pair of old jeans; the stiff newness had worn into a snug comfort.

I left the car on the street and stepped into the crisp March air. A deep inhale: the foretaste of spring tickled the bottoms of my lungs. The cloudless sky was a Caribbean blue; glints of sunlight shot off car windows; streams of runoff from dirt-encrusted snowbanks trickled down the street. *I'm home*, I thought. *This is my parish now. This is my place. Where I belong.*

Despite its affluent Westchester County zip code, St. Dominic's was not a wealthy parish. It wasn't poor, but it wasn't wealthy. It also wasn't very large. Average Sunday Mass attendance hovered around seven hundred people spread across three Masses. It used to be bigger. It also used to have a school, which had closed a good decade or so before I arrived. Now the building was used for sundry adult educational efforts: English-as-a-second-language classes, how-to-do-your-taxes-without-an-accountant classes, teach-me-to-paint-like-Bob-Ross classes. It was used for religious education too—Bible studies, Sunday school, and the like, a requisite to keep people's donations out of Uncle Sam's pocket.

Historically it was an Irish parish, though few true Irishmen still inhabited the neighborhood. The Italians had their own church, St. Philomena, six blocks away. That church closed a couple of years before I arrived. So technically, the parish name was St. Dominic–St. Philomena, but everyone still called it St. Dom's.

This was my third assignment, and my first as pastor. Before, I was the help; now I was the boss. It's what every priest wants to be—in charge; that is, every priest except me. I liked not being in charge. In my second assignment I had been associate pastor at St. Rocco's in the Bronx, a large parish with a school. I got to do the glamorous stuff: run to the hospital to minister to a dying patient, be the youth *padre*, prepare couples for marriage, and so on. I didn't have to sit in an office and count beans, worry about the leaky pipes, or arbitrate a standoff between the school's kitchen and janitorial staffs. And even better, I didn't have to deal with the schoolkids' parents.

Generally, if parents have an issue, they deal either with one of the teachers or with the principal. But sometimes they want to escalate the issue to the pastor. Once, in my first assignment, at St. Clement's, the principal expelled a kid after he had broken into the teachers' lounge and urinated in the coffeepot (and this wasn't his first infraction). The parents demanded to meet with the pastor.

Doomsday came—the meeting was scheduled for high noon, if I recall correctly—and the parents arrived wearing T-shirts displaying a portrait of their cherubic little devil surrounded by the words "We Stand with Stevie". I was helpless to support the pastor much beyond entertaining a few aunts and uncles who made up the entourage.

Despite chaotic episodes like that one, I missed having a school. It was sad for me to go from St. Rocco's, a bustling Latino parish with a grammar school of five hundred students, thirty-three different ministries (one for each country in Latin America), and a huge annual festival that was *the* summertime attraction, to St. Dominic's, whose only claim to societal relevance was that the rectory (not the church, mind you) had made the National Register of Historic Places. At St. Rocco's we were an essential part of the neighborhood, the center of everything. The pastor was king and his vicars were princes, doling out blessings and benevolence to every passerby. St. Dominic's, nestled in the middle-class New York bedroom community of East Springdale, was one more storefront on Main Street—a quaint relic that, to the patrons looking out the Starbucks window, seemed to fit in well with the 1950s hardware store and the 1960s diner. The priest, the hardware store clerk, and the barista were all members of the same class of service personnel. *Thank you for all you do. Keep the change.*

No, this sleepy little parish was no St. Rocco's. But it was mine. All mine.

After I left Mrs. O'Brien, I came back to my castle on Main Street. My staff would be expecting me.

The offices were on the first floor of the rectory—a large Second Empire Victorian across the parking lot from the church building. The upper floors were reserved for the priests' quarters.

Every time I stepped into the main office, it was as if I were walking onto the set of a nineties sitcom. The cast of characters on the St. Dom Show could compete in complexity and quirkiness with anyone on *Friends* or *Cheers*. Whenever I flung open the rectory door and crossed the threshold, however, no friendly *Norm!* would ring out; rather, I'd get a pointed *"Father Hart!"* from Rita, the sassy parish secretary. (Her sass, though, was always undermined by her inadequate use of metaphors—some mixed: *"C'mon, Father, this isn't rocket surgery"*; some hitched together: *"There's light at the end of the tunnel just around the corner."*)

"Whatcha got for me, Rita?" I'd say. Her retort was always the same: a list of my undone to-dos shot at me one by one

like darts, then a dive into fresh gripes about Jerry, the som-
nolent maintenance guy, or Gretchen the despotic sacristan
(who's also the organist, the cantor, the wedding coordi-
nator, and the bereavement committee chairperson). Rita
was fair, though. She would split her complaints between
the two evenly and never slam them both at the same time.
And Rita wouldn't touch Maria, the housekeeper, for
Maria was a saint.

Santa Maria started her day at Mass and ended it on her
knees in the Marian chapel, rosary in one hand and prayer
book in the other with yellowed holy cards slipping out
from between its worn pages. Puerto Rican by origin, she
looked like a plump version of Rita Moreno, and when
she hugged you—she was a hugger—she felt like one of
those giant teddy bears you get at the carnival for popping
out all ten beer bottles. She was grandmother to the world,
confidant to all, a shoulder to cry on. To Maria you could
talk as if to a cup of hot cocoa, if cups of hot cocoa had
ears; she was warm and sweet, and no matter how harsh
the subject, she'd respond in her broken English, "*No you
worry. Everything gonna work out good.*"

Every whisper of parish gossip found its way to her ear,
yet she never had a disparaging word to say about anyone. Even when scandal hit—such as when an associate
priest, who was already a little off, got drunk one night and
thought it'd be fun to roam the neighborhood dressed like
Adam before the fall singing "Wild Rover" at the top of
his lungs—Santa Maria just said, "That Padre Finney, he
always was a free spirit."

🕊 🕊 🕊

One last character rounded out the playbill, our very own
Archie Bunker: Monsignor John S. Leahy, the pastor
emeritus. "We just call him Monsignor," Rita told me. I

called him Jack. Priests generally don't call each other by their titles in private unless they mean business, kind of like when Mom got upset and called out my full Christian name: "*Christopher Francis Hart, get over here!*"

At eighty years old Monsignor, a.k.a. Jack, had been forced to retire, despite his sharp mind and decent health. Ordinarily a retired pastor will move to another rectory, live on his own, or move into assisted living. Not Monsignor. He had been pastor for thirty-five years, this was his parish, and he was going to die with his boots on, right here, and that was that.

Monsignor was plump—the kind of plump where neck and head meld into one. Pictures I saw of him in his younger days—that is, when he was in his early sixties—reminded me of Winston Churchill, complete with cigar and brandy. At eighty he reminded me more of an old bulldog.

As for our relationship, I'd like to say he treated me the way old Father Fitzgibbon treated Father O'Malley in *Going My Way*: suspicious at first, but then warm and paternal after that. But that wasn't quite the case. Civility abounded for sure. "*Good morning, Reverend Pastor,*" he'd say, bowing his head at *pastor*. "*Are the eggs cooked the way you like them, Reverend Pastor? May I do anything for you today, Reverend Pastor? Shine your shoes for you, Reverend Pastor?*" Then he'd chuckle to himself, stick his nicotine-stained fingers into his shirt pocket for a pack of cigarettes, and remember he had quit smoking. The Reverend Pastor bit was mildly amusing the first two hundred times he did it; the next couple hundred felt excessive.

Eventually Monsignor accepted reality; the time had come to hand over the keys of the kingdom, literally. He handed me an enormous ring with thirty or forty keys. I suspected, however, that he had held on to two or three figurative keys, keeping some "doors" accessible only to him. It was a feeling, a suspicion, an inkling, but hard evidence was elusive.

He insisted, for example, on taking all after-hours calls. To be fair, he didn't have a cell phone or a private line; maybe that was the only way to keep people out of his personal life. He's allowed to have a personal life, isn't he? Another incident: he came back late one night, exiting from the rear door of a shiny black SUV. He claimed it was a sick call and the hospital sent a car for him since it was late. Why shouldn't I believe him? And when he saw me pick up a white envelope from beneath the mail slot, with his name handwritten and misspelled—Father Layhee—and barked, "That's mine," should I have wondered why he was so sensitive? If he wasn't eighty years old, I would think he was having an affair or running drugs. Stranger things have happened, but I was pretty sure in his case it wasn't a woman. And drugs, really?

I tried broaching the topic once. I prepared. I planned out what I would say. Present him with the facts, ask him point-blank, *Tell me, what's really going on with you?* He would then explain everything, the mystery would be solved, and those two or three keys he had held on to would be back on my keychain. It didn't shape up that way.

He sat in front of me, a lump of gray, his sunken, expressionless eyes and stern lips rendering his face illegible. "So, Jack," I began. "I imagine it's been difficult adjusting to your new situation." I smiled. He didn't. "I wanted to ask you about a few things. I'm sure there's an explanation." I detailed my observations, waiting for him to come out with it.

"You know I was ordained in 1962? How old were you then, Father?" he asked, employing my title. *Not good.*

"I wasn't born yet. I think you know that."

"Oh, that's right. How old are you, by the way?"

"Thirty-eight."

"So you were just three years old when I became pastor here. Hmm. Let me ask you, did you notice Bea Dunne this morning?"

"Who?"

"Bea Dunne. She shows up five minutes to six every morning, waiting for someone to open the church."

"No, I didn't see her."

"Right, I didn't think so. She waited a long time."

"Oh, okay, yeah. I remember. There were a few people waiting when I opened up. Jerry overslept. He's supposed to unlock the doors in the morning."

"Right. And I noticed you got new hymnals."

"Well, Gretchen got those."

"She did, did she? Was that in the budget?"

"I'm not sure, honestly. But I mean, she had a point. The old ones were ratty and needed to be replaced."

"Did you notice the kind of hymnals she got?"

"Didn't really pay attention."

"Didn't pay attention. Reverend Pastor didn't pay attention. Uh-huh. And that plumber you had over here. He screwed up, didn't he?"

"Yeah, what's your point?"

"Are we getting reimbursed?"

"They're sending another guy out to fix it."

"Oh, and that's it? Our people are freezing to death, and you're content with 'We'll send another guy out to fix it'? Now, these are little things, Reverend Pastor. But they become big things. Jerry oversleeps and you say, 'Oh well, better not do that again'; meanwhile, poor Bea Dunne is shivering out in the cold. Soon Jerry's taking naps in the broom closet while neighborhood junkies are stealing chalices to pay for their next hit. Gretchen goes and spends fifteen hundred dollars on a bunch of German hymnals no one can sing along to and ends up spending ten grand to hire some Austrian boys' choir to sing at Christmas because 'We need music, and the parishioners aren't good singers.'

"I haven't even started with the big stuff. You heard the police chief's got it in his head to start cracking down on the homeless sleeping behind the Columbus Avenue shopping center? Where are they going to go? Are you going to do something about that, Reverend Pastor? And when was the last time you checked in on Rick Brady? You know his daughter, his only daughter, the one he was left with when his wife died of cancer? She's in the hospital recovering from an attempted suicide. You call him recently? Go visit the kid?"

That pretty much sums up my intervention with Monsignor. The moment I said "thirty-eight", I knew I had lost any high ground in the conversation. I didn't even put up a fight. I just waited for the lecture to come.

※ ※ ※

Thirty-eight. The age when most men either are coming into their stride—finally independent, feeling competent in their profession, the major hurdles of life overcome, world conquest firmly undertaken—or are teetering on the edge of midlife crisis—rethinking their career path, wondering whether they married the wrong woman, staying later and later at work, reengaging in pastimes once forsaken. Thirty-eight. Only two years away from the point of no return, when all sales are final. Or so it seems to the thirty-eight-year-old.

Before my conversation with Monsignor, I had felt solidly a member of the first group: the kind of thirty-eight-year-old that feels confident, the follies and naïveté of his first years of priesthood out of the way; seasoned and smart but still young and dynamic. Monsignor put me in my place, at least for a time.

I tried to shake it off, pull myself together. True, I never wanted to be pastor. *But now that I am, I will accept my mission*, I thought. *I'm not here just to keep cranking the gears on this machine. My life is not about getting the right hymnals or making sure the doors open on time.* No, I had big plans. I was going to make this parish grow, inject new life into the place.

⚜ ⚜ ⚜

"Imagine," I said to Rita, standing next to her, sweeping my hand toward the empty parking lot, "a huge parish festival the likes of which Westchester County has never seen." She looked at the melting snowbank, the water glistening on the cracked asphalt, and then back at me. "The weekend of August 8, feast of Saint Dominic, that's when we'll do it. People will flock from all five boroughs for the rides, the music, the food—and the devotions, can't forget the devotions. A big procession maybe. It'll boost people's faith, and our bottom line too." Wide-eyed and smiling, rubbing my fingers together as if I had the bottom line in my hand, I gave her an expectant look. She shrugged and reminded me the checks she had piled on my desk two days before were still there, unsigned.

Everyone on staff had pretty much the same reaction to my candied-apple dreams, especially Monsignor. "Sure, kid. When you wake up, I've got a new jacket for ya. It's got really long sleeves. Matches the padded walls I'm installing in your room."

That's why I needed to enlist someone who could help me bring this dream to life, someone who would share the dream. I needed a friend, a priest who could fight by my side. Yes, I had Monsignor, but I couldn't count on him. If he was really going to die with his boots on, he'd have to go before lunch, because the rest of the day he wore slippers.

The announcement to the staff that I would be requesting an associate was met with groans and excuses: we can't afford it, we're not big enough, the archdiocese will never assign another priest here. But I had a plan, and that plan required that I go to Rome.

2

Andrew

It was billed as a pilgrimage to the tomb of Saint Peter, and it had come to me in a dream—well, it had come as I woke from a dream. Working late one night trying to reconcile discrepancies in the parish finances, I'd fallen asleep at my desk. Somewhere around midnight, chin buried in chest, shoulders slumped forward, I cracked open my eyes and saw a bulbous saliva bead dangling from a strand of drool, a fractional second away from splashing down on the financials. I snatched the spreadsheets out of the way just before it detached. With the jerk, the drop flew up and over my desk lamp, landing on a stack of unopened correspondence in an in-basket. The principal casualty: a postcard depicting St. Peter's Basilica at night, with its warm glowing lights recessed in alcoves adorning the facade, its illuminated saint statues standing vigil above the colonnade, and its needly cupola now magnified by a bubble of spittle.

The sender was Andrew Reese, the Reverend Andrew Reese, a classmate from seminary, a companion in my first assignment at St. Clement's, and a dear friend. He was a doctoral candidate studying in Rome. He'd been there five years, and according to his sister Trish, it was high time he got his rear end back here.

Two thoughts came to mind: one, a pilgrimage to Rome would create a buzz, spark enthusiasm, and light a fire under complacent parishioners; two, it would give me an excuse to see Andrew and convince him to spend the next semester—and hopefully the next several years—in my parish.

Besides being my friend, Andrew had a gift for preaching that was unmatched. That's what I needed him for more than anything. At St. Clement's, people in the local diner or the neighborhood barber shop would be talking about his Sunday sermons well into the week. The parish saw a 20 percent increase in attendance during his first year, when he was still wet behind the ears. I could only imagine what he'd be like now that he had honed his skills.

Insecure priests don't like having him around because he steals their show. I'll admit, I used to get a little jealous now and again too. Parishioners would call the rectory: "*Excuse me, who's celebrating the ten thirty this Sunday?*" When I'd respond, "*I am*," I would inevitably hear a disappointed "*Oh*," followed by "*What Mass is Father Reese celebrating?*" He's not. He's away. Forever, I'd think, and then tell them the time.

I needed Andrew to come to the parish, but I knew I had to make it a sweet deal. He was settled in Rome. He liked it there. It was just his kind of scene: luncheons with cardinals on rooftop verandas overlooking the cityscape; lofty academics philosophizing over a plate of gnocchi while sipping Chianti, then strolling through antique shops near Piazza Navona haggling with vendors in his fluent Italian; and shopping for gifts for wealthy friends on the Via dei Condotti. And, yes, spending time in the many exquisite churches that pepper the old part of the city like pointy jewel boxes waiting to reveal their priceless contents—he was a priest, after all. But this last activity, praying in churches, was a less frequent occupation than it should have been. If I search my heart, I suppose that was the chief reason I wanted to bring him to my parish. I worried about him. I feared the bourgeois lifestyle in Rome had snuffed out so many positive qualities he had exhibited in his seminary days and in his first assignment. Qualities that balanced out what some consider grievous flaws. Qualities I now hoped to reignite.

❧ ❧ ❧

Why do I feel so disgusting? Scratchy face, crusty eyes, hair matted on the side, I landed in Rome after my first trans-atlantic flight. I had managed to sleep five of the eight hours. Kim, a parishioner and former travel agent put out of business by the internet, congratulated me on the feat. "I can't sleep on planes. I usually watch movies the whole time," she confided. I had roped Kim into organizing the parish pilgrimage's logistics. Why pay a tour company when you have access to such talent?

Suitcases and duffel bags plopped, tumbled, and rolled onto the conveyer belt in baggage claim. One by one our forty-four pilgrims, the exact capacity of a Roman tour bus, took up their luggage while I stood staring at the chute, as if by concentrating hard enough I could make my bags appear. It didn't work. Neither did a prayer to Saint Anthony, nor an attempt at haranguing an Alitalia repre-sentative in broken Italian. How do you say, *How can you lose a bag on a direct flight, you idiot?* in Italian? It turned out the rep spoke English perfectly well but enjoyed watching me flip through my dictionary to find the word *idiot*. Kim said it's what I get for reinforcing the Obnoxious Ameri-can stereotype.

Resigned to spending the next forty-eight hours in the same clothes, I boarded the bus that shuttled our band of jet-lagged but espresso-hyped sojourners from Leo-nardo da Vinci Airport to the Hotel Romulo, an econ-omy auberge "only a five-minute bus ride from Vatican

City", according to the website—thirty-five according to the laws of physics.

Check-in. Pilgrims off to their rooms. Peace. At least for the next two hours, when we're supposed to meet up for lunch.

Lying on the twin bed in my closet of a room, I promised myself I would close my eyes for just a minute. "*The trick is to stay awake as long as you can*," Kim had said. I awoke four hours later, my body heavy, my head hurting, and the digital alarm clock displaying 14:00 in blurry red numbers. After a minute, the fog waned. Then the realization hit: *I'm in Rome! I'm actually in the Eternal City. This is amazing!*

I jumped out of bed, staggered over to the window, and hoisted the strange bunker-style blinds, hoping to see the Roman skyline. Instead, an overweight elderly man in a T-shirt and bathrobe leaned on his balcony, jowls drooping and a cigarette dangling from his lips, entirely undisturbed by my voyeurism.

Of course I was excited to be in Rome—the city of popes and emperors, poets and painters, the capital of Catholicism. I had dreamed of visiting this city ever since I saw *Roman Holiday* as a kid. Sure, part of it was the crush I had on Audrey Hepburn, as if she'd be waiting for me at the airport. But it was also the history, the architecture, the artwork, and, of course, the food.

Roman Holiday. The thought of it brought me back to seminary. Old movies bonded Andrew and me. We had met informally during orientation, but it wasn't till sometime late in the first semester that we became friends. A group of us were running to make it to class on time, and a student ambling in the other direction announced class was canceled. Stopping, I said in my best Marlon Brando impersonation, "You don't understand. I coulda had class."

Snickering, another seminarian continued, "I coulda been a contender." It was Andrew.

"Instead of a bum, which is what I am," I said, finishing the quote.

We both roared. Apparently, the other seminarians had never seen *On the Waterfront* and looked at us as if wondering whether we needed professional help.

A weekly ritual of classic films, jazz, a little scotch, and a cigar became our coping mechanism after a week of stale lectures and abstruse theology studies. Seminary authorities probably wouldn't have been supportive had they known. That tradition had continued through the years. For both of us, old movies, especially noir detective films, became a healthy escape from the pressures of pastoral responsibilities.

That brief reminiscence reminded me to call Andrew. He lived at the Casa Santa Maria, affectionately known as the Casa, a residence for English-speaking priests studying in Rome. My call went to voicemail, so I left a message with my temporary Italian cell number and the number to my hotel. He knew I was coming and already had my itinerary.

🕆 🕆 🕆

After three days I had my luggage back, and the pilgrimage was going well—and by that I mean people weren't complaining, no one had gotten lost, and we hadn't missed a meal. But still no call from Andrew. I tried him again. No answer. I left another message. We were to be in Rome eight days. By the fifth day, I still hadn't heard from him, and now I was nervous. I was not returning to the States without a face-to-face with Andrew. I was on a mission.

Finding myself at the Trevi Fountain one morning, fighting off flashbacks of *La Dolce Vita* and a dazzling Anita Ekberg wading through the waters in her backless evening gown, I remembered Andrew telling me the Casa wasn't too far from there. I deputized Kim, leaving the group in her charge, and went in search of it.

Twisting and turning down narrow cobblestoned streets swarming with tourists, past dubious street vendors with their rows of imitation designer handbags spread out on blankets, and ignoring the advances of waiters standing outside their restaurants, I finally emerged onto a large open piazza in front of a towering facade. It wasn't a church, though. A papal flag hung from the loggia above the main door. A row of columns formed a crown for the building. Between the flag and the crown, the inscription *Pontificia Vniversitas Gregoriana* stretched across the building's face. It was a landmark: the Pontifical Gregorian University, colloquially known as "the Greg", a half-millennium-old Jesuit institution considered the most prominent ecclesiastical university in the world. Andrew had said the Casa was between the Trevi Fountain and the Greg. I was close.

Clouds had been building overhead all morning. I felt a raindrop hit my cheek, and as if on cue, an Indian immigrant (or was he Pakistani?) approached, handing me an umbrella. From his other arm hung at least a dozen more. "Five euros," he said in English.

"No thanks." I turned and walked away. And as if the Far Easterner had a weather-control app on his phone, the moment he was out of sight, it began to pour. I darted into a souvenir shop to wait it out.

"Should've taken the umbrella," said a voice from behind me, also in English. I turned. Leaning against the counter was a priest—young, tall, with blond hair. Not Andrew, but clearly American; he had that dapper look, like he had just walked out of a clergy apparel catalogue. Hand outstretched, he said, "Kevin Duffy, Diocese of Little Rock."

"Oh, hey. Chris Hart, New York."

"New York ... City?"

"Yeah. Well, just a bit north. Like twenty-five minutes."

"Huh." I could see the wheels turning. Pause. *Is it my turn to say something?* His lips parted. "You looking for Andy Reese?"

"Yes, actually. You know Andrew?"

"Sure do. If you want, I can take you over to the Casa. He left you a note."

"He did?"

"Yessir. Saw him tape it to his door before he went out this morning. Said it was for a friend who'd be stopping by this afternoon. Must be you." He pulled a crumpled handkerchief from his pocket and honked.

"But how? He didn't know I was coming. I mean, *I* didn't even know I was coming today." People were crowding into the store seeking refuge from the rain. Several bumped up against me. I checked my wallet. *Still there.* "I was just over by the Trevi Fountain and thought I'd stop by and see if I could catch him. Weird. How did he know?" I said that last part more to myself.

Andrew loved the unexpected. One time he burst into my room screaming that my car was on fire. I tumbled downstairs, out to the street, only to see my car unharmed. It turned out he just wanted to use my laptop to send some emails; his was on the fritz. He could have just asked. *But that would be boring,* he'd have said.

Duffy shrugged. "Beats me. Let's go. I gotta get back there too. I don't want to miss *pranzo.*"

The rain was brief. Duffy explained it was odd to have an isolated shower so early in the day that time of year. I told him my theory about the umbrella peddler having an app that controls the weather. I was joking, but I think he took me seriously.

He led me down a narrow street lined with scooters and tiny cars. Square windows with iron grates punctuated the mustard-colored walls.

"Y'all classmates?" he asked.

"Yes."

"You thinking to come study too?"

"Oh no. That's not my thing. I'm here to steal him away from you." I winked.

We stopped at a door adorned with Latin inscriptions. He buzzed the attendant. I peered farther down the street and recognized a shop I had passed just before getting to the Trevi Fountain. Go figure. I had been only a block away.

"That's mighty kind of you," Duffy said. "The boys'll be happy to say good-bye."

"Really? His eccentricities getting on your nerves?"

"You could say that."

Duffy ushered me through the main door, into a courtyard, and up a flight of stairs to a hallway. He pointed. "Down there, third door on the left."

Right in the center of the door, at eye level, as if suspended by some magic force, was a four-by-six-inch bone-colored envelope with "Reverend Christopher Hart" written in solemn black calligraphy. As I peeled the envelope from the door, the magic trick was revealed: double-sided Scotch tape. I broke the red wax seal on the back and pulled out a heavy-stock card. The envelope had royal blue lining matching the trim on the card's edge. Again in black calligraphy—surely from his Montblanc fountain pen—Andrew had written:

+JMJ

C.

Eight o'clock
Trattoria da Peppino

A.

Duffy still lingered by the stairs, staring at his phone. I approached him. "Any idea where Trattoria da Peppino is?"

"Oh, sure. One of Andy's favorite hangouts. It's at the end of Via Giulia, over by the Vatican, but on this side of the river. Here, I'll show you." He went to work on his smartphone.

"He lets you call him Andy?"

"Nah, he hates it. But that doesn't stop me from calling him that," he said with a snicker. "Where I'm from, everybody's got a nickname. Some of the guys whistle the *Andy Griffith Show* theme when they see him coming."

"That's not nice."

"Yeah, well, we needed an alarm. Seemed to fit."

"He's a good friend of mine."

Duffy looked up from his phone. "Sure. I understand. No harm meant."

"No, I know. He can be a little much sometimes."

"A little much. Yep." Duffy leaned against the wall, sliding one leg over the other, studying his phone again.

"You know, he's not all what he seems," I said. "To hear him talk, what with his patrician accent and ramblings about wine pairings and trips abroad, you might think he was a well-heeled Manhattanite—an Upper East Sider— shipped off at age ten to a New England boarding school." I chuckled at the image sharpening in my mind. "Yeah, then on to Europe for college, maybe Oxford or Louvain. You can see it, can't you? Tweed jacket, pipe, Edith Piaf playing on a record player?"

"Who?"

"Anyway, he wasn't any of that. His mom was a cashier at a grocery store in the South Bronx, and his father was a UPS driver. They're divorced now, from what I've heard."

"He's embarrassed about his family?"

"Sort of. I guess. I don't know. I mean, he's never told me about his upbringing, really. I only know about his parents from his sister. He's super tight-lipped about it."

Come to think of it—and I didn't tell Duffy this—I really didn't know much about Andrew's life before seminary. I had heard stories—a fortuitous acceptance to Regis High School, an academic scholarship to Dartmouth—but they were devoid of any real color, just details I had tweezed from anecdotes he'd dropped occasionally.

"Found it." Duffy said, showing me the phone. "Where are you staying?"

"Hotel Romulo."

"No idea where that is. Anyway, the restaurant's about five minutes from the Vatican."

"Is everything five minutes from the Vatican?"

He laughed. "This really is only five minutes. Look. Just walk down the Conciliazione, then cross the river. You won't miss it."

3

Allison

Trattoria da Peppino had no curb appeal. A chintzy backlit sign more suitable for Atlantic City than Rome announced the restaurant's location tucked behind a bus stop, over-shadowed by the looming facade of some grand church I didn't catch the name of.

Once inside I found proof of what I call the Kim Theory. In Italy, Kim told me, the drabness of the exterior is directly proportional to the extravagance of the interior. Indeed. Wax candles with green lampshades lit intimate tables. Dark mahogany wainscoting complemented cream-colored walls adorned with glowing sconces and impressionist prints in gilded frames. A ceiling with exposed rafters and beadboard and hardwood floors with Persian carpets created that rustic yet elegant ambience that was very much Andrew Reese. He loved quaint bistros that felt part restaurant, part manorial library. The charming atmosphere was a stark reminder of how hard it would be to unmoor him from this cozy life and bring him back to New York.

"*Prenotazione, signore?*" asked the round-faced maître d'hôtel.

"I'm sorry? I don't speak Italian."

"Do you have a reservation, sir?"

"I'm not sure. I'm meeting a friend here. Andrew Reese?"

"*Padre Andrea, certo.* This way, please."

He showed me to a table in a corner of the restaurant, not far from the kitchen. As he handed me the leather-bound menu and I noticed the embroidered tablecloth, I was suddenly conscious of my wallet.

A little after eight fifteen, the door opened and in walked Andrew with a flourish. Everything Andrew did was with a flourish. In this case, the flourish was his getup: ankle-length black *cappa*, or cape, covering a button-down cassock, completed by a *saturno*—an exaggeratedly wide-brimmed clergy hat that looks like Saturn, hence the name. The *cappa* and the *saturno* went out of style in the 1960s.

I watched him greet the maître d' with arms outstretched, just out of earshot. *Ciao, Francesco*, I imagined him saying. *Tutto bene?*

Tutto benissimo, padre. Welcome back. It's good to see you, Francesco seemed to say, his accent thick. *How you studies coming along, eh?*

Oh, why must you dampen my cheerful spirits with such an unhappy reminder? Andrew probably said.

The maître d' took Andrew's hat and cape and pointed my way.

Andrew marched over, and as I stood, he crossed his arms over his chest. "Well, of all the gin joints in all the towns in all the world—"

"I had to walk into yours," I said.

"Good to see you, Christopher, old man."

"Likewise, *old sport*," I chaffed.

"Now, now, no need to mock."

"You look good, healthy," I said.

"Well, you don't look good at all." He eyed me up and down. "Quite gaunt, I must say. Have you been sleeping?"

"Not enough. You know, jet lag, keeping up with the group—"

"Worrying."

"Yes, that too."

"You're always worrying. When will you learn to let go and let God?"

We sat down, and Andrew pushed the menu aside. He unfurled his napkin over his lap like a beach blanket and scooted his chair in, only to notice something on a glass. He picked the glass up, held it to the light, and shook his head. "I suppose you've had a chance to peruse the menu? Everything here is delectable," he said.

"And expensive."

"Tsk, tsk. Never mind that. We're celebrating tonight. Let's forget all our mundane cares, shall we? Money and pilgrim groups and studies and all that weighs on us?"

"I wish I had your *laissez-faire* attitude," I said with a smirk.

"Good show. A little French to sound more sophisticated. I'll pull the aristocrat out of your plebian bones yet."

"Sophisticated, or pompous?"

"Pompous? Excuse me——"

The waiter interrupted, "*Benvenuti, padri. Volete qualcosa da bere?*"

"Ah, Giancarlo, I'm so glad it's you. The boy who served me the other night was awful. Granted, he was a nice enough fellow, but he missed all the details. My glass was empty for at least five minutes—and that happened several times. He brought me a side of spinach with pine nuts when I specifically told him I didn't want the pine nuts, and then he completely forgot about the *digestivi*." He pushed the water-stained glass he had examined earlier to the edge of the table. "Oh, and this."

"*Scusi, padre. È questa nuova generazione*," he said with a shrug. "*Questi ragazzi hanno perso il loro apprezzamento per i dettagli più fini.*"

"Quite right. This generation has indeed lost its appreciation for finer details," he replied, translating for my benefit. "But it's also a question of training, Giancarlo, and that's your job."

"*Certo, padre,*" he said with a nod. "*Volete qualcosa da bere?*"

"Yes. We would like something to drink. Christopher? What say you?"

"I'll just have some water to start."

"*Naturale o frizzante?*" asked the waiter.

Andrew interjected, "Water? Bring us a bottle of that Brunello I had the other night—no, wait, something lighter to start, then we'll go heavy with the main course. How about prosecco?"

"Andrew, I really can't drink that much." I looked at the waiter. "Plain water to start, please. *Naturale.*"

"You're such a bore," Andrew said.

"You know me."

The waiter left to get our drinks.

"So, I have a question for you," I said. It wasn't going to be *the* question. Not yet. That was for later. This was practice.

"A question? This sounds intriguing. Proceed."

"How did you know I would show up at your door today?"

"Oh, Christopher, you're so predictable. You left me three messages, but you had called at least five times trying to get ahold of me. I knew by now you would be exasperated. Your itinerary had you visiting the Trevi Fountain today, and you would surely recall me telling you the Casa is not far from the Trevi. And so, spurred on by your exasperation, you would make all attempts to find me. And sure enough, you did."

"Well, I might not have, if I hadn't run into your friend from Arkansas."

"Duffy? The hillbilly? Not my friend. But I'm glad he proved to be a Good Samaritan to you. And yes, you would have figured it out. I know you. You're quite resourceful when you want to be. And I know you want to be tonight."

"How's that?"

"Please, Christopher. I can hear it in your voice. I can see it in your tapping fingers." I dropped my hands to my lap. "Out with it. What is your request? What benevolence may I bestow upon you?"

"Well," I said, clearing my throat. "I wasn't planning on bringing it up until later."

"I know. And I was going to let it fester in your bosom all evening. It would have been great fun to watch your expression change as you got engrossed in our conversation, forgetting your little mission, and then suddenly remembering, trying to think how to steer the conversation to your ends. Am I right? When were you going to do it? At dessert? That's always the best time. Me all liquored up, defenses down, in a nostalgic, pliable mood. But I was ready to exact payment this evening for whatever favor you're going to ask. I was going to play coy, erect levies and bulwarks and conduct the flow of conversation in another direction entirely. Then, plates cleared, check settled, *adieus* paid, as I was getting into my cab I was going to call back to you, 'Was there something you wanted to ask me?'" His eyes wandered; he was clearly imagining the scene with glee. "But, frankly, I'm tired, Christopher. I just don't have the energy to play tonight. And you should enjoy the evening too. Of course you should. Why cause you so much stress? I'll exact payment another way. So, what is it? What can I do for you?"

I hesitated. I hadn't rehearsed this. I had been caught up in just trying to find him, and once I did, I had to rush to change all my plans for the evening and forgot to think exactly how I would phrase it. *So, Andrew, how'd you like to get out of this sleepy truck stop and come to bustling East Springdale, land of adventure and endless opportunities?*

"So," I said, "I was thinking. You know I'm no longer at St. Rocco's, right?" He nodded. "I'm now a pastor. Can you believe that?"

"Spit it out, Christopher. The waiter will be back soon. I want none of this business talk to sully a single moment of our festivities."

"All right. Here it is. I want you to come help me out at St. Dominic's when you finish the semester. You can use Fordham's library. You'll have your own bedroom and sitting room in the rectory. It'll be part-time, but I'll pay you full-time."

"Yes. I'll go."

"Really?"

"Yes, really." He sat back, his shoulders dropped. "To be honest, I'm a bit tired of Rome. The fellows at the Casa are beginning to get on my nerves, and the Vatican set got all shaken up recently, a long story I won't bore you with. Suffice it to say, it is time for me to weigh anchor and set sail for bluer waters."

"That's great. I'm so relieved."

"I'm sure you are. Now, you know I'll have certain demands ..."

"Yes, I know, we can work that out."

"Of course we can."

I really was relieved. I had thought it was going to be impossible to convince him. What did I have to offer him in East Springdale that compared with the glories of Rome?

By this point Giancarlo had returned with the prosecco and water and was filling our glasses. It was time to order. When I opened the menu and saw that my intuition about the pricing was right, I decided on an appetizer and thought to leave it at that. Andrew would have none of it.

"Giancarlo, be a sport and bring us a selection of antipasti. The good ones, you know, the *musciame di tonno e pomodoro*, the *fiori di zucca alla Sanremese*, and some focaccia." Andrew looked over at me. "You can get focaccia anywhere, but here it's to sell your soul for."

"And I'm sure you already have."

"Now, Giancarlo," he said, looking away from me in feigned indignation, "what else do you recommend this evening?"

The waiter lifted an eyebrow and paused for a moment. "*Primo piatto, vi raccomando le trenette col pesto, patate e fagiolini—*"

"Do you have fettuccine Alfredo?" I interrupted.

His face went stern. "*No. Alfredo no. È per i turisti.*"

I turned to Andrew, confused.

"He says fettuccine Alfredo is for tourists, and I agree."

"But I like fettuccine Alfredo."

"One thing you need to learn about Italy is that the customer is never right, especially when it comes to food. Now stop being a tourist and trust me." Andrew turned to Giancarlo. "First course, the *trenette*. And then?"

"*E poi, secondo piatto, vi raccomando—*"

"Wait—*secondo piatto*? Second plate?" I asked.

"Yes, of course. This is how it's done. First the antipasti, then the first course, usually a pasta dish—though risotto and gnocchi are also *primi piatti*, and they are technically not pasta. Anyway, the second course comes next, usually a meat of some kind or fish accompanied by a side dish—a vegetable. Then dessert and finally a delectable digestive, grappa, to help it all down, or if you prefer, *vin santo*, port, Sauternes, or some other dessert wine."

"You're paying, right?"

"Christopher, please. What did I tell you? We're celebrating."

"Okay. I'll follow your lead."

"Good." He then rattled off some instructions in Italian to Giancarlo, who scampered off to the kitchen.

A few minutes later the waiter returned balancing several plates on his arms, placing them gingerly on the table: little bits of smoked tuna with tomatoes, fried strips of something Andrew told me were zucchini flowers (I didn't even know zucchini had flowers), and a pizza crust with no sauce, no cheese, nothing except what looked like olive oil and spices. The presentation was delightful; the taste was magnificent. *And these are just the appetizers.*

As we started our antipasti, the customary chitchat ensued. He asked whether I was surviving the pilgrimage; I asked how his studies were going. I extolled the spiritual benefits of a pilgrimage for the parishioners; he lamented the dearth of decent books in English.

Soon enough the first course was served. By this point Andrew had already finished a glass of prosecco, and by the end of the first course he had finished another glass and a half; meanwhile, I hadn't finished even one glass. He whispered something to Giancarlo, who cleared our plates and glasses and returned a moment later with another bottle of wine and fresh glasses, these larger than the first. Giancarlo ceremoniously presented the bottle to my host, who tilted his head, inspected the label, and then nodded. With a few twists of the screw, our waiter uncorked the bottle and poured a dash into Andrew's glass. A swish and a swirl, a whiff and an airy sip. Eyes widened, then the utterance of approval: "Yes. Good. This will do just fine. *Grazie*, Giancarlo."

I sipped, and my face went flush. "I have never had anything this good in my life," I said. "I mean, this is incredible."

Andrew lifted his glass. "Here's to Italia, here's to friendship, here's to priesthood."

🍸 🍸 🍸

As the meal progressed, I waited for the inevitable. Maybe I'm too harsh toward my own kind, but whenever two priests get together in such intimate conversation, gossip is soon to follow. Gossip is a sin, to be sure, like alcohol abuse or lust. If alcohol is your vice, you go to a bar; if lust, you go to a strip club; and if gossip, there's no better place than a rectory. But don't think the gossip is about parishioners. Certainly not. Still less is it about penitents. No, the gossip is almost always about other priests— especially the bishop. While I'm usually not one to serve a dish of scuttlebutt, I never fail to gobble it up once it's on the table. And I knew it was only a matter of time before Andrew would dish up a generous portion.

The second course half-devoured, Andrew took his wine glass by the stem—the only proper way, he explained— leaned back in his chair, swirled the wine, held it against the candlelight, and began.

"Did you hear about Jenkins?"

"Nothing special," I said. "Last I heard he just had to defend his dissertation, and then they're going to give him some cushy job at ten-eleven." (Ten-eleven, I should explain, is not a convenience store; it refers to the previous location of the chancery offices for the Archdiocese of New York: 1011 First Avenue in Manhattan.)

"He left," Andrew said.

"He left Rome? Went back to a parish?" I asked, hoping.

"Oh no, he's still in Rome. Just not with us. He met some *bella ragazza* and moved in with her."

"What? That's nuts."

"Nuts it may be, but it's true." He sipped his wine, keeping an eye on me, surely to see my reaction.

"Why would he do something like that? I mean, he had it made: doctorate almost in hand, well respected by everyone, good position lined up. And he was a good priest. I mean, he loved his parishioners and they loved him. Give it up for some chick?"

"Oh, but you should see this chick."

"I don't care if she looks like Cindy Crawford. After so many years, so much hard work? I mean, this isn't a job. You don't just quit and move on."

"Cindy Crawford? You're dating yourself, my friend. She's certainly still quite attractive—for a fifty-year-old. But I digress. The thing is, he fell in love, and that's that."

"I could never do it."

"Fall in love?"

"No. Leave. I could never give this all up. It would be like a father abandoning his kids. Like cheating on your wife."

"Happens all the time."

"Yeah, but I'd expect more from a priest."

"Are you still so naïve, Christopher? How about Tim Connors, Eric Wicklow, Rob Murphy? Shall I go on?"

"Look, I know it happens. And I guess I shouldn't be so surprised, but Jenkins was a classmate. He was one of the best and brightest—and holiest. I thought if anyone would make it, it'd be him. It just doesn't make sense."

"You just haven't fallen in love. That'll change your perspective."

"Yeah I have."

If Andrew were a deer, his ears would have pricked up and turned toward me. As it was, his interest was expressed in the upward tilt of his head, an arched eyebrow, and a slight puckering of his lips.

"The name Allison Stradler ring a bell?" I asked.

"Oh yes, your high school sweetheart."

"And college. We went to CUNY together. I was going to marry her."

"And what happened?"

"I heard the call. I couldn't shake it. Even when I was with her, I knew we weren't going to last because I had to follow the call. I felt so insincere. Eventually I had to tell her."

Though I had drunk only two glasses of wine, with the intimacy of the setting and the joy of Andrew's unexpected acceptance of my offer, my guard was down, my inhibitions waning. "That was hard, Andrew. To look her in the eye and tell her I had to break it off. The tears, the anger. I thought she'd understand. I really thought she saw it coming. I mean, all those retreats I went on. The fact that I started going to church during the week. She didn't see it coming. She had big dreams of wedding dresses, white picket fences, little Bobby playing catch with his dad, and little Susie having tea with Mommy. I crushed those dreams. I thought she'd be flattered when I told her the only one who could take me from her was God. Flattered wasn't the word."

Andrew feigned a sad face.

"Was that it?" he asked. "Did you ever see her again?"

"I ran into her a few years ago."

"And?"

"And nothing."

"So you see the love of your life for the first time in what, ten years? And ... nothing?"

"Let's change the subject. How about your favorite topic: juicy Vatican scandals. Got any new tales to tell?"

"Oh no, you're not getting away that easily."

"Drop it."

"I shall not. I want to hear about it. Every salacious detail."

"Forget it."

"You owe me. This has been so easy for you. I let you have what you came for without exacting the least payment."

"Yet."

"And who's paying for this dinner? A little *quid pro quo, s'il vous plaît.*"

I really didn't want to tell him. I had learned the worst thing I could do was give Andrew access to my private life. Google had nothing on him. He could recall the minutest detail in just the right moment to use it against you. I once confided my Achilles' heel: I have an irrational fear of night crawlers. So what did he do? Two years after my indiscretion, when I had completely forgotten about it, he offered to cook dinner, made a nice linguine primavera, and mixed in, yes, night crawlers.

But I'm a glutton for punishment. The wine had loosened my tongue, and so had Andrew's charm. And, truth be told, I could never say no to him.

"All right," I said. "It was when I was at St. Clement's—"

"When *we* were at St. Clement's."

"Right. When *we* were at St. Clement's. Remember Dr. Morris?"

He nodded. "I've never had whiter teeth since I left that parish."

"Well, he moved into a new office. Asked me to come over and bless it. Turns out Allison was a hygienist there. I couldn't believe it. I felt like Rick in *Casablanca* running into Ilsa."

"Was there a jazz pianist named Sam playing 'As Time Goes By'?"

"There should've been," I said with a chuckle. "I tried to act nonchalant, but I couldn't hold the *Book of Blessings* still. I avoided looking at her, but I thought of nothing and no one else the whole time. Dr. Morris could tell I was distracted, but he didn't know why. He was good about it. Allison could tell too. When I had taken my leave from Dr. Morris, she walked up behind me. 'Howdy, stranger,' she said. She had that voice, you know, like she just walked out of a 1940s film."

"Like Lauren Bacall?"

"No, more like Barbara Stanwyck. Sophisticated, not too sweet, just a little sultry, you know?"

"Sounds like a real charmer," Andrew said.

"And how."

"Now *you* are sounding like someone from a forties film."

"Now, listen here, bub. Watch it or I'll give you a knuckle sandwich." If only I had a fedora. "So anyway, after the office blessing, we go for coffee. We get a chance to catch up. I tell her about my life; she tells me about hers. She had gone to Chicago after college and worked for a corporate real estate broker for a while. She met a guy, but it didn't work out. She tried dating different people, but she was restless. She ended up going back to school to become a dental hygienist. Her dad was a dentist, so it was all familiar to her.

"As she spoke, all the old feelings came back. Like nothing had changed. And I remember at one point she was talking and I wasn't paying attention to a word she was saying. I was just looking at her. She still had that look. I don't know how to describe it. It's not that she was drop-dead gorgeous or anything. She was cute, for sure. And age was only helping her, like a late-blooming flower. Those freckles ... she had these faint freckles sprinkled across her nose and cheeks, and they were so adorable. And her hair. Silky and flowing. It kept falling down, covering part of her face like a velvety curtain, teasing me. But that's not it. I mean, there are lots of pretty girls around. It was something else, her personality. She had a vivacity, a luminosity, that was, well, contagious. To be in her presence was to be happy. And as I stared at her, I knew I still loved her." In my reminiscence I had forgotten Andrew was even there. I just saw her in my mind's eye, winking at me.

Andrew coughed. I snapped to.

"And you know what the killer was?" I continued. "When I asked her if New York was any better than Chicago as far as male companionship was concerned, she just looked at me and said she never found anyone who could replace me."

Andrew winced and plunged an imaginary dagger through his heart.

"I knew I could walk off with her right there. And I'd be happy. At least for a while. But then I'd regret it."

"Maybe not today, maybe not tomorrow . . . ," Andrew started.

". . . but soon, and for the rest of my life," I said, finishing the lines from *Casablanca*. "But do you know what?"

"You'll always have Paris?"

"No." I chuckled. "Do you know what shook me out of my trance? And believe me, I was mesmerized. I was seriously considering leaving everything for her."

"Oh, I believe you."

"It was the thought of Tim Cook."

"The guy from Apple?"

"No. Timmy Cook. The kid from Mrs. Sayers' class I semi-adopted."

"Doesn't ring a bell." He was lying. I knew it. He remembered everything. He just wanted me to keep talking.

"Mrs. Sayers was the sixth-grade teacher at St. Clement's, and there was this kid, Tim. He was a good kid."

"They all are at that age," Andrew said. "It's in seventh grade that someone injects them with some sort of nastiness serum. Hormones, I suppose."

I glared at him. "Anyway, this kid Tim was acting up, and Mrs. Sayers couldn't deal with him. One day I found him in the boys' room, and he was crying. It turned out his dad had walked out on him and his mom. He was an only child. So I talked to him for a while—"

"Right there in the bathroom?"

"Well, yeah. I was a young priest, inexperienced. I wouldn't do that now, but you know, the kid was sitting on the floor leaning up against a wall, face in his knees, sobbing. I wasn't going to stand over him and tell him to come to my office. So I just sat down on the floor next to him. I know, gross, right?

"We talked a long time, and at one point he said, 'I promised I'd pay him back.' I dug into that phrase, and it turned out he thought his dad left because Timmy had stolen five bucks from his dad's wallet to buy a pack of Pokémon cards. I tried to reassure him his dad didn't leave because of that. I don't think he believed me. Then I said something I regret. Like I said, I was young and inexperienced. I said, 'Don't worry, I'll be your dad.' You should have seen his face light up. I said, 'Yeah, you already call me Father, don't you? So just consider me your dad here at school.'"

"You didn't. Please tell me you didn't, Christopher."

"Yeah, I know. Stupid. I had to explain to his mom what I was trying to do. She was good about it, but she was a little standoffish after that. I did build up a rapport with the kid, and a lot of his friends were in the same boat. So I started taking a group of them to Mets games and movies and that sort of thing."

"Dangerous nowadays," Andrew said. Giancarlo passed by, refilled our glasses.

"Yeah, I know. But look, besides that time in the bathroom, I was never alone with the kid."

"Christopher, may those words never come from your mouth again."

"Andrew, these kids need fathers. They need men in their lives that can teach them how to be men. They need examples. We can't let the threat of lawsuits and all these 'safe environment' rules stop us from being mentors to these boys. We'd be letting the devil win."

"If Dante were still alive, he'd have me in the first ring of the Inferno, for I will not risk even being on a first-name basis with a human being under the age of eighteen."

"Excuse me, what about that Rafferty kid you were all buddy-buddy with? What was his name? Michael?"

"That was different."

"How?"

"Never mind that. It just was."

"You spent practically every weekend with that kid. People were beginning to talk, you know."

Andrew sniffed at the wine in his glass and sipped. "So what, pray tell, does little Master Cook have to do with the enchanting Miss Stradler?"

"Well, as I looked at that bright face and imagined myself carrying her over the threshold, my mind's eye saw past the doorway, into the living room, and there was eleven-year-old Timmy Cook sitting on the floor, back against the wall, head buried in his knees, sobbing. And I told her, 'Allison, I love you. I will always love you. There is nothing I want more than to walk out of here with you right now and live happily ever after. But you know, that's not how life works. You make your choices, and you live with them. I've made commitments; I have people who depend on me. I must be faithful to that commitment.'"

Andrew pretended to wipe tears away with his napkin. "You're a good man, Christopher Hart. Better than I. To stare temptation in the face and walk away. Now, that is an *homo integer*, a real *vir fortis*. I, on the other hand," he said, elbow on the table, wrist suspending a forkful of veal scaloppine over his plate, "must distract myself from those kinds of temptations by indulging in others."

"You're an embarrassment to the priesthood." I was only half joking. He was a man of extremes. Over our three years at St. Clement's, I watched as Sunday after Sunday he drew in a crowd and then sent them away beating their breasts in repentance, or charging forth to change the world, or marching off to be better husbands or wives or mothers or fathers. I'd overhear quiet whispers about how charming, how charismatic he was. Yet no one had quite the knack for eliciting an eye roll from the school principal, raised eyebrows from the housekeeper, or a facepalm from the pastor.

"Excuse me. I don't see you rejecting this fine fare in favor of bread and water," he said.

"No, but I also don't do this every night as you apparently do, and I don't throw money around like it's water—or wine, in your case."

"I do not eat like this every night. Maybe once a week, but always socially, never alone."

"So that makes it better?"

"Have you turned Jansenist?" he asked. "We're Catholic. Ours is an incarnational religion. We're not Manichean dualists who say, 'Spirit good, matter bad.' No. We enjoy the fruit of the earth and the work of human hands— God's creation and man's ingenuity together. Money is simply a means. I happen to have some at present, but I don't keep it. I put it out there to benefit others. Look at Giancarlo and Francesco. They have jobs, they have homes, they support their families, all because of my generosity to you and to others." He raised his glass in toast. "Tonight we celebrate God's goodness, man's creativity, and our friendship. We're Catholic. One day we fast; the next day we feast. No remorse. No guilt. All things in moderation. Here's to our faith and our—"

Giancarlo laid a narrow leather folder on the table.

"What's this?" Andrew asked.

"*Il conto, padre.*"

"Just put it on my tab," he said, pushing the check to the edge of the table. "I'll settle at the end of the month, as usual."

"*Scusi, padre, ma ...*" Giancarlo leaned over and whispered in Andrew's ear.

"No. Not acceptable. Where's Peppino?"

"*In cucina.*"

"Christopher, would you excuse me a moment?" He stood, not waiting for an answer.

"If it's about the check—" He silenced me with a wave of the hand and marched toward the kitchen, calling out the owner's name in a singsong rise and fall—pey-PEE-no.

4

Numbers

"Mission accomplished, Jack."

"Pass the salt," Monsignor said, voice grittier than usual.

"Aren't you excited?"

"I'm more excited about this stew." He slurped a spoonful of the chunky beef stew Maria was famous for. We were at supper in the formal dining room. I had just returned from Rome.

Evening supper in the formal dining room was a ritual. Breakfast and lunch were informal events at a little table in the kitchen, sometimes the two of us together, sometimes not. But supper was a solemn affair, always together, always in the formal dining room.

"Now I just have to convince the guys downtown," I said. "I don't think that'll be too hard."

Monsignor let out a hacking cough, little tendrils of meat spraying the tablecloth.

"You all right, Jack?"

"Fine," he said, wiping his chin, then blotting the table. His eyes were glazed.

"You're sick."

"I'm not. Pass the salt."

"It's right in front of you."

He doused the stew with enough salt to preserve his body for decades after his death. Surely this was part of his master plan to become a permanent fixture in the parish.

"Well, *you* might not be excited, but *I* am. We're making progress."

"Toward what?"

"Toward saving the world. Isn't that the business we're in?"

"The world's got a Savior, and you're not him."

"Well, we do our part, don't we? Seriously, open a newspaper, turn on the news. There's so much we have to do. We're small, but we can have an impact."

"So this new vicar of yours is going to help you save the world, is that it? Where'd you dig him up? Last I heard, the Arch wasn't assigning priests to little shops like ours."

"I dug him up, as you call it, in Rome."

"Rome, huh?" He shoved another spoonful of stew in his mouth and continued, his speech now garbled. "I went to Rome once, when I made monsignor. Took a bunch of people with me too. Grand old time. But those Italians"—he pronounced it EYE-talians—"they don't know what pizza is over there. That flat crusty stuff. I bet all the guys who really knew how to make pizza came over on the boat and opened joints on Arthur Avenue." Again, a sustained hacking. I expected a lung to land on the table.

"You gotta take it easy. Why don't you let me take the morning Mass tomorrow?"

"It's my day. I'm taking it."

"Well, go to bed early then."

"I might. We'll see."

I was hoping to get to bed early too. My eyelids were heavy even though it was only six o'clock. Kim had told me to expect the jet lag to last one day for every time zone crossed. That meant six days till normalcy.

"So what'd you do?" he continued. "Promise him season tickets at Yankee Stadium?"

I rolled my eyes. "He's a friend who's finishing his doctorate," I said. "He's done with his classwork, so he'll come here and help while he works on his dissertation."

"Oh great, an intellectual. That's just what the parish needs. Last time I had a brainy associate, I got nothing but complaints. Long, boring sermons. Sounded like Mr. Rogers on Valium. I kept telling him, 'This isn't Springdale, it's *East* Springdale. The Harvard types live on the other side of the tracks. We're simple people over here.' He didn't listen. They never listen. It's all about 'orthodox catechetics' and 'reverent liturgy'. As if a cassock and some Latin will bring 'em all back in droves." He wiped his mouth with his napkin. "But I'm not the pastor. If the pastor wants an intellectual, that's his business."

"I need help. No offense, but I need someone with a little more pep, and he's got it. I know it's a small parish, but it's going to grow—it has to grow—and I'm going to need help. God gave me this mission, and I will fulfill it."

"You do that. But careful not to throw your back out while you're at it."

I snorted, stood up, and grabbed my empty bowl.

"You want some more stew to go with your salt there, Jack?"

A crock of stew sat on the sideboard. As I began to serve myself, the kitchen phone rang. There's nothing unusual about a phone ringing, but as I recall it now, I shudder. Over the years, whenever I replay the movie of my life, this scene goes to black and white. My inner Hitchcock frames the shot from within the kitchen looking out into the dining room, the rotary telephone large in the foreground, shrouded in darkness, its ring shrill and startling. In the background, Monsignor is seated, his back to the camera, and my profile is in the distance dishing stew into a bowl. Hairs stand on end with each foreboding ring.

Of course, it wasn't like that. The ring wasn't the trilling bell of a rotary phone. Rather, a cheap RadioShack cordless bleeped in crescendo like an electronic canary, as it did incessantly throughout the day. The swinging kitchen door was shut, and the fluorescent kitchen lights were on. No, it wasn't dramatic or foreboding. It was ordinary. So often, the catalyst for traumatic life events is not some raucous explosion but a faint spark that sets a long fuse blazing, the explosion to come later.

"I'll get it," Monsignor croaked.

"You will not."

"Sit down. It's for me." His octogenarian arms and legs pushed him up as fast as they could, but not fast enough.

"Relax," I said. "Whoever it is, I'm telling them you're not available."

The caller ID said "Unknown". *Great. Telemarketer.* I reluctantly took the receiver. "St. Dominic's."

No one answered at first. Distant chatter. A faint crescendo of laughter in the background. Finally a voice spoke—masculine, coarse, reinforcing my resolution not to take up smoking. "Father Leahy there?"

"Monsignor isn't available right now. Can I help you?"

"Who's this?"

"This is Father Hart. I'm the pastor."

Again no response, just the sound of metal on metal in the near background, a whisk against a mixing bowl perhaps, and then someone speaking Spanish calling for more pepper.

The voice started again, this time hushed. "I got somebody. Needs last rites."

"Okay. Yes, well, I can help with that. Is the person in imminent danger of death?"

"Death? Yeah, he's gonna die. Soon."

"Can you give me a little more info? A name, hospital, room number?"

A rustling sound followed by total silence. Now the husky voice again. "We'll come pick you up."

"Look, just give me the address. I've got GPS. I can find my way."

"We'll come pick you up. Be ready in ten minutes."

Before I could protest, he hung up. I stood there for a moment, the receiver still in my hand.

"Jack!" I shouted from the kitchen. I went out to the dining room; he was gone. I pounded on the door to his room. No answer. No light from beneath the door. *What is going on?*

🙟 🙟 🙟

Ten minutes later a black SUV—a big one, Ford Expedition maybe?—pulled up in front of the rectory. A barrelchested man in a dark gray suit stepped out of the passenger side, opened the rear passenger door, and stood, legs shoulder width apart, hands folded low like fig leaves. The ensemble—silent man in a dark suit with a black SUV—was a photo for a funeral home brochure, the undertaker waiting patiently for the bereaved.

Now, I know what you're thinking, because I was thinking the same thing: *Don't get in the car.* You see this setup in movies, and you think, *What kind of an idiot would get in the car?* Just turn around, go back inside, close the door behind you, and call the police. Of course, it's a lot easier to analyze the situation when you're sitting in front of your home entertainment center munching on popcorn. The suspenseful music helps too.

I didn't have any music. I didn't even have an ominous raven cawing from atop a telephone pole. Only neighborhood sounds: a loose muffler of a passing car rattled, a boy on a bike yelled after another boy on a bike, traffic from the parkway groaned in the distance—all ordinary, and all drowned out by the *ba-thump, ba-thump, ba-thump* of my heart. No, I didn't need any scary music.

Just take the first step. The rectory has five front steps, then ten feet of pavers leading to the street. If I could just take the first step, the rest of me would follow. Deep breath. *Someone is dying. I need to do this.*

Down the rectory steps I went, straight to the SUV, nodding to the Grim Reaper as I got in. Words were superfluous at this point. I placed myself in their hands and just went with it.

The Grim Reaper, instead of getting into the front seat, motioned for me to scooch over and got in next to me. Now this was getting uncomfortable.

As he closed the door, he said, "Thanks for making this easy, Father. Don't worry. We're not going to hurt you." He could evidently see my unease. "We just need to put this on you." He held up a black cloth bag as the SUV pulled away from the curb.

"Really? Is this necessary?"

"I am afraid it is, Father. For your sake. It's best you not know where we're going. But, like I said, don't worry. We're not going to hurt you." This reassurance wasn't reassuring. That he even felt the need to reassure me suggested he had made trips like this before, giving no such assurances.

With the bag over my head, I tried to feel where we were going. We stayed on surface streets and crossed one set of railroad tracks; that much I could tell. I concentrated on how many turns we took and in which direction, but after four or five I lost track. Besides, I thought, they probably weren't taking a direct route.

After a good twenty minutes, the car stopped, the door opened, and I was extracted. The pleasant smell of leather interior gave way to the pungent odor of garbage. They left my head covered.

Whoever was guiding me—*Is it Grim?*—steered me like a shopping cart for about fifteen feet and then told me to watch my step, oblivious to the irony of his request. I stepped up and through a doorway. The temperature warmed, the stench of garbage faded, and the scent of garlic and onions assailed my nose. The sounds of a kitchen rang in my ears: the chopping, the frying, and the chef yelling at the sous-chef, or maybe the other way around.

My guide—*It's Grim, it has to be*—turned me to the left and again warned me to watch my step as we ascended a series of stairs. Another set of footsteps squeaked ahead of me, Grim still behind me, now with one hand gently pressed against my back. The staircase was steep. It was also narrow. My hands glided against the walls as I attempted to steady myself.

One tight landing, then a few more stairs, and I was at the top. Grim nudged me into a hallway, steered me about twenty feet, and pulled me to a halt. To my left the snap of a deadbolt, then the creak of an opening door. Despite the bag on my head, an unexpected blast of cigarette smoke forced me into a gagging cough. A tug on my left shoulder, a prod forward, and I was in a room. A hand from behind yanked the bag off, snagging some of my hair.

"I'll leave you here. Knock when you're finished." The door slammed shut, and the lock clicked into place.

My eyes adjusted slowly as I tried to get my bearings. Looking around, it was as if I had been transported to a government housing block in Soviet-era Stalingrad. The walls were drab, decorated with ghostly outlines of missing pictures; pea-green wallpaper curled into suspended scrolls near a closet door, exposing patches of laths. Plaster from the ceiling flaked into piles on the abraded hardwood floor. The last rays of daylight filtered through plumes of cigarette smoke hovering overhead.

My ears also adjusted: from the noisy street, to the clattery kitchen, to the creaky floors of the hallway, I came into silence. A distant police siren rose and trailed off.

The room was relatively empty. A cot with a bare mattress sat in one corner, and a folded chair leaned against the opposite wall. Near the window, a man sat at a card table staring blankly at a heaping ashtray.

The man, midfifties, with silvery black hair slicked back, seemed unperturbed by my sudden entrance. His brown leather Florsheims were scuffed, and his parchment-colored dress shirt, probably once a crisp white, had the sheen of wax paper.

Was this my suffering soul, the one who needed last rites?

His hand trembled as he brought a cigarette to his mouth. Oblivious to my presence, or indifferent, he took a big draft and let the smoke out long and slow, breath quivering, as he stared out a curtainless window.

"Do you mind if I turn the light on?" I asked, but received no response.

I flipped the switch. A circular fluorescent bulb in the middle of the ceiling flickered and crackled, replacing the warm nostalgic glow of the setting sun with the stark glare of reality. The man winced, hung his head, rocked back and forth, then stopped and stared out the window again. With the interior light on, the window became a mirror, our eyes meeting in the glass for a moment. I grabbed the chair leaning against the wall, placed it on the other side of the card table, and sat, silent. He took another drag. His skin was pale, his eyes red-rimmed and bloodshot.

In front of him, along the edge of the table, nine cigarettes were lined up parallel to each other, exactly one
inch apart, like railroad ties. The filters alternated: the first
pointed toward him, the second away, the third toward,
and so on. Two Marlboro packs made bookends for this
artistic design. The ashtray, another work of art, was in the
exact center of the table. Ten half-consumed cigarettes,
spaced equidistant from each other, circled a pyramid of
ashes, jutting out like the ramparts of an early American
colonial fort. If lacquered, the ashtray would be ready for
exhibition at the Guggenheim.

Hesitant to disturb his monkish aura, I leaned forward
and put out my hand tentatively.

"My name's Father Hart. I'm a priest from St. Dominic's ..." I tried to keep my voice steady and soothing,
despite the adrenaline coursing through my bloodstream.

Either not seeing the hand or just ignoring it, he took
a last drag on his cigarette, now half-finished, tapped it
overtop the pyramid, and stuck it, filter up, along the edge
of the ashtray, rearranging all the other half-smoked cigarettes so they were evenly spaced.

I thought about the guys outside. Would they make an
untimely entrance? How much time were they giving me,
anyway?

Sitting back, I caught his reflection in the window staring straight at me. "When was the last time you slept?" I
asked the reflection.

His eyes looked up and to the left. Then in one motion,
he tilted his head to the side and down, then away from
me, then snapped it back looking at me, again by way of
the window.

What was that all about?

"Three, sixteen, twenty sixteen," he said. His voice was
at once monotone and erratic, like a bad Siri impersonation.

"Seven hours, eighteen minutes. One twenty-two A.M. to eight thirty A.M."

"Well, that's pretty exact."

He nodded. It was a rapid, jerky nod.

"Three, sixteen, twenty sixteen," I said, maintaining eye contact with him through the reflection. "March sixteenth? Last Wednesday? So you haven't slept in two days. Not good, my friend. Listen, I want you to be able to sleep, peacefully. I think I can help you with that. Would you like that?"

Again he tilted his head, twisted it down and away from me, and snapped it upright.

"I guess you're not sleeping because of whatever it is that's going on right now." I had no better name for it than "whatever it is that's going on". Was he sick? Did he have cancer? I wasn't ready yet to accept there might be an alternative. "I think I can help bring you a little peace."

"Five. Last rites. Five. Last rites send me to heaven," he said, putting emphasis on *five* and saying the rest so quickly I could barely make it out.

I searched his face, trying to understand his meaning.

"Five last rites?" I asked. "Well, *rites* is plural, but there's only one rite, actually. So, are you the one who needs it? Last rites?"

Another jerky nod. "Five. Fifth. Last rites send me to heaven. Fifth."

"Yes, well, they could send you to heaven. But you know something? They don't call it that anymore. Last rites. They call it anointing of the sick now." I placed the little book of rites on the table, opening it to the page where the prayers begin. "Because they're not really *last* rites. The prayers all ask for healing. See ... for people to get better. So let's focus on that. Getting better. What do you say?"

His reply was an absent stare.

"You are sick, right?"

He shook his head slowly, then did that thing again, lunging his head sideways and snapping it back.

I don't know why I asked whether he was sick. I knew he wasn't. The situation was clear: the mysterious SUV, the black cloth bag, Grim Reaper standing guard at the door all reeked of mobsters, Mafia, godfather stuff. But I was partially in denial. I didn't want to believe they were going to kill him. I hoped he was one of them, but sick. And since he was a mobster or whatever, they couldn't just take him to a hospital. As the minutes passed, my hope in that hypothesis dimmed.

"You're not sick. Okay."

"Fifth. Last rites send me to heaven. Fifth."

Fifth? What is it with the five, fifth thing? ... Oh, of course.

"The fifth sacrament," I said.

He didn't respond or even nod, but a glint in his eye told me he felt understood.

"Anointing of the sick—or last rites, same thing—is the fifth sacrament. So you want me to give you the sacrament?"

He gave me another nod.

"Because you're going to die?"

A more vigorous nod, then head tilt, twist, and snap back.

"One. White Death," he said.

"One white death? What's that?"

He pressed his forefinger to his temple and pretended to shoot himself, mouthing the word *pow.*

"Fifth. Last rites send me to heaven," he said.

"So they've brought me here to prepare you to go to heaven." I said it more to myself than to him.

Now an intense nod.

"That's the White Death? I give you last rites so when they kill you, you go to heaven?" Well, at least they were pious mobsters. "Is there a Black Death?"

A grim nod, then a head tilt, turn, and snap. He thumbed back toward the cot.

"I don't get it. What's the bed got to do with—" My film noir–trained imagination started working. "Oh, I *do* get it. That makes sense, in a twisted sort of way. Ugh." I leaned forward, placing my elbow on my knee and my chin on my palm. "So, if the White Death is when the priest prepares you for heaven, then the Black Death must be when they want to send you to hell. They catch you in the middle of some sinful act, like sex with a prostitute or something, and then—"

He repeated the gun-to-temple simulation.

"Right. Sick." I looked at his reflection in the window again. "So, there's no way out of this?"

He shook his head.

"How about if I just call 911 right now?" I pulled out my cell phone, but there was no signal. "This is ridiculous. They expect me just to come in here, administer the sacraments, and leave?" My voice was rising. He put his finger to his mouth to quiet me.

I stood and paced. The room had two doors: the one leading to the hallway, and a closet door. I opened the closet hoping to find a duct or something to escape through. It was empty save a triggered mousetrap on the floor with rat droppings next to it. The only ways in and out were the door and the window. The door was guarded, and the window was painted shut. Besides, we were at least twenty feet up, with nothing to land on except the roof of the SUV. Jumping out of a building might work in movies, but even when facing potential death by gunshot, I wouldn't try it in real life.

A pounding erupted from the door, followed by a muffled voice. "Hurry up in there, Numbers. We ain't got all night."

Sitting again, I asked, "Numbers? Is that what they call you?"

He signaled affirmatively.

"Okay, Numbers, listen. I don't know what you did to deserve this, but I'm going to do my job. You don't need last rites, okay? What you need is confession."

"Fourth. Reconciliation. Fourth."

"Right," I said, surprised he knew the word. "That's right. Reconciliation. Reconcile with your Creator before you meet him face-to-face. You ready to do that?"

He assented, and I pulled a purple stole from my breast pocket.

"This means you have to tell me your sins. Do you know what a sin is?"

He turned toward me, breaking from the mirror filter, and gave me a look as if to say, *Do I look like an idiot?*

"Right, of course you do. Well, let's be—" I stopped. "Wait ... this is important. Whatever you tell me *in* confession, I can't use *outside* confession. Even if it's not a sin, I can't allude to it. So if I can't get you out of here, you can at least tell me what's going on, who these people are, who's taking your life. Then maybe I can figure out a way to bring them to justice."

His lower lip pushed up into a pout. Then he made the sign of the cross, saying, "One, two, three. Three. One."

"No, seriously. Tell me what's going on, and I'll help you as soon as I get out of here."

Again, he made the sign of the cross.

"Numbers, please. At least a name of the boss or something. Something I can use to tip off police."

He didn't move. He had become more animated in the exchange, but now his face resumed the wooden expression from before.

"You just want to start then. Okay. Fine. Let's start." I made the sign of the cross. "How long's it been since your last confession?"

"Three, seven, twenty fifteen. Four fifteen P.M."

"March 7, 2015. So, a year ago. All right. Well, tell me all the things you've done in the past year or anything you want, anything you think may have offended God, anything you want to get off your chest."

"Ten. One, two, three, four. Eight, nine, ten. Ten."

"I don't get it. What do the numbers mean?"

"Ten. One, two, three, four. Eight, nine, ten. Ten."

"Ten? Ten what? ... Oh, ten commandments?"

A nod.

"Can you repeat those numbers?"

"Ten. One, two, three, four, eight, nine, ten. Ten."

I ran through the commandments in my head. "So basically you haven't killed anyone, slept with anyone else's wife, or stolen anything, but you're guilty of the rest?"

Another nod.

"Okay. That's good. I mean, it's not good, but it could be worse. What else?"

"Seven. One, two, three, four, five. Seven."

"Seven. Seven what?" I scanned the room as if there were a clue somewhere on the walls. "Wait, that's easy. The seven deadly sins?"

Affirmative.

"Okay, so no envy or gluttony."

No, that wasn't it.

Seven deadly sins, hmm ... pride, greed, lust ... envy, gluttony ... "Oh, I know, wrath and sloth. All of them except wrath and sloth. So you're not vengeful or lazy. That's good."

"Five. One, four, five. Five."

"Five? Five what?" I stroked the beard I didn't have. "Five, five, five. Gimme something more. Five. Five wounds of Christ. Five sorrowful mysteries. Five Guys. Jackson Five. I don't know ... What's five?"

A pounding on the door again, then Grim's voice. "You got two minutes, Numbers. That's it."

"Five. One, four, five. Five," he said, his jaw tight, urgency in his eyes.

"Hey, you said more than numbers before. Why not now?"

"Five. One, four, five. Five."

I stood up and paced to the door and back.

"Oh, that's it. The five precepts of the Church."

He exhaled, and his face loosened.

"Oh geez, what's the order of them? Go to Mass on Sundays ..."

He nodded.

"Confess once a year. Communion once a year."

He shook his head.

"Fast and abstinence on certain days?"

He nodded.

"Provide for the needs of the Church?"

He nodded.

"So you've missed Mass, you haven't observed fast days, and you haven't plunked a dime in the collection plate?"

He nodded vigorously.

"Good. Anything else? ... No? ... Okay."

At this point I was supposed to share some wise words, wax profound, and usher up an eloquent discourse about God's mercy, how Numbers was now forgiven and no matter what he'd done, God wouldn't hold it against him. But then I was also supposed to give advice on how to live a better life from here on out, how to shed bad habits or adopt new attitudes. As I looked into his red-rimmed eyes, I saw a glimmer of hope, but I felt the despair of his situation. There was no future for him except death. The only consoling words I could now share were about the beauty of the afterlife, the fulfillment of all desires, Jesus' loving embrace on the other side.

Just as I had mentally formulated all I needed to say, Grim's pounding came again, followed by his muffled voice. "Thirty seconds."

So I didn't say any of it. I just asked whether he was heartily sorry for having offended the Lord, to which, of course, he nodded. Then I told him to say a Hail Mary as his penance, and I said the words of absolution. Thus the rite was over, his soul cleansed. And as I heard the key turning in the lock, he grabbed my arm and said, "Three, fifteen, fourteen, fourteen, nine, five. She knows. She knows." He said it clearly, urgently, and forcefully, as if trying to press the numbers into my brain. "Three, fifteen, fourteen, fourteen, nine, five. She knows."

I looked at him, confused. "Too fast. I couldn't catch all those numbers."

The door swung open. "All right. Time's up."

"Three, fifteen, fourteen," he said quickly, still intense. "Three, fifteen, fourteen."

I repeated the digits to myself, then whispered, "March 15, 2014?"

He shook his head, his face tense with frustration.

"Sorry, Father, gotta put the bag back on. You understand."

5

Maria

I opened an eye and glanced at the clock for the eighth time—4:32 A.M. Kim's second law of transatlantic flight dynamics states: the effect of jet lag from an east-to-west flight is a rapid transition from lucidity to dormancy the moment one's head hits the pillow, then an equally rapid transition from dormancy back to lucidity, usually around three in the morning, regardless of when the head hit the pillow. I found an exception to this law. If, upon return, one is temporarily abducted by the Mafia to hear the confession of a man targeted for execution, no matter how tired one may be, one shall not sleep.

The sheets lay in a pile on the floor, my body sprawled stiff on the bed. My mind panted in exhaustion from having worked all night, turning events over as if trying to solve a Rubik's Cube. Every turn that successfully matched a row of oranges on one side disrupted a completed row of blues on another. But, like an obsessed adolescent working over the enigmatic cube, my mind would not quit. Even when my inner child would hurl the cube against the wall out of frustration, shattering it into a million pieces, he'd find it only a moment later back in his lap, intact, and would go at it again.

Many times I reached for my cell phone to call the police and dropped it again, realizing I couldn't call them. What would I tell them? A nicotine addict with silvery black hair and a numbers fetish will be killed, most likely by a tall man with a crew cut in a dark suit. Oh, and the suit drives a black SUV.

License plate?

Um, I don't know.

Where will this take place?

Um, I don't know.

So how do you know he'll be killed?

Um, I can't tell you.

And that's the piece that kept my thumb off the green button. I'd get as far as hitting 911, and then I'd think, *I can't tell them how I know. I really shouldn't even tell them I was there.*

"*It is absolutely forbidden for a confessor to betray in any way a penitent in words or in any manner and for any reason.*" That's what Church law says. Even if my sparse details could lead some Sherlock Holmes in the local police precinct to find the perps, they'd want to know how I was so sure. And I couldn't tell them. I knew only because Numbers had told me in confession. Never had I felt the confessor's cross so acutely, for a confessor—the keeper of secrets, the guardian of intimacies—will die before he lets those confidences slip from his lips. That's his cross: carrying the sins of his penitents to the grave with him so they don't have to.

I could have just said the truth: I was called to give last rites to a dying man, and the whole setup wreaked of a hit job. *That's it. That's what I could say.* A row of blue squares on the Rubik's Cube locked into place.

And if it worked? If the police figured it out? Wouldn't I get fingered as the stool pigeon? Wouldn't that put my life at risk? Yet, I wasn't so worried about that. As strange as it is, I was worried I'd be breaking the mobsters' trust. Those thugs placed a certain confidence in me. There was a respect, however macabre, for the sacred. They brought me in because they wanted Numbers to go to heaven. Twisted? Sure. Hypocritical? Definitely. But they trusted me to perform my duty. I was bound by that trust. I couldn't rat them out. Orange squares aligned, blue now broken up.

Another glance at the clock—4:47 A.M. *That's it. I'm done.* My feet landed on the carpet. I grabbed a pair of sweatpants, slid on a sweatshirt, and laced up my running shoes. Time for a jog. Jogging was almost better than coffee at clearing my head. Almost.

The crisp air stung my lungs as my legs, still stiff, lumbered down Main Street. While my aching muscles soon warmed and my blurry eyesight cleared, my mind stayed muddled.

At that hour there was no traffic. No one stirred in the dark houses. Merchandise in closed-up storefronts was obscured by the reflection of streetlights. Even the birds, recently returned from their Florida vacation, were sleeping.

I ran my route. Always the same. A four-mile loop through town. Even though I had been running four miles every other day for the last six months, I found it hard. But today it was impossible. In the homestretch I had to slow to a trot, my hamstrings burning.

Headlights from behind me lit up a speed limit sign. The murmur of an engine and the crackle of tires on the dirty street disrupted the predawn stillness. A car driving down a street is normal. Why was I suddenly wary? The car, still behind me, was going too slow for this neighborhood. I didn't turn to look, didn't change my pace, but my muscles tightened, my already-pounding heart beat a little faster, and my ears were now so alert I thought I could pick up the local NPR station.

Yet it wasn't just a car. It was an SUV. *Now what do they want?* It crawled past and turned the corner. I notched down to a walk.

A moment later, headlights shone from behind me again. Same muffled engine noise, same slow pace.

I had done what they wanted; why were they following me? *Now what do I do? I should run. No, I didn't betray anyone. Forget it. They won't intimidate me.*

I stopped and turned to face the oncoming vehicle, arms folded across my chest. I wanted to stare into the driver's eyes, show him I wasn't afraid, but all I could see was headlights. I stared anyway, past the lights, at the spot where I figured the driver was, knowing he'd see me. As the SUV rumbled by, I kept staring, watching my own reflection glower back at me in the tinted passenger windows.

Three car lengths down the street, the SUV stopped. The back door popped open. Giggles and screechy female laughter burst out. Two women stumbled onto the sidewalk holding on to each other, one steadying herself on stiletto heels like a newborn foal, the other groping at her, trying to keep her balance, both whooping hysterically. As they gained their footing and started to hobble away, the SUV's horn blasted through the quiet neighborhood, and a hand held a purse out the window. A sober male voice came from within: "Forget something, ladies?"

My muscles slackened; my blood pressure normalized. Relief. Just two party girls returning from their Friday night soiree. In retrospect, maybe I should have offered to hear their confessions.

I was just jittery. A hot shower and some prayer time were what I needed.

Turning the knob to the rectory door, about to pull it open, I stopped and turned back, as if someone had just tapped me on the shoulder. Standing on the corner of Main Street and Ash, about fifty yards from me, a stocky, bald man in a leather jacket, blue jeans, and work boots popped the lid off a coffee cup, steam pouring out. A shiver ran through me and, once inside, I locked the door.

⚜ ⚜ ⚜

After a warm shower, I got dressed, snatched my keys from the bureau, and sloughed across the parking lot to the church. It was six fifteen. Bea Dunne waited by the door, her mittened hands clutching her purse, her face buried beneath a knit hat, fluffy scarf, and billowy coat collar.

"Morning, Bea."

"Good morning, Father."

"Can you do me a favor?" I asked as I unlocked the doors. "Can you pray for a special intention?"

"Of course I can, Father." Bea was great. I didn't need to explain. Just a "special intention". No questions asked.

Bea made her way to her spot in front of a statue of the Blessed Virgin Mary, which was lit up.

Three lights always stayed on: one on the statue of Mary to the left of the altar, one on the crucifix above the altar, and one on the statue of Saint Joseph on the right. I marched up the main aisle to the altar, a concrete trapezoid with the words "Let Us Break Bread Together" etched in golden block letters along the base. Thank you, 1970s.

I knelt on the carpeted steps immediately in front of the altar, hands pressed together, gazing up at the tabernacle just below the crucifix. I was waiting for a bright light to burst out of the gilded box and the crucified Jesus to turn his head, jump down from the cross, put his arm around me, and speak consoling words. Instead, my attention waned, my body tilted forward, my forehead pressed against the altar, and I fell asleep.

It was a cough that woke me. Jerry's cough. I opened my eyes to find that my body had slumped down and curled up into the fetal position.

"Jet lag's a killer, ain't it."

"Yeah, it is. Sorry." I sat up, cross-legged, and took a bleary-eyed look around the church. It was half-full, people waiting for the 8:00 Saturday morning Mass. I felt the blood rush to my face. "Monsignor's got this Mass, right?"

"Nope. Some missionary priest. He's doing a morning retreat. Legion of Mary or something."

"Right. I forgot. Is he here yet?"

"Nope."

"Good. I'm not presentable."

"No, you ain't."

"Help me up, would ya?"

Jerry gave me a hand, and I exited through a side door, quickly scanning the parking lot to make sure I wouldn't run into anyone who might want to chat. The coast was clear. I slipped between parked cars and into the rectory without being noticed.

"*Bienvenido, padre*," Maria, our housekeeper, said as I entered the kitchen. So much for going undetected.

"Oh, hi, Maria." I was surprised to see her. She didn't work Saturdays.

"Jesus wake me last night."

"Did he?"

"Yes. To pray for somebody. Looks like is you. You okay?"

I sighed. "I've been better."

She let out a sympathetic "Come here, *mijito*," wrapped her flabby arms around me, and squeezed. Maybe Jesus didn't come down from the cross, but at least I had Maria.

"Is that why you've come today?" I asked.

"No, padre. I come because I left my mixer in the kitchen yesterday. Yours is burnt out, had to bring mine. I want to bake a cake today for my niece. Is her birthday tomorrow."

"Oh."

"*Hay café*," she said, pointing to the coffeepot. "You look like you could use a cup, or two."

🕈 🕈 🕈

As I nursed my cup of joe and slopped up my Raisin Bran, I heard the shuffling. Monsignor was coming. Monsignor shuffled. He didn't walk. A widowed parishioner once dared to offer him the walker her late husband used. She's now an Episcopalian.

In all my mind's toil to solve the Rubik's Cube, I hadn't even thought of Monsignor. *Thank you, God. The answer to my prayer.* Of course he knew about Grim Reaper and the White Death and ... everything ... He knew everything. He must. Why else would he have insisted on taking *all* after-hours calls?

"Feeling better?" I asked as he shuffled into the kitchen. He didn't answer, probably because he didn't hear me. Instead, he splayed the morning paper on the counter and ran his finger along the headlines, most likely the obituaries. It was the first thing he looked at every morning.

He cleared his throat and spoke, not looking up from the paper. "Did you know Rita scheduled some missionary for the Mass this morning?" he asked.

"Yeah, I forgot until Jerry reminded me."

"You forgot. I schlepped all the way across that parking lot. Ended up getting harangued by Lisa Stillman about Gretchen's singing. Too high-pitched, she said. I told her to take it up with you."

"Sorry about that."

He folded the paper, tossed it on the kitchen table in front of me, and began his breakfast routine.

"Communication, Reverend Pastor. A lot of problems are avoided with good communication."

"Tell me about it."

"I just did."

He pulled two mugs from the cupboard. From the fridge he plucked two hard-boiled eggs Maria had made the day before. Into one of the mugs he slid the eggs, shells still intact, and into the other he poured coffee. He pulled a spoon from the drawer, set it all down on the kitchen table opposite me, and went to work.

"You know, Jack, we young priests need role models. People who'll demonstrate these important principles of parish management, like communication."

"I always tell you when I need to change my schedule. And you can ask any of my former vicars if I ever once surprised them or forgot to inform them someone else was taking a Mass." He cracked an egg with his spoon and began flaking off the shell.

"I mean beyond the Mass schedule."

"When I was in charge, this place had better information flow than a gaggle of country club housewives. And if there's been any slippage, it's not my fault. For instance, I gave you important information the other day: Bea being left out in the cold. And the mayor's plan to run the homeless out of a perfectly unintrusive space while giving them no alternatives."

"Touché. But I don't think you're sharing everything."

"Where's the salt shaker?" He started spinning the lazy Susan, impatiently shuffling around the oil and vinegar, the five different kinds of hot sauces, the jar of pickles—shouldn't those be refrigerated?—and everything else that had once held its own designated spot in the pantry. "So I give you all that information, and you never ask my advice. I do know a thing or two about running a parish. But you need to go all the way to Rome and get some golden-tongued traditionalist to come help you."

"Fine. Can I ask you some pastoral advice?"

At this point he was up and searching the spice cupboard. "Where's the damn salt? What did she do with it?" He didn't hear me. I waited till he found it and got back to the table.

"Jack," I said, "can I ask you for some pastoral advice?"

He looked up at me over his glasses. "Oh, now the pastor wants to ask me for some advice. All right, sure. Whaddya got?"

"Remember that call we got at supper yesterday? It was a sick call. But it was different."

"Sick calls are sick calls. Don't worry about it."

"The caller had a gruff voice saying someone needed last rites but that they'd come and pick—"

"Stop. Don't talk about it."

"You know what I was going to say?"

"I said don't talk about it." He scooped up a piece of egg and put it in his mouth.

"So this has happened to you?" I put my hand out, trying to get him to stop focusing on his egg and look at me. "The White Death? It's a thing?"

That got his attention. He let go of the spoon and glared at me. "Look. People die. Everybody dies. Some die peacefully in their sleep; others have a heart attack while they're mowing the lawn; others get knocked off. Everybody dies. Our job is to get them ready for it. It's a helluva lot easier when they know it's coming."

"That's it? Just turn a blind eye to everything else?"

"We do them a service. We don't ask questions. We don't get involved. We just do our job."

I stared at him a moment, amazed at his Machiavellian rationale. "I can't do that. I mean, yeah, sure, we all die, and it's nice to know when it's coming, but not like this. Sure, we worry about the victims' poor souls, but what about the murderers? What about their souls? You just let them go to hell?"

"And what choice did I have? You think I should've called the police? And said what? 'Hey, policeman, somebody's gonna get killed, but I don't know who, and I don't know where, and I can't tell ya how I know, but I do.' Yeah, that'll work."

Apparently he never solved the Rubik's Cube either.

"Well, you could have just not participated," I said.

"You think so? You think then the guy wouldn't die? 'Oh, the priest won't come. Darn, guess we can't kill him now.' Is that how it would go?" He started working on the second egg; a bit of shell stuck to his forefinger. "At least I kept the door open. What if this were ten years ago and we still had the death penalty? Would you go confess an inmate on his way to the chair?"

"That's different."

"What's different? Nothing. One's the government; the other's the mob. The guy in a cell on death row and the guy in that room at ... at ... the guy in that room are both preparing for death, and we're there to walk 'em through the door."

"At where? Where's the room?"

"I'm done with this conversation."

"Come on, Jack. Tell me. What room? Where did they take me last night? Is it always the same place?"

He pounded his fist on the table, his eyes boring into me. "I said I'm done talking about it. Do you understand?" I nodded sheepishly. He pushed back from the table, got up, and shuffled defiantly out of the kitchen. I sat motionless. Fifteen seconds later he shuffled back in, grabbed his coffee cup and the cup of eggs with the spoon sticking out, and left again.

Over the next five minutes, still sitting at the kitchen table, cold coffee and soggy Raisin Bran in front of me, I cycled through every negative emotion from frustration to consternation and then landed at resignation. What could

I do? Maybe Monsignor was right. Maybe he wasn't. The only thing I knew for certain was that I needed to let it go. Forget about it. Get it out of my head. The more I thought about it, the more confused I was. Clarity would come when I'd be thinking about something else. With every brilliant idea I ever had, every puzzle I ever solved, the answers had come in the shower, or during my morning jog, or while sitting in traffic. So forgetting about it became my mission. I'd focus on my weekend duties. Confessions at four o'clock, Mass at five, three Masses the next day. Focus. Focus and forget.

And it worked. Almost.

As I headed over to the church that afternoon for confessions, I noticed a white envelope on the ground beneath the mail slot. I picked it up. Someone had scrawled "Father Layhee" on the front with a black Sharpie, then with a Bic had crossed out "Layhee" and written "Heart". I tore it open and found four crisp one-hundred-dollar bills. That was it. Nothing else. My stipend for services rendered, I guessed. My hand trembled just a little.

When I returned after the five o'clock Mass, I tucked the envelope in a random book, stuck the book back on the shelf in the living room, had a light dinner, and went to bed. I slept—not soundly, but I slept.

6

Lupita

"Check your voicemail."

"Good morning to you too, Rita."

"I'm serious."

"I will, I will. Gimme a minute."

I should really have taken Mondays off. People think a priest's job is easy. What does it take to celebrate a few Masses on Sunday? I do the same thing three times in a row. Even the homily is the same all three times (although any priest will tell you, it's never the same homily—and the second one is always the best). Yet, in some strange way, the huddled masses in the pews seem to drain me. Then there's the post-Mass meet and greet on the front steps, trying to remember whether it was little Tommy or his brother who slipped on the ice and broke his wrist. And is that Tina Bertelli in the flowery chiffon dress, or is it Cathy Sawyer ... no, wait, Saylor ... no, Taylor? I ended each Sunday wiped out, and Monday morning came too quickly. This Monday in particular.

The light on my office phone blinked. I hit speaker, dialed voicemail, and powered up my computer.

"You have ... five ... messages ... First ... message."

I clicked open my Gmail as the first voicemail rattled on. It was the plumber. Turned out the check I gave him bounced. *Great. Would it be ethical to try to renegotiate?*

"Second … message." Now a long-winded voicemail from my sister about possible gifts for our mother's seventy-fourth birthday. But it was still three months away.

I skimmed the email headers on my computer screen, my sister's stream of consciousness droning in the background, every so often her children's fingernails-on-chalkboard screams piping up.

One email jumped out at me. It was from Andrew.

Subject: My demands

C.

Lovely spending time with you, old man. Hope you arrived safely.

As discussed, I am happy to assist in that parish gentrification project of yours.

Now my demands:

1. Upon arrival I expect to be furnished with a suite on the third floor of the rectory. The suite shall consist of a bedroom, a full bathroom, and a sitting room. Don't tell me you don't have the space. I know that rectory.
2. My furniture is to be retrieved from storage. The key is with Trish. Use Morgan's Movers out of Tuckahoe. I don't trust anyone else. Ask for Josh and tell him whose things you're moving.
3. Remove whatever tawdry IKEA trash you have in the sitting room and place my burgundy armchair in the corner facing the window, and the leather armchair in the adjacent corner, also facing the window. The Chippendale bureau plat shall face the door, but on an angle, the two Hepplewhite chairs on either side.
4. My bookcases may be left in storage for now since the sitting room has built-ins. By the by, the built-ins are rather shoddy. We'll have to talk about renovations once I'm over there.

5. Make sure any cool lightbulbs are replaced with warm. And please, none of those gawdy LEDs.

6. Replace the bed you bought at Bob's Discount Furniture with my Belle Époque bed frame. I've ordered a mattress, and it'll arrive in five days.

7. All the rest—the knickknacks, boxes of books, side tables, and such—shall be placed in the sitting room for me to arrange upon arrival.

I appreciate you, Christopher. You are a true friend. I don't know where I'd be without you.

Cheers,
A.

I clicked the Forward icon, inserted a shrug emoji, and sent it to Rita.

"Third ... message."

I jotted a note on a Post-it—*Call sis*—and pressed it to the bottom of my monitor, next to a half dozen more, as the next voicemail started to play.

"Uh ... yes. This message is for Father Hart." A female voice, nervous, trying hard to maintain composure. "Father, this is Maggie. Maggie Spencer. Maggie O'Brien Spencer? We met a couple weeks ago at my mother's? She asked me to call. It's Richie, my brother. He passed away on Saturday. It was sudden. A heart attack. Um ... anyway, my mother asked me to call and arrange things. Could you call us back? I think you have the number. Thank you. Good-bye."

Mrs. O'Brien was one of the shut-ins I had visited only a week before the Rome trip, the one with the schizophrenic husband. I remembered the visit fondly. On the drive over that day, my mind had conjured up a blue-haired, blue-eyed granny wrapped in a crocheted shawl—a defensible hypothesis given the ethnic surname O'Brien and Rita's intel putting her in her mideighties. And I was close: silver hair, arthritic hands twisted around a walker, a faded blue housecoat with a pattern of little pink roses (provenance: Sears mail-order catalogue, circa 1977). She was the quintessential granny, but not an Irish granny.

On that visit, a liver-spotted hand, skin the color of a baseball glove, had pushed the screen door open.

"You're not Monsignor," she had said, her voice scratchy yet sweet. I still remember her round brown eyes looking up at me. It turned out her first name was Lupita, her maiden name Ramirez, and she was from El Paso, Texas. Her husband, Richard O'Brien, had been in the military, stationed at Fort Bliss.

Maggie had come in at the end of the visit, right after Lupita had finished telling me about Maggie's no-good ex-husband who had left her for a woman half his age.

When I heard the voicemail say, "He passed away ... it was sudden," my instinct connected Lupita's dead son with my Friday-night penitent. But the connection was unlikely. I get calls like Maggie's all the time. And wasn't Numbers going to be shot? Wasn't that what the whole imaginary pistol-to-the-temple thing was about? Just because I met Numbers on Friday and Lupita's son was found dead on Saturday didn't mean they were the same person. No, there was no reason to think the two deaths were in reality one death, but I thought it nevertheless.

I decided I wouldn't call back; I'd just go over and see them.

🐦 🐦 🐦

"Oh, Father, you didn't have to come all the way over." Maggie opened the front door. The skin around her eyes was pink and puffy.

"I figured I'd stop by. I'm really sorry for your loss."

"Thank you. I know, it's so sad. Please come in." She held the screen door with her arm, moving her body out of the way. "Don't mind the mess. Have a seat anywhere."

The dilapidated couch in the living room received me with an achy twang. My nostrils twitched at a potpourri of Lysol and litter box, and an antique clock ticked away on the mantel. Lupita had repeated over and over how she had been living in this house for sixty-three years. The matted shag carpet and burlap wallpaper, as well as the furniture, threadbare and sagging, must have all been original.

"My mother's in the bedroom. I called her when I saw you drive up. She'll be coming shortly." Maggie, a redhead, was probably in her early fifties but managed to appear midfortyish. She sported a Martha Stewart look— untucked mint-green button-down over tan slacks, sleeves rolled up below the elbows, a circus of gold bangles on her wrists, sensible yet stylish shoes—that clashed with the Dickensian surroundings.

From the kitchen emerged another woman, older than Maggie. Her shoulder-length hair was silver, and she wore a navy pantsuit and a pair of reading glasses looped around her neck.

I stood.

"This is my sister, Connie. Connie, this is Father Hart from St. Dominic's."

I extended my hand. "A pleasure to meet you, Connie. I'm sorry for your loss."

"Thank you," she said. She had stern features—a slight resemblance to her mother but without the sweetness. And she had a mole. Not a cute pin-dot mole by the corner of her mouth but a hairy honker of a mole on her upper cheek. The kind you try not to stare at and wonder why she doesn't have it removed.

Maggie had smiled warmly when she saw me, despite her grief. Connie didn't.

"Father, can I get you something to drink? Maybe some coffee?" Maggie asked.

"Sure. Love some."

"Cream or sugar?"

"No. Black. It matches my outfit." Maggie smiled at that. Connie maintained her flinty demeanor.

"Con?"

"Thanks, Mags. I'm fine."

Maggie left the room. No sign yet of Lupita. Connie and I sat. A moment of awkward silence passed.

"I imagine this is quite difficult for you," I said.

"Yes, well ... it's sad. I can't say I'm surprised, though. But still, when it hits you, it's hard."

I nodded sympathetically. "Why do you say it doesn't surprise you?"

"My brother didn't take care of himself. He chain-smoked, only ate what he could microwave, and never exercised. It was either going to be a heart attack or lung cancer. I told my mother to expect the call any day. I told *him* that too. He didn't listen. He was a lot like my dad that way."

"Your mother told me about your father."

"Did she? And what did she say? 'He was such a good man.'" She mimicked Lupita's voice. "'He had his ups and downs, but he was a good man at heart, and he so loved his children.' Is that what she told you?"

"Well, more or less. She did explain his illness to me. I suppose that can account for, well, a lot, you know? It's hard enough being a parent when you're mentally stable. I can't imagine what it's like when you have schizophrenia."

She gave me a searching look. "I'm not sure if my mother told you, that I'm a psychologist?"

"Yes. She did." She had given me the whole run-down of the family. There were four kids. Connie was the oldest. Lupita had told me she was a psychiatrist. Close enough, I guess. Josefina, the second oldest, had died fifteen years before from cancer. Richie was next. He was an accountant at a restaurant in town, which Lupita couldn't remember the name of. Maggie was last. She was a real estate agent with Coldwell Banker. "Your mother is very proud of you," I said. "She says you're very good at what you do."

"She would say that. My mother has a good heart. And she paints a rosy picture of people, that's for sure. Listening to her, you would think she's never met a bad person in her life." She fixed the pillow to fit better in the small of her back. "Have you ever met a bad person, Father? I mean really bad?"

"Yes. A few."

"In my line of work you meet a lot of bad people. But you meet victims of bad people more. My mother's lived a sheltered life. It revolves around her kids, the grandkids, and this house. She's never been west of the Hudson or south of the Bronx. I, on the other hand, have been around."

Connie wasn't turning out to be the grief-stricken sister I'd expected. She was in full mason mode, laying brick on brick, erecting a wall of defense mechanisms. If there had been another psychologist in the room, I would've asked for some insight.

"What kind of psychology do you practice?"

"I'm a clinical psychologist. I work with women. Trauma survivors mostly. It's amazing what women suffer. Did you know, Father, that one out of every five women is the victim of abuse?" Oh, this wasn't going to be just a wall—it would be a fortress. I could hear the portcullis clattering down, the cannons rolling into place, the guards goose-stepping to their posts.

"I knew the number was high," I said, "but I didn't think it was that high."

"And that's just sexual abuse. It gets higher when we talk about physical, emotional, and verbal abuse. You know, I counsel some former nuns. Now, talk about abuse. We call that spiritual abuse. The Church has its fair share of abusers. Were you aware of that, Father?"

Warning shot. *Do not engage. Do not engage.* I cleared my throat. "Well, of course, anytime there are human beings involved, there will always be—"

Trumpets blared in the distance: the hollow clanking of Lupita's walker. *Thank God, the cavalry has arrived.*

"Margaret, did you offer Father something to drink?" she asked, still plodding down the hall, her voice raspy.

"Yes, Mother, I did," Maggie yelled from the kitchen.

I stood as Lupita came in. "Your daughter was very gracious, Mrs. O'Brien."

"Oh, I see you've met Connie. She's good for conversation, isn't she?" Lupita trudged over to what was evidently *her* chair. "My Connie's so smart. She's a psychiatrist. Did I tell you that?" With effort she lowered herself into the recliner. "She can tell you all sorts of things about how the brain works." Lupita tapped her temple. "She got straight As in school."

"Yes, I see that," I said. "She certainly knows a lot." Turning to Connie, I attempted a pleasant smile, though I'm not sure what actually appeared on my face. She wasn't making the same effort.

Maggie came in with two cups of coffee and handed me one.

"Thank you," I said as I sat back down. "How are you hanging in there?" I asked, scooting to the edge of the couch so I could take Lupita's hand.

"I'm all right. Connie had been telling me to expect him to go soon. She's a doctor. She knows these things. I told poor Richie he should listen to her, but he didn't. Of course, I'm sad to lose my boy. He'd laugh if he heard me call him 'my boy'. He's a grown man, you know. But he'll always be my little boy. Anyway, he's with the good Lord now. Is there a better place for him to be?" Her gaze was distant. "Why should I be so sad when he's where I want to be? I'll see him there too, soon enough. And I'll see my dear Dickie." She turned to look at me. "Won't that be wonderful, Father?"

"Yes, Lupita. That will be wonderful." I patted her hand. Her eyes were clear and bright; any tears had long since dried up. In her eighty-six years she must have seen so much. "I have to tell you, I am very impressed by your faith. You're taking this remarkably well."

"Her faith or her denial?" Connie whispered to Maggie.

I shot her a disapproving glance and then said to Lupita, "Do you have a photo of Richie?"

"Oh, somewhere, don't we, Margaret?"

"Sorry, Father," Maggie said, "we aren't picture people." I hadn't noticed before, but scanning the living room, I saw that the only photographs were a black-and-white wedding picture on an end table, presumably Lupita and Richard, and a portrait of Richard in his army uniform over the mantel. Otherwise, only an oil painting of a ship at sea over the couch and a print of the Sacred Heart of Jesus on the opposite wall adorned the room.

"Check in the kitchen, sweetie, under the counter where the toaster is. You'll have to pull out the phone books and the coupon box. I think Dickie's old album is there."

Maggie went and came back with an oddly shaped picture frame. She handed it to me. The frame was shaped like the outline of Mickey Mouse's head, except in place of Mickey's face, there was a photo of the smiling O'Brien kids huddled in front of a concession stand.

"This is the last picture taken of the four of us. Don't be fooled by the frame. That's Playland down in Mamaroneck, not Disney World. We could never afford Disney."

The smiles on the kids' faces were forced, their bodies rigid. I could imagine the before and after: complaints of the heat, unmet demands for cotton candy, name calling, hair pulling, threats to tell Mom.

"That's Richie in the middle," she said.

I squinted, trying to make out the face. My jaw went loose. "Numbers," I said under my breath. It was an eleven-year-old version of Numbers. The photo was slightly out of focus and he hadn't aged well, but it was definitely him.

"What was that?" Connie asked.

"What was what?" I said.

"What did you just say?"

"Oh, um ... numbness," I said, not sure she bought it. "Numbness. That's the impression I get when I look into his eyes. Like there's a lot of pain there. Repressed. Like he's numb."

"He was autistic," Maggie said. "He always looked like that."

"You said 'numbers,'" Connie insisted.

"You just heard that, Con," Maggie said. "You see, Father, our brother only spoke in numbers or words associated with numbers. Connie can explain it better, but I guess it's due to a mix of his autism and childhood trauma. We always thought he'd grow out of it. But it just became how he was. Like it was safer to hide behind the numbers."

"He was such a smart boy when it came to math," Lupita said. "He was really good at math. He wasn't good

at English or social studies or any of the other subjects.
And he wasn't good at sports. That's hard when you're a
boy. I remember he used to come home crying. He was
always the last one picked for teams and such. And during
recess he would just sit by the wall playing with his Match-
box cars. The kids would make fun of him. They could
be pretty cruel. He didn't have people skills either. Dick
used to say that Richie was a late bloomer, that it would
take time but he'd figure things out and do something
he was good at and do it really well. And that's just what
happened. Dickie told me to give him some time and he'd
find his way. He was right."

"Actually," Maggie said, "there was that time—
remember, Con?—when Dad almost got hit by a car.
Richie screamed, 'One car! One car!' And it worked. Josie
grabbed Dad and pulled him out of the street."

"True," Connie said. "When things were serious,
Richie would find a way to say more than just numbers, as
long as a number was in there somewhere."

Words like *White Death, she knows*. Words that meant
life and death. What was he trying to tell me at the end, as
Grim walked in? Another 'one car' moment? A chance to
yank someone else out of the street before a car careened
into him? *Three, fifteen, fourteen. She knows*. Who was this
she? There were three females in that living room. Was she
one of them?

"Connie's really the only one who could communicate
with him easily," Lupita said.

"She cracked the code," Maggie agreed, chuckling.

"If you'd had more patience, you could have too,"
Connie said. "It's just a matter of listening. Thinking.
Making connections. It's what I do all day. Listen and
make connections. And you could have done it too, if
you'd tried."

Connie had cracked the code. Connie was the one who could make connections. Connie knew how to talk to him. Connie was the *she who knew*, wasn't she? Even if she wasn't, she was my best lead.

"Connie got him the job at Stefano's," Maggie said to me.

"Stefano's? That place on Grant Street?" I asked.

"That's right. Connie convinced them he'd be a good employee."

Connie interjected, "Not exactly. They put an ad out for a bookkeeper, and Richie applied. I just took him over for the interview and translated. I taught them how to work with him. Nothing more."

"Father," Lupita interrupted, "do you think we could have 'On Eagle's Wings' at the funeral?"

The comment jolted me back to the reason I had come in the first place.

"Oh, sure, Lupita. That's a classic. In fact, if you're up to it, I thought we could go over the funeral details. I'm happy to do that with you. If you're ready, of course. No pressure."

"Oh, that's fine, Father. We can do that. I've got nowhere to be."

"I have a booklet here. It has the different readings you can choose from and the songs. Shall we all look at it together?" And maybe I could work those numbers into the conversation and see whether Connie would bite. She could crack the code.

"All right, we can do that."

"They're numbered, see—"

"Mom," Connie broke in, "I have some errands to run this morning. I need to meet with the people at Cassidy's. They want us to pick out the casket, headstone, whatever. I'll leave you three to work on this." She rose and picked up her purse.

"No, Connie, I want you to be here. You know I can't read very well anymore. I need you to read these things for me."

"I'm sure Maggie can help you with that."

If Maggie's eyes were pistols, Connie would've been dead.

"All right. You can go. Margaret and I will take care of the rest. But promise me you'll come to the funeral." Lupita turned to me and said, "She doesn't go to church anymore, Father. It breaks my heart, and she knows it."

"Mother, I don't think this is the time to talk about that. Of course I'll be at Richie's funeral. I'll even read if you want me to."

As Connie started for the door, I stood.

"Allow me to walk you out."

"Thanks, Father, I think I know my way."

"I insist."

She shrugged, and I walked her out to her car.

"Connie, I enjoyed our conversation ... when we were alone there for a moment. I know you weren't trying to make it enjoyable, but I like having a sparring partner now and again. I'd love the opportunity to continue our conversation sometime. Would you be open to that?"

She scoffed. "Look, I'll be at the funeral. I don't want to make any more commitments than that right now. This is a distressing time, as you can imagine." She pulled the keys from her purse and opened the car door.

"I'd like to talk about what happened to your brother. Why were you expecting him to die so soon?"

She looked at me, then across the street, and then back at me. "Yeah, maybe we can talk. I need some time. You understand. I'll call you; don't call me."

"Sure. Right. Call me whenever you want ... or not. Whatever. If it works out, it works out. Here, take my card." I fished a business card from my wallet, set it on the hood of the car, scribbled *3*, *15*, *14* on the back, as if I were jotting down my private line, and handed it to her. "Please call me sometime."

She got into the car and started the engine. I stood there and watched her back out and drive away.

7

Ashley

Blond cat fur blanketed the back of my suit coat and, from what I could tell, the seat of my pants. The lint roller I kept in my glovebox pulled off only the loose stuff. I'd need a brush, or better, a vacuum cleaner. I never saw the cat, just the litter box in the corner of Lupita's kitchen. And I smelled it. No amount of Lysol could ever cover up the pungent odor of cat urine in that house, which told me more than one cat lived there.

Now, standing next to my car parked along Grant Street, I flung the roller onto the passenger-side floor mat in resignation, tossed my jacket on the back seat, and clicked the locks.

I had finished with the O'Briens. The funeral details were set. Work awaited me at the office. But I wasn't at the office. Instead, I stared down the block—Shiny Cleaners on one corner, Fast Cash Payday Loans on the other, and sandwiched between them, a three-story brick building: Stefano's Italian Bistro. Why was I standing down the street from Stefano's? Why hadn't I just gone back to the rectory? I wasn't looking for clues, I told myself. I wasn't searching for something that would solve the riddle the dying man had left me. No, I had promised myself not twenty-four hours ago I wasn't going to pursue it. I was simply passing by the workplace of the man whose funeral I was to celebrate in a couple of days. Why not? If I were to give a homily, I'd need details, stories about his life. Where better to get them than at his work? And it was lunchtime. It's a restaurant. A man can eat lunch at a restaurant, can't he?

By the time I reached the door, I had worked through the denial and leveled with myself, the situation laid bare before me: On Friday night two goons brought me to some undisclosed location to hear a man's confession. On Saturday I was spooked, but at least it was over. By Sunday evening I was resolved to drop it. Now, midday on Monday, the man they called Numbers had been revealed to me as one Richie O'Brien. Richie had a family, and in particular a sister who seemed to know how to decipher his cryptic codes. I had a code that needed deciphering, but I couldn't tell anyone—the whole Rubik's Cube conundrum. I was on my own. From Friday night to Monday midday, I had gone from a movie extra to a supporting character. The momentum now carried me into a leading role. Next scene: snooping at Stefano's.

The only thing elegant about the place was the name: Stefano's Italian Bistro. Yet it was clearly a new name; the restaurant's former moniker, Skip's Place, was still faintly visible beneath the sign's shoddy paint job.

Inside it was Tuscany meets Denny's. The warm saffron-and-vermilion stucco walls and the plastic grapevine strung over the bar were a halfhearted attempt at Italian ambience, undermined by Formica-topped tables and beige vinyl booths—probably repurposed from more glorious days at a diner somewhere upstate. An operatic rendition of "O sole mio" played just a bit too loud overhead.

Though it was lunch hour, the place was empty. No one stood at the hostess stand. A bartender clicked through channels on a wall-mounted TV.

Without looking over, the bartender said, "Sit wherever. Someone'll be right out."

I chose a spot next to a window so I could keep an eye on my car. *Yep, still there.* I turned back toward the empty restaurant and started a bit—a young waitress with streaks of purple and pink in her otherwise blonde hair had appeared from nowhere, pad in hand.

"Hi, I'm Ashley. I'll be your server today." Her voice was dreary, as if I were a phone call that had just woken her up. Her appearance was also dreary: chipped black fingernail polish matching a black T-shirt, black lipstick, and black eyeliner over metallic pink eyeshadow; she looked like a character out of *The Rocky Horror Picture Show.* "Can I get you something to drink?"

"Just some water with lemon. Thanks, Ashley."

She turned robotically and plodded away. She wore a short black skirt. Blotches on the back of her leg caught my eye. A birthmark? Or maybe an injury?

The five-page menu she left me featured three pages of Italian cuisine, faded pictures interspersed: pasta primavera, veal piccata, *pollo francese* and, of course, fettuccine Alfredo. I scoffed. These ersatz dishes were beneath me; I had been to Italy. I flipped to the back—the American Classics section—my fingers sticking to the plastic pages.

Ashley soon returned with the water, but no lemon. As she approached, I got a better look at her leg, taking staggered glances so as not to stare. It wasn't a birthmark after all but a pant leg of tattoos: thick vines embedded with fleurs-de-lis, ying-yang symbols, and little stars or maybe suns with smiley faces, all forming the background for a scaly serpent slithering up out of her Doc Martens. The snake's head, just over the knee, was that of Marilyn Monroe staring salaciously at a skull. And vertically along the outer calf ran the name BRIAN etched in three-dimensional block letters.

"Have you decided?" she asked.

"Yes. I think I'll just have a club sandwich."

"You want fries?"

"No, not really. Actually, can you get me a side of spinach?"

She gave me a look that matched my impression of her tattoo, then shrugged and scribbled on her notepad.

"Anything else?"

"Yes."

She looked at me warily, as if bracing herself for a picky customer, this guy who just ordered a side of spinach.

"I have to tell you," I said, "that tattoo is fascinating."

She smiled in relief, her slit eyes turning wide and round like a manga character's. "Do you like it?"

"The artistry is amazing. It is *so* intricate."

"Right? The guy did a great job."

"It must've taken forever."

"It did! But I didn't get it all done at once. He made me come in like three times."

"Did it hurt?"

"Everyone asks that! Yes, it hurt *a lot*. Especially the part around the kneecap. That was the worst."

"So, the symbols ... do they mean anything?"

"No, not really. The guy like had this little booklet, and I could pick stuff. My mom grew up in New Orleans, so the little cornstalk thingy is for her."

"The fleur-de-lis?"

"Yeah, that. And my dad's a black belt, so the ling-lang is for him."

Ling-lang? I decided not to correct her. She was smiling now, and I didn't want to ruin it; she looked like she needed the practice.

"Can you see the little suns?" she asked. "They're really cute. At least I think so."

We were both looking down at her leg admiring the artistry, but my gaze wandered up to her face. I saw something new in it. Perhaps it was the angle, how the light hit, or the soft skin, her pure, youthful complexion. In that brief moment, beneath the heavy eyeliner and the faded black lipstick, an aura of natural innocence radiated. She was young, for sure, probably no more than twenty-two. It was clear the goth aesthetic was just a grasping for an identity. It wasn't the real her.

"Well, I better get your order in," she said. She was off again, this time with a slight bounce in her step.

"Could you bring some lemon?" I called out after her.

Ten minutes lapsed. I imagined Richie O'Brien in some office behind the kitchen updating profit-and-loss statements. Given his penchant for numbers, he must have done his job well. A model employee. No complaints out of him—nothing that anyone would take as a complaint, anyway. But who would hire a guy like Richie? The manager must have been a decent guy, or desperate. I'm sure Connie did her best to sell him. But still, it would have taken a special person to accept someone with his disability. Then again—and as this thought occurred to me, I could swear the theme song from *The Godfather* came over the speakers—if the place was run by the Mafia, what better person to have managing the books than a guy who can't snitch. He could see things or overhear things and not tell a soul since no one could understand him, except Connie. *But if Connie brought him for the interview, is she also mixed up with the—*

A club sandwich and a side of spinach plunked down in front of me. Still no lemon.

"Thanks, Ashley," I said, not looking up, keeping my train of thought on its rails. *Could Connie be mixed up in all this? I'll admit, she was quite the—*

"So, are you like a priest or something?" Ashley asked, derailing the train just in time.

"Um, yes. I am like a priest or something. What gave it away?"

"Well ..." She traced an invisible collar around her neck. "Does that mean you can't get married?"

I wanted to say *Everyone asks that!* but I resisted. "Yeah. Pretty much," I said.

"That sucks."

"You're not married, are you?"

She chuckled. "You've got something against marriage?"

"No, no, not at all. That's not what I meant." That was the second time I had stuck my foot in my mouth today. The first was the whole *Numbers/numbness* thing. Now this. "I just noticed you're not wearing a ring, that's all."

"No. No ring. I've been with a guy for like seven years, but he's ... we're not ready."

"Is that Brian?" I asked.

"Yeah. How'd you know?"

"I figured the tattoo on your leg was either for your boyfriend or your brother, and I figured it probably wasn't your brother."

"Oh yeah. I forgot about that."

"How old is Brian?"

"Thirty-five."

"But you're not thinking about marriage."

"I am. He's not. I mean, we've talked about it, but he says he wants to pay off his college loans first."

"Brian is thirty-five and he still hasn't paid off his college loans? What does he do?"

"He's a mechanic. Works at the Ford dealership in Scarsdale. He does deliveries for this place too, as a side hustle."

"Do you know where he went to college?"

"No, come to think of it." She snickered a little.

"Might be a good question."

"Yeah. I'll ask him that."

"So he's thirty-five and you're ..."

"Twenty-three."

"You're young." Too young. What was I talking to her about marriage for? When she said she had been with him for seven years, I figured she just *looked* young. Now I started doing the math. Seven years ago. A twenty-eight-year-old hitting on a sixteen-year-old. Something wasn't right. My paternal hackles were raised.

"Well, I'm not *that* young. I mean, I've already got a head start on my career. Better than a lot of my friends."

"Not a career in waitressing, I presume." She glowered at me. "I mean, there's nothing wrong with service as a career. I just don't sense a lot of opportunities for upward mobility in this place."

"Oh no. I'm only here till I get the job I really want."

"And what's that?"

"The theater." She drew out the word *theater*, feigning a dreamy-eyed look upward.

"Aren't you a little far north for that? I thought all the aspiring actresses waited tables down in SoHo."

"No. I don't want to act. I want to design! I'm going to be a set designer on Broadway. I'm taking online classes. My cousin has an in. She met this guy that builds sets for *Saturday Night Live*."

"Well, I wish you luck there."

"I'm serious. I've already been working with a production company setting up shoots for ads and stuff."

"I'm serious too. I love your dream. Go for it."

"I just have one semester left. Then I'll start applying for jobs."

This conversation wasn't going the direction I was hoping. I hadn't come here to talk about marriage or set

design. I had come here to find out about Richie O'Brien.
But what did I expect? My life is full of conversations like
this. It's part of being a priest. An eavesdropper might find
it strange that Ashley and I went from zero to sixty—from
tattoos to her romantic relationship—in five seconds flat.
But if that eavesdropper was a priest, he wouldn't find it
strange at all. People become remarkably candid with a
man of the cloth, and in the oddest places.

For example, at the supermarket, as I reach for a jar of
Tostito's chunky-style salsa, a middle-aged woman might
say, *Excuse me, are you a Catholic priest?* A half hour later
she's unloaded about her wayward son, apathetic husband,
and Alzheimer's-ridden mother-in-law, right there in aisle
seven. That's why many priests don't wear a Roman collar
when they run errands. It's also why I do.

"So, back to Brian, if I may. You're going to ask him
about where he went to school."

She nodded.

"You want to know another good question? Kids. Ask
him if he wants to have kids someday."

"Oh no. He doesn't. He already told me. We had a dog
for a little while, but he said it was too much work. He
didn't like having to walk the dog in the winter, when it's
cold out. It also barked a lot during the day. Brian works
the night shift and wants to sleep during the day. So we
had to get rid of the dog. I got my cousin to take it. Sandy,
you know, the one who met the *SNL* guy? Her dog died
the year before, and she told me she didn't want another
one. But then I told her that if she didn't take it, Brian
would shoot it. So she took it. Now she can't stand being
away from the little guy. Funny, isn't it?"

"So, does that tell you anything about him?"

"Um, that he doesn't like dogs?"

"No. About the kind of man he is."

Confusion flitted across her face.

"Never mind. Just think about it, would you? Also, when you have a chance, could you get me some lemon for the water?"

"Oh yeah. You asked for that. Sorry, I forgot."

"No problem. And another thing. Maybe when you get back with the lemon, you could tell me a little about Richie O'Brien?"

She screwed up her eyes. "Who?"

"Richard O'Brien. Didn't he work here?"

"Not that I know of. At least not the shifts I work. But he's not on the board either. So I don't think a guy by that name works here, no."

"Who's the bookkeeper?"

"I really don't know. All the back-office stuff is in Yonkers. They don't do that here."

"Okay. If Richie was the accountant, then he would work out of an office in Yonkers?"

"Yeah. Mr. Cardelli runs everything from there. That's where he started. Now he's got like three or four restaurants. But the one in Yonkers was the first."

"And what's that place called?"

"Cardelli's."

"Of course. Thanks. And don't forget the lemon."

"Right. Be right back," she said with a wink, then practically skipped away.

So why did the O'Briens say Richie had worked here? Maybe this is where the interview took place? Did I have to go to Yonkers now? Forget it. I had to drop this whole thing. I wasn't a detective, and I couldn't call one. And I was not going to Yonkers.

She brought the lemon and asked whether she could get me anything else. After I declined, she added, "By the way, standing policy, meals for clergy are on the house."

"Really? That's very kind."

"Yeah. Mr. Cardelli's a real religious guy. He wears a ring with this little cross on it and one of those scalpers."

"Scapulars?"

"Yeah, that. Sal says Mr. Cardelli has all these holy pictures in his office. Sal's the manager here. He's like, 'Instead of going to church, I just go to Mr. Cardelli's office.'"

"Sounds like a religious guy, all right."

"Sal? No way. He doesn't believe in anything."

"No, I meant Cardelli. You said he was a real religious guy. I was just agreeing."

"Oh. Yeah."

"Well, look, next time Mr. Cardelli comes in, let him know that Father Hart at St. Dominic's says he's always welcome at our church."

"Will do."

I smiled. She smiled back, looking at me as if she was expecting me to say something else. Awkward silence. Finally she said, "Well, I'll let you enjoy that food." She winked again and left me with my club sandwich.

It seemed I had made the trip in vain. But Ashley was nice, and it was a good chance to be alone and think. By the time I finished my meal, I had decided to get through the funeral and then let the whole Richie O'Brien affair go. I really didn't need to get involved with the mob, assuming that's who was behind this, and I had a parish to revive. I needed to focus.

I got up to leave. Ashley sat at a nearby booth intently tapping away at her phone.

"Hey, Ashley," I said.

"Yeah." Her eyes were still glued to her phone.

"Do the numbers three, fifteen, fourteen mean anything to you?"

"Nope."

"Okay. Just checking." As I reached the door, I called back, "And another thing. You're a pretty girl."

She tilted her head up and cocked an eyebrow.

"That's a gift. Don't squander it. Make yourself a gift for someone who deserves you."

❦ ❦ ❦

I was outside, walking to my car. The tug-of-war between winter and spring was still raging, the bright sun warming one side of my face, the chill air freezing the other. My mind continued to crank away at the Rubik's Cube.

Literature and TV provide abundant examples of detective priests. There is G. K. Chesterton's Father Brown (now the BBC's Father Brown), and then there's Ralph McInerny's Father Dowling (now ABC's Father Dowling). While in Italy, I discovered Don Matteo (now and always, Rai 1's Don Matteo), a streetwise parish priest played by Terence Hill, who winds up in all sorts of neighborhood crime-fighting adventures.

While these characters are quaint, I have one major issue with them: none of them seems to have a day job, as if one can just go off on some escapade and leave his parish duties for an angel to take care of. I was not a Father Brown or a Father Dowling or a Don Matteo. I was Father Hart, a man with a mission to rebuild St. Dominic's. Rather than figure out who may have killed Richie O'Brien, I could do more good by revamping my parish, turning it from some cute relic that people vaguely recall from childhood—like a dial-up modem or an eight-track tape—into a component of life as essential as their smartphones.

A big reason the Mafia has mafiosi to begin with is because the Church failed in some part of her mission. There were neglected poor who got swept up in easy money;

fatherless boys looking for belonging, ritual, meaning; people wallowing in a culture of fear, trapped in a prison of shame; men staring down a dead-end street, the only door propped open by the foot of a mob boss. If the Church is positioned right, she can provide opportunity to people who can't get a break otherwise, shine rays of hope on other doors, reveal to darkened eyes new possibilities.

The Church's mission on earth is to be a ship to carry people of all kinds to safe harbor. I needed to focus on building a bigger boat, not fighting organized crime.

As I stepped onto Grant Street again, I had almost convinced myself that I really was just a minor character in this crime thriller, already exiting stage right. Then I passed the alley next to Stefano's. I wouldn't have noticed it if I hadn't caught a glimpse of a car heading down the alley. No, not just a car. An SUV. A black SUV. I stopped, paralyzed, staring straight ahead, the alley to my right. *No, I'm not going down there. Forget it. I'm done with this.* But I couldn't walk forward. I looked down the narrow passageway, just wide enough for the SUV not to scrape its mirrors. The vehicle turned the corner around the back of the building. I followed, hugging the shady side. *I am so stupid. Why am I doing this?*

The sound of the vehicle's doors opening and shutting bounced off the building wall. Two indistinct male voices talked casually. I reached the end of the alley and peeked one eye around the corner. The two men were gone, apparently already inside the building; the SUV was parked by the restaurant's service entrance, a good forty yards from me. A sudden breeze blew dumpster stench in my face. I looked around, especially up, at the surrounding buildings. Yes, everything was familiar. I marked the position of the sun and imagined where it would go if it were setting. This was the same place, the same scene.

That was the dumpster I had passed; that was the door where I was told to watch my step; those were the buildings I saw through the second-story window when I confessed Richie O'Brien before he died—was murdered. *I can't forget, he was murdered.*

I memorized the tag number and retreated.

Good enough for ya? Yeah, I'm satisfied. I got back to my car unnoticed, as far as I knew. My next stop was home.

🦗 🦗 🦗

In the time it took to get from Stefano's to the rectory, the sky darkened; gray clouds like clumps of freshly sheared wool cropped up overhead. This wasn't in the forecast. Little did I know it was an omen for the storm brewing inside.

"Whatcha got for me, Rita?" I said, entering the main office.

"Oh, you got something ... coming. But not from me." She smiled and tore up some form she had been reviewing. She ripped it up slowly, as if she was enjoying it, then tossed it in the wastebasket.

"What's up?"

"Monsignor's in your office, and he's about to blow a casket."

"You mean gasket? What'd I do now?"

"I think it has something to do with that email you forwarded me this morning." She grabbed another form, ran her eyes across it, then looked at me over her reading glasses. "You know, I'm here to help you. You could've told me who this new priest was."

"Why? What about him?"

"Never mind. You'll find out." She held the form up with both hands and tore slowly, smiling, still looking at me.

Bracing myself, I walked into my office and found Monsignor sitting in my chair.

"Make yourself comfortable, Jack," I said, closing the door.

"Sit down."

"I would, but you're in my chair."

"*Sit. Down.*" He spat out each word as if it were its own sentence.

"Okaaay." I sat in the chair in front of the desk. I was taller than Monsignor, much taller; yet when I sat, he was looking down at me.

"You didn't tell me it was Andrew Reese."

"You know him?"

"Do I know him? I fired him. Five years ago. Why do you think he's in Rome?"

"He was assigned here? That was you?"

I remembered something about Andrew's last assignment before he went off to study in Rome. It had been short, maybe a year. But I always pictured him at St. Philip's in the Bronx. He used to gripe about the pastor, a suspicious, controlling monsignor who was always jealous of Andrew's success. Toward the end of that school year, every time we got together it was story after story about the lengths to which this man went to undermine him: taking him off the Sunday Mass schedule except for the 7:00 A.M.—the Mass only elderly people and golfers attended; canceling his evening Bible studies; pulling him off the liturgy committee; and demanding he tender a weekly expense report. The last straw was insisting he submit his homilies for review.

That was when Andrew requested a transfer—he was not fired, as Monsignor claimed—and proposed the idea of getting a doctorate in canon law so he could work in an office downtown rather than be subjected to another tyrannical pastor. As bad as his new boss in the chancery might potentially be, at least the two of them wouldn't be living under the same roof.

Six years ago, as we sat drinking cognac and smoking cigars on the back porch of my mother's house in Staten Island, he kept talking about St. Phil's, and only now did I make the connection. He meant St. Philomena's, our now-defunct mission church. For several years it had operated under the auspices of St. Dominic's, until the archdiocese finally decided to deconsecrate it. It was a wonder he accepted my invitation to come here. Maybe he thought Monsignor had moved or died—a reasonable assumption. Or maybe he wanted revenge—another reasonable assumption.

"You call him up right now and tell him it's off," Monsignor demanded.

I folded my arms over my chest, crossed my legs, and leaned back.

"Come on. He's not that bad."

"I already called the chancery and put the kibosh on it. Now, you get on the phone. Call Reese."

"You had no right to do that. Besides, the chancery won't listen to you. You're not the pastor anymore."

"I've still got pull."

"Jack, listen to me. Andrew is coming. Deal with it."

He looked at me as if I were the first person in his life to tell him to deal with it.

"I'm sorry," I said. "Look, I know he can be kind of eccentric, but he's a good priest. He loves the people. He gives his all to the parish. I should know; I lived with him for three years."

"*Eccentric*'s not the word. *Egocentric* is more like it. I've never met a more self-centered, stuck-up glory hound in my life. And trust me, I've met a lot."

"Glory hound? Oh, so that's it. You're jealous."

"I am not jealous. He's all show and no substance. He only makes an appearance when his adoring fans are around. I was the one who rolled up my sleeves and did the dirty work. I went to the hospital, I went to the nursing home—hell, I even went to Bingo Night. And where did he go? He went to lunch and to dinner and to the club."

"There's another place he went I bet you don't know about. Do you know where he went on his day off?"

"Golfing."

"That too, sometimes. But every week on his day off he went up to Sing Sing to visit the inmates. On his day off! Who does that?"

"He's just picking out his future cell."

"Oh, so now he's a criminal?"

"Where does he get all that money?"

"A trust fund."

"You know that for sure?"

"No. But that's what his sister told me. Some old lady took a liking to him when he was in sem and left him a tidy sum. His sister says it's all locked up in a trust so he only gets a certain amount every month."

"You believe that? He told me he inherited real estate upstate and gets income from it. And, by the way, that's where he goes on his days off. To check on his real estate."

"Well, there you go. He told you that because he didn't want you to know where he was really going. He's humble that way. The uppity attitude is all show. Deep down he's a good priest. I know he goes to the prison. I followed him there. Gary McLeod—he was our pastor back then—thought something was up too, and to prove Andrew was a good man I followed him four weeks in a row. A whole month. I got pictures."

"You don't understand. He's bad news."

"No, *you* don't understand." I uncrossed my legs and leaned forward. "I need to resurrect this parish you've let deteriorate due to your micromanaging and your conceited, condescending attitude." Blood rose to my face, and my fists clenched reflexively. "If you didn't play pope and fire every good soul that had a little more talent than you, maybe we wouldn't be where we are. Maybe we'd still have a school, maybe we'd have more than church ladies at daily Mass, and we'd certainly be in the black. But as it is, somebody's gotta do something and this is what I came up with."

That was harsh, and on the surface, unmerited. An overreaction on my part. But Andrew had told me about the old monsignor who had kicked him out so hard he landed in Rome. And now that I knew whom he meant, I was incensed. Andrew was my friend. And as capricious as he could be, he was not a scoundrel, and I wouldn't let him be treated as one.

Monsignor stood, pulled up on his belt, straightened his shirt, and started for the door. "Don't say I didn't warn you."

8

Sal

Lupita wanted the funeral on Tuesday, the day after I sat on her dilapidated couch sipping coffee and collecting cat hair. "That's how we did it back home," she told me. Wake, funeral, and burial in twenty-four hours. "We'd keep vigil over the body all night," she said. Keeping vigil is an ancient tradition still observed in places where the faith runs deep. In the United States, we tend to plan the funeral for the most convenient moment. Though some take it too far: A friend of mine's father died one January. He had the body cremated and then stuck the ashes in his closet. "We'll do Dad's funeral in May when it's warmer. We'll time it with Maddy's graduation."

To be fair, the pious take it to their own extreme. If you don't keep vigil, they say, the soul might not go to heaven. It'll end up haunting its former residence: slamming cupboards, flipping lights on and off, and pacing the attic, humming and snapping the *Addams Family* theme song. A bit of superstition is always mixed in with popular piety. I should mind that, but to be honest, I don't. The world could use more enchantment.

The funeral couldn't happen that fast. Not in twenty-four hours. The best I could do, I told her, was Thursday at eleven. She nodded. "That'll be all right, Father. You're sweet for trying."

At ten forty-five on the morning of the funeral, the church was a beehive of activity, and one bee buzzed louder than the rest. It was Gretchen, the sacristan, organist, cantor, and bereavement committee chairperson. At a funeral all those titles kept her wings flapping. She had to light the candles on the altar and the charcoal for the incense, then set out the books, the chalice, and other sundry liturgical paraphernalia, then dash over to the organ, where she'd pound out such timeless classics as "Be Not Afraid" and "How Great Thou Art" (all one octave higher than anyone could actually sing).

Next she'd dart over to the parish hall to light the cans of Sterno under the catering platters, then scuttle back to play "On Eagle's Wings" or, if it was an Irish funeral, "Danny Boy". As the ceremony finished, she'd race down to the sacristy, stow everything, and dash back over to the hall, making sure people were behaving themselves around the punch bowl. She did a lot of darting, dashing, and racing—not to mention scuttling. I suggested once that she recruit helpers. Why not get the other ladies on the bereavement committee to chip in? She waved off the suggestion as if shooing a fly. "No, no, Father. I don't want to bother them." In time I understood: she was as territorial as Napoleon.

Now she stood in the sacristy, holding a piece of charcoal over a lighter with a pair of sooty tongs.

I was in the sacristy too, dancing. I had to use the bathroom.

I had a lot of dreams for the parish—some grandiose, some more modest. Among the modest dreams was installing a lavatory in the sacristy. It's standard nowadays to have a place in the sacristy for the priest to be alone, a refuge from the hubbub, a quiet oasis where he can find comfort and relief from bodily pressures. But not when they built St. Dominic's. Perhaps back in the day they thought priests didn't need to use restrooms.

But the architects knew parishioners needed them. Two spacious public restrooms had been installed in the vestibule next to the main entrance—about five miles from the sacristy. I could use those, but it'd be chancy. Venturing out before Mass, I risked running into a parishioner who "just needs a moment", thwarting relief and ensuring another hour of abdomen tightening and teeth clenching.

The other option was in the basement. A stairwell just outside the sacristy twisted down to a dank storage room lit by a single 60-watt lightbulb. If St. Dominic's were haunted, that's where the ghosts would live. And in the back of that musty room, behind a paper-thin door, sat a toilet and nothing else—no sink, no mirror, just a toilet. I didn't like to use it for two reasons. First, the room gave me the heebie-jeebies. Second, I worried churchgoers using the side entrance at the top of the steps would be startled by the sonorous echo of my tinkle emanating from the stairwell.

Given I had only ten minutes before Mass, and there were surprisingly few mourners, I chose to brave the ghost-infested basement and risk potential embarrassment.

Just as I was about to flush, the rapid *click-clack* of high heels coming down the concrete steps reverberated through the thin door. Then a hushed voice cut through the clammy air.

"Okay. Now I can talk." The voice was Connie's. Was she on the phone? "I'm in a church."

. . .

"Yeah, I know. It's my brother's funeral. What do you want?"

. . .

"Well, no kidding, Randy. The timing couldn't have been worse."

. . .

"No, it was a heart attack."

. . .

"How in the world do you fake a heart attack?"

. . .

"Yeah, but are they that—"

. . .

"Yeah, well, maybe. Anyway, you need someone else."

. . .

"Isn't that *your* job to figure out? I don't have any more brothers, Randy."

. . .

"You're all heart, thanks. Listen, they're gonna start this thing any minute. Can I call you back?"

. . .

"But answer my calls, will you?"

. . .

"Okay. Bye."

I waited. I wanted to be sure she had made it to the top of the stairs before I flushed and stepped out. I also needed time to absorb what I had just heard. Connie was somehow involved in all this. That was clear. She knew his death wasn't just a heart attack. Or at least, whoever she was talking to knew. But wait—what were the chances I'd overhear that call? A convenient coincidence? Too convenient. Did she know I was in the bathroom? Maybe she did. Maybe she saw me go downstairs. Was this a secret way to confirm for me that she knew I knew about Richie? That she saw the numbers I had written on my business card and wanted to tip me off, but indirectly, intuiting why I couldn't talk about it? Or was she throwing me off the scent? Maybe there was no Randy. Maybe she wanted to stage this ruse to derail me. She was a psychologist. She knew my type. She knew I'd start fixating, try to find out who this Randy guy was. I'd look her up on Facebook and see if she had any Randy friends. Failing that, I'd google all the Randalls in Westchester and try to figure out connections. All the while, she'd use the time to further bury her tracks, maybe take off for Panama or something.

I shook my head. *Absurd.* She had no idea I was there. I had overhead a conversation. It was that simple, that serendipitous. Yet now I had no doubt: Connie was involved, somehow. But how? And whom had she been she talking to? *Focus. You must focus on the funeral, on the mourners.* I took a deep breath and went upstairs.

෴ ෴ ෴

The mourners. There weren't many. As I peeked out the sacristy door into the church, I could see Lupita, Maggie, Connie, and at most ten others, all elderly women, little puffs of gray hair scattered throughout the pews like dandelion seed heads. They must have been Lupita's friends. The sparse turnout would be typical for the funeral of an older person but not for a fifty-four-year-old.

When people die young, the funerals are full; friends and family come from all over. It's a tragedy. When elderly people die, unless they are prominent figures or had a lot of kids, their funerals tend to be small affairs. Of course, Richie probably didn't have many friends. He certainly wasn't the social type.

"You're always pushing it," Gretchen said. "We start in two minutes, and you're not even ready." I've met a lot of Germans over the years, and none of them fit the Teutonic stereotype—except Gretchen. She had arrived in New York circuitously through Vermont, where she

had been a maid for the von Trapp family—yes, the one
from *The Sound of Music*. She had shown me a Polaroid of
her getting off the boat in Boston Harbor in 1976. That
face. I had an old movie poster for *Witness for the Prose-
cution* in the rectory basement. I swear Gretchen was the
spitting image of Marlene Dietrich, the German actress
who played the lead: same high-arched eyebrows, same
heavy eyelids, same thin nose that points at you accusingly.
Her whole countenance bore the air of being perpetually
unimpressed.

"Don't you have to get to the organ, Gretchen?" I
asked, pulling my vestments on.

⸙ ⸙ ⸙

The funeral began as all funerals begin and ended as all
funerals end. It was the middle that was a little different.
Just before the homily a man slipped in through the main
doors of the church and slumped into the back pew. From
that distance his features were indistinct—I could see
only that he was bald and stocky, wearing a leather jacket
and jeans. And a watch. I noticed the watch because he
kept looking at it.

The homily went well, I thought. Maggie made eye
contact with me, smiling and frowning and laughing at all
the right times; Lupita maintained a placid, motherly, I'm-
so-proud-of-you look; and Connie was expressionless. I
did get her to smirk at one clever comment, a comment
that had made Maggie and Lupita roar. The guy in the
back, however, just looked at his watch.

After the final commendation prayers, the pallbearers
loaded the casket into the hearse, the three O'Briens got
into Maggie's Lexus, and I ran back to the sacristy to change
and join the family on their way to the grave site. All this

according to age-old custom. What was not according to custom was the man I found in the sacristy. It was the watch-man.

"Hey, fatha," he said in a distinct Bronx accent. "Nice to meet ya." He reached out his hand. "I'm Sal Grisanti. I work for Mr. Cardelli, Richie's boss. It's a shame what happened, so young and all." He had squinty eyes, one of which wandered; his eyebrows were upside-down check marks over an aquiline nose. He reminded me of a cross between Julius Caesar and Sam Eagle from *The Muppet Show*.

"Nice to meet you too," I said, shaking his hand. "I hate to be rude, but I need to change so I can go with the family to the burial site. I hope you—"

"You did a nice job, a real nice job," he said, as if he didn't hear me. "Loved that sermon. It was great. Funny too. You gotta sense o' humor, that's good. You gotta have a sense o' humor. Life's rough. If you don't have a sense o' humor, you know, you can go crazy."

I smiled and nodded as I pulled off my vestments.

"Listen, you gotta go, I understand. Mr. Cardelli just wanted me to stop by and thank you for taking care of Richie and his family. He thinks it's a real shame what happened, you know. He's glad you're here for them. He wanted to come to the funeral himself, but ... you know ... he's got a lot goin' on.

"He also wanted me to tell ya he's happy you stopped by Stefano's. You're always welcome at any of his restaurants. Just know that. He always says, 'The padres eat free.' That's what he always says. Men of the cloth, you guys do good work. Real important stuff. He believes that, he truly does."

"That's generous of him. I appreciate it," I said, sliding my coat on. "And he's welcome here anytime too. Now, if you'll excuse me, I have to go."

"Sure. I know. You gotta get with the family. I understand. Just one more thing. Mr. Cardelli says your car
needs new tires. He thinks it's important you get them
replaced. He says you gotta drive places because when you
walk, you can get lost, go to the wrong places. You know?
So he wanted me to give you this." He handed me a white
envelope. "It's for new tires for that little Honda Civic
you got. The silver one. That way nothing happens to you
by walking to the wrong places. He says your work is too
important. You can't take any risks."

❧ ❧ ❧

I got in my car and tossed the envelope on the passenger
seat. *Was that supposed to be a threat?*

Funerals are supposed to bring closure. Richie's funeral
did not bring me closure. No, everything was still wide
open, exacerbated by overhearing Connie's conversation
and receiving veiled threats from what I assumed was one
of Cardelli's henchmen. Where do they get these guys,
anyway? Some sort of mob headhunting agency? Maybe a
trade magazine where they advertise? "Now hiring: Thug.
Must have experience with brass knuckles and intimida-
tion tactics. Nice guys need not apply."

The funeral didn't bring closure, but I wanted it to be
closed. I wanted it to go away. Sal the Thug had intim-
idated me successfully. I knew what he meant: I'm not
about to go messing with the mob.

And I took the money. Why did I do that? I don't
know. He handed me an envelope; I took it. It didn't
occur to me to do anything else. I was nervous. I was
holding up the funeral procession, and I was in front of a
guy I imagined killed people for a living. So I just took it.
Was I now complicit? Was someone hiding somewhere

in the sacristy, secretly filming me taking the money? I didn't know. I just wanted it to be over and closed and done with.

And I thought, why not? Why can't it be over? Did I promise Richie anything? Do I really need to confront this Cardelli guy? What could I do? Nothing. I would do nothing. Just go on with my life.

That was my resolution, and it lasted all day. Busy office work that afternoon, evening confessions and Mass, a rewatch of *Double Indemnity* accompanied by a glass of scotch (just one), and it was all out of my head. But that night, as I knelt in the little chapel we had in the rectory, the noises and events of the day swirling in my head, my nightly conversation with God degenerated into a conversation with myself. Strenuous attempts to turn back to prayer were futile. Eventually, I slammed my breviary shut and said out loud, "Lord, what do you want me to do? There's nothing I can do. So, please, may Richie rest in peace, may his murderers repent, and may I forget about it so I can get some sleep tonight. Thank you. Amen."

God always answers our prayers. Sometimes it's yes, sometimes it's no, and usually it's *Wait*. On my first two requests, that Richie might rest in peace and the murderers repent, I couldn't know how he'd respond, but on the last, that I might sleep, his answer was a resounding no.

As I lay there staring at the ceiling, Richie's sad face was all I could see. Now that I knew the location of that fateful encounter, that Connie was definitely the *she who knew*, and that Richie's boss was most likely responsible, my indignation boiled over.

In the darkness of my bedroom I relived the scene. I heard Richie's erratic voice rattling off the enigmatic numbers; I smelled the stale cigarette smoke; I saw the pain in his swollen, red-rimmed eyes; and I felt his hand

on my arm, stopping me from getting up, that last desperate cough of numbers, *three, fifteen, fourteen, she knows,
she knows.* But what kept my eyes open, staring into the
blackness, was nothing my five senses picked up; it was
the gut-wrenching feeling of utter helplessness. After the
encounter with Richie, I did nothing. I just went back to
my rectory for a sleepless night.

And once again, as on that first night, I grabbed my
phone off the nightstand, about to dial 911. *Not again.* I
tossed the phone on the carpet. I was not going to work
the Rubik's Cube again. I balled into the fetal position.
Think of something else. I couldn't. My mind was untam-
able. The urgent need to do something came over me.
But what?

Confront Cardelli. That's what I'd do. He was responsible. Sal left no doubt of that. Ashley said Cardelli was
religious, that his office was a shrine. He wouldn't hurt
me. I'd just march in there and ... and what?

I rolled onto my back. *Who am I to go up against the mob?*
My body went limp in resignation. *I can't do this. It's point-
less. Just fall asleep, will you? Please.*

My bed became a boxing ring. It was a repeat of the
match held in the same bed six nights before—the night I
confessed Richie. This bout lasted a good ten rounds, but
the contenders were different. Last Friday I had, in one
corner, my duty to be a trustworthy confessor and, in the
other, my duty to bring the murderers to justice. Tonight's
match: an obligation to act—to decipher what Richie was
trying to tell me, to figure out who murdered him, to somehow stop future assassinations from happening—versus my
helplessness. As round ten started, Helplessness landed a
fierce uppercut on Obligation's jaw: *No, I'm not going to
Yonkers, where Ashley said the back-office operations were. No,
I'm not marching into Cardelli's holy office and interrogating him.*

I am not a detective. This is absurd. I'm dropping the whole thing. Done. Decided. Now fall asleep, will you?

The referee counted away, slamming his hand on the mat: *One ... two ... three ...* I now lay on my stomach, an arm hanging off the bed, saliva pooling on the pillow. But just as the referee's count reached nine, I felt a sudden resurgence, a second wind. Obligation was back on its feet. *Connie, I'll go see Connie ...* a quick jab to Helplessness' body. *Yes, that's it. I've overheard her conversation with this Randy guy ...* a left cross. *I now have information I learned outside confession. I can demand she explain herself ...* a right hook. Helplessness was down for the count. Knockout. I resolved to go see Connie in the morning. Peace came, and so did sleep.

9

Connie

Dr. Constance O'Brien-Katz—Westchester Women's Center. It was written on a plain white business card I found tacked under a Domino's Pizza magnet on Lupita's fridge, along with Maggie's card from Coldwell Banker. I had snapped a picture of them with my phone that day I visited the O'Briens, just in case.

I'm not sure what I expected, but I certainly didn't expect the Westchester Women's Center to look like a Jiffy Lube waiting room: exposed fluorescent bulbs on a whitewashed ceiling, thinly padded stackable chairs, a Keurig machine but no K-Cups. I guess I expected flowers, at least, and maybe instrumental versions of Dionne Warwick's greatest hits playing in the background.

The waiting room was full, mostly Latina women. A baby cried, a woman prattled on her cell phone in Spanish, and the others either flipped drearily through back issues of *Elle* or scrolled mindlessly on their smartphones.

I approached the receptionist's window. A sandy-haired woman in her midtwenties with a dolphin tattoo on her neck pecked away on a computer. I cleared my throat, but she continued typing.

"Excuse me," I said.

"Just sign in on the clipboard." Her eyes were fixed on the screen. "Left side, Dr. Blandel; right side, Dr. O'Brien-Katz."

"I'm a new patient," I said.

She looked up. "Sorry. We're not accepting new patients." She squinted. "And um ... not to discriminate or anything, but this is a *women's* clinic?"

"I know. I was just joking. I wanted to see if Connie— Dr. O'Brien-Katz—might have a moment."

"She's booked solid. Sorry." Her attention was back on the screen.

"All right if I just have a seat and wait here?"

She shrugged. "Free country."

"Thanks. And if you have a chance, just let her know I'm waiting." That remark didn't get a reply. "Um, the name's Hart, Father Hart."

I had thought of calling ahead, but I figured she wouldn't want to see me. So I spent the morning in my office with the idea of arriving around noon, to catch her on her lunch break. My plan was derailed when Gretchen caught me on my way out the door and asked for just five minutes. The look on her face told me it was going to be at least thirty, and it ended up being fifty. By the time I arrived, Connie had already taken her lunch break. But I was prepared to wait. And wait I did.

I stood in a corner for three-quarters of an hour. A door yawned, and the huddled mass of expectant patients looked up in unison. A young woman emerged. She was almost a teen and looked about ten months pregnant; a nurse trailed her with a clipboard. All eyes were on the nurse.

"Carmen?" she called out. The eyes fell back to the magazines and cell phones. A petite woman grabbed her purse and followed the nurse. The door clicked shut behind them; the atmosphere of anxious boredom resumed.

I leaned against the magazine rack, first answering emails on my phone, then leafing through a brochure for the clinic that I grabbed from the rack. The Westchester

Women's Center was an all-in-one clinic for low-income women, mostly on Medicaid or paying cash. On staff were a social worker and three doctors—a general practitioner, an OB-GYN, and a psychologist.

At one point I spied Connie through the glass, behind the receptionist. She had just finished with a patient who now rejoined the gray pool of humanity in the waiting room. She handed the receptionist a piece of paper, said something inaudible, and disappeared again. The receptionist merely received the paper, nodded, and went back to typing. No mention of me, no pointing out the conspicuous gentleman dressed in black.

Three hours passed. A dozen patients came and went. Every so often I caught a glimpse of Connie, but she never glanced my way. The throng of patients had thinned considerably. Only three or four women remained. I was no longer standing conspicuously but now sitting, slumped over, my forearms on my lap, my hands joined. I was tempted to give up, but something kept me there. Obsession?

The receptionist looked out at me, and her eyes bulged as if she had just remembered a pot left on the stove. Hopping to her feet, she disappeared into the back office. Flames of hope were stoked, but when she returned, eyes glued to the floor, and resumed her station, the embers slowly died down again. But not out. I had sat there this long; I would not leave till I got in front of Connie.

My thoughts wandered to the eventual showdown. What would I say? How should I approach this? When you're in a spot, not sure what to do, you should ask, *What would Jesus do?*, so they say. I had asked myself that question, but the answer didn't come readily. I don't remember Jesus ever having to confront the sister of a dead man about his involvement with the Mafia or, more delicate still, her own involvement.

I remembered the Samaritan woman at the well from John's Gospel. I could see some parallels. At least, I thought I could borrow Jesus' technique. He started slowly with mundane chitchat about Palestinian water sources, then worked his way gradually to her personal life. But he had an advantage I didn't have: he already knew her secret. That's what tipped her. "Go call your husband," he had said. She said she didn't have one. "You're right to say you have no husband," he said. "You've had five husbands, and the one you're with now is not your husband." What could she say to that? Nothing. She tried to change the subject, but by that point he had her, and she knew it. When all was said and done, she became his biggest promoter in Samaria. A genuine Jesus freak. All because he knew her secret.

My problem was, I didn't know Connie's secret. That's what I was after.

No, WWJD didn't work in this situation. But what about WWPMD: What would Philip Marlowe do? I was no Humphrey Bogart, but I could play the part. I'd seen *The Big Sleep* at least five times, and plenty of other hard-boiled detective movies.

The nurse would call me, then show me to Connie's office door, the psychologist's curvy silhouette in the frosted glass with her name arched in black letters. Connie would invite me in. The office would be spacious with a big mahogany desk, a matching credenza on the far end of the room, and in an open space between them, a leather club chair and a low-profile davenport separated by a coffee table. She'd motion for me to sit in the chair as she asked, *May I offer you a drink?* And without waiting for a reply, she'd pour me a brandy from the crystal decanter on the credenza. Meanwhile, I'd pull a cigarette from my silver case and strike a match on the sole of my shoe.

Mind if I smoke? I'd ask.

Smoke 'em if you got 'em, she'd say, her tone almost playful. Then she'd place the glass of brandy on a small side table next to me and recline on the davenport, elegantly crossing her legs. (She'd be wearing a pencil skirt, of course.) *To what do I owe the pleasure?* she'd ask.

I think you know why I'm here.

Do I? What makes you think I know anything? Her coy eyelids would flutter in an attempt to distract me, but it wouldn't work.

Quit the act, missy. You know darn well why I'm here. The name Randy mean anything to you?

Randy? I don't know a Randy. She'd try to keep up the playful tone, but it would falter.

I think you do. I overheard your little conversation in the church basement. Now fess up. What was Richie involved in? What's that code mean? Three, fifteen, fourteen. I know you know. Give it up. I'd blow smoke confidently in the air.

How dare you come in here and make demands of me. Any playfulness in her voice would vanish. It'd be all irritation.

It's no use, sister. I'd place the cigarette coolly in an ashtray on the side table and pick up the brandy. *Either you tell me, or I'm callin' in the law.* I'd sip the brandy.

You can't threaten me.

I just did.

It's a bluff.

You wanna try me? I'm holdin' a royal flush, and I'll lay 'em down unless you give me what I came for. I'd down the rest of the brandy and pick up the cigarette again.

All right, you win. I'll tell you. Her face would be filled with consternation but then break into a solicitous gaze. *You gotta promise me you'll take this to the grave.*

Scout's honor, I'd say, then take a long drag on the cigarette and slowly release the smoke.

Three, fifteen, fourteen is a secret code that gives you access to—

"Father Hart?" The film reel sputtered, the houselights came up, and I found myself back in the waiting room, empty except for a heavyset woman playing some sort of bubble-popping game on her phone. The receptionist's voice rang out again. "Father?"

"Yes, I'm sorry." I shook my head. "Is she ready to see me?"

"Yes. Please follow me."

I stood. Beads of sweat formed along my hairline as my pulse quickened. I felt less like Humphrey Bogart and more like Jimmy Stewart.

A deep breath, a straightening of my suit coat, a resolute march forward, and I was through the door. I went from a Jiffy Lube waiting room to every doctor's office ever: a white-walled hallway, with undiscernible decorative art hung between examination rooms, and the pungent scent of air freshener and disinfectant.

I was led down the hall to a nondescript door with a blue plastic nameplate: Constance O'Brien-Katz, Ph.D. But I was not brought through that door. The nurse motioned me into an adjacent room.

Two examination rooms had been joined to create a kind of living room. The sun filtered through long sheers. Two table lamps on either side of a flower-patterned couch and a standing lamp next to an armchair added a warm glow to the room. Clearly the soft lighting was considered more conducive to therapy sessions than stark fluorescents. It also set the mood for a Marlowesque encounter. But I still wasn't feeling the spirit of Bogart rising within me.

"Have a seat. Dr. O.K. will be with you in a minute."

Dr. O.K.? Really?

I headed for the armchair. The nurse stopped me.

"On the couch, if you would."

I plunked onto the couch. Dust billowed up, and I sneezed into the crook of my arm. The door didn't open again for another twenty-five minutes. This time it was Connie, and I was reminded that she was no Lauren Bacall: gray pantsuit, blouse buttoned up to the neck, shoulder-length gray hair, reading glasses hanging around the neck, and her distinctive mole. I stood.

"Hello, Father. I wasn't expecting you," she said in a voice that seemed to want to say, *What are you doing here?*

"Yes. Sorry to drop in unannounced. I happened to be in the neighborhood, and I thought I would stop by." I held back a grimace at my cliché.

"Did we forget to pay?"

"Pay?"

"The funeral. We were told to do everything through the funeral home. We didn't make a check out to the church. Were we supposed to?"

"Oh, no, that's all right. You did it right. The funeral home takes care of all that. Don't worry. I'm ... I'm not here about payment."

"Okay ... Is there something else I can help you with?" We were still standing. I had expected this question, but we were getting down to brass tacks too fast. I thought there'd be a longer prelude of pleasantries first, maybe even an invitation to sit down. Somehow, *Quit the act, missy. You know darn well why I'm here* didn't seem appropriate right now.

"Well, I wanted to see how you're adjusting, you know, postfuneral," I said. "It's often *after* the funeral, when things settle down, when the rush of getting everything ready for the out-of-town guests is over—you know, when things go back to normal—that it can all come back and hit us.

So I just wanted to see how you're doing." Plausible. And true. I did honestly have a heart for the whole family.

"Fine. I'm fine. Thank you for checking in on us. That's very thoughtful. Actually, it's been very busy, and I really haven't had time to think about it. Long days, short nights, you know. In fact, I just had a marathon of appointments today, making up for the ones I had to cancel. So, again, thank you. Maybe you could stop in and see my mother. I'm sure she would appreciate that."

"Right, of course. Yes. I'm glad you're all right."

"Just fine. Thank you."

"Good. Well, I don't want to keep you." What? What was I saying? Yes, I did want to keep her.

"I'm glad. I've still got a lot of work to do before I can go home. Judy can show you out." She started for the door.

"Wait, wait," I blurted. "Look, yes, I wanted to come and check in on you. I really am concerned, but there are other things I wanted to talk about."

She gave me that flinty glare I had come to know, but I wasn't sure whether she was trying to say *I'm waiting, spit it out* or *If I have to endure your existence another minute, I think I'll explode.*

"When we first met at your mother's house," I said, "you gave me the impression you suspected your brother might, well, die earlier than expected."

"I told you, he was a typical bachelor who lived on macaroni and cheese and microwave pizzas. He was a heart attack waiting to happen."

"Yes. You did say that. In fact, verbatim, I think. Listen, I overheard your conversation in the church basement with Randy." I hadn't expected to play that card so soon, but she was about to walk out the door. "I just want to know what happened."

She stared into my eyes, searching, as if the answer to what she should do next was somehow written in them.

"Sit," she said.

She motioned me to the couch as she crossed to the armchair. Obediently I sat; another puff of dust and another sneeze, this time into my handkerchief. She sat erect, noticeably higher than me, crossing one leg over the other, her forearms resting on the arms of the chair, less like a coy dame in a noir crime film and more like a dour empress on her throne.

She paused, probably calculating exactly what she wanted to say. Her face twitched as if she had chosen one tack, reconsidered, and decided on another. "I have to tell you up front," she started, face stern. "I am not fond of your profession."

"I could kind of guess that, yes." *Where's she going with this?*

"I am glad religion has provided some comfort to my mother and my sister, but it has never had a place in my life. I find it all a bit too hard to swallow. With age, my incredulity has only taken stronger root."

"Right, I understand that. I'm not here to—"

"In particular, I find the priesthood—the celibate priesthood—to be an obsolete, misogynist institution that does society no apparent good and more than a little harm." I think my jaw dropped. If not, she could tell I was shocked. "Please do not take that personally. I am sure you are a noble-hearted man who wants to do good—so I have nothing against *you*—but know that your coming here dressed like that is only an obstacle to our mutual understanding."

Strange. I've met plenty of nonbelievers, some antagonistic, but none so in-your-face. Usually they throw a snide comment into an otherwise friendly conversation—

a passive-aggressive jab that happens so quickly you can't respond. But most people simply avoid the subject altogether. Connie was downright bellicose; the first salvo was launched before I even knew we were in combat.

And I hadn't come to do battle. I had extended a hand, and I thought she was going accept it like a lady. When she had invited me to sit, I saw it as a distress flare shooting up on the dark horizon. She had been holding on to this secret of hers, and now she could finally let it out. But I was naïve. The flare was no distress signal; rather, it was an incoming rocket. My presence was a threat, and she just blasted a warning shot over my bow.

"Look, Connie," I said, attempting to maneuver out of the way, "I didn't come here to talk religion. I respect where you're at with that, and I'm not going to try to convince you otherwise. Not today, at least. I honestly wanted to make sure you were okay. And see if you could help me resolve a doubt I just can't seem to shake. I don't know why, but I just have a feeling there's more to this and you know something that could help me come to peace with it. I put those numbers on my business card. Not sure you saw them. I can't explain how I got them, but I need to know what they mean and what's going on. Really, you could give me so much peace if you could help me."

"Peace? Hmph." She shifted in her chair slightly, repositioning her cannons. "I have a lot of clients that come to see me looking for peace." Her broadsides turned toward me, I prepared for the next salvo. "They try all sorts of things. They do yoga, they pray rosaries, they listen to New Age music or waterfall sounds. All in search of peace. But peace comes when we look at reality as it is and embrace it, when we face the raw harshness of it and accept it with all its consequences. The other things—yoga, rosaries, religion in general—are coping mechanisms aimed at

avoidance, distraction. Cheap forms of self-narcotization."
Her voice was calm, detached.

I needed to run up the white flag. I'd come here for
a reason, and it was not to engage her. I needed to seek
peace terms. "Okay, I see, so that's your doctrine. I get it."

"It's not doctrine. It's simply empirical truth. Look, up
until a couple hundred years ago, religion was useful. People needed it to help come to terms with what they didn't
understand. I don't blame them. There was no compre-
hension of how science worked, and—"

"That's not true," I interjected. "The scientific method
dates back hundreds of years, and it was actually developed in the monasteries—you know, by monks. Catholics have been at the forefront of scientific research for
centuries." Forget the white flag. Something in the prim-
itive part of my brain lit up. The fight-or-flight switch
had been tripped. I yelled to my internal shipmates, *Prepare to return fire.*

"Please, a couple hundred years ago doctors were still
blaming epileptic seizures on demonic possession. They
filled all the gaps in scientific knowledge with religious
explanations. As true scientific knowledge—knowledge
based on empirical evidence—started to grow, the gaps
began to disappear, and religious explanations along with
them. And so did religion itself. It's simply no longer useful. Look at Europe. Entire countries are basically athe-
ist, and you don't see rioting in the streets or utter moral
chaos. Indeed, you see the opposite."

"I'm not a Fundamentalist," I said. "There's no com-
petition between faith and science in my book. Sure,
some people jumped to superstitious conclusions, but not
serious-minded religious people."

At this point our guns were going full blaze. What I had
intended to be a peaceful encounter about getting to the

bottom of her brother's situation had turned into a full-on apologetics firefight. We continued debating for another thirty minutes. Back and forth, all the old arguments came out. She went on about Freud and Jung; I quoted Aquinas and C. S. Lewis. She talked about priests' manipulation of religious sensitivities to maintain power; I retorted that good priests don't seek power but seek to serve.

But as the battle wore on, I felt the tide turn against me. It became harder and harder to rebuff her attacks. I tried going on the offensive: Western atheists are just living off the moral capital built up by Christian culture; the great technological and artistic advances of the Renaissance were possible only in a Christian culture that promoted exploration and free thinking. She replied by asking what happened, then, in South America and Africa? Why don't we see a similar renaissance on those wildly Christian continents? I pointed out the racism in her remarks, which won me some points, but still, I couldn't give a satisfactory answer. Then I said, if she was so sure God didn't exist, she should prove it. She replied that the burden of proof is on the believer. You don't disprove the existence of the tooth fairy or Santa Claus or Bigfoot; on the contrary, those who purport their existence must give some evidence.

I was waiting for her to bring up Galileo or the Spanish Inquisition—these I was ready for. Instead she talked about the Catholic religious persecution of Protestants in England under Mary Tudor, to which I could give no reply since I had known only about the Elizabethan persecution of Catholics.

Then it hit me. The Samaritan woman. There was something to learn from Jesus' encounter with that poor thirsty soul after all. Sure, Jesus had an advantage; he knew the woman's past, her sins. But more than that, he knew what she needed, what every soul needs. She needed love, acceptance, forgiveness. She was an outcast. He didn't need to know her sins. He knew her predicament just by watching her come draw water at the hottest time of the day, when no one else would be around, avoiding the company of other women, judgmental women.

The woman at the well acted tough, like Connie. But when Jesus gently spoke to her need, her wound, she started to open up. What was Connie's wound? Why so much aggression? Why did my presence cause so much agitation? Something inside her must be hurting; my mere presence had poked at some festering abscess deep within, and now she was reacting. My artillery had been aimed at the head when I really needed to go for the heart. Time to change tactics.

"Listen, we could go back and forth like this all day," I said. "You're a smart woman, and these intellectual arguments are interesting, but I think we can find some common ground. People out there suffer a lot. I think we can agree on that. I mean, you see it every day in your practice. I see it too. Every day. So many people live such dreary lives without meaning and without hope. Some people suffer because of a situation they're in; others suffer because of something that happened to them in their past or that they did to someone else, something they carry around wherever they go, never able to let go. Don't you see that? Maybe you yourself have had to carry something around like that. But I'll tell you, my God is a God of hope. My God makes sense out of suffering. He gives it meaning. He's a God of love. A God of forgiveness. A God who says, No matter what you've done, I still love you. A God who says, No matter what was done *to* you, I'll be with you." I had a soft, almost imploring look on my face, or at least that's the effect I was going for.

She leaned back in her chair, uncrossing and recrossing her legs. Her lips pursed into a tight grin, and the skin around her eyes crinkled. I half expected her to crack her knuckles. And then, on the horizon, I saw the aircraft carrier pull into view, and on it was a single plane, a large bomber. I knew from the moment of takeoff the ordnance type it contained. I sat back and crossed my arms over my chest.

"I had a client come in last Thursday," she started, calmly, deliberately. "Twenty-five years old. Pregnant. Immigrant from Guatemala. She had come to see me before, but I couldn't make much headway with her." The bomber circled overhead menacingly. "She kept talking about her *Diosito*, her little God. She had upset her *Diosito*. And I tried to get her to tell me how she had upset him. She talked in circles and never got to it. Finally, yesterday, I had a breakthrough. She told me her story." Bomb bay doors open.

"Olivia—let's call her Olivia—grew up in a remote village," she continued. "The youngest of four, and the only girl. When she was eight, her oldest brother, who was fourteen, started to touch her—they all slept in the same bed, you see. She didn't know what he was doing at first. And it was only every once in a while in the beginning. But soon it was almost every night. Then he got her to touch him. Am I making you uncomfortable, Father?

"Well then, like a good big brother, he showed his little brothers the ropes. At thirteen years old she was pregnant. She miscarried. It wouldn't be the last time, though. In fact, she got pregnant three times and miscarried each time—at least that's what she told me. For ten years she was her brothers' playground.

"And where were the parents, you ask? Mom was working; Dad was drunk. And why didn't she say anything to anyone? To whom? The police? In rural Guatemala you don't call the police. Child Protective Services? That doesn't exist there.

"So finally Olivia gets up the courage to run away. She's eighteen by this point. Walking alone along a dirt road, she gets picked up by some gentleman in a pickup truck. Real nice guy. Big smile. Courteous. She tells him she needs help. 'Happy to help,' he says. Next thing she knows she's on a bus, then a boat, then in a van; then she's in an Atlantic City hotel room with a sweaty overweight white man who has just passed a wad of cash to the van driver.

"After a year and a half of hotel rooms in various parts of the Northeast, she was finally discarded somewhere down in Hunts Point. She was all used up, you see. No good anymore.

"Then one day a chef—we'll call her Jenny—from a fancy restaurant in Manhattan was down at Hunts Point looking for fresh fish and produce for her restaurant. The chef was famous, Olivia told me. She had seen her on the Food Network, which she used to watch on the hotel televisions in between 'clients'.

"Now, I'm sure Jenny had seen plenty of homeless people, but there was something that caught her eye as she walked by this little Guatemalan woman sitting up against the side of a warehouse. 'You're too young,' she said. 'You're too young to be on the street. Come with me.' So she brought her to her restaurant, then took her to her brownstone in Brooklyn for the night, then called a friend of hers who volunteers at a halfway house.

"You can imagine Olivia telling me this story, Father. Big brown eyes, tears welling up. She gives me every detail as if it happened yesterday. So sad."

"Right, I get it," I said. "How could a good God let such a horrible thing happen to a girl like that? But God did act. He inspired that kind chef to reach out. You see, there's an innate goodness in people, and desperate situations bring it out of us. God works through each of us."

"Oh, I haven't finished the story yet." Bombs away. "The halfway house got her back on her feet. She got a job at a restaurant in White Plains busing tables. That's where she met a man we'll call Dionisio. Dionisio was a Honduran cook who dealt drugs on the side.

"It was from Dionisio that our little Guatemalan picked up her drug habit, a habit she couldn't afford. Dionisio, however, was a gentleman. If she couldn't pay, he wasn't going to hurt her. No, he would take payment in other forms—forms she was well acquainted with. But at one point he was hard up for cash himself and needed her to pay for real. She couldn't, but she told him she knew who she could get the money from."

Oh no.

"Yes, Father," she said, reading my mind. "One evening Olivia showed up at that fancy restaurant in Manhattan where kind Chef Jenny worked. She told Jenny that the boyfriend she had been living with was beating her, that she didn't feel safe, that she couldn't go home. The shelter would not have an opening till the next day, she said, so would Jenny mind taking her in just for one night? The softhearted chef said, 'Of course.'

"That night, when Jenny was asleep, Olivia unlocked the back door. Dionisio and two friends came in and rummaged through the house looking for valuables. The two friends made off with a laptop, some cash, and who knows what else. Jenny, unfortunately, woke up and discovered Dionisio going through her closet. She didn't scream. Instead, she stealthily snatched pepper spray and her cell phone from the nightstand, slid out of bed, and shouted, 'Don't move!' Dionisio spun around. He glared at her, unfazed. He slid his hand up the back of his untucked shirt. He wasn't armed, but he pretended to be. He told her to put the pepper spray down and he would leave quietly. Jenny refused and fumbled with her phone to dial 911. She didn't hear Olivia come up behind her, but I suppose she felt the brass handle of the fire poker hit the back of her head—I really hope not, though.

"Olivia and Dionisio ran, but then, that night, Olivia made her way back to the brownstone. From there she called the police. She told them Jenny had taken her in because Olivia was afraid of Dionisio, that he and his friends forced their way in and Dionisio killed Jenny using the poker. The lie worked. She was connected with a social worker and was offered outpatient therapy paid for by the state of New York. The social worker sent her to me.

"Now, Father. This God of yours. You call him good, loving, forgiving. Tell me, is he going to forgive her for that? Is he going to forgive her brothers? Are you going to tell me that in his providence he allowed all that to happen?" Her voice was more and more intense. "Are you going to tell me that this all-powerful, all-loving God, the one who cares for each and every life, just sat there and watched all that happen?"

"Yes," I squeaked.

She scoffed. "No, I'm sorry, I can't believe that. I cannot accept that someone who has the power to intervene, the power to change the course of history, would allow all that to happen." She had told Olivia's story dispassionately, clinically, with utmost propriety. Now her face went red, and a vein I hadn't noticed before protruded along her left temple. All semblance of culture and erudition disappeared. "Your God of justice and love is a fraud. I'm sorry. And don't give me any of that 'greater good' nonsense. There is no way this evil can lead to a greater good." Her volume increased with each word. I could almost feel the heat of her breath from several feet away. I was waiting for fire to shoot out. "You may think you're making people feel better by selling them all that bunk, but you're deceiving them. Olivia's story—that's reality. No happy ending. No superman flying in to save the day. That's what happens in this hellhole. And it happens all the time. Believe me. I wade through it all day long."

I sat there, speechless, mouth agape. The bomb had gone off. It was the ordnance type I'd expected. It's not that I had never considered the problem of evil before. I had. To be sure, it's hard to refute, but I did have an answer. I just didn't have an answer for *her*. The words didn't come. She was like kryptonite to me. I knew nothing I could say in that moment would convince her of my position. I just sat there, staring at her, still reeling from the bombardment.

That was the end of our interview. Connie stood up, thanked me for stopping by, and made excuses that she needed to get back to work. I walked out, deflated, forgetting why I had even come. The waiting room was empty. The section of the parking lot in front of the clinic was also empty. I schlepped to my car and laid my head on the steering wheel, then back on the head rest, staring at the visor.

❧ ❧ ❧

I would replay that conversation in my head for days to come—no, years. Indeed, every time I think of that interaction, what I could have said, should have said, but didn't say all comes back. I don't just rewatch as if it were a wedding video; it's more like reenacting—having the whole conversation over again, hearing her voice, seeing her cold demeanor, her erect torso in that gray business suit, that wicked-teacher face methodically laying out her arguments. Then me giving her new arguments, playing my chess pieces in a new pattern, finally putting her in check. Yet in all the mental reenactments, I never win. I can never convince her. And then I start to wonder: *Can I convince myself? Do I really believe it all?* How often I've asked God, *Where are you?*

I had been defeated not just in the debate. That wasn't her game. I had been defeated in the real contest, to which I was oblivious. She wasn't being a witch. She was being savvy. The debate was a diversion tactic. She had provoked the argument on purpose to avoid talking about her brother and Stefano's and whatever it was she knew. And I fell for it. How could I have been so naïve? That word came back. *Naïve.* That's what I was.

I turned the key to battery power, not quite ready to go. The fan kicked on; the dashboard clock lit up: 5:12. More than four hours in that place. What a waste of time. Now I was done. I was really done. She was my last shot.

Looking in my rearview mirror at the clinic, I imagined her staff wrapping up final paperwork before heading home for the night. Then I shot my head up in a sudden realization. Connie hadn't left yet. She'd be in her office wrapping things up too. Why couldn't I just go back in there? What was stopping me?

I snatched the keys from the ignition, jumped from the car, and marched back to the office. The glass door was already locked. I looked in, blocking the fading sunlight with my hands. The receptionist was still at her desk. I pounded on the glass. She turned toward me, annoyance written across her face, and then she composed herself. I gave her a pleading look back.

The lock snapped open, and she leaned out. "Back so soon? Here you go." She handed me an envelope, stationery from the clinic, my name written in large cursive letters on the front.

"What's this?"

"Oh, I thought you were expecting it. Dr. O.K. told me to give it to you when you came back. Thought it'd be tomorrow or next week or something, the way she said it."

"What is it?"

She shrugged. "Dunno."

"Right. Thanks." I half smiled, confused, as I examined the envelope.

"Have a good night."

"Yeah, you too ... good night," I said, still looking at the envelope. I drifted back toward my car, slicing the envelope open with my key. The business card I had given Connie at her mother's house slid out; nothing else was inside. On the back she had written in tight block letters above the numbers—the cryptic numbers I had received from her brother, the numbers I was hoping would be a clue to unravel the mystery of the mob or a clearer indication of whatever Richie was expecting me to do— *For your own good, stay out of this, and never come near me again.* Then, under each number, she had written a letter: 3 = C, 15 = O, 14 = N. I quickly did the math. *C* is the third letter of the alphabet, *O* the fifteenth, *N* the fourteenth. CON ... Con ... Connie. Her name. She knows. Con knows. *No. It can't be.* That was the big mystery? Something I already knew? Something I had figured out on my own? No way. Not possible. All this time the clue was that I needed to speak to Connie because *she knows,* and now she wouldn't tell me anything, wouldn't even see me again?

A horn blast broke me from my stupor. I was standing in the middle of the lane. I waved apologetically at the guy in the steel blue Mustang giving me the finger and got into my car.

Back at the parish, I slipped into church, knelt, and prayed: *God, what am I doing? Why do you have me here? What do you want from me? I went to see Connie because I thought that's what you wanted. I thought that's what I was supposed to do. And now I don't know what I'm supposed to do. I tried and failed.*

My prayer got a response this time. A little voice. A whisper in a deep corner of my heart, barely audible to my spiritual ears. *I'm not finished.*

Part II

Suburban Noir

10

The Third Man

It was bigger than a bread box, much bigger. The cardboard packaging had THIS END UP stamped in black and a stick figure bent over, hand on his lower back surrounded by little ouch marks shooting out. The box sat obtrusively on the floor in the main office.

"Rita, what is this thing?"

"I think it's a minifridge for Golden Boy. I told the guys to bring it up to the third floor with the rest of his junk, but they just left it here. Jerry knows. He'll figure it out."

Golden Boy? Andrew? If I were a good boss, I would have reprimanded her for the epithet, but I was too surprised.

"Father Reese's furniture is here already? I'm not expecting him till—"

"Yes, and not just his furniture." She shot a glance toward my office.

"No, you're kidding. He's in there?"

Two weeks had passed since my showdown with Connie, and three since I had gotten back from Rome. It felt like centuries since the Rome trip, but still, Andrew's arrival was too sudden. I needed to work on Monsignor, tenderize him, let him marinate in the idea. I also needed to make sure Andrew's room was set up right. Everything needed to be perfect. I couldn't risk a finicky backpedaling on our deal because his Chippendale was slightly off center.

I entered my office and there he was, leaning back in my chair, feet up on my desk, eyes closed, hands folded on his chest.

"Comfortable?" I asked.

"Not even a little," he said without opening an eye. "You need a new chair, Christopher. This one is tired."

"I'll get right on that, boss." I smiled.

Lazily he dropped to his feet, arched his back in a stretch, then lurched at me, giving me a big hug with hearty slaps on the back. "Surprised to see me, old man?" he asked. He gripped me by the shoulders and held me out at arm's length. "You've lost weight."

"I wasn't expecting you till the end of the semester."

"I know, but I thought, why wait? There's work to be done." He stepped back and half sat on the desk, one leg dangling off. "Yes, indeed. I thought, Poor Christopher's over there slaving away with that octogenarian ball and chain scowling at every new idea, pooh-poohing every fresh venture. Who needs the devil to whisper discouragement in your ear when you have Jack Leahy. Am I right? Yes, Christopher needs my help. That's what I was thinking. So I booked a flight, and here I am. And just in time too. I haven't been back twenty-four hours, and I've already saved you from disaster."

"How's that?"

"Look at this." He grabbed a flier I had on my desk for our annual Lenten mission—a long-abandoned tradition I had decided to resurrect. In the old days, the parish would invite a guest speaker to give a series of talks on some Lenten theme. It was meant to get people into the spirit of the season, help them turn their hearts back to God. For me, it was an opportunity—I was grasping for excuses to bring people together. This was low cost, low commitment, low maintenance, and high return on investment since the only investment was a speaker's fee and the cost of heavy hors d'oeuvres for the post-talk reception. My guest speaker was Father Anselm Rotterman, O.P., a renowned Dominican theologian and a rising star in the circle of American Catholic intellectuals. Dominicans get their name from their founder, Saint Dominic. The initials O.P. after their names stand for *Ordinis Praedicatorum* (Order of Preachers). Our parish is St. Dominic's, and I needed a good preacher. So, what better combination? Wasn't I clever?

"Rotterman? Really?" Andrew said. "I thought you were smarter than that."

"What're you talking about? He's brilliant. *The Five Wounds of Contemporary Families* was genius."

"Brilliant, no doubt. And indeed a spunky writer, if you don't mind hackneyed metaphors. But an orator? A voice to rally the masses? Convict the unconvinced? Penetrate hardened hearts? No, my friend. He's not that. He's a droning academic blowhard. And he's not coming."

"What? Why not?"

"He was told not to."

"He was told? Who told him? You? You called him?"

"No, of course not. Who am I to do such a thing? No, *you* called him. Well, all right, technically I called him, but he thought I was you ... Don't give me that look. If you knew the error you made, you wouldn't mind my using your name in vain."

I wanted to punch him. I had worked hard to get that event organized, and we were only two weeks away. I held my fists at my side and wanted to shout, *Who do you think you are?* but all I could muster was, "I can't believe you would do that."

He plopped into the desk chair, twisted the computer monitor to face me, pulled up YouTube, typed in "anselm rotterman op", and clicked on the first video that came up.

It was a homily for a graduation Mass at some little Catholic college in Illinois. I watched. He was right. Rotterman had a lethargic, nasally voice, a sort of Deep South version of Kermit the Frog. He also had the skin-crawling habit of clicking his tongue against the back of his teeth with every pause: "We gather today to celebrate a very important moment in the lives of these students." *Click.* "Very important." *Click.* "How important?" *Click.* "So important, they will remember it for the rest of their lives." *Click.* "The culmination of four years"—*click*—"or maybe five or six?" *Click*, as he waited for laughter that never came. "We have many important moments in our lives. Many, many important moments." *Click.*

"Okay, stop it. Please," I said.

"Never heard him speak, had you?"

"No."

"Now aren't you glad I'm here?"

I had no response. I was still irritated he hadn't checked with me, and even more that he had impersonated me. But he was right. We couldn't bring Rotterman in. It would have snuffed out any flickering flame of enthusiasm I had managed to kindle in the parish.

I turned away, looking at nothing in particular. "I just had fifteen hundred fliers printed. What am I going to do with those?"

"Return them."

"I can't return them. They aren't a pair of jeans."

"There was a printing error. Look at this. Is this the shade of blue you wanted? Of course not."

"They won't accept that."

"Well, they must. What are they going to do, sue you? The order's too small. Three billable hours for an attorney would cost more than the whole print job."

"Yeah, but it'll kill our relationship with them. They do our bulletins."

"Bulletins? You still use bulletins?" He held up his watch and tapped it. "Is it still 1986? I could have sworn it was 2016. Or has e-marketing not made it to Westchester County? No matter. I'm sure you can find another printer. They abound."

"I don't have time to look for another printer."

"I'll do it, then, when I have the new fliers ready." He scrutinized the old flier. "You did this yourself, didn't you? Not to worry. I have a friend. Terry. A graphic designer. Terry ... Terry ... MacConnell ... MacDonnell ... something like that. Anyhoo, leave the new fliers to me."

"Yeah, well, before we can do new fliers, I need a new speaker."

"Done. Did you think I would cancel your speaker without a substitute in mind?"

"Who?"

"Me, of course. What better way to showcase your new acquisition? The people will be tickled. Give me three nights and I'll have Sunday Masses packed again."

I stared at him.

"That reminds me. Free yourself up for this Saturday night. There's a welcome-back party at the Giordanos'. You're hosting it. The mayor will be there, and Congressman Sheltz. Keep your words short, though. Nothing spoils the mood like a babbler. Remember the three Bs: be brilliant, be brief, and be seated."

"You've already organized a welcome-back party? You just got here."

"No, no. It's been in the works for a while. At least two months. It's black tie, so wear your nice suit. Do you have a nice suit?"

Leave it to Andrew to give me emotional whiplash: irritation, because he had usurped my parish mission event, and now confusion, because he had organized a party for his return from exile well before I had even invited him to the parish. Had I missed something?

"It's only been three weeks since we talked about you coming here," I said.

"I can recommend a tailor. He's a little slow, so something from scratch won't work, but he might have something on hand he could just alter a bit. You're a forty-two long, right? That's pretty standard."

"How could you start planning a welcome-back party two months ago if I just asked you to come here three weeks ago?"

"The Giordanos planned it. Not me. I wouldn't throw a party for myself." He chuckled.

"Yes, you would."

"Well, maybe. But in any case, I didn't have to. As soon as I told the Giordanos I'd be back at St. Phil's—St. Dom's, rather—Gina G. said, 'Oh, you must come by the house. No, no, I have a better idea—we'll throw a little something for you. Get the whole gang together.' Christopher, how could I decline an offer from Gina G.?"

"My point, Andrew, is how did you have any idea you'd be coming back two months ago if I brought the idea to you only three weeks ago?"

He looked at me perplexed. "It was obvious. You kept pining for me to come back. Why else the random phone calls, the emails lamenting how lonely your new assignment is, how hard it is to get people excited about anything?"

Had I come across as that needy? Granted, I did try to warm him up with a few emails about how well things were going, how exciting St. Dominic's was. I appealed to his nostalgic sensibilities, painting myself as a Father O'Malley—not from *Going My Way* but from *The Bells of St. Mary's*: a priest entrusted with a huge project full of endless possibilities but also enormous obstacles, with faith that God would provide and that miracles would happen. Instead of showcasing an exciting venture, however, my missives came across as pleas for help, smoke signals coming off a desolate island. *SOS, I'm stranded, help!*

"I knew it would take you forever to ask," he continued, "and I wasn't going to wait around. I don't dawdle on things like that. Sorry, but I'm decisive. I act. However"—he held up his index finger—"you cannot accuse me of breaking decorum. I waited for you to get up the courage and make your pitch. I must admit, I didn't expect you to fly all the way to Rome. That was a bit excessive, but I was touched. And, as I told you, I had even planned to have a little fun with you, play hard to get, but I was so anxious to get it over with that I just couldn't delay it anymore. Besides, it wouldn't have been the right way to start, don't you agree?"

"Is *this* the right way to start?"

"This? What?"

"This!" I pointed at him with both hands and then around the office.

"You seem agitated."

"I *am* agitated. You just swirl in here unannounced. What do you expect?"

"Christopher, I'm here to help you," he said, as if scolding a small child. Then, as if trying to soothe that same child, he said, "I take my role seriously. Please. Allow me to help you."

"Right, of course. I do appreciate that you're here. It's just that—"

"And we're going to get this place shipshape. Trust me. The Giordanos' party is the start. It's not about me. It's about St. Dominic's. I'm the excuse, but it's your night. Then the parish mission. That'll be dynamite. Then—"

He cut off abruptly, as if he had just thought of something, swiveled toward the computer, adjusted the monitor, and started drafting an email.

"Andrew?"

"Don't worry about me," he said without making eye contact. "If you see people traipsing about, they're here to arrange the furniture in my rooms. I'll look in on them later. Run along now, I've quite a few emails to dispatch, calls to make, all that." He waved the back of his hand at me. "We'll catch up at supper."

"Andrew," I said. Now I was the one using the parental tone.

"Something the matter?" he asked, still typing.

"This is *my* office. That's *my* chair and *my* computer."

He stopped and turned toward me. "And I suppose you want to use them now? Of course you do. Right." He typed a bit more, clicked Send, shot up, turned the chair to face me, and graciously motioned to the empty seat. "All yours."

⚓ ⚓ ⚓

Alone, I sat at my desk and scanned the room. Everything was still in place, yet it felt like a tornado had ripped through, my head still spinning. *What just happened?* Then I sighed, peered over at the crucifix on the wall, and smiled.

"Well, Lord," I said out loud. "Would you look at that. You did it. You worked it out. It's all coming together nicely. Andrew's here. He'll be a pain, sure. But he's here. He's already getting social events going, spreading the word. The parish mission is going to be great. Things are going to be all right. Thank you, Jesus."

Shadow of a Doubt

The Giordano event was a Great Gatsby affair, and I was Nick Carraway swimming in a sea of bubbly socialites and jet-setters. Faces I had never seen before and would never see again strobed before me in a blur. Everyone either had just gotten back from or was about to go off to some exotic destination: a week of skiing in Vail, taking the kids to the Virgin Islands for spring break, a business trip to Hong Kong. I was out of my element, the natural wall-flower trying to bloom where I was planted. *Find a group of two*, I read once. *At least one will feel trapped, and your interruption will be welcome.* It worked. But after a minute, one of my interlocutors would leave, and I'd find myself in that awkward twosome, diligently trying to be interesting and finding my partner's eyes flitting around the room, looking for someone more engaging.

And who were all those people? Apparently parishioners of St. Philomena's, until Andrew left. Did they move on to some other parish? Maybe. Probably not. Would they start coming to St. Dominic's now that their beloved Father Reese was back? We'd see.

The night was a success, or at least Andrew thought so. "You were charming, Christopher. They all loved you. That bit about how you needed only mention the wonderful people of St. Philomena's to compel me to leave the glories of Rome behind—that was smooth. Nice. The whole thing was a success. An absolute success."

The parish mission was a success too. Well beyond my expectations. The first night a tolerable crowd of seventy-five people came, but by the third night it was packed. And, as promised, Sunday Mass attendance saw a significant uptick after that—or maybe it was just wishful thinking on my part, since I never actually counted.

Then there were the donations, the sudden influx of tax-deductible contributions, all thanks to Andrew. He convinced a generous friend to underwrite the St. Dominic's Day Fair, though it meant I had to commit to sitting in the dunking booth for a few hours. He also got several pledges to replace the roof, quite a challenge since roofs aren't sexy—not like a prominent stained glass window with your name etched at the bottom so people will pray for you for the next hundred years (or perpetually judge you for being vain). And on my birthday, April 17, he gave me a very special gift—two cashier's checks, each for nine thousand dollars, to install a new bathroom in the sacristy.

It was all going according to plan, everything falling into place. But I knew it was too good to be true. The other shoe would surely drop, since there's no such thing as a free lunch. And sure enough, the shoe fell with a mighty thud, and the waiter came by with a pricey check.

In seminary and in our first assignment, Andrew and I had been friends. I watched gleefully as he got away with murder—or maybe manslaughter, since none of it seemed premeditated. Despite all his superiors' efforts to box him in, head him off at the pass, or tie him down, he always seemed to escape their grip. He didn't do anything immoral, of course; he just didn't do what he was supposed to be doing. He walked many old ladies across streets, rescued plenty of cats from trees, pulled gaggles of babies from burning buildings—all garnering the desired accolades—but his superiors just wanted him to show up on time for Mass, sit in the confessional at the appointed hour, and attend a parish council meeting for once. So they'd try to force him. But if they put a fence around him, he'd jump it; if they built a wall, he'd burrow underneath.

I always played the enthralled spectator, bucket of popcorn in hand. Often I was an unexpected beneficiary of his escapades, like landing on the Community Chest square in Monopoly: box seats at the Met, dinner at La Grenouille, Cuban cigars, Louis XIII cognac, and the best of all, free dry cleaning (that's a book unto itself). But now the roles had changed. I was his superior, and despite deep friendship, fraternal sympathy, and the derivative benefits, I was compelled to wrangle him in.

This compulsion came from the staff's complaints, increasing in number and intensity over the course of the first few months. He managed to trample over every piece of turf anyone in the parish laid claim to. Rita's phone calls, texts, and emails went unanswered. If ever he spoke to her, it was only to tell her to ask Jerry to empty the overflowing trash in his office. Gretchen bemoaned numerous occasions when he had canceled a wedding or a funeral she'd been scheduled to play for, only to find out they hadn't been canceled after all; he had paid some *Fräulein* under the table to play instead of her.

Jerry's beef with him was minor. He complained Andrew left lights on all over the place, forgot to lock the church on several occasions, and discarded "organic material"—mostly orange or banana peels and the occasional half-eaten sandwich—in the recycle bin, thus rendering the other contents unrecyclable, not to mention attracting flies. Of all the members of the staff, the only one who didn't complain about him was Maria. Of course, if she had any complaints, she probably offered them up for the salvation of his soul, which might have been the only thing that could save it.

All those offenses could be dismissed as pretentious Andrew being pretentious Andrew. But his behavior toward Monsignor had no excuse. It was at times juvenile, at times downright cruel, but always intentional and spiteful.

One day we were sitting at dinner. As usual, Monsignor attempted to empty the salt shaker onto his food, this time veal cutlets, but the shaker was already empty. He huffed, dejected, like a boy who discovers his favorite toy's batteries are dead. He shuffled into the kitchen, mumbling something about "that woman" under his breath. I looked at Andrew, who held a glass of wine up to the light. (Drinking wine with dinner had become a regular thing for us after his arrival.) Sounds of slamming cupboards and crashing drawers filtered through the kitchen door.

"He'll need a chair," Andrew said, cocking his ear toward the door. "Five, four, three, two—"

The door burst open. "Bring that chair in here," Monsignor demanded.

Andrew smirked.

"What do you need?" I asked, knowing full well what he needed but not why he needed a chair to get it. In the kitchen I found the large Morton's salt container on the highest shelf, well out of Monsignor's reach, and almost out of mine. He snatched it from my hand and grunted, "Thank you, at least someone has some decency."

Returning to the table, he salted his veal, cut it, and put it in his mouth. I took a mental note to make sure he got an eye exam soon; even from across the table I could see it wasn't salt coming out of the shaker, but sugar.

That was just one instance of several pranks, equally juvenile, if mildly amusing, had Monsignor been a good sport about them.

🕊 🕊 🕊

"Yes. I did that," Andrew admitted when I finally confronted him. "I couldn't resist. I saw the salt shaker was empty, and I simply fell into temptation. Forgive me, Father, for I've been sophomoric." He hung his head in mock shame.

"Andrew, you can't treat people like that. This isn't elementary school." We were sitting in my office. I was in my chair, Andrew on the other side of my desk. I was firmly in control of the situation, ready to do what no other boss of his had ever been able to. I was confident that I would succeed because I knew him better than any of them.

"Right, of course not. I've just been in a silly mood lately. Was there something else you wanted to see me about?"

"Well, what about everything else I just said? Rita feels like you don't give her the time of day, Gretchen thinks you purposely work around her, and Monsignor ... really, why do you pick on him?"

He looked at me with big droopy eyes, which at first I took for contrition. Then he sighed, and I realized it wasn't contrition but pity.

"Christopher, Christopher, Christopher," he said. "I'll overlook the fact that you swallowed their stories hook, line, and sinker without considering there may be another version of events. I understand the pressure you're under. I do. So I won't take offense. We're still friends." He had an ankle over his knee and was buffing a scuff on his shoe with his handkerchief. "Now then, as a friend, I must lift the wool from your eyes and tell you"—he dropped his foot to the floor and leaned forward dramatically—"you're being fleeced."

I gave him a confused look.

"What does Rita do all day?" he asked.

"She does a ton. Takes all the calls, handles the registrations, deals with the accountant, schedules stuff—you know, weddings, baptisms, funerals. What every parish secretary does. Not to mention keeping the archdiocese off my back."

"Well, she certainly does sound busy. So why does she take such long lunch breaks?"

"She doesn't. I mean, not every day."

He lifted an eyebrow.

"She works hard."

"Yes, I can see that. She practically has no nose left since it's held so firmly to the grindstone."

"What's your point?"

"She arrives on time, I'll give her that, around nine. And she leaves promptly at five, not a minute before; I'll give her that too. But in between she does about three hours of work. You pay her for eight, if I'm not mistaken. I also heard she requested to switch to salary."

"Yes, what about it? I already told her no. She's staying hourly."

"Have you done anything about the photocopier?"

"What?"

"Oh, you don't know. Does the parish own the copier, or do we lease it?"

"We lease it."

"No. We don't. We own it."

"Trust me, we're leasing it. I sign the checks every month."

"Yes, you do. And the payments go to a company owned by her husband, that has one employee, and it's not her husband."

"You don't know that."

"Who's the business manager?"

"What does he have to do with the photocopier?"

"Who's the business manager, the accountant, the one who does the books, prepares the checks?"

"We outsource that. All the accounting, the bookkeeping, it's all outsourced. I just get the reports and make sure they square."

"What's the name of the company?"

"It's not a company, it's a guy. A CPA—Henry Mancini or something like that."

"Henry Massotti?"

"Yeah, that's it."

"And Rita's maiden name is . . ."

"I don't know."

"Right. You might want to check."

"Is it Massotti?"

"Then there's Jerry. Nice enough guy. Not very productive, but kindhearted."

"Look, I know he's kind of lazy, but I need someone I can trust."

"Oh, you trust him, do you?"

"Yes. Why?"

"No reason. I just think that when a guy cheats on his wife, you might not know who else he's cheating."

"Stop. You're making this up."

He shrugged.

"Look, even if he is cheating on his wife, his personal affairs are none of my business."

"Unless his personal affair is with an employee. Haven't you ever wondered where Rita goes those days she takes an extra half hour at lunch?"

"No. Quit it. They hate each other. And more important, they're loyal employees. I trust them."

"You trust them because you hired them?"

"No, Monsignor hired them."

"Uh-huh."

"So now you're going to tell me Monsignor's their ringleader? And is Gretchen his enforcer?"

"No, no. Gretchen's clean. Just controlling. I have no time for controlling people. Monsignor, on the other hand ... You know I was here before? I ask because you never brought it up. I was beginning to think you forgot."

"No, I know. I had forgotten, but I was reminded the other day."

"You don't know why I left, do you? Because I certainly never told you."

"Jack told me, sort of. He didn't want you around because you weren't pulling your weight." He was about to speak; I held up a hand. "Those are his words, or something like that. I'm not taking sides. I wasn't there. Basically he complained you were a loose cannon, and he can't deal with that. He's a control freak." I could deal with it, though. I was ready for it. I knew if I gave Andrew sick calls or asked him to visit shut-ins, he'd find an excuse not to show. So I did all that. I wanted him as my associate for a few very specific things: increasing attendance, improving community relations, rekindling parishioners' faith through his preaching. I knew if I gave him a stage, he would work his magic. He was the charmer; I was the worker bee. I was comfortable with that arrangement. And it was working. I just didn't expect him to be getting into it with the staff. That's where my foresight had failed me.

"Yes, 'tis true, he couldn't control me. I was—am—uncontrollable." He gave me a self-satisfied grin. "But that's only part of it. I could tell something was rotten in St. Dominic's. I snooped around. Played Sam Spade. I found the receipt for the copier purchase. Researched the bookkeeper. Followed Rita on her lunch breaks. I brought it all to Monsignor, well documented—photographs, receipts, spreadsheets, everything. He thanked me, patted me on the back, and told me he would take it from there. Just like a corrupt government agent from a B movie. That's when I knew. After that he clipped my wings, feather by feather. At first I thought I might go to the Arch, but then I decided against it. I don't have a lot of friends down at ten-eleven, and he does."

"And all that's still going on? Are you sure?"

"Well, if you're still writing checks to pay the lease on a copier, and Mr. Massotti is still your CPA, and Rita is still taking ninety-minute lunch breaks, I would suppose so."

"Wouldn't Jack have cleaned things up before I took over?"

"Maybe. Maybe everything *is* on the up-and-up."

"Well, I better find out."

"No, no, you better not."

"Yes, yes, I better. We can't have irregularities like this."

"My advice, Christopher? While everything functions properly, just let it go. Be careful how much you confide in Rita and Jerry and, especially, Jack. But it's best not to kick the hornet's nest."

"If any of this comes to light, it's on my head."

"It started before you came here. You wouldn't have figured it out had I not told you."

"Andrew, I have to be responsible."

Andrew was silent a moment, putting hand to chin. "There's something else. Another reason to let it go."

"That is?"

"It's about Jack. I'm not sure I can really say. He's ... he's involved in something that ... let's just say it would be rather dangerous if you got involved or knew anything about it."

"I know about it."

"You do."

"Yes. I do. The Mafia. I figured out he was tapped as their go-to confessor."

"And?"

"And what?"

"So you don't know everything."

"There's more?"

"No. Nothing more. Not at all. Forget I ever said anything. Now you must give me a penance."

"Andrew, tell me. What else is he involved in?"

"Nothing. Sorry I ever said anything; forget it. Now please give me a penance. If you don't, your authority will be undermined. No one will respect you. They'll walk all over you because you don't hold people accountable. So please, tell me, what is my punishment?"

"I don't believe you. Jack isn't involved with the mob. You're just trying to cover your derriere."

"You're absolutely right. Jack isn't involved with the mob. Your staff is completely trustworthy. I have been hallucinating. Now, shall I get a ruler? Would a nice rap across the knuckles do? Or do you want to dock my pay or have me peel potatoes for a week? What is it? What shall I do?"

I stared at him for a moment. I didn't buy it. Any of it. The copier, the CPA—it was all a game. A diversionary tactic. Or was it?

As a penance, besides demanding Andrew apologize to all the staff, even Maria, I ordered him to take Monsignor out to dinner. I knew it would be a penance for Monsignor too, but I needed them to become friends. For Monsignor the enticement would be the location: the Old

Fitzgerald, a beloved Irish pub. The pub would probably be a bigger penance for Andrew than the company, but it served him right.

※ ※ ※

Our little tête-à-tête had been in the morning. I ate lunch in the kitchen alone, except for Maria, who had already started preparing dinner.

"Padre, what is wrong?" Maria asked. How did she know something was wrong? Perhaps she had a gift, like those saints who could read souls. More likely it was because I had been staring blankly at the opposite wall the last ten minutes, sandwich untouched, my hands in my lap.

"It's nothing," I said. "Just had an uncomfortable conversation, that's all."

"With Padre Andrés?"

"Yep."

"He's *especial*, Padre Andrés."

I looked down at my sandwich. I wasn't hungry, but I didn't want to offend Maria by not eating. I grasped the BLT firmly and before biting into it said, "Maria, where does Rita go on her lunch breaks?"

"*No sé, padre*. At lunch I'm in the kitchen. She don't come here, I know that."

"Right." Besides, even if Maria knew, she wouldn't tell me. She divulged people's secrets only if it made them look good.

"You know," she said as she chopped carrots, her back to me, "is no easy to tell when a papaya's ripe. They say me, 'Maria, is the color. It gotta be yellow, no green.' Oh, and they say it gotta be a little soft and smell a little sweet, then is ready." She wagged her finger in the air, her back still to me. "Not enough. Could be yellow, and you open it up and is still hard, no good. Maybe still have some green, and you think, is no ready. But you never know, it could be, in fact, perfect ripe ... *en su punto*. You squeeze the papaya and smell it, but it don't always tell you. People can be like that. Rita could be like that. Monsignor ... Monsignor is like that."

I sat up a bit as Maria approached and stood across the table from me, knife still in her hand. She could tell I wasn't comprehending and wanted to make her point.

"*Por ejemplo*, that Padre Andrés?" Maria continued. "Everyone think he so selfish, so presumed—no, that's not the word—a showoff, no? But you know what? He could be like a ripe papaya that still a little green on the outside. You look inside and is all pink and soft and juicy. Like what he do for Kendra, no? *La pobre*. Where would Kendra be without Padre Andrés?"

I gave her a questioning glance.

"You know, *esa chica*, the one who plays the organ for him? She work two jobs and has that *niño* to take care of. She won't take money. Padre Andrés, he try to give her some money one time. He didn't tell me nothing, but I find out. She won't take it because she 'ain't a charity case'. That what she says. Padre Andrés knows she play the piano, so he have her play the organ at his things— you know, weddings, funerals. It don't sound good, but, you know. And he pay her twice what he pay Gretchen. Oh, and Gretchen, she don't like that. But Padre Andrés don't care. He just want to help Kendra. And he find out Kendra's *niño* has a birthday, and he buy presents and have her bring to him. And he pay her rent twice, and she don't know where it coming from."

"Andrew—Father Reese—does all that?"

"*Sí*. You see, sometimes the papaya is a little green, but you open it, and is sweet."

12

I Confess

I wasn't entirely convinced Andrew's parochial conspiracy theory had merit, but it planted a seed. I was more reserved with Rita after my talk with Andrew. I started to count the breaks she took. Some of her lunch breaks were excessive, but she got stuff done. I was going to follow her one day but caught myself. Even if she and Jerry were having an affair, I didn't need to know. Her maiden name *was* Massotti; the CPA *was* her cousin. The copier leasing seemed to be legit, but I could never get a human being on the phone when I called the company.

All this weighed on me, and Maria could tell. In an attempt to cheer me up, a few days later she made her famous empanadas, these little crunchy half-moon-shaped turnovers I loved. And I had them all to myself because that was the night Andrew fulfilled his penance, taking Monsignor out to dinner. It was also the night the phone rang, again.

It was another call for last rites. The fifth, actually, including Richie. That's right, there had already been three other calls for last rites after Richie. They all came at seven o'clock on the dot, but the days of the week varied—sometimes a Tuesday, sometimes a Thursday, but always a weeknight, never a Saturday or Sunday.

The second call came the night before Andrew arrived. Monsignor and I were at supper.

"All yours, Reverend Pastor," he said.

I picked up the receiver. "St. Dominic's."

"Father Hart?"

"Yes." My heart rate had already shot up. I wasn't sure who was calling—this was only the second time—but the look on Monsignor's face clued me in.

"I got someone who needs last rites." I recognized the voice now. It was Sal Grisanti, the ostensible manager of Stefano's and the guy who had cornered me in the sacristy after the funeral.

"We'll pick you up. Expect us in ten minutes." He hung up, but I still held the receiver, dazed, listening to the airy sound of nothing, then the repetitive *mamp, mamp, mamp*, and I breathed out a soft "No." But it was too late.

Back in the dining room, Monsignor was spooning a lump of chocolate pudding into his mouth.

"Jack, it was them."

"Do your job, Father," he said with his mouth full.

"I can't do this again."

"He's gonna die whether you go or not. You have an opportunity here. You miss it, who knows what happens. You want that on your conscience?"

I didn't. But I also didn't want to get involved in another murder. What was the right thing to do? Just "do my job"? Was that my job? Was I just supposed to go along with this? Wasn't I enabling the cycle of violence to continue, a cog in this mad death machine, helping it to churn? Or was I making a bad thing a little better? Was I saving a soul who would die whether I was there or not?

In a war, if I were living behind enemy lines and they were going to execute a soldier, one of their own, for treason let's say, wouldn't I hear his confession? Would I be condemned for aiding and abetting the enemy, or would I be lauded for ministering to a man in his final hours? Maybe Monsignor was right. Maybe this was my job.

By the time the SUV pulled up, I had decided. I'd be a humble priest. I would go behind enemy lines and tend to the soldier sentenced to death. They would kill his body, but I would save his soul.

The setup was the same. Grim Reaper and his pal picked me up, brought me up to the same room on the second floor, and took me home when I was finished. And so it happened with the next three, with one exception: they canceled the shuttle service after the second trip, when I told them to skip the blindfold since I knew we were going to Stefano's. After that I took my own car, and Grim met me at the kitchen entrance.

The three penitents after Richie had little in common. They were all men; two of the three were Catholic (one was Methodist, which was kind of awkward); and they were all criminals. But that's where the similarities ended. One guy was a truck driver from Baltimore; another was an IT specialist living in Queens; the third was a used car dealer from Camden. None of them was Italian, strangely enough, and I didn't detect any shared ethnic roots. Some were more talkative than others, but no one was particularly contrite. Years of silencing one's conscience has that effect.

Ordinarily I would end up walking them through the Ten Commandments. When I asked about the first commandment—"Have you loved God above all things?"—each one, without fail, nodded in affirmation.

It was hard work prying out any recognition, even a slight one, that their crimes just might be morally wrong, that is, sinful. Facing certain death was a good lubricant, though, and grace a solid crowbar. By the end of each session I was satisfied when I saw a tear drip along a tough guy's face or a look of relief wash over a cumbersome penitent, his shoulders slumping, his breath escaping in a sigh, as if decades of pent-up fear and anger had been released.

An unexpected by-product of these forays behind enemy lines was a better knowledge of the organization. This was not just some Westchester County thing. The network of ne'er-do-wells ran the length of the Eastern Seaboard. No one gave it a name, like the Cardelli Crime Family. They just talked about "the guys". "So, the guys asked me to rough him up a little" or "The guys called, and you knew what that meant."

"The guys" dabbled in the usual Mafia rackets: extortion, prostitution, corruption of public officials, the placement of horse heads in beds, and the mailing of care packages of dead fish. But their specialty was brokering deals between other crime organizations. Every group has its specialty, its share of a given market, and its turf. But some schemes need a joining of efforts, an invasion of turf, or an outsourcing of operations. That's where "the guys" came in. Cardelli's guys were the go-between, a sort of Switzerland of Mafiaworld. And Stefano's, it turns out, was Geneva. That's where rival bosses could meet without fear of a snub-nosed revolver hidden in the john, à la Michael Corleone.

None of the four guys I met was a broker himself. Only direct relatives of Paul Cardelli could be brokers. My penitents were all either first contacts who vetted potential clients for the brokers or low-level functionaries within the organization. And they all messed up. Each one, somehow, lost the trust of somebody and became a liability. Since they weren't traitors, just victims of dumb luck, there was no need for the Black Death. That's how they got to sit in front of me.

🙢 🙢 🙢

The night Andrew took Monsignor to Old Fitzgerald's, I received what I expected to be an ordinary last rites call.

It was a Tuesday night in mid-August. I was still recovering from the St. Dominic's Day Fair, which was a success despite serious cost overruns. When I answered the call and heard "Father Hart?" on the other end of the line, I simply hung up, got in my car, and drove to Stefano's.

I was almost looking forward to this one. Not that I wanted anyone to die, but I had come to accept I needed to do my job, and I was starting to get the hang of it. Each time, I managed to take my penitent a little deeper, coax a little more contrition. As I drove over, I rehearsed my approach. Going head-on never works with guys like these. You have to start asking about where they grew up, what their home life was like, first girlfriend, best day of their life, worst day of their life—sort of like that speed-dating icebreaker I had to do at a ministry conference once. Then you talk about regret. "What's your biggest regret?" That gets them in the right frame of mind. Next you use the Ten Commandments as a framework to mine for regrets, and eventually sins, and by that point Grim is banging on the door.

When I arrived this time, Grim wasn't there. Instead, a short, stocky guy with a pug face, bug eyes, and slick black hair with a razor-sharp part stood at the back entrance. A few strands of hair on the back of his head stuck up, which reminded me of Alfalfa from *The Little Rascals*, rendering him less intimidating. He walked me upstairs and down the corridor, and just before I crossed the threshold, he stopped me.

"No funny business. Just do what you came for." *Did he just say* funny business? *Who says that?*

But I was indignant—as if I had ever been anything but professional. "You're new, aren't you?" I said. "Check with your predecessor about me. You've got nothing to worry about."

He gave me a huffing snicker as if he knew something I didn't.

I walked into the room, and just before he closed the door behind me, I looked back at him, eyebrows raised: *Are you sure? Hasn't there been a mistake?* He shrugged and closed the door.

She sat, blonde hair with purple streaks frizzy from the humidity. Two lines of tear-smudged mascara ran down her cheeks, stopping short of her faded black lipstick. A pant leg of tattoos crawled out of a Doc Martens boot.

"Ashley?" A pile of wadded-up tissues sat under the card table next to her.

"I thought it'd be you," she said.

"Well, I had no idea it would be you." My imagination attempted to make sense of the situation, trying on theories and then tossing them aside, like shopping for clothes at Goodwill, nothing looking quite right. Was this the same Ashley, the same sweet goth-girl waitress who shared her dreams of Broadway set designing? Why was she sitting in the perp's chair? Why were they going to kill her?

I sat in the folding chair in front of her. "What are you doing here?" I asked.

She sniffed back tears, dabbed her eyes with a Kleenex, and blew her nose. "They call it the White Death," she said, her voice faltering and hoarse.

"Yes, I know, but why you?"

My imagination was still working through theories: Maybe she wasn't simply a waitress. Maybe that was her cover and she worked for Cardelli. Maybe she served spaghetti and meatballs at the mob boss meetings and one of the bosses didn't like the way she looked at him. Or more shameful involvement—perhaps she had slept with one of "the guys" and he talked in his sleep, and now she knew too much.

"He lied to me," she said. "He told me he just did deliveries. I thought, like pizza and stuff. I was *so* wrong."

"Who? Who lied to you?"

"Brian," she said with a certain exasperation, as if I should have known.

"Right, Brian. Your boyfriend. He lied about doing deliveries for Stefano's?"

"I asked Sal if Brian could have his birthday off so we could go out. He said no, because it was going to be a busy night. He needed him. Busy night, my ass." She clasped her hands to her mouth, eyes wide in embarrassment. "I'm sorry. I shouldn't talk like that."

"It's all right. You're about to go to confession."

"Confession? Oh, right. Yeah. We have to do that." Her body tensed. Tears began to stream.

"We will. In time. Let's just talk about what happened. Sal wouldn't give Brian the night off?"

She shook her head as if she didn't want to continue, then pulled a new Kleenex from the box, tossing the used one onto the pile under the table.

"It's okay," I said. "I want to know. I want to understand."

"I thought he was cheating on me. And Sal was covering. That'd be just the thing a jack—a jerk like Sal would do. Cover for his buddy so he could go screw some other chick. I'm sorry, I didn't mean—"

"And?"

"And I ... I ... I can't. I mean, I can't. I'm here 'cause I know something I shouldn't. If you know too ..."

I looked into her eyes. "It's okay. Keeping secrets is my job. They know that. It's part of the deal."

She hesitated, then continued. "I followed him. I was going to catch the prick. And I did. But it wasn't ... he wasn't ... I mean ... there was no other chick."

She stopped. Her eyes searched the room, looking for the words.

"It's okay. Take your time. Breathe. Deep breaths."

"He ... he shot someone ... with a gun. Killed him."

"Did he see you?"

"No ... worse. Damien saw me."

"Who's that?"

She leaned over the table, burying her head in her arms.

"It's okay, Ashley. Don't worry, don't worry." I rubbed her back gently. "Listen, I want to help you. You don't need to die tonight." I don't know what spurred me to say it, but once I did, it became a conviction. I couldn't let her die.

A muffled voice responded. "You can't ... You can't help me."

"I can. I want to. Just tell me what happened. Give me a chance. Who's Damien?"

"The cook. One of the cooks." She sat upright, wiping her eyes with her forearm, leaving a stripe of mascara across it. "Brian dropped off his car at the restaurant and then went with Damien in his truck."

"His truck? Was it an SUV?"

"Yeah, the black shiny one. Damien loves that truck." She blew her nose again. "I followed them to the Stop & Shop. The truck—the SUV—disappeared behind the store, and then I saw Brian drive out in a beat-up old Chevy Cavalier. But just Brian. And it had fuzzy dice. He hates that. I was like, *He must really love this chick.*

"The SUV didn't come out. I followed Brian to some motel. I thought I had him. I thought that's where he'd meet the bi—the girl he was going to hook up with. But he just sat there in the dark across the street. After like fifteen minutes this guy came out of the motel. He was totally nervous. I saw them talk for a minute, the guy still on the street speaking through the passenger window. Then Brian got out and they switched places—the guy got in the driver's seat, and Brian got in the passenger's seat. It was weird. It was really weird, like I thought, what's going on, you know? The car started, and *bam!* Blood splattered all over the window. Brian must have shot him when the guy was distracted starting the car."

"What did you do?"

"I sat there. First in shock, but then ... I didn't think Brian saw me following him, but I was afraid if I pulled out, he would spot me. Then Damien drove past real slow. He must have seen me. But he didn't stop. He drove up to the Chevy. Brian jumped into the SUV, and they drove off.

"That night, he got home and chewed me out. That's how I knew that Damien must have seen me and said something to him. Brian chewed me out so bad. Worse than ever. I thought the neighbors would call the cops."

"Did he hit you?"

"No. Brian doesn't hit. I'm always waiting for it, but it never comes. He probably can't risk it. You know, like he'd be afraid I'd show my bruises to somebody. But what he doesn't do with his fists he makes up for with words. Sometimes I wish he'd just hit me. It'd be over faster."

"So you're here because you saw him murder someone. You're a witness, and they can't have that."

"Yeah."

"And Brian can't do anything to get you out of this?"

"He tried. I was actually kind of flattered. He stood up for me in front of Sal. Nobody does that. Brian can be such a sweetie. I guess that's why I love him. I mean, he's a jerk, but then he does stuff like that."

I put my hand on her shoulder. She dropped her hands to her lap. They were trembling.

"I'm so scared."

"Don't worry. I'm not going to let anything happen to you. You do not deserve to die." I was whispering.

She matched my whisper. "You can't. There's nothing you can do."

"Yes, there is."

"What? They've got guns. You gonna take them out? You gonna go all Jason Bourne on 'em?"

"No. I'll call the police. Once I get out of here, I'm calling the police. I don't care."

"You think the police will come? When you give them this address?"

"Why wouldn't they?"

"Everybody knows the cops don't go to Stefano's."

Right ... of course they wouldn't. A place like that couldn't operate the way it did if they didn't have protection.

I stood and paced the room. At this point my imagination had finished with the Goodwill bargain bin, having tried on everything, its assessment complete. Ashley, sweet goth-waitress Ashley, was just a waitress. She didn't serve at mob boss rendezvouses in Stefano's back room or moonlight as a prostitute. She was nothing other than a cute girl taken in by an older man who she just learned was a hit man for the Mafia. Which gave me a thought.

"Ashley, tell me what your boyfriend looks like."

She described him. He was unmistakably my erstwhile escort, Grim Reaper.

"When was the last time you saw him?"

"Yesterday, when Sal locked me up here. That's when they had their little fight."

"Brian wasn't at the door tonight. He's always at the door."

"You know Brian?"

"Yes. I didn't know his name, but I know him. He wasn't at the door, but I guess that's not surprising. He doesn't want you to die. So they probably have him on another assignment or gave him the night off or something." I took her hand. "All right. Here's the deal. I'm going to find Brian. We'll work together and find you a way out of this."

"Please don't, Father. Don't. I mean, I'm already worried about what they're gonna do to him. Like, Sal was pretty pissed. If Brian pushes, I don't know what they'll do to him."

"I can't just—"

She put her other hand on mine. "Father, can you hear my confession?"

13

Rear Window

My little Honda's dim headlights were burning a hole in the back of the rectory garage. I stared at my cell phone, the engine still running. After Ashley's confession, when Alfalfa banged on the door warning me time was almost up, I slipped my phone out of my pocket, opened the notes app, and wrote, *Did they tell you when they'd do it?*, handing her the phone. I didn't think they were listening in, but I couldn't be sure.

Tonight, she wrote and handed it back.

Me: *Did they say how?*

Ashley: *No.*

Me: *Did they say where?*

Ashley: *No. But I overheard. Not here.*

Me: *Any idea where?*

Ashley: *No.*

Me: *Okay. Don't worry. I'll figure something out.*

Ashley: *Thank you.* She tacked on a heart emoji.

Now I sat in my garage, figuring something out. Andrew and Monsignor hadn't come back yet. That was a good sign. It meant they were having a good time, or service was really slow. It also meant I was alone on this. Monsignor would have probably told me to let it go, but Andrew was street-smart. He'd know what to do. But I didn't have time to wait, and Old Fitzgerald's was in Port Chester, a good twenty-five minutes away.

I thought to call 911 but then reconsidered after recalling Ashley's warning that the police might be in cahoots with "the guys". Maybe the FBI had a hotline? But what if the FBI relied on local law enforcement? I didn't want to risk it.

An idea: gangbangers. I knew a bunch from my time at St. Rocco's. But how would I contact them now? And how hypocritical would that be? I had been trying to get those kids *out* of gangs, and now I wanted to leverage their gang muscle against another gang? Rather Machiavellian of me. Besides, the Mafia was a different beast. Those kids weren't the sophisticated organized crime types; they were just fatherless boys looking for a tribe.

So much for figuring something out. When I replay that night in my head now, a bunch of solutions come to mind. For one, I really should have called the FBI. It was the obvious thing to do. But I didn't. Why call in experts who are trained to deal with this kind of thing when you can do it yourself? Yes, I'm that guy who, if his left arm hurts and he finds himself short of breath, googles "how to treat a heart attack" instead of just calling an ambulance.

So I would handle this myself. But I couldn't go back to Stefano's in my car. They knew my car. Andrew's forest-green Mini Cooper, however, sat idle in the garage. It was brand-new. There was no way "the guys" knew about it.

I ran up to Andrew's room, snagged the spare key, and charged down to the garage, only to charge back up to my room and grab the baseball bat I kept next to my bed.

Hoping I hadn't arrived too late, I parked a few blocks away, facing the restaurant. Thirty-five minutes had passed from the time I had left Stefano's till the time I got back. The sun had fallen behind the buildings. The early evening shadows had dissipated into a warm dusky twilight. I had a clear view of the alley, and I waited for the SUV to pull out. If those thugs were going to bring her somewhere, I was sure they would take the SUV. But I was wrong.

Ashley walked out the front door, alone. She clutched her purse and skittishly crossed the street, fumbling with keys, dropping them, picking them up, searching for the lock fob. Finally the lights on a red Corolla flickered. She looked up and down the street, then got in.

Strange. Why was she alone? And why wasn't she starting the car? My skin began to tingle, and my stomach knotted. Something was wrong. But what? I instinctively slipped my seat belt off and tugged at the door latch. *A bomb. Of course.* Her brake lights came on. *Wait ... no ... no no no no ...* I launched out into the night air about to scream, *It's going to explode!* as I heard the ignition turn and saw her pull out. My mother was right. I watch too many movies.

I jumped back into my car and waited a few seconds to see whether anyone would follow her. Nothing. No black SUV, no other car. The light at the end of the block was red, so I didn't lose her. As it turned green, I eased onto the road, checking my mirrors constantly to see if I was being followed.

She drove for about fifteen minutes, out of East Springdale, onto the Cross County Parkway. I let a couple of cars get between us so it wasn't obvious I was following her, but remaining inconspicuous proved harder than I thought. She stayed in the right-hand lane and went five miles per hour under the speed limit. Every car that slid between us eventually got exasperated and went around her. I tried to hang back but almost lost her when a tractor-trailer illegally merged onto the parkway in front of me. I would have gone around, but I was blocked by a guy having a heated conversation on his phone. She pulled onto the Hutchinson Parkway, heading south, exiting soon after into Pelham Manor.

Eventually she turned into a neighborhood dotted with small 1970s homes, mostly ranches, a few colonials. She pulled into a driveway on the right side of the street. I kept going and took a left at the next corner, rounded the block, shut my lights off, and pulled back onto the same street just in time to see her get out of her car, look around nervously, and approach the house. I parked on the side of the road at a safe distance. She stopped on the front walk just before the picture window in the center of the house and tried to look in.

At this point, I slinked out of the car, observing her from behind an oak tree. The street was quiet. No cars. No nighttime strollers, no dogs barking. It was silent, except for the crescendo and decrescendo of cicadas. The air was August sultry. I was sweating.

In one house, the blue-and-green flashes from a TV reflected off a wall. In another, drapes glowed warmly. Otherwise the neighborhood was dark. No faces in windows. No lurking shadows.

Ashley was now at the front door. She rustled around in her purse and pulled out a set of keys. It must be her house if she has keys. A moment later she was in. The door closed behind her.

I scurried up to the house, checking for potential assailants as I went—through car windows, over at the other houses. No one, not a soul. I held the baseball bat nonchalantly at my side. *Just me, your friendly neighborhood priest, with a baseball bat.*

Through a white sheer covering the narrow side window, I detected Ashley's silhouette move cautiously to the right and then disappear. There were two windows on the front of the house, but the shades were drawn in both. I moved around to the side. A window toward the back was open, the venetians lowered but not completely closed.

The ground sloped downward, and the window was too high for me to see in.

Looking around for a solution, I spotted one: a three-foot statue of Saint Francis gazed prayerfully at me from a flower bed on the side of the neighbor's house. I leaned the bat against the house and lugged the statue over. With one foot on Saint Francis' head (*Sorry, Frank*) and my hands pressed against the siding, I peered through narrow slits in the blinds. Before I could pull myself up and lean in, a shard of light from an opening door slowly widened, revealing a body slumped in a chair and blood splattered on the wall behind. It was Brian. He was dead.

A scream rang out loud enough to wake the entire Hudson Valley. Ashley had just opened the door. A stern male voice shouted from somewhere in the room. The man was berating her. "I told you, never do that. Never! That's it. That's the last time!" Ashley tried to respond, her voice weak, confused. He shouted over her. "I told you there'd be consequences."

Then another male voice, older and loud, from behind me: "Hey! Knock it off!" I turned quickly, almost losing my balance. The voice came from the neighbor's screened-in back porch; it was dark. I stared, frozen in place. I could barely make out the patio furniture. Was that the back of a head breaching the top of one of the chairs? Could he see me?

"Ron, mind your own business," said a whiny female voice from farther inside the porch.

"They're always going at it. Somebody's gotta say something. One of these days he's gonna put her in the hospital." The red smoldering end of a cigarette tapped an ashtray on a little table next to the tepidly concerned citizen.

"Let it go, Ron."

His indignation wasn't strong enough to overcome his laziness. If he had gotten up to check out the situation, he would have seen me. The circulation in my leg was starting to cut off, but I didn't move. A slap from inside the house caught my attention, and I turned back to the window. I saw Ashley stagger. Then two flashes—*bang, bang*, pops like firecrackers. Then a thud.

I dove onto the ground.

"Gun!" Ron yelled. "Joan. Call 911."

Moments later a third shot rang out. I flattened myself into the grass, hoping my black clothing would be enough to camouflage me if either Ron or the shooter looked out. The sharp sound of metal scraping on cement clattered out of the porch. Ron must have bashed into a table as he raced inside.

Now. I have to move now. Before they turn the lights on, before police arrive. I leapt up and darted for the woods, disappearing into the full summer foliage.

Leaning up against a tree, I tried to catch my breath. Another body broke through the foliage farther down the tree line. Was it the shooter? Short and stocky build—it had to be Alfalfa. He couldn't see me. He was scanning his surroundings, waiting for his eyes to adjust.

I was torn. If I was going to do something, it had to be now. Do I confront him? He's got a gun. Do I pull out my phone and video him? The light from the phone would give my position away. I hesitated, and he skulked away. I did nothing, except watch him fade into the darkness. The faint wail of sirens blared in the distance. Acid released in my stomach, and self-loathing in my soul.

14

The Man Who Knew Too Much

"I squished up in the back seat of the Mini until the commotion died down. I couldn't stay in the woods, and I couldn't just drive away. I mean, there were cops all over the place. So I hid." That was what I told Andrew after I explained everything else, and when I say everything, I mean everything.

I had zombie-walked into the rectory around one in the morning wanting to crawl under my bed—door locked, shades drawn—and die. A light was on in the living room. Out of habit I went to shut it off and found Andrew, bourbon in hand, the bottle on a side table with an unused glass next to it. A book sat on his lap; his finger traced a line.

"'I love the silent hour of night,'" he recited. "'For blissful dreams may then arise, revealing to my charmed sight, what may not bless my waking eyes.'" He held his glass up to me. "Anne Brontë, Charlotte and Emily's lesser-known sister. But quite a poet in her own right."

Shut up, Andrew. Just shut up.

"Hmm ... pale," he said. "Bloodshot eyes. Something like Hamlet after seeing his father. I hope it was worth it."

I wished he would just go away. I wanted to be alone. My mind projected me walking away, up the stairs, crawling into bed. My body just stood there. Dazed. Blinking slowly.

"Did the car work out? The brakes are a little squishy, aren't they? I've been meaning to complain."

I sort of nodded, sort of shook my head, not really sure what I was responding to.

"I thought so too. I will have to have a word with the dealer. I specifically chose not to go preowned. It should be mint perfect."

I started for the stairs.

"Christopher, what's wrong?"

"Nothing. I need to think." The words came out robotic, droning.

"Nonsense. You need to talk. Come. Join me for a nightcap."

I plodded up the stairs, consciously lifting one foot after another as if I were in high altitude.

"Christopher." He said it loud. Commanding. "Come. Sit."

I stopped. Like an obedient dog I reversed course, slogged back down the stairs, and plopped onto the couch.

"I hope you like it neat," he said, pouring a couple of ounces into the glass on the side table. "Michter's. Single barrel, small batch. See if you can pick up the hint of chocolate truffle." He handed me the glass. "So, out with it. What happened?"

"I just saw someone get murdered," I said, surprised at myself for saying it out loud. But after I said it, I knew I needed to, as if I were dehydrated and had been offered water. He was right. I needed to talk.

"Murdered? As in the intentional, premeditated ending of another's life?"

I nodded, staring straight ahead.

"What happened?"

"I'm still trying to figure it out." Maybe this was why Andrew had come—not to help me with the parish as I had planned but so I wouldn't be alone in all this. "I need your help, Andrew," I said.

"Of course you do. A friend in need and all that. Tell me."

And I told him. Every last bit. I held in reserve only what might identify the penitents and their sins. With Ashley I had to be even more careful. Andrew may have met her since she worked in town. Not that Andrew would have stooped to dining at Stefano's, but you never know.

"The others were all players in their stupid little game," I said. "They were insiders. Soldiers in the war. She wasn't. She was a bystander. They had no right to take her life. Not that they have a right to take anyone's life, but at least the others knew the rules. And for the most part, they took it honorably. But she was different."

"So you just lay on the floor of the car. No one saw you?"

"I don't think so. I got back to my car—"

"*My* car."

"Right. I got back to it before the police arrived. I ran along the tree line to the end of the street, then backtracked to the car. I was shaking. I thought for sure they'd check the cars on the street. I waited for the flashlight to shine on me, but I guess they just focused on the house."

"Well, Christopher. That's a harrowing tale." He sipped his bourbon. "There's one thing I still don't get. I understand why you didn't call the police, but it's not clear to me why you didn't call the FBI."

"Like I said, it occurred to me. I don't know why I didn't, really. I guess I should have, but I had to act quickly. I couldn't wait for the FBI to come."

He twisted his head and raised an eyebrow.

"Yeah, that's lame. You're right. I don't know. I figured I could rescue her, I guess."

"You wanted to be her knight in shining armor."

"No. Not at all. It wasn't like that."

"Well?"

"Well, I failed. And now I'm an accomplice to murder."

"No, you're not. You're a witness to a murder, but you're not an accomplice."

"That's reassuring." I downed my bourbon in one gulp. It left a satisfying burn. I grabbed the bottle and poured myself another glass.

"What are you planning to do now? Are you going to call the FBI?"

I wasn't listening. I was replaying the scene in my head. "I just don't get it. What was Alfalfa trying to do? I mean, he started yelling at her—things that didn't make sense, like they were out of context—then he shot her twice and maybe even a third time, then ran out into the woods. But the window was open. Even the screen was open. I'd think he'd be more circumspect, you know. Or it was intentional. My first thought was he wanted the neighborhood to hear what was going on. That makes no sense."

"Of course it does, Christopher. Think about it."

"I have. I spent hours scrunched up in the back of your car thinking about it . . . and beating myself up for failing."

"You need some sleep, old man."

"I need to call the FBI."

"You're sure you want to do that?"

"What choice do I have? I witnessed a murder. I was there. There's proof I was there. There's a knocked-over Saint Francis statue. And my footprints all over the grass, I'm sure. Maybe a neighbor did see me. I've got to go to the FBI before they figure it out and come for me."

"You could do that. But what if these guys of yours come after you?"

"I've been thinking about that. I think it's worth the risk. I mean, they have witness protection programs for this kind of thing, don't they?"

"You really want to live like that? On the run from the mob the rest of your life? You couldn't continue in ministry, that's for certain."

"Are you suggesting I just forget about this? I sweep it under the rug or something?"

"I'm not suggesting anything. I'm just helping you ponder your options." He sipped his bourbon, not taking his eyes off me. "Christopher, it's late—no, rather, it's early. You've had a distressing evening. I suggest you lie down and let the morning sun bring you clarity. Don't make any moves till you've had a good eight hours."

I knew he was right. I didn't have a clear head, I wasn't sure what to do next, and I needed sleep. Fear and guilt and remorse stabbed me, paralyzing me. Could sleep be the remedy? Could I act in the morning?

I went up to bed, stopping before a print of the Immaculate Heart of Mary that hung just outside my bedroom. I looked into the deep blue eyes of Our Lady. "Help," I whispered. Then I blew her a kiss and receded into my bedroom.

❧ ❧ ❧

I awoke the next morning, groggy, my body heavy. I hadn't really expected to sleep, so before going to bed I had taken some NyQuil, the closest thing I had to sleeping pills, hoping it would knock me out. I spent most of the night in and out of sleep, haunted by every sort of dream.

I sat in the kitchen staring blankly into my coffee cup. Andrew came in, iPad in hand. "Mystery solved," he said. "This is what your Alfalfa was up to." He propped the iPad in front of me.

It had the Eyewitness News 7 broadcast from earlier that morning. The headline read: LOVERS' QUARREL TURNS DEADLY, ALLEGED MURDER-SUICIDE.

The video showed scenes from the night before, paramedics pulling dead bodies from the house, then coverage from that morning, police tape around the perimeter. The reporter's narration described "early reports of a squabble turned homicidal and finally suicidal".

"Brian McAuliffe and Ashley Napier," she said, "had lived in this sleepy Pelham Manor neighborhood for the past five years. They were known to have a rocky relationship, according to neighbors."

Cut to neighbors. "Those two were always going at it." A balding man in his early sixties; a banner beneath read RONALD PERLMAN, NEIGHBOR. "He was worse than she was. Always barking at her. I told my wife I was going over there to say something. That was just before we heard the gunshots."

Switch to a fortysomething man in a navy-blue hoodie: "I'm not surprised. He lost his job at the Ford dealership a couple months ago, and he'd been depressed ever since. It's tragic, though. She was a nice girl."

A woman in a bathrobe, with damp hair, hands self-consciously tugging at her lapels: "I'm absolutely shocked. You never expect something like this in your own neighborhood. It just goes to show, you never know."

"There you have it, Christopher," Andrew said. "They made it look like a murder-suicide." Tracks covered.

Then I saw an update posted below the video: "Police will not confirm murder-suicide; third party not ruled out." It was a paragraph-long post. "Signs of a third party who had recently been at the location call initial assessment into question. The investigation is still ongoing. No more information is available." The case was not closed.

"I've got to go to the FBI now," I said. "Look at this."

"It certainly doesn't look good for you, if you are the presumptive third party. But maybe you're not. Perhaps the article is referring to, ahem, Alfalfa," Andrew said.

"And what if it's not? I'm sure he was careful about not getting caught. I wasn't even thinking about covering my tracks. My fingerprints are on the windowsill, on the Saint Francis statue. What if someone saw me sneak into my— your—car? Or maybe saw me drive away. I can't risk it. I've got to go and tell them."

"Indeed. Indeed." He squinted, thoughts churning. "Might I suggest you be careful about how you do it?"

"What do you mean?"

"Well, what are you planning to do? Will you simply call the toll-free number on the FBI's website?"

"I guess. How else?"

"What if your phone is tapped?"

"I'll use my cell phone."

"Let me ask that again. What if your phone is tapped?"

"They can't tap an iPhone, can they?"

"My dear friend, this is not 1945—much to my chagrin. I would suppose the Mafia has gotten more sophisticated since the times of Al Capone. If they are as big an operation as you seem to suggest, they may be listening to us right now."

"I have no idea how big or sophisticated they are. I just know they operate up and down the East Coast."

"And you told me they are quite diversified. No matter. I am only giving a word of caution: if you're going to the FBI, I suggest you go in person."

"And they can't just follow me?"

"For all we know, they have no suspicion that you saw anything. If you make a phone call and they are listening, they will know. If you go down to the FBI offices in Manhattan, you can at least watch to see if you're being followed. You take the train, not your car."

"There are cameras all over the place in Manhattan."

"Yes. Police cameras. So?"

"So, maybe they're tapped into those."

"Don't be ridiculous, Christopher. This isn't Hollywood."

"But—"

"Listen. I'll take you to the train station; I have to run some errands anyway. You look up the address for the FBI in Manhattan. I need to powder my nose and get my keys. I'll meet you in the driveway in seven minutes. All right?"

"Yeah. Okay. I guess."

"Good."

"By the way," I said. "I still have your keys."

15

Strangers on a Train

What does a mafioso look like? I huddled in the last seat of the last train car, watching for fedoras and trench coats. It was a sweltering August day. Only a few baseball caps and no trench coats. The most suspicious person was a plump guy with a faded blue button-down shirt, steel-rimmed glasses, and a pathetic comb-over. He stood next to the door and picked his nose with his pinky, sucking his treasure off like it was Mom's cookie batter. Hmm. No, not a mafioso.

It was an off-peak train. We missed the last peak train thanks to Andrew's seven-minute nose powdering that turned into seventeen, then his insistence we take an indirect route to make sure we weren't followed. To be honest, the indirect route didn't bug me. It meant he was taking it seriously. He believed me. Something I wasn't sure the FBI would do.

As a pastor, I get all sorts of complaints of ghosts flipping bedroom lights on and off, or demons possessing the neighbor's Chihuahua, or the Blessed Mother appearing in cereal bowls. I can only imagine the kinds of calls the FBI gets. What if the officers didn't believe my story? Or what if they were just hesitant to provide me protection? That would be worse. If they believed me only halfheartedly, said they'd look into it, and sent me off on my own, then what? I'd be sitting in my rectory waiting for the drive-by shooting, or at Mass sniffing the altar wine wondering whether it might be poisoned.

I'd have to give them something concrete but something I could talk about—nonconfessional material. I'd start with Ashley. *You know that murder-suicide in Pelham Manor last night? I was there.*

I was. I was there. I saw it happen. I saw Ashley pad up to her house, her shaking hands finding the key and apprehensively opening the door. Me and my baseball bat. We were there, ready to come to the rescue. The priest-avenger determined to bash in the head of anyone who dared attack her. Then seeing her boyfriend's dead body slumped in a chair, hearing her screams echo into the night air, paralyzed in fear. Me and my bat. Not doing anything. Letting the poor girl get shot and not doing anything. We were there, all right. Me and the bat.

The bat. I didn't have it when I got to the car that night. *What did I do with it? I must have dropped it. Did I leave it at the scene? Oh no, I think I did.*

Blood rushed out of my face, and my muscles tensed, an appropriate reaction when you realize you left a piece of yourself at the scene of a crime. It's also an appropriate reaction when a mafioso walks into your train car from an adjacent one. Over six feet and a good two hundred fifty pounds of body mass were covered in a leather jacket, jeans, and tactical boots—the modern-day equivalent of a fedora and trench coat.

How'd I know he was a mobster? Perhaps it was that over-the-top, almost cartoonish appearance, obviously meant to intimidate, like the main henchman in a James Bond flick. But more likely it was the way he scanned the seats like a spotlight looking for an escaped prisoner. When his light fell on me, he made a beeline for the back of the car.

I thought I was smart sitting in the last seat of the last car. I wasn't. I was cornered. The nearest person was seven rows away. Jaws the Henchman could take me out with a quick jab to the jugular or a palm to the bridge of the nose, or whatever moves these guys do, and leave me in that back seat, and no one would be the wiser.

I started to get up, maybe make a commotion, alert other people to my presence. He signaled me to stay seated. I did. Funny how a simple motion of the hand was enough to keep me in place. No touch required.

The conductor's voice groaned over the intercom, "Next stop, 125th Street. Next stop, 125th Street. Doors open right side. Doors open on the right." Just one stop away from Grand Central. Lots of people. That would be good. More people, more witnesses. If I managed to escape, I could disappear in the crowd.

The train rocked, forcing the big lug to brace himself. He plowed forward. I expected him to grab me. He didn't. He stood blocking any possible escape, one hand clasped to the overhead luggage rack, alternating glances from me to the front of the car and back. I thought to introduce myself, get his name, but by this point I knew the drill. He wasn't here to talk. I should expect another. And I was right. Moments later the door between cars opened, and another mafioso walked in. This one I knew.

"Good to see ya, padre. I hope you've been well," Sal said when he reached me. He motioned to move over and sat next to me. "I'm glad I ran into you. I've been meaning to show you something." He pulled out his cell phone. "I got this picture I thought you should see. It's a pretty picture." He swiped through photos. "Here it is. Pretty, right?" It was a picture of my sister and my nephew outside their house on Long Island. It was a candid shot, probably taken from across the street, maybe from within a car. I clenched my fists. "There's more. Look." He swiped through several photos of my family members in different places—my brother at work, my sister-in-law picking up my niece at school, my mother gardening. I glowered at him. "Mr. Cardelli thought you'd like to see these photos. Good thing I ran into you. What are the chances, right? Mr. Cardelli hopes he can count on your continued service. He's been very pleased with your work so far."

"How did you know I would be on the train?" I asked. The words came out in a low guttural tone I wasn't expecting.

The conductor's voice again: "One Hundred Twenty-Fifth Street station. One Hundred Twenty-Fifth Street. Doors open right side. Watch the gap."

Sal gave me a tight grin and stood up. "This is my stop. Have a good day, padre."

🐟 🐟 🐟

Thwarted. Marching to the FBI field office was now out of the question. The only option I had left was to figure out who Cardelli's rival crime family was and enlist their help. Okay, an absurd idea. Besides, the Cardellis probably didn't have a rival since their shtick was to broker deals between different crime organizations.

I had thirty minutes to kill before the next train north. I decided to kill them in St. Agnes, a little Forty-Third Street church I considered my Manhattan refuge. Tucked between two skyscrapers only half a block from Grand Central Station, St. Agnes is the commuter parish par excellence. With confessions offered at lunchtime and rush hour, as well as five daily Masses, it's a way station for sinners and a pit stop for spiritual refueling. Just what

I needed. The church was empty. I sank into a shadowy back pew.

A priest emerged from the back, genuflected, and picked a discarded MetroCard off the floor. He puttered around, straightening flowers, restocking devotional candles. He didn't see me, and I had no intention of introducing myself. I just envied him from afar. What I wouldn't have given to be worried about church aesthetics right now.

Behind the altar a mural prominently displayed the child martyr Saint Agnes robed in white, a symbol of her purity and martyrdom. I thought of Ashley, not that they shared many similarities. Ashley was no twelve-year-old virgin dragged naked through city streets to a brothel and decapitated for refusing to give up her purity. But she was innocent. Innocent in the way most people are innocent.

For most people, sins are bad choices that inflict their own punishment: the guy burdened by guilt for exploding at his wife but too proud to apologize; the pregnant girl abandoned by the tough guy she fell for; the working mom who indulges in a glass of wine after work every day, then two glasses, then three, then finds herself sneaking off to AA meetings during her lunch break. These are the "innocent sinners", people who want to be good but believe the little lie, the whisper in the ear: just one more, no one will notice, you're not hurting anyone (else).

Yet each of those self-inflicted punishments is a secret lever, a catalyst to conversion, a pair of shears to cut the binding chains. The honeyed sweetness of sin turns sour, creating momentary revulsion for the act and lingering self-loathing. The small voice of conscience whispers, *There's got to be another way*. The pathway to freedom opens up, a desire to reorder one's life, put things in their proper place. Then a new discovery: the love of the One who makes all free. So the innocent sinner confesses his sins and starts on that path, sure to fall off again but able to pick up right where he left off, drawn by the ever-merciful love of his Creator. Ashley was in this lot. Not a pure lamb, but not a malevolent goat either.

My eyes fixed on Agnes' wholesome little face, and soon all I could see was Ashley's. I remembered giving her absolution, saying the words that have brought so much joy to so many repentant sinners. A huge smile burst from her tear-laced lips. This girl with the tattooed leg, the innocent sinner, was contrite. She was ready to change her ways.

How easy it would have been for her to escape the life in which she was trapped. How I wanted to whisk her away and set her on the path to freedom. Like a dad imagining what his daughter would be like all grown up, I imagined what Ashley could be doing. Set designing in Manhattan during the day, Bible studies at night, planning with her new set of friends how she could bring a bit of Jesus into the theater world. That dreamy flame was snuffed out as I recalled her screams and the shots that dropped her to the floor with a soft thud.

Absolving a penitent of his sins normally sparks exuberance in the confessor—the worse the sin, the greater the joy. But I did not feel joy that night at Stefano's. I strained to hold back a fiery rage as I said the words of absolution over her. I was angry that night. And in that little Forty-Third Street church, I was angry again—at myself for failing her, at Alfalfa for killing her, at Cardelli for setting up the whole sick system.

The priest was still in the front of the church, now fiddling with the lights, looking for burned-out bulbs, I supposed. I thought about asking him for confession. That would be the right thing to do. I could confess my stupidity, my cowardice, my failure to protect an innocent life.

But I wasn't ready. I didn't know what I would do next, but it might not be the holiest thing in the world. I might need to tag it onto the list. In any case, I wasn't going to roll over and go along with Cardelli's plan. I remembered Sal's words: "*Mr. Cardelli hopes he can count on your continued service.*" Yeah, I don't think so. Not after this. I'm done.

16

The Wrong Man

Andrew rolled up to Springdale Station just as I descended
from the platform. He was in a heated phone conversation,
his brand-new AirPods jutting out of his ears like little lolli-
pop sticks. His left hand was on the wheel, his right flailing
about—a mannerism he picked up in Italy. I tapped on the
window for him to unlock the passenger door.

"I know, I know," he said to the windshield as I got
in. "But first things first. Go to the bank and secure that
capital. If you do not, he will leave you high and dry." He
gave me a wink and pulled away from the curb. "That is
precisely what I mean. Don't think he hasn't prepared for
this, my dear. He has his plan."

As he conversed with heaven knows who, I watched the
Springdale storefronts go by: the diner, the Häagen-Dazs,
the Stop & Shop. My thoughts drifted to the bat. Should
I tell Andrew to change course, to go to Pelham Manor
so I could search for my bat? Or was that too risky? It was
probably still considered a crime scene. There would be
cops for sure.

"What about the house in Bonita Springs?" Andrew
continued. "Is that in both your names?"

Melville Park drifted by, full of young parents chatting
as their toddlers romped carefree on the playscape. Going
back for the bat would be a bad idea.

"You see," Andrew said, "he probably sank the four million into that place planning to cash in later."

And how did Sal figure out I was on the train? He didn't follow me from the rectory. That's impossible. Someone tipped him off. The only person who knew I was headed to the FBI field office was Andrew. Did my best friend give me away?

"Of course he can. Florida taxes are like that." Andrew tilted his head and gave me a what-can-I-do shrug.

I couldn't bring myself to believe Andrew would tip them off. He had no motive, and as far as I knew, he had no connection to them. But what about Monsignor? He had a connection. I never told him where I was going, but he knew I was going somewhere. I saw him as we backed out of the driveway—the curtain in his room pulled aside, his stern face peering out. But he couldn't have known the destination.

"Clarissa dear, you are wasting time. I'm hanging up on you now. Take care of your future, then call me. Okay? ... All righty. Buh-bye."

"Who was that?" I asked.

"Oh, Clarissa LeBlanc. She finally caught Hal cheating. Poor thing. She didn't see it coming. Strange, isn't it? She could live with him day and night and not suspect a thing. Seems that everyone knew but her."

"And she was calling you for financial advice?"

"No, no. Of course not. She wanted spiritual advice. Typical. These girls always need a little smack."

"If anything, she needs comforting, not a smack." Andrew, always a paragon of pastoral sensitivity.

"Christopher, how long have you been at this? In situations like these, one needs a friendly slap on the cheek to wake up. It's like being in a plane crash. Statistically, you have ninety seconds to evacuate before the plane is

consumed in flames. But most people just sit there looking around, not doing anything useful, thinking they have
all the time in the world. Sure, they're upset, anxious,
confused. But they don't act. That's because they haven't
thought through what they would really do if the plane
were to crash."

"Is that so," I said.

"The phenomenon has a name. It's called normalcy
bias. Your brain tries to fit abnormal scenarios into a normal framework. It strains to make the unpredictable predictable. Happens when a woman catches her husband
cheating, or vice versa. If she didn't see it coming, she
goes through all those phases: denial, anger, regret ... I
forget the rest. In any case, she might get upset and angry,
but then she just sits there and thinks about all the signs
she missed, what she did wrong, what she can do to get
him back or get back at him or whatever. But what she
should be thinking about is protecting her assets—making
sure she doesn't get left in the lurch." He shot a glance at
me. "Why are you looking at me like that? Yes, yes, the
spiritual counseling will come in time. 'Trust in God; he's
got a plan; he'll see you through this.' All that. But first
things first. You know I'm right. And, more important,
so does she."

"Andrew, you need help."

"I need help? I'm not the one being chased by the mob
and the police. Speaking of which, what happened? You
couldn't have been in the city more than thirty minutes.
Certainly not enough time to spill your story to the Feds.
Get cold feet?"

"They found me," I said, looking out at the passing
houses again.

"Before you got to the FBI?"

"Yes. They knew I was on the train."

"Did they hurt you?"

"No."

"Did they threaten you?"

"Not me, but my family. Funny thing was, he didn't have to say anything. He just showed me photos of my family members. Each one. Vulnerable—at work, at home, at school."

I turned and studied Andrew's face. I couldn't read anything in it, not a single emotion, except maybe concentration—he was driving, after all.

"How did they know?" I asked. "That I was on the train, I mean."

"You're asking me?" When I didn't respond, he turned to me, then back to the road. "Sorry to disappoint you, Christopher. I did not tell the Mafia your plans to rat on them. Here, check my phone." He pulled it from his breast pocket and tossed it on my lap. "You won't see Vinnie the Mobster on speed dial. Besides, your house was infested well before I moved in."

"I'm suspicious of everyone, Andrew. You can imagine. I mean, how could they possibly know?" I reached over and tucked his phone back in his pocket. "Have you seen Monsignor?"

"Not since before I dropped you off. I was on my way out the door, and he asked where we were going."

"What did you tell him?"

"That I had convinced you a new suit was in order and I was taking you to my tailor in Midtown. Seemed to buy it. You suspect he's the tattletale?"

"How else? It was either you or him."

"Maybe they didn't know. Maybe it was a random scare tactic. Or maybe they have our kitchen bugged. Or they're tracking your phone. Do you have location settings turned on?"

"Location settings? How can you tell if they're on?"

"Oh, Christopher, please. Join the twenty-first century, would you?"

I pulled my phone out and scrolled through the settings. "Anyway," I said, "it doesn't matter. I'm out. I'm done. And I'm going to tell Cardelli personally. Tonight."

"I wouldn't do that. Once you're in, they won't let you out. At least that's what TV logic says." We had crossed the East Springdale town line. In three minutes we'd be at the rectory.

"I am. I've decided. I looked up his place in Yonkers on the train. I'm going. Tonight."

"And how, pray tell, do you know he will be there?"

"Because I called and asked. He's not there during the day, but he's there for the evening rush. Oh, and by the way, you're coming with me."

"No, sir. I am not getting involved in this."

"Please. Just tonight. Come to the restaurant with me. I've made reservations. You don't have to say anything; just be there. It's a nice place, your style. Oh, and I'll pay."

"My dear friend, as much as I enjoy dining with you—and the novel idea that you should pay does pique my interest—I think I'll pass."

We pulled into the rectory driveway. Andrew put the car in park, and we both stared at the house, the car idling.

I gave him a sidelong glance, then clasped his shoulder. "Andrew. Friend. I'm all alone in this. I need you. Please come."

He stared at the garage door for a moment and sighed. "All right. Call ahead and have them decant a bottle of Brunello 2006 about an hour before. If we're going to do this, I may as well enjoy it."

"I said I'm paying for this. So, no."

"Well then, we'll just have them unscrew a bottle of Yellow Tail when we get there. Or shall I run out and grab a six-pack of Milwaukee's Best?"

❧ ❧ ❧

Cardelli's was not a dive like Stefano's. It was classy, sophisticated. Tripadvisor gave it three dollar signs and four and a half circles. Like Stefano's, it was on the ground floor of a multistory building, this one a high-rise filled with lawyers and hedge fund managers and venture capitalists—or at least that's what I imagined.

The interior design was industrial—high raftered ceilings that seemed to disappear into the night, lots of metal and knotty wood surfaces, sharp edges, and a subdued color scheme. Yet it wasn't all warehouse chic: a classic Dean Martin song—"Sway", I think it was—gave it a touch of vintage charm.

A brunette named Taylor in a form-fitting black dress showed us to our table, and a slick twentysomething in a white shirt and black vest named Ricardo took our drink orders. I asked for sparkling water with lemon, but Andrew scratched that and insisted I have a Sazerac.

"What's that?" I asked.

"Trust me. It'll help."

I panned the room, searching for my target. I was going on instinct. Months before, I had stood at the top of the rectory's front steps, the SUV waiting at the curb for the first time. I had tipped myself forward and plunged down the stairs, across the pavers, letting gravity lead, and it led me into a world I now wanted to escape. This evening it wasn't gravity but my desire for the truth leading me, and I had to hush the little inner voice telling me I was crazy, I was walking into the lion's den, I was to face the guy who sends people to their deaths for a living.

"That table over there in the corner," I said. Andrew peeked over at the corner booth and saw a rotund man in a three-piece suit, sixtyish, with two girls a third his age, one under each arm.

"So that's the man, is it?" he said.

"You don't get any more godfatherish than that."

Another man, well dressed, elderly, with a vulpine face, round glasses, and a cane, approached the booth, made a reverential bow, and smiled. *Don Cardelli, I come to pay my respects*, he seemed to be saying. I expected him to kiss the don's hand, but he didn't. They exchanged a few words; then the elderly man gave another bow and, with a slight wave of the hand, retreated.

"Hmm ... I see what you mean," Andrew said, hooking his forefinger between his chin and bottom lip. "Yes. Look at those Etruscan features—the aquiline nose, the sunken eyes with permanent bags. A veritable reincarnation of Marlon Brando. And those two beauties—why, a man who looks like that must have a lot of money or power or both to attract such bombshells."

"Right? Maybe I'll have the waiter introduce us."

"Interesting idea. But I advise against it."

"Why's that?"

"It may not have the effect you desire. The waiter's introduction might serve to tip him off. He's five steps from the emergency exit. He could disappear, and then what? Or what if your godfather simply sends the waiter back with a negative response? Would you dare seek an audience again? No, I think you better just sashay over there and confront him directly. Don't give him a chance to escape."

I thought about it. He was probably right, but as I imagined myself actually doing it—rising, steeling myself for the encounter, marching over to the Mafia boss—acid washed over my stomach and a Parkinson's-level tremor developed in my left hand. Still, I knew I had to do it. This is what I had come for. The waiter idea was just a stall tactic, a maneuver resurrected from middle school when I had used my best friend to tell my crush I liked her.

Ricardo came back with our drinks. I downed mine, told Andrew to order for the both of us, and sidled up to the fat man's table. He was in the middle of some story that held the younger of the two girls in rapt attention and bored the other to tears, or at least to spaced-out hair twirling.

"Mr. Cardelli," I said. "It's nice to finally meet you."

He didn't look pleased at the interruption.

"Who are you?" he asked.

"Father Hart. I'm the priest from St. Dominic's that's been doing those services for you?"

His female companions both giggled.

"Oh really." He smirked. "And what services might those be?"

"I don't think I need to explain. Not here in public, anyway."

"Please do. I keep no secrets from my daughters."

"These are your daughters?" Of course they were. Why would I have thought otherwise? "Nice to meet you, ladies." I nodded to each of them, smiling. "Mr. Cardelli, do you think we could have a word in private?" The women giggled again, exchanging knowing glances. I began to feel like I was on the outside of an inside joke.

"This is too good." He chuckled and squeezed the girls a little. "Too good. But I just can't. Can't keep it going." He let go of the women and put his palms flat on the table. "Hate to break it to you, Father, but the name's Geller, and I'm Jewish. You haven't been doing any services for me." He gave a big belly laugh.

I felt a tingly surge of blood to my face and was sure my cheeks were redder than the glass of wine on the table.

I looked for a hole to crawl into and, not finding one, simply let out a titter. "My apologies. I'm truly sorry to bother you. Please, enjoy your dinner." The threesome broke into laughter.

As I returned to the table, Andrew patted me on the back. "Good show, old man. Well done indeed. You certainly know a mobster when you see one."

"You knew, didn't you?"

"Of course I did. Hyman Geller is one of the most successful private equity investors in the country. Number two hundred eighty-seven on the Forbes 400, if I'm not mistaken. He was on the March cover of *Westchester Magazine* after he bought the Crownsfield Estate in Bedford Hills for thirteen million. Of course, you would know these things if you ever read something other than your email. You're not quite prepared for this tête-à-tête, Christopher. Had you thought of maybe googling dear Mr. Cardelli? I'd think a photo of him would be somewhere on the internet, don't you?"

"Why didn't you tell me?"

"You were so convinced, how could I dare? Anyway, I took the liberty of ordering you the osso buco. It's to die for—sorry." He took a sip of his Manhattan. "And I did you another favor. I asked Ricardo to arrange a meeting with Mr. Cardelli. It turns out he's in the kitchen and will be right out."

As if on cue, a figure approached—or rather waddled—from the direction of the kitchen.

"Ah, that must be him now," Andrew said.

"You're enjoying this, aren't you?" I said.

"Immensely."

The waddling man came into focus. If he was Paul Cardelli, the only accurate part of my imaginary character sketch was the swollen gut. It bulged beneath an untucked baby blue Izod shirt, smeared handprints decorating it like a kindergartner's art smock. In his midthirties with messy blond hair and baggy jeans, he was a colossal man with a merry demeanor, looking more like a reincarnation of Chris Farley than Marlon Brando.

"Hey, guys," he said, his tone chipper and brisk. "Hope you're enjoying everything. Is that a Sazerac? Nice choice. And you? A Manhattan? What are you doing with that? This is Yonkers!" He chuckled and jostled Andrew's shoulder. "So you guys are priests, huh? That's great. Hey, Ricky," he called over to the waiter, "what's the special price for clergy again? Oh yeah ... double." He chuckled again, but harder, making his gut bounce; then he gave me a punch on the upper arm—*I'm just joshin' ya.* Now a hand gripped each of us by the shoulder.

"Great to have men of the cloth in the house," he said, squeezing and massaging our shoulders. "Really, you guys do so much good work. I gotta tell ya, my dad always had a thing for priests. You know Monsignor O'Banion? Yeah, he was a great guy. Used to come over for dinner every so often." His face bore a nostalgic grin. "Wow, that was great. It was like having God almighty visit your house, you know."

I did know Monsignor O'Banion, or at least of him. He had died a good fifteen years prior, in prison. Not one of New York's finest. The city has a storied past of holy residents: Saints Elizabeth Ann Seton, John Neumann, Frances Xavier Cabrini, Isaac Jogues. A baker's dozen more are on their way to canonization: Solanus Casey, Dorothy Day, Fulton Sheen, and even a Haitian hairdresser named Pierre Toussaint. But the New York Catholic world has also had its share of sinners, and Monsignor O'Banion topped the list.

"Too bad you guys weren't here last night," Cardelli continued. "Rabbi Fleischmann was here. And Pastor

Wendy from that new church over on Kimball. Can you imagine? It'd have been like the setup of a joke: 'Two priests, a preacher lady, and a rabbi walked into Cardelli's.'" He laughed, playfully shaking Andrew by the shoulder and me by the scruff of the neck. Ricardo forced a smile, and Andrew rolled his eyes. "So, which of you men wanted to see me? Hope you're not looking for a handout. My pockets are empty."

"That would be me," I said, raising a hand. "And I'm not looking for a handout."

"Well, well, Father. What can I do you for?" Didn't he recognize me? Was he so removed from his operations that he had no idea who I was? Or was he just playing games?

"Is there somewhere private we can speak?" I asked.

"Private? Oh, this must be serious. Did somebody die? Are you coming to tell me someone died? Geez, I hope not. My *nonna* died last February. I can't deal with another death."

"Um, sort of, not exactly." He really didn't know who I was. Maybe Sal was the guy who found the priest and organized the hits. In that case, this was going to be easier than I thought. Cardelli didn't care who did the job. He just needed a priest. If I pull out, he'll just get Sal to find another one. "It's about something else," I said. "Do you have an office or something?"

"Yeah, sure, come on." He released his grip and waved for me to follow.

I trailed him to the kitchen, through the swinging door with its circular window, leaving the staid world of soft lighting, gently clinking glasses, and soothing golden-age crooners. We entered a fluorescent chaos of slicing, dicing, stirring, and whirring.

Though waiters zipped here and there, dropping off orders and snatching up steaming entrees, an element was missing: muscle, that is, protection. No guards, no big men in suits with pistols in shoulder holsters or tucked at the small of their backs or in their socks. Maybe they were outside?

"Hey, Pepe! Get ready. The padre's gonna be hearing confessions in a minute." Cardelli's voice bellowed over the cacophony. "You too, Cassie. Just 'cause you don't remember last night doesn't mean it didn't happen." He cackled and pushed open a door next to a large plate-glass window. "In here, Father."

He showed me into a tiny office that barely accomodated a desk, a couple of chairs, and a filing cabinet. A whiteboard behind the desk had a hand-drawn calendar of the week with different restaurant-related to-dos under each day. His chair faced the window, through which he commanded a view of the entire kitchen.

"Have a seat, Father." He pulled his cell phone from his jeans pocket, scrolled a bit, and rolled his eyes. "You get a hundred texts a minute too? People can't wait anymore. They need everything now now now. Drives me nuts." He placed the phone face down on the desk. "Well, they can wait. You're the only one who's important right now. I'm all ears, Father."

"Look, Mr. Cardelli—"

"Call me Paul." He picked up a plastic cucumber, which turned out to be a letter opener, and started to clean his fingernails.

"Okay. Look ... Paul ... I'm sorry, but you've gone too far. I was going along with it for the sake of those poor souls, but Ashley was too much."

A look of confusion. "Come again?" Now I knew he was putting on a show. *Come again? Ashley who?* Oh please.

"I know about Stefano's. I know about the White Death. I'm the priest. I'm the one who's been hearing the confessions, preparing these people to die. And I've come to tell you I'm out. Killing Ashley was too much."

"Ohhh, oh, oh, oh. I get it, I get it. No, no. You've got the wrong guy. You're looking for my dad. That's not my gig. I got nothing to do with that stuff. Pop keeps us out of it. I just run the restaurant. That's it. None of us are involved in that stuff. Phew, I was scared a minute there."

"Wait, what?"

"Yeah, my brothers and me, we got nothing to do with that side of the family business. I got a half sister. She's a little involved, like a real little. But that stuff is all Pops and Uncle Tommy and those guys. The Feds know that ... That doesn't stop 'em from sitting in their van outside my restaurant, but they know it; we're clean. Me and Lou and Steve, we just do restaurants."

"Well, what if I told you I know for a fact your dad runs operations out of Stefano's?"

"Upstairs?"

I nodded.

"Yeah, well, probably. Pop owns the building, like he owns this one. We just run the restaurants. I run this one, Lou runs Luigi's in Mamaroneck, and Steve runs Stefano's. Steve's place is kind of a dump. I'm surprised it's still open, to be honest." I was now convinced: I was not Philip Marlowe or Sam Spade. I wasn't even Father Dowling.

"Well, then. I guess I need to talk to your dad."

"No you don't."

"Yes, yes I do."

"No. No you don't. Really. It's not a good idea. Just go back to church and fuhgeddaboudit." He put the letter opener down and started to shuffle papers around.

"A young girl was killed. A waitress from Stefano's. One of the places you said was not involved. Are you okay with that?"

He shrugged. "Listen, padre, like I said, I don't know anything about that stuff. I don't know about a waitress or anything. I'm just telling you, for your own good, forget about it. Go back to your church and pray for my dad, and for me, would ya?"

"Can you get a message to your father?" I said, determined.

He squirmed, turned, glanced into the kitchen, then looked back at me.

"Tell your father I'm done. I'm out. He can find someone else to play priest for him. I'm not doing it anymore."

"Nah, padre. I'm not telling him that. No way. You don't know my pop. You're it. You're the priest."

"No. I'm out. I'm watching these people go to their death. And now this girl. I saw her get killed with my own eyes."

His hands went limp. "What?"

"Yes, I saw her. Murdered in cold blood. Set up to make it look like her boyfriend killed her."

"Nuts," he said.

"What?"

"You're done. You saw it go down; you're a serious liability. That's it for you."

"What? That's ridiculous. He's going to kill me? Your father's going to kill a priest? A man so religious he gives people a chance to go to confession before he kills them? How's he going to kill a priest?"

"I don't know. I mean, right, he probably wouldn't kill a priest. But maybe he would. I don't know what he's gonna do, but you're done."

I took a deep breath. The thought of Cardelli eliminating me sank in. It made sense. In his worldview, the priest knows things but can't say anything because of the seal of confession. But the priest had never actually witnessed the deed before. This was a first. I'd become a liability.

"You know what?" I said. "It was dark. I was ten feet from the guy who did it, and he didn't see me. I know he didn't. So your dad doesn't know."

"Yeah, well, my pop has a way of finding things out. He probably knows you're here."

"How? Does he have someone following me twenty-four seven?"

"If he knows you're here, he knows we're having this conversation." He said this more to himself than to me. "Since he knows we're having this conversation, he'll think I'm in cahoots with you, were anything to happen." Pause. He stared into space. "Huh. Nope. Not gonna happen. He's gotta hear this."

"No he doesn't. Look, I'll leave right now, not say a word."

He flipped his cell phone face up. It had been recording our conversation. "Sorry, padre. I'll pray for you. I will. But I gotta keep clean. You understand."

17

Trouble along the Way

Over a week passed. Eight full days. After three days I had reduced the number of times I checked for strange vehicles outside to once an hour, and the frequency I checked the internet for updates on the investigation into Ashley's murder to once every two hours. So far, no news. It was as if it had never happened. Election season was heating up. Both the Democratic and Republican national conventions had already happened, and the Trump-Hillary Armageddon commanded the media's full attention—it was 2016, after all. That accounted for some of the silence, but not even local news outlets carried the story.

Cardelli Junior had said I was done. I didn't know what Senior would do to finish me, but my working theory was he wouldn't kill me. He was superstitiously religious. The White Death ceremony proved that. So killing a priest, according to my theory at least, wasn't an option.

I suspected, instead, it would involve Ashley's murder. Maybe he was working a way to frame me for it. Evidence that I was at the house that night could be easily produced—my fingerprints on the siding, maybe the bat—but proof I committed the murder would be a lot harder. For one thing, there was no motive. For another, Cardelli knew I could identify the real murderer. But he also knew I couldn't prove it. If he managed to develop some scheme to make it look like I was guilty, my unsubstantiated claims the Mafia was behind it would just make me look silly.

On the eighth day, I received a call at 10:33 A.M. I remember exactly. I had just finished an excessively long contract negotiation with Jerry. He had tried to convince me he was actually doing two jobs—custodial engineer and facilities manager—and thus should be paid the combined salaries of both. He had even brought in printouts of Jobs.com pages showing the income ranges for each position and explained that he was willing to go for the lower end of each since he had been working at St. Dominic's for only two years. After an hour and fifteen minutes we agreed I would give him a 6 percent wage increase this year instead of the usual 2 percent cost-of-living increase. He smiled triumphantly as he walked out the door, and I slumped back in my chair wondering why I was always such a sucker.

When he left, I picked up my cell phone to check the time, and it rang in my hand. It was a 212 area code, a landline in Manhattan.

"Chris, it's Pat. Pat Lynch." Monsignor Patrick Lynch was the vicar for clergy. He's the guy you want to hear from only when you've initiated the contact and you're just waiting for him to call you back. If he's calling unprovoked—and calling your cell phone, not your office line—it's probably not a good thing.

"Hello, Pat," I said. "To what do I owe the pleasure?" I put the phone on speaker, set it down, and put my feet up on the desk. Stretching back in my chair, I glanced out the window and saw a police car pull into the parking lot.

"How was your weekend, Chris?" Lynch asked, his voice full of contrived joviality.

What were the police doing here? Maybe they'd just cruise around the parking lot to make sure things were okay and drive off. They do that now and again. Maybe? No. The car was stopping.

"Chris? You still there?"

"Yeah, yeah. Sorry. My weekend ... umm, well, it's Wednesday. The weekend was a long time ago." I moved closer to the window. Two people got out of the car, one uniformed officer, another in plain clothes. Had they figured it out? Yes. They must have. They knew I was there the night of Ashley's murder. I strained to see whether one carried a baseball bat. No, of course not; that kind of evidence would be locked away somewhere.

"Sorry, Chris, just trying to make small talk," Lynch continued. "Listen, we need to chat. We have a situation."

"Right, okay," I said. "But now isn't really a good time." I started pacing. *Do I run? No. Don't be stupid.*

"That's fine," Lynch said. "Anyway, I'd rather not talk about it over the phone. Actually, I need you to come down."

"Yeah, sure. Well, I've got a lot going on today. Maybe we could set something up for Friday?" I said.

I would just tell the police I can't speak to them until I have a lawyer. They'll back down. On *Blue Bloods*, whenever someone "lawyers up", the cops get all frustrated and they have to let the guy go. But what if they were coming to arrest me? In front of my staff? That would be so embarrassing.

"No, Chris. It's going to have to be a little sooner. Actually, I need you come down ASAP."

Now he had my attention. "Really? What's the rush?"

"Just come down, and we can talk about it here."

"I can't do that, Pat. Maybe in the afternoon? I've ... I've got the noon Mass—"

"Actually, I've taken care of that. Jack will take it. Don't worry. You just come down."

"You've taken care of that? Okay then, well, I'll do my best. But some people just showed up, and they're not the type I can just send away."

"Do your best. I'll see you in a bit."

"Wait. Will the cardinal be in this conversation?"

"No. But he's given me instructions. We'll talk when you get here." He ended the call.

My head was spinning. What was going on? The desk phone rang.

"Father?" It was Rita. "There's a Detective Senape and an Officer Vlansky here to see you."

"Okay. Tell them I'll be right out." Deep breath. *Lawyer. I can't talk till I have a lawyer.*

I stepped out of the office into the main area, where I saw Rita handing a cup of coffee to a tall, lanky guy that looked a lot like my high school shop teacher, and next to him a uniformed officer, female with pulled-back black hair and strong eastern European features.

"Gotcha!" said the tall man, a wide smile on his face.

"What? No, I'm sorry. I really can't speak to you without my lawyer present."

He gave me a curious look. "Relax, guy. We're not here to arrest you." He chuckled, looking over at his partner. She was relaxed and also smiling. "You're Father Hart, I take it?"

"Yes. Yes, I am. How may I help you?"

"We're here about the PBA dinner? We called earlier—last week. Did you get the message? Anyway, sorry we didn't make an appointment. We got a call this morning from somebody here, said a personal invitation would go a long way. We happened to be in the area, so we thought we'd drop by."

"PBA dinner?"

"Police Benevolent Association. For the invocation?" Senape said.

What was this all about? Someone called them? Was this a Cardelli scare tactic?

"Um, sorry," he continued. "Let me start from the beginning. Officer Vlansky and I are on the organizing committee this year, and we were looking for someone to give the invocation. We sent an invitation and followed up with a call last week—well, Vlansky called."

"Yeah, I called. Twice, actually," the woman said. "Spoke to one of the priests. He said he couldn't do it but that Father Hart—that's you, right?—could do it. You love opportunities like this? That's what he said." *Andrew. I'm going to kill him.* "You were out, I guess, and we expected a call back. Anyway, this morning someone called and said to come by in person since you get a lot of mail and stuff and don't return phone calls very quickly." She chuckled. "Sorry, I don't mean to laugh. You just look so stunned. I mean, if you don't want to do it, that's okay. No big deal."

"Sorry," I said. "It's just that I've been dealing with a tough situation, and you kind of came in at the wrong time. I'm sorry, I'm completely distracted. Rita, am I free on—when did you say the dinner is?"

"Saturday, September twenty-fourth at six o'clock," answered Officer Vlansky.

"Rita, am I free that night?"

"Yes, Father. As of right now you're free. I'll make sure not to put you on the Mass schedule for the vigil that night."

"Thanks. Well, officers, I think we're good, right? I hate to rush you out the door. You guys do so much for us. Thank you for your service." They simultaneously pressed their lips and nodded in appreciation. "If you don't mind, I've really got to get going."

"No problem," said Detective Senape. "Whatever issue you're dealing with, Father, I can relate. We see a lot of stuff in our line of work, but you know, there's always a silver lining. Something good always comes out of it in the end. That's my experience." I could swear he taught shop at my high school. The name wasn't coming to me, but our shop teacher was also the baseball coach, and every time a kid struck out he'd say, "You're just getting the bad swings out of your system. Keep at it, kid."

"Thank you for your words, Detective. They mean a lot."

"If there's something we can do to help, please let us know."

I hesitated. "Well, I kind of do have something, but . . ." What could I say? The police were right there in front of me. I could tell them everything right then and there. This was my chance. They could protect me. But I was uneasy about it all. Something just wasn't right. It was too strange that they just happened to show up like this. Could this be a test? Were they baiting me? "You know what, never mind. There are some things a man's just got to take care of himself."

"I hear ya, Father. You ever need anything, you let us know."

"Thanks," I said as I showed them out.

Closing the door behind me, I turned to Rita, who was now at her desk. "Did they really call last week?"

"Yes, Father. Twice. Officer Vlansky. I put her through to voicemail as usual."

"Oh."

"Yeah, and as usual, you didn't listen to your voicemail."

"What do you mean, as usual?"

She gave me her are-you-kidding-me look.

"All right. But why didn't you tell me? You always tell me when someone's left an important message."

"I'm not getting involved. I've made that mistake before." She was squeezing a tea bag over a mug. The officers' arrival had put her midmorning tea ritual on pause.

"What do you mean?"

She was silent. She tossed the depleted bag into the trash, pulled a plastic bear-shaped honey bottle from her desk drawer, and proceeded to let the honey drip slowly into the mug.

"Rita, what do you mean?" I repeated slowly, emphasizing each word.

She delicately tipped the bottle upright again, ensuring not a drop of honey got on the cap or the bottle or her desk. She put the bottle back in the drawer and slid it shut. Then she took the mug in hand and slowly oared her teaspoon back and forth.

"Rita!"

"All right already. Monsignor used to get those calls too. So I figured you were into the same thing."

"What thing?"

"You don't know? The pastor doesn't know. Oh, that's rich."

"Go on."

She hesitated, then muttered something to the effect of, "What the heck, the old man doesn't sign my paycheck anymore." She put down her spoon. "Well, you didn't hear it from me," she said. "There was a time when Monsignor was getting a lot of calls from this certain detective. Not Barney Fife here, but some other one, not a local. I think he was FBI or IRS or whatever. So, after a while I get curious. What are all these calls about? And, we could say, I happen to overhear a conversation.

And, let's say, Monsignor, well, he used the wrong detergent." She peered up at me over her glasses as if to say,
You know what I mean?

"I don't follow."

"Boy, you're not the sharpest bowling ball in the pack,
are you? Detergent—you know, like laundry detergent?
Money laundering? Sheesh."

"Through the parish?"

"No, through a laundromat. Of course through the parish; where else? We were getting tons of donations all of a
sudden, and it must've tripped some IRS alarm or something. Anyway, they gave Monsignor the third degree."

"Over the phone?"

"At first, yeah." Holding her warm tea with both hands,
she proceeded to describe how she had eavesdropped on
three phone calls and two office visits, had written out
all the details, not understanding a word, and had gotten
her cousin Hank Massotti—the purportedly unscrupulous
parish accountant—to give her a crash course in money
laundering schemes. He wasn't involved with any of it, he
swore. According to him, all the transactions were legitimate. And that's what he told the FBI or the IRS or whoever it was he handed all the books over to. Rita swore now
too, on her mother's grave, that she never eavesdropped on
any of *my* conversations. No, that was just a special situation, due to a clear and present threat to her moral reputation. She didn't want to be found guilty by association.

"So, what happened?" I asked.

"I don't know. The Feds just stopped calling, and that
was it."

"And this happened when?"

"Maybe five or six years ago? It was around when we
mothballed the north wing of the school and stopped
doing Masses over at St. Phil's."

"When Father Reese left for Rome?"

"Yeah. About then."

"Were donations pouring in then as they are now?"

"Yep. They stopped when he left and started when he came back." A self-satisfied smirk emerged on her face: *I told you so.*

My heart sank. Andrew, my dear friend, a shiftless fraudster. I didn't want to accept it. But I also didn't want to accept what I had learned about the others: Monsignor the Mafia informant, Rita and Jerry the adulterous duo, Henry Massotti the darknet spreadsheet master. I could not accept that I, the pastor, the head honcho, presided over a den of iniquity.

No evidence. There was no proof that any of it was true. It was all circumstantial, hearsay. Monsignor's continued involvement with the mob was just a hunch. I had yet to catch Rita and Jerry in the act. I had checked out Henry Massotti after Andrew told me about the copier thing; no irregularities were found. And just because Andrew was pulling in a lot of donations didn't mean he was a crook. The IRS was suspicious but had found nothing. And that was five or six years ago. No word from them since.

I let Rita know I had to go downtown and I wasn't sure when I'd be back. Monsignor Lynch didn't give a reason for the summons, but now I was looking forward to it. I had my own business with the chancery. Surely they had information about the IRS investigation. And if I couldn't divulge my secret to the FBI, at least I could let someone in the Church know. That way, if I suddenly died of food poisoning or mysteriously drove off the Triborough Bridge, someone would know what really happened.

18

The Harder They Fall

When I stepped out of the elevator at the archdiocesan offices, I was greeted by Marcia Tillman, Monsignor Lynch's secretary. She showed me to a meeting room. It was small with a conference table for six. On one wall hung a black-and-white print of St. Patrick's Cathedral from the early twentieth century; on another, portraits of the current and two former cardinals. A window looked out onto First Avenue. The noise from the street was muffled but still audible.

"Coffee, Father?" she asked.

I hate to be a coffee snob, but I've learned office coffee and gas station coffee are just not worth it unless it's a real emergency. "No thank you, Marcia," I said. This mysterious convocation was causing enough jitters to keep me alert anyway.

"Monsignor Lynch will be in shortly."

A few minutes later the door opened. Bruce Chesney, the archdiocese's general counsel, walked in.

"Oh, hello, Bruce," I said. "I wasn't expecting you."

"Hello, Father. Monsignor Lynch asked me to join the meeting."

"So this is serious," I said.

"'Fraid so, Father."

Yes, the archdiocesan attorney wasn't a good sign, but if anyone would know about an IRS investigation into St. Dominic's, he would. But I wouldn't bring it up yet.

I'm not sure how much time passed before Monsignor Lynch arrived, but it was just enough for Bruce and me to exhaust the topics of common interest: "When will this heat wave end? ... What's up with the Yankees this year? ... Oh, you didn't get away this summer either? That's too bad."

"Chris, good to see you," Lynch said, taking the chair at the end of the table. "Thanks for coming down on such short notice. Listen, I'm just going to come out and say it—"

My cell phone went off, loud, obnoxious, dance song ring. I started patting down my pockets, trying to get it out, shut it off. "I'm sorry. How do you—oh, I got it. There. Sorry about that." Lynch's face tightened in consternation.

"So, as I was saying, I'm just going to come out with it. You've been accused."

"Excuse me? Of what?"

"Sexual abuse of a minor."

I didn't respond. I couldn't. The shock squelched my voice—not just my vocal cords but my inner voice, my thoughts. Lynch went on, but everything he said after that was incoherent. Nothing registered, just words: *accusation, police, investigation, victim, anonymous.* Words. He droned on, and I struggled even to keep my eyes focused.

Sexual abuse of a minor. It was like walking into a glass door: the sudden bash, the stagger backward, then staring at smeared face grease, trying to process what had happened: *Oh, do I need to clean that now? Is that blood on my shirt? Oh no, is my nose bleeding? It is. Wait—oh, ow, that hurts.*

In its attempt to process, my mind replayed all the events of the last months: walking down Stefano's upstairs corridor, absolution after absolution, face after face of now-departed souls, Paul Junior flipping over his cell phone, saying, "You're done." Then flashes from my life as a priest: my ordination, the baptisms, the funerals, the schoolchildren laughing, the penitent crying with joy, the patient dying in his hospital bed. All these images flooded to mind because I knew in an instant it was all over. These were memories, events I was not to relive. I was done. Paul Senior didn't need to kill me. This was worse. I wished Alfalfa or Jaws or Sal Grisanti had just walked in the room and shot me.

"Does that make sense, Chris? Do you understand what I'm telling you?" Lynch asked.

"I'm sorry, Monsignor. I'm having a little trouble taking it all in." I rubbed my eyes and tried to focus. "Who did you say is accusing me?"

"The victim prefers to remain anonymous. I suppose for you it's better that way. We notified Child Protective Services this morning, but if the victim won't come forward, I doubt they'll follow up. They've got a backlog longer than a papal ceremony." He looked over at Bruce with a smirk. "Did you get up early to watch Mother Teresa's canonization, Bruce? I know you did." He looked at me. "Bruce loves the pomp and circumstance."

"Wait. Victim?" I said, still dazed. "There's no victim. I didn't abuse anyone."

Lynch's smile disappeared. Bruce looked down and started to fidget with the papers in front of him.

"No, seriously. This is a setup. I know who's setting me up. There was no abuse," I said.

"Right, of course. Look, we're not questioning you here about what happened. There's going to be an investigation, and you'll have a chance to tell your side of the story. All in due time. I'm sure there's an explanation." He shot a knowing glance over at Bruce.

"Yes, there is an explanation. I'm being set up. This is a false accusation."

Lynch tugged at his Roman collar. "False accusations do happen. That's true. There was one I can remember. It wasn't an issue with a minor; it was with a woman. But honestly, false accusations aren't very frequent. I mean, most guys say they didn't do it ... there must be a mix-up ... it didn't happen exactly as they're saying ... all that, you know. And those guys believe it. They really do. I know they do. Actually, that's part of the therapy, getting guys to understand what they did.

"So anyway, you start to scratch the surface, right, and maybe in Father's mind he didn't do anything wrong; he was just playing around, you know? But in the mind of the victim, it's a whole other story. Especially when the kid grows up. I mean, things start to go sideways on him, and he can't figure out why. If he's lucky, he goes to therapy and figures it out; but some don't, you know. It's all a game when they're little, and maybe they're laughing and Father's laughing. But the damage is permanent. The victims are affected for the rest of their lives, and no one's laughing anymore. As you can see, I've been through this before."

"No. I'm telling you, this is different. I'm being set up. I know child abuse is horrible. I've dealt with victims myself—this teacher at St. Roc's ... unspeakable what he did ... I spent a lot of time counseling the family. But this is different. I didn't do it. I'm being set up." I looked away, grimacing in frustration. "I got involved in something somehow, something I shouldn't have." Lynch looked at Bruce, who in turn picked up his pen. "Nothing illegal. Not on my part, anyway. It's just that, well ..." Could I tell them? Could I say I witnessed a murder? I had already made that mistake once. "I saw something illegal, and now they want to shut me up. They want to ruin my reputation, I guess. Take away my credibility or something."

"Who's *they*, Chris?" Lynch asked.

"The mob."

Lynch nodded slowly and crinkled his face, trying too hard to look like he believed me. "The mob," he repeated.

"Yes. Well, I don't know. I guess it's the mob. I mean, it's organized crime for sure. They're guys involved in illegal activity, and they take orders from this Italian American guy that owns a bunch of restaurants. Well, I'm not sure if he owns the restaurants or just the buildings. Anyway, they're after me."

"Italian guy. Okay. Hmm. I mean, we shouldn't stereotype, but I can see where you might get that impression. Did you call the police?"

"No. I couldn't. I think they're in on it."

"Right. Of course, they would be. How about the FBI? I think organized crime is in their jurisdiction, isn't it?"

"I tried. I was on my way to the FBI field office in Lower Manhattan, and these Mafia guys followed me and then threatened my family."

"This sounds serious, Chris. You better take care of yourself."

"Thanks. Great advice, but what am I supposed to do? I don't know who to trust or where to go. I've already said too much to you guys. Who knows, maybe they're listening in on this conversation. I mean, maybe you guys are in on it. I know Monsignor Leahy is."

"Really? Jack Leahy, huh? Man," he said, shaking his head.

"Yeah. He used to help them out. He was kind of their go-to priest. And I'm pretty sure they knew I was going to the FBI because he tipped them off. In fact, I wanted to ask, did you know about an IRS investigation of St. Dominic's like six years ago?"

Bruce was writing furiously.

"Chris, I think some time off will do you good." Monsignor Lynch's voice slowed and became gentle. "Recalibrate, you know? You're stressed; it's obvious. Maybe you need to get out of here. Just take off, get the weight of the parish off your shoulders, breathe some fresh air. There's a place in Maryland, just north of Washington, D.C., in Silver Spring? It's for guys that are going through a hard time and need to take a step back. Maybe you should check it out. In fact, I'd be willing to go down there with you, get you situated."

I looked at him, then at Bruce, then back at Lynch. "I see. You think I'm crazy. Okay, whatever. Look, forget I said anything. Please. Bruce, do me a favor and rip up what you wrote." I sighed. "Can we just pretend this conversation didn't happen? I'll cooperate with whatever you guys want me to do. I'm not worried about this. I know I'm innocent, and I'm happy to cooperate. Just forget I said anything about a setup or the Mafia or anything like that, would you?"

"Okay, Chris. Well ..." Lynch tapped his fingers on the table, pinky to forefinger, pinky to forefinger, then stopped. "I know this is a lot to take in. Your mind must be racing. So I think we've done enough for today." He looked over at Bruce for confirmation. "You need to process this. Maybe spend some time in church. Sit with it, you know? From our end, we're good. There's only one more thing. A formality. I just need you to read and sign this document." He pushed a folder across the table. I opened it. "It's basically everything that I just told you but in writing."

I started to read it. "So I'm officially on administrative leave?"

"Just till we can finish the investigation."

"I thought you said the police wouldn't investigate."

"They might not. I don't know, really. But we need to investigate. It's in the Code. Canon seventeen-seventeen. It's protocol. The cardinal will appoint an investigator—I suppose it'll be me—and a notary, probably Bruce. No, I think it needs to be a priest. Father Kerrigan, the judicial vicar—he'll do it. Anyway, we'll do some interviews, check your personnel file, you know, make sure we get a complete picture. We'll do an official interview with you, like I promised. If the accusation turns out to be bunk, well, you're in the clear, and we'll make sure there's a note in your file that says so, and we can forget this ever happened. Now, if it turns out the accusation is credible, then we'll send it to the CDF in Rome, and they'll decide what to do. All right?"

I exhaled, slumping my shoulders. "Are you going to put out a press release or something?"

"No, no. Definitely not. Not yet. We need to do the preliminary investigation first. We wouldn't make a big announcement at this point. We would only make a statement if the investigation shows the accusation is credible. For now we'll just make an announcement at the weekend Masses. Verbal. Nothing in writing."

"You're going to announce to my parishioners that I've been accused of sexually abusing a minor?"

"Yes, Chris. We need to. We've got to tell them why you've been removed from ministry. We can't just say, 'Oh, Father Hart is going to be off for the next couple months taking care of himself.' That doesn't cut it anymore. Best to get it out there. Let people know what's going on so they don't let their imaginations go wild, you know?"

"No. I don't know. I haven't done anything, and you have no proof that I did. You just have some anonymous accusation."

Lynch sat up straight; his face tightened. "The victim isn't anonymous. This person didn't want to go to the police and instead came to us. We encouraged the victim to go to the police, but he or she wasn't ready. But we do know who the person is. He or she is an adult now. We know when and where it all took place, the circumstances. It's plausible, Chris. Otherwise you wouldn't be here."

"And you won't tell me."

"The person is afraid of reprisal."

"Reprisal? I can't believe this. You know me, Pat. You know I wouldn't do anything to hurt anyone. This is ridiculous."

Bruce was still writing.

"All right, whatever," I said, irritated. "Give me that pen."

I went to sign the document but realized I hadn't read past the first part, where it said I was being put on administrative leave.

"Wait," I said. "It says that I can't wear clerical garb or present myself as a priest in any way, and I have to vacate the rectory? What the—"

"*Ad cautelam.* These are precautionary measures only—temporary measures—not punishments. Once the investigation is complete, assuming the conclusions are favorable, everything goes back to normal."

"Except it doesn't. Do you think people are going to believe I'm innocent after you announce this to the whole parish and I'm nowhere to be found, not able to tell my side of the story?"

"Chris, we're under a microscope on this stuff. You understand, we can't take any chances. I'm sorry. Just please sign the document."

I put the pen down and picked the paper up; it trembled in my hand. My cheeks and ears burned, and I could feel tears starting to well. I took deep breaths to calm myself. "Where am I going to go?" I said, now with a tone of resignation. I placed the paper back on the table. I looked at them. I picked the pen up again. "All right," I said. "I know abuse happens. It happens way too often. I get it. The Church is under a microscope, as you say. You're just doing your job. I get it. I get it. I don't get it, but I get it." Another deep breath. "I'm going to sign it. I'm going to sign it for all the people who really are victims. Who knows, maybe this person who came forward is somebody else's victim. I'm going to sign it for him. Or is it a her? And I'm going to sign it for the bad apples that never got plucked from the barrel. I'll take it. I'll take it for them."

I said that, but I didn't mean it. At least not then. It was a noble sentiment for sure, but what I really wanted to say was, *Screw you*. I wanted to rip up that piece of paper and toss it at him—no, better, roll it up, shove it up his nose, and pull it out his ear and then cram it into Bruce's mouth and make that orifice useful for something. But of course I didn't do any of that. I made a good show of it. I took the high road, the noble path. I signed the document, and I wanted to throw up.

The tension in Lynch's face broke; a smile cracked on his still-joined lips. "Good. I think that's the right attitude. Don't worry. We'll get this investigation done quickly, and we'll try to keep it as quiet as possible."

❧ ❧ ❧

At the parish again, having skipped lunch, I entered the church. It was empty and quiet, illuminated only by the early afternoon sun filtering through the stained glass. Multicolored streaks of light dappled the main aisle in front of the altar like autumn leaves, and I fell prostrate among them. I was a cadaver lying there, my heart empty, barely able to squeeze out a prayer. But something in me, a piece of my soul, crawled up to the altar, lay upon it, and resigned itself to God's almighty will. *What are you trying to teach me, Lord?*

An hour later, a bit more at peace but still shaken, I went to the only other place where I knew I'd find solace: Maria's kitchen. There she stood, kneading ground beef into hamburger patties, and there I stood, in the doorway, looking like I'd seen a ghost, as she'd later describe me. But in that moment she spoke no words. She just put her big fluffy arms around me and let me cry.

I avoided everyone that afternoon and began packing. In the evening, at dinner, I explained the situation to Monsignor and Andrew. Andrew wailed, "This is preposterous" and "Of all people to be accused" and "No one's safe anymore." Monsignor also protested in his dry way. "I'm calling ten-eleven and getting this straightened out." I calmed them both down, surprised I was able to remain calm myself. The courage and energy could have come only from my hour spent bespeckled in stained-glass-filtered sunlight. I told them what I had understood: my absence would be brief, and the archdiocese would do an investigation and then reinstate me once they discovered it was all contrived. I told Andrew and Monsignor not to do anything except hold down the fort. They agreed to cover for me, for both my responsibilities and my reputation.

The next morning, I told the staff I was leaving for a time. No made-up excuses about a dying uncle or something. I told them I had been wrongly accused, I was pretty sure I knew by whom, and not to worry because I'd be back. The archdiocese would surely give them more details and tell them what to say if anyone should ask. For my part, I said, "Tell people I'm fine. In my own heart I know I did nothing wrong, and I trust in God, who always stands with the innocent."

I thought there might be tears or a shout of protest like I got from Andrew and Monsignor, but they only stared at me blankly, as if they were trying to take it in, make sense of it, decide whether I might actually be guilty. Finally, Rita said, "Father, don't worry. We'll take care of everything here. You take care of yourself."

Part III

Femme Fatale

19

Sentimental Journey

Drip. *One hundred forty-two.* Drip. *One hundred forty-three.* Drip. *One hundred forty-four.* I watched the water gather at the right corner of the AC unit, then bead and drop. *One hundred forty-five.* Something was wrong. *One hundred forty-six.* Condensation should collect outside, not inside. *One hundred forty-seven.* As mechanically disinclined as I was, the best I could do was put a bowl under it and watch. *One hundred forty-eight.* And why would it accumulate in the corner like that? Maybe it's tilted somehow. *One hundred forty-nine.* And that's the dog's bowl. The water is basically distilled, so it shouldn't harm the dog, right? *One hundred fifty.*

Five weeks after my interview with Monsignor Lynch, I found myself in the kitchen of a priest friend's rectory in Newark, New Jersey, my hands flat on the table, layered one over the other, and my chin resting on top as I counted the drops. This was my second residence since I moved out of St. Dominic's.

"*We'll get this investigation done quickly, and we'll try to keep it as quiet as possible.*" That was the last thing Monsignor Lynch said to me. Ever. Two weeks after our meeting, the archdiocese announced that Monsignor Lynch was taking on a new role as director of the Sudanese Refugee Foundation based in Washington, D.C. In an email, his secretary notified me my case would be handled by his replacement, who had yet to be named. Needless to say, the investigation was not being done quickly.

Nor was the episode being kept as quiet as possible. Bishop Ketter, an auxiliary or "vice" bishop, read a statement at all the Sunday Masses at St. Dominic's. Smart move: have someone in authority read a statement, but don't put out a press release. Potential victims would see the archdiocese taking it seriously, yet there would be no website article or email blast, nothing to kick up dust in the press. But times being what they are, someone had surreptitiously trained his cell phone on the bishop, recorded a video, and posted it on YouTube, which then made the rounds on Facebook, Twitter, Instagram, and other social media platforms. A few hours later I was getting calls from local media.

My brother Bill told me not to worry too much. News cycles these days were getting shorter and shorter, he said. I had moved in with him by that point, having been banned from the parish premises "out of an abundance of caution". But the arrangement was short-lived. I figured it would be. Bill and his wife had three kids under twelve and no guest room. I was sleeping on the couch, which was fine by me since I wasn't really sleeping anyway, or eating for that matter. Then the neighbors found out about me.

What harm could a walk through the neighborhood do? It was mid-September. I needed fresh air. The air couldn't have been fresher. The humidity was gone, the sun shone with brilliant clarity, and the gleaming red and orange canopy of maple leaves evoked a Fourth of July fireworks display. As I strolled down the sidewalk, a young mother stepped out of her house, her eight-year-old son trailing behind. Our eyes met briefly. She turned, blocking her son's advance, and started fishing through her purse. "Honey, Mommy forgot something inside. Let's go back in and see if we can find it, okay?"

I was tempted to stand and glower at her front door for the rest of the morning, but I kept walking.

That afternoon I thought I'd be a champ and offer to help with grocery shopping. I took one of my nephews with me and caught pairs of eyes darting from me to the boy. Was I *that* infamous?

The clincher was when my sister-in-law, who indiscriminately accepts every Facebook friend request, got a direct message from someone she didn't know asking how a mother of three boys could possibly allow a man like that in her house.

So I left.

I was reluctant to go to another New York parish. The day the news broke, Father Hugh Kennedy, a pastor at an inner-city parish in Newark and a friend, had texted me a few times to check in. He told me to let him know if I needed anything. Well, now I did.

Hugh was in and out, and he was out more than he was in. At lunch he'd make a quick sandwich and eat it standing in the kitchen. He'd bring me takeout or prepared meals from Stop & Shop, saying he'd grab something for himself later. He was clearly overworked. It pained me to see him busy and to know I couldn't help. When he would drag himself through the front door after a marathon round of confessions or after having celebrated three Masses back-to-back, I had to stifle the urge to say, "Hey, I'll take a couple Masses for you."

Hugh had no vicar and no housekeeper. And I had no one to talk to. After the experience at my brother's house I was afraid to show my face outdoors, so mostly I moped around the rectory.

But I wasn't wired for a monk's life either. I tried. God knows I did. I resisted the temptation to binge-watch old movies while sucking hamster-like on a bottle of scotch.

Instead, I took a stab at those great works of literature everyone says you should read, starting with Dostoevsky's *Crime and Punishment*.

Bad choice. Raskolnikov and I shared the same predicament: we both sat on a couch in brooding melancholy, unable to leave for fear of being caught. The difference, of course, was that Raskolnikov—spoiler alert—had actually murdered the old hag, while I was innocent.

I didn't finish the book. The three hundred or so pages I did manage to read, half-distracted, sent my thoughts spiraling downward into the deepest dungeons of my soul, revisiting dark sentiments that had been locked up long ago, sentiments I thought were dead.

My rational thoughts paced the dungeon corridor, twirling their keys and glancing over at Anger, who was rattling the bars of his cell, muttering foul curses at the Cardellis and Sal and Alfalfa. And next to him, Revenge, his face pressed through the bars, whispered, *Let me at 'em, let me at 'em. I'll rip 'em apart.* Farther down the hall Despair slumped against the wall of his cell, rocking back and forth, repeating, *It's no use. What's the point?* Across the corridor Self-Contempt, beating his breast, joined the desperate chorus, lamenting, *You idiot. You're so naïve.*

My legal counsel—if you can call a tax attorney I knew from St. Dominic's my legal counsel—told me I was rushing to conclusions. No one was pressing charges; the police wouldn't investigate. The only entity investigating me was the Church, and since I was innocent, the Church authorities would eventually come to that conclusion too. "Chin up, you'll get through this." Smile. Wink.

But I knew Cardelli's guys were good at framing people, and the priests who do canonical investigations, while professional, aren't exactly protégés of J. Edgar Hoover. If the Church investigators found I was guilty, that'd be it. I'd be out of the priesthood. I'd be finished, just as Cardelli intended. Oh sure, I'd live. I'd find a job somewhere, maybe in Montana. I'd make a life for myself, but it wouldn't be *my* life, because my life—not my job, not my career, but my *life*—was the priesthood.

Then again, would I live? Would he let me? A foggy sensation hung in the air, nebulous but unshakably present: Cardelli wasn't quite done with me. Granted, if I were found guilty, I'd be discredited—an unreliable witness. But I was still a threat to him. I still saw what I saw. My brain still held the secret in its coils, and if those coils were plucked the right way, the truth could still spring out.

No, I couldn't be sure I was safe. My theory was Cardelli wouldn't have me killed because I was a priest. If I were laicized, would I be fair game? Was I fair game now because I was prohibited from acting as a priest? Technically, once ordained, a man is a priest forever in the eyes of God, even if he doesn't wear the garb or administer the sacraments. But I couldn't expect a mobster to know the finer points of sacramental theology. For all I knew, he'd think it sufficient for me to hang my collar up for the night.

When a FedEx package arrived—addressed to me, even though I had told no one where I was—the distinct sound of chattering teeth echoed from the far end of the dungeon of my soul. It was Fear, curled up in a ball and whimpering. I sliced open the package and fished out a baseball bat. A small card hung off it that read: *You dropped this. Sincerely, P.C., Sr.*

Despite the words on the card, I read a different message: *I know you witnessed Ashley's murder, and I know where you are.* Fear erupted in cataclysmic convulsions: "No no no no no no."

Yet fear is not from God. I knew that. And by fear, I'm not referring to the instinctive reaction at a vicious dog's growl or at the crack and whiz of gunshots over-head. I mean the existential fear that all the world's forces are against you, that no matter what you do, utter doom is inescapable. That kind of fear is not from God, because nothing lies outside the scope of Providence. Nothing can definitively thwart God's plan. God is omnipotent and competes with no one. That kind of fear is a betrayal of hope. It is to deny the power of the One who resur-rected Lazarus, a man the Gospel tells us had been dead for four days.

This truth about fear I preached from the pulpit and counseled in the confessional and believed with my whole heart. Still, sitting on that couch contemplating the bat on my lap, it rang hollow. It's so easy to wax profound in a homily and whisper sage words to a penitent, but now that I was in the pew, Fear's moaning wouldn't let me focus on the sermon I tried to preach to myself.

Only one thing was clear: I had to leave that house before I went mad or before I was murdered.

And I had an out. It was Andrew's idea. On one of my darkest days, he called me.

"Christopher, I have an offer you can't refuse."

"Not funny," I said.

"We're going to Palm Beach."

"Florida?"

"Yes. You need to get out of the Northeast. You need sun and ocean breezes and piña coladas. That will snap you out of your stupor."

"I hate Florida. You know that. It's just strip malls and gated communities built on a swamp."

"Remember the Giordanos?" He wasn't listening. "I ran into Gina at the Catholic Charities ball. They had it at the Pierre this year instead of the Waldorf. Terri-ble idea. Anyway, she wondered how you were doing.

I told her. So, she has graciously offered us her home in Palm Beach for as long as we want. She and Bob won't be going down till after New Year's. Thus, you and I shall be heading down on Monday to wait out this storm. Hold on—before you object, I know what you're going to say. I've got things at the parish covered. Don't worry about a thing. I'll have to come back for the weekends, but that's not a problem."

"I don't know," I said. "It sounds nice, but you know I prefer the mountains. Give me a cabin in the woods, next to a lake, and then ... maybe."

"Unfortunately, Christopher, the Giordanos do not have a ten-thousand-square-foot house overlooking the Atlantic Ocean—with an indoor pool, sauna, wine cellar, tennis court, and movie theater—in the mountains next to a lake. They only have one in Palm Beach."

"Andrew, I appreciate it. I really do, but I'll need to think about it."

That's where we left it. I couldn't deny it was a clear ticket out. And I would have snatched it up if the invite hadn't come from Andrew. I was suspicious. It was hypocritical of me: here I was, the victim of a false accusation, drawing conclusions about someone else based on hearsay. But my suspicions were confirmed when Monsignor called.

"Don't go," he said, his voice raspy and phlegm filled.

"What?"

"He's taking you to Florida. He told me this morning. Don't go." *Andrew, I told you I'd think about it.*

"Why not?" I said.

"Listen and don't interrupt. I don't know what you did, but I know you didn't touch any kid. You probably tried to go to the cops or something. Doesn't matter. Just so you don't think I'm indifferent, I'm telling you ... don't go."

I never thought Monsignor was indifferent. When I was packing my things to vacate the rectory, his lumpy silhouette appeared in the doorway to my room. He tossed a book on my bed—*Abandonment to Divine Providence* by Jean-Pierre de Caussade—then gave me a pat on the shoulder and a squeeze on the arm. He didn't need to say anything; his pressed lips and knit brow said it all: *I care. I can't help you, but I care.*

"Why? Because of Andrew?" I asked.

"I said don't interrupt. I need to tell you something. Something I should've told you the day I found out Reese was coming." Then began Monsignor's confession. His voice was cracking, hesitant, as if he was trying to maintain his devil-may-care facade but wisps of contrition and humility were seeping out along the edges.

Six years ago Monsignor had dreams for the parish like I did. While I wanted to make St. Dominic's a spiritual beacon in Westchester, his dream was to apply a defibrillator to the parochial school, which was still open at the time but mired in debt and sitting on the archdiocesan chopping block. He thought he'd be smart and hire a consulting firm. Said firm, recommended by a friend of a friend, turned out to be run by a couple of grifters that siphoned a clean two hundred fifty thousand dollars from the parish accounts. Legally Monsignor could do nothing except cut his losses.

That's where Andrew came in. Late one night, lips loosened by two vodka martinis, Monsignor confessed his error. Three Sundays later the parish coffers had been replenished. Just like that. "I took up special collections at my Masses," Andrew had said when Monsignor asked how he did it.

The ingress of funds didn't stop at two hundred fifty grand. Sunday collections—generally composed of cash donations—skyrocketed from seven thousand dollars a week to upwards of sixty. The excess amounts were paid out to a so-called Montalcino Foundation.

"Father Reese told me it was to help schools in Haiti," Hank Massotti had said. "He asked me to cut checks to this foundation. I checked it out online. Sure enough, their website says they support educational efforts in third-world countries. We've got tax receipts from them."

As I listened to Monsignor tell the story, I imagined him staring up at Andrew, arms folded across his chest, as if to say, *What's going on?* Then Andrew shrugging. "The first two fifty that came in was a loan. What's coming in now will pay it back."

The second-collection revenue streamed in, and then out again, for another nine months, until the IRS started snooping around. Monsignor told Andrew it was time to part ways. Andrew went to Rome, and the two agreed to keep their lips sealed about the whole thing. That's what Monsignor should have told me. He didn't because he wouldn't break his promise. How noble of him.

I asked him whether the people he was laundering money for were related to the Cardellis. He didn't think so, but he never asked because he never wanted to know. From what he could tell, it was an independent family, maybe a rival.

I was torn. Should I stay, or should I go? I could stay local and risk death by either cabin fever or Cardelli, whichever came first, or I could escape to Florida with a dear friend who happens to be a money launderer. The scale tipped when a new local threat was placed on the balance. It came by way of text message.

Hey, Chris, it's Allison. I know it's been a while, but I heard you've been through a lot lately, and I wanted to reach out. The note was followed by a red heart emoji.

That was sweet of my old girlfriend, and dangerous. Oh so dangerous. Here I was, depressed, thinking my priesthood was over, my whole life project washed up, and in walks an angel who could whisk away my troubles faster than a Calgon bath.

As my thoughts drifted down the dungeon corridor of my soul, they tripped over one more emotion tucked away in an isolated recess: loneliness. I knew Allison wasn't married yet; I had checked her out on Facebook. Relationship status: single. Her only companion, from what I could tell, was a cocker spaniel named Rowlf (*so* her). She appeared to have a nice house, an active social life, and no boyfriend—which inappropriately brought joy to my heart. A post showing a new couch delivery had said, "Allison is feeling excited." That sofa would be perfect for snuggling on, like we used to. *I hope she puts it in front of the fireplace.*

I opened my laptop, turned it on, clicked on Facebook Messenger, and started to type, coaxed by the little guy on my shoulder with the red suit, pointy tail, and horns. But then the guy on the other shoulder with the white wings and halo punched me in the arm, and I slapped the laptop shut, pushed it aside, and focused on the dripping AC unit. *One hundred fifty-one.*

Now the balance tilted firmly to one side. A potential hit job, death by boredom, and romantic temptation outweighed the dangers of a Florida vacation with a suspected money launderer.

I grabbed my phone and texted Andrew: *I'll go. When do we leave?*

Andrew: *I knew you'd change your mind. We'll fly out of LaGuardia on Monday at 10 A.M. I already emailed you the reservation.*

Me: *You had Allison contact me, didn't you?*

Andrew: *Moi?*

20

Beyond the Sea

Four strokes by Andrew on a keypad and the iron gate opened, revealing a tropical seaside estate that would impress even Robin Leach.

"Welcome home, Christopher," Andrew said as he got back in the Uber that brought us from the airport. Rajesh, our driver, carted us along a palm-lined driveway, past manicured shrubbery and Greek statues, to my own private Xanadu—the set of *Citizen Chris*. I could just see myself now, rambling listlessly around the colossal mansion like Charles Foster Kane, just before he died. As I lay dying, the name falling from my lips would be not Rosebud but Cardelli—or maybe Allison?

Andrew wouldn't let me tumble back into the doldrums of despair, however. As he took me from room to room, showing off every luxurious detail—"Look at this pillowtop mattress, like sleeping on a cloud ... Have you ever seen a Jacuzzi this big? ... And what is this in the garage? A Porsche?"—he assured me this was the beginning of a different movie: *Father Hart's Day Off*. Whatever I wanted, all I had to do was say the word, and it was mine. Of course I knew regardless of what I wanted, he'd drag me through a planned itinerary: a forced march from golf course to beach to fine restaurant, with the goal of anesthetizing me by entertainment.

I should have been happy, right? What a privilege to
live like a prince, at least for a while—to bask in the sun
on sandy beaches and sip daquiris by the pool. Yet this
just wasn't me. I'm not a prince; I'm a pauper. I don't do
luxury well. This felt foreign, awkward, and sterile. My
idea of a getaway was sneaking down to the homeless shelter where no one knows me and dishing out food in the
soup line, or walking the halls of my old parochial school
and chatting with the kids, or slipping in to hear confessions at one of the Hispanic parishes where people come in
droves. But that was all considered ministry and thus barred
to me.

Andrew installed me in my room, the master suite, with
its wall of glass overlooking the Atlantic. I sat on the edge
of the bed, contemplating the ocean, its gentle waves falling silently over the beach, my gaze drifting out to the
horizon where cotton-ball clouds soaked up the cyan sea.
And I prayed. I talked to God. It's something priests do,
you know. It's something I had been doing all along, but
for a long time now it felt as if I were talking to a wall.

Since my seminary days I had spent the first hour of
every morning in prayer. And during the day too, I'd pray,
little informal invocations: *O Jesus, give me all green lights
so I can make it to the hospital before this guy passes away.* Or,
*Lord, I have no idea what to tell this couple. If you don't do
something, they may very well kill each other.* And I always got
a response. No booming voice from above, but an interior
word or a newfound confidence: he's got me.

Then, sometime after I arrived at St. Dominic's, he
stopped talking to me. I didn't know why. Did I do something wrong? I was so excited to build up the parish for
him. He finally trusted me enough to give me something
big, and I was determined not to let him down. But when
I slid into church in the wee hours of the morning or knelt

in the little upstairs chapel at night, I found only silence. My mind wandered to my to-do list, then to conversations from earlier in the day. He was gone, and nothing I did could make him come back. When the events at Stefano's started, the distractions took on a tinge of angst. But no consolation came, no inner confidence sprang up to convince me everything was going to work out.

The one thing about this Florida trip I was looking forward to, the only thing, was the prospect of letting my eyes drift over the flat ocean stretching to infinity, searching the soft pastels of a sunrise or the pacifying blues of a clear midday sky or the woolly clumps of overcast clouds, and somewhere in there finding God. When all else failed, nature brought me to God. The Divine Painter's brushstrokes always leave unmistakable evidence that he is there, in the midst of all life's turmoil; he is there in a rainbow, in a sunset, in a silvery birdsong, or even in the croak of a frog. I so hoped that finally, here, seaside, my parched soul would be quenched.

Yet now, propped on the edge of the ocean-sized bed, looking over the balcony past the beach, I saw water, just water, plain and simple. H_2O. Water in full liquid form, resting in an earthen basin, its tidal ebb and flow explained by the gravitational pull of the moon. Water in gaseous form suspended in the air, not by angels, but by the standard laws of physics. No awe was inspired. No handiwork of a Master Creator was found. It was as if I held a seashell to my ear and heard not the still-crashing waves of the beach it was plucked from but the sensible sound of air resonating off its curved interior and reverberating in the drum of my ear.

"*The priesthood is an obsolete institution that does society no apparent good and more than a little harm.*" That's what Connie had told me. Maybe she was right. Maybe my whole priesthood, everything I did as a priest, was just delusional superstition dressed up in theological pseudo-science: convenient spiritual palliatives to numb people's existential pain.

🙣 🙣 🙣

As expected, the next day Andrew had a plan. Our first activity was set for ten o'clock: mimosas on the veranda with fresh berries, croissants, eggs to order, and bacon. Andrew would cook. Then we would unhook the bicycles from their perches in the garage and ride along the ocean, arriving at the Bath and Tennis Club, where we would lunch, followed by a leisurely afternoon of reading on the beach or poolside. We would cap the day off with a jaunt in the Porsche, ending up at the Palm Beach Country Club, where we would dine. And who would pay for these diversions? Andrew held up a shiny black credit card. "My account's been padded. Aren't the Giordanos generous?" he said.

Things were going as planned, at least till lunch. I sat facing the bar. On the television I expected to see highlights of the latest PGA tournament, but instead the Weather Channel broadcast news of a hurricane watch for southeast Florida. I overheard a waiter ask a busboy whether he had stocked up on bottled water yet.

Back in LaGuardia, as we were checking our bags, I had called Andrew's attention to the tropical storm brewing in the Caribbean, but he had said not to worry; the likelihood of its heading up to Florida was low. Besides, he said, tropical storms are wonderful. Often, after they've blown over, the weather is gorgeous. I had pointed out that, often, tropical storms don't stay tropical storms; they turn into hurricanes. Now I nodded toward the television as if to say, *I told you so.* He shrugged and said, "We'll keep an eye on it."

In the afternoon, I found it too muggy to sit by the pool and longed again for New York's dry October air. When it was time to head to dinner, the Porsche wouldn't start. It had gas, but the battery was dead. It had sat unused a tad too long.

Uber brought us to dinner and back. I pumped the leathery-skinned driver with questions about the brewing storm, but he was dismissive. "They always get their panties in a bunch about this stuff, man," he said. "Last really big one was over ten years ago. Wilma, 2005. They say we're due. I dunno; maybe we are. Gotta follow the drill just in case, man. Stock up on bottled water, board up, all that crap." He tossed an empty Zephyrhills water bottle at me. "Those dudes, they got the action, man. They make a killin' in Florida. Forget that Evian and Deer Park junk. Those Zephyrhills guys are everywhere. I wanna get me some of that action, know what I mean?"

We arrived back at the house well into the evening. The skies had cleared enough to see the full moon cast a shimmery streak across the ocean. Dinner had been fun. Andrew was his charming self, bantering with the waiter, showing off his wine list savvy, even stealing into the kitchen to congratulate the chef on the foie gras: "Not at all easy to do well, my good sir." Now in my room, my head spinning from the Chartreuse Andrew had insisted I consume, I planted myself on the plush carpet, leaning against the foot of the bed, and stared out at the moonlit sky. The plan was working. I was forgetting.

And moments later, toothbrush in hand, I remembered again. Just when I felt dry, the realization of my situation crashed over me like a wave, and I was soaked by it: I was finished. That's how the feeling came, in waves. First the tsunami—the meeting with Lynch, the social media blitz, the reporters, my exile—and then small surges of awareness at random moments in the middle of mundane tasks. *I'm finished.* Like a widower who turns to ask his wife where the dustpan went and realizes, again, she's gone.

※ ※ ※

The next day, more of the same. Breakfast—Andrew made waffles—was a bit earlier because we had a ten o'clock tee time at the Breakers. I told him I didn't play golf, but he insisted. After the second hole we agreed it was best I stick to driving the cart while he finished the round. Occasionally I'd toss a ball on the green and putt. Without the little windmill in my way, I found it rather easy to sink a shot.

Lunch was also at the Breakers: Bloody Marys and gourmet grilled delights. That was the first time I ever saw a twenty-five-dollar hamburger, much less tasted one. We spent the afternoon at the house lounging by the pool. Andrew made mint juleps served with water biscuits and a sort of pâté. We dined at the Palm Beach Grill, where a hot dog–deviled egg combo went for sixteen dollars. I would never complain about Yankee Stadium again.

If the days were filled with fun and diversion, the nights were filled with sadness and depression. As if a variation of the same melancholic song played in the background, a sort of slow-tempo blues piece, maybe an African American spiritual: "Nobody knows the trouble I've seen. Nobody knows but Jesus." Or did he?

As I snuggled into bed on my cloudlike pillow-top mattress, amid a half-dozen cloudlike pillows, hoping not to suffocate, I reminded myself it would be appropriate to sleep now. But neither my body nor my mind were listening. Something like sleep eventually came, and when it did, dreams, vivid and alarming, came with it. On the second night when I awoke drenched in cold sweat, I jotted down the experience:

Floating heads yelling, and disembodied fingers pointing.

Faceless figures in cocktail attire whispering about me as if I wasn't in the room.

My first pastor, Father McLeod, approaching, smiling, putting a drink in my hand. "Why are you naked?" he asked through a haughty laugh. Was I naked? I couldn't tell.

I tried to explain, but my voice was garbled.

He gave me a sympathetic nod, but then it wasn't him—it was Mrs. Aiello, my third-grade teacher.

I politely waved good-bye to everyone as I stepped out a door and onto a pier. Heavy clouds swirled above; the ocean churned below in a whirlpool. Sea spray dappled my white shirt with blue ink. At the end of the pier sat a young woman. Auburn hair blew in the wind, but her body was motionless. I sat beside her. She turned and looked at me. It was Allison. Suddenly a warmth came over me; the wind had stopped, and we were standing now in a botanical garden, a ray of sunlight breaching the green foliage overhead.

Allison would listen. Allison always had a way of knowing when something was bothering me. She would be good about it. She wouldn't pry. She'd just say something like, *Hey, guess what? I got my ears checked. Turns out I've got perfect hearing.* I was always slow on the uptake. *And I got my heart checked too,* she'd say, *and turns out it works even better. Oh, and my shoulder. Turns out it's great for leaning on and even crying on.* Then I'd smile, and she'd smile back. Then she'd kiss me tenderly on the corner of my mouth; then I'd melt and spill it all. And she'd just listen. And if I cried, so would she. If I was frustrated, she'd rub my chest and hug me, and the tension would go away. Then she'd kiss me full on my lips, and I'd forget my troubles and feel renewed.

In my dream, she didn't speak but just put her hand on my chest and smiled as if to say, *Silly, you worry too much.* I looked down at the hand and back up to the face, and it was now Sal's face. A shock went through the hand into my chest.

My body twitched and I awoke, the blanket twisted tightly around me, three pillows and the comforter on the floor. I lay staring at the ceiling, the room spinning.

21

Bewitched, Bothered, and Bewildered

Another day, another set of fun, distracting activities. Today: museum day. Andrew fanned before me two tickets to the Henry Morrison Flagler Museum, tour starting at 10:00 A.M. "It's a Gilded Age mansion, like Kykuit. You'll adore it."

How would we get there? The previous day our Uber driver kindly gave the Porsche a jump, but nothing happened, just the pathetic clicking of the starter. Andrew texted Gina to let her know. *Sorry about that, darling,* she responded. *The old thing mustn't hold a charge. Bob will look after it when we're down in January. Feel free to use the bicycles in the garage.* Bicycles, again?

"You can use this one today," Andrew said, a smirk on his face, as he rolled over a pink beach cruiser with a little white basket in front. But I wasn't paying attention. I was looking at my phone's weather app.

"Um, Andrew?" The tropical storm had, as I expected, turned into a category 1 hurricane and was currently pummeling the Bahamas. It would make landfall on Florida's east coast by Saturday. The app predicted a chance it might veer east and hit land around the Carolinas, but only a slight chance, like 3 percent.

Andrew tried to reassure me. "Gina has her man coming to put up storm shutters. Large ones, impregnable.

There's a generator too, in case the power goes out. You'll be perfectly safe. It'll actually be rather exciting, don't you think? I mean, Christopher, when was the last time you were in a hurricane?"

※ ※ ※

We arrived at the museum just after ten and hitched our bikes to the wrought iron fence at the entrance. Henry Flagler had dubbed his Beaux Arts–style mansion White-hall. Fitting. It sat, a large mass of white amid palm trees on PGA-grade lawns, with its massive white fluted pillars, its white symmetrical facade, and its numerous white chimneys protruding like battlements along its red tiled roof. The windows were white too, but I could barely tell. Large corrugated sheets of metal hung over half of them, and men with hammers and ladders were in the process of covering the others. Apparently I wasn't the only one checking the forecast.

I supposed Mr. Flagler's idea in making his mansion look like a marshmallow castle was to give an airy feel to the hundred-thousand-square-foot behemoth, a sort of light fairyland refuge for rich industrialists escaping the bleak Northeast winter. Now, however, with the curtain of clouds as a backdrop and the storm shutters, it took on the ominous feel of Manderley—the eerie estate in Du Maurier's novel *Rebecca*, which Hitchcock adapted master-fully for the silver screen.

As Andrew and I sidled up to the small tour group just forming on the front steps, I imagined Mrs. Danvers standing in the doorway, just as Du Maurier described her: "tall and gaunt, dressed in deep black with prominent cheek-bones and great, hollow eyes that gave her a skull's face, parchment-white, set on a skeleton's frame".

No, we found no one matching that description. Instead, we met our tour guide: a plump, giggly faced graduate student in an Orange Julius–colored blouse and cream slacks a size too small. She welcomed everyone with a neon-bright voice, as if she had just downed thirty-two ounces of Starbucks' strongest.

"Hi, everyone! Welcome to Whitehall. I'm Dina, a docent here at the Flagler Museum." Her purple cat-eye glasses kept slipping to the tip of her nose. "Today I'll be taking you back in time to the Gilded Age, when robber barons ruled the land and built fabulous estates like this one, opulent in design and rich in detail." Then, as if an ulcer had started acting up, her buoyant face turned sullen. "But we can't forget, this was all built on the backs of people who couldn't dream of living in a house even the size of the dining room. So, as we walk through these halls, it's a good chance for us to keep our own privilege in check." Pause for consideration. "Okay now, everybody, let's hop into the grand hall, shall we? Here we'll find our first treat, the domed ceiling depicting Apollo's pretty little nymphs!" Oh boy.

Dina the Docent led us room to room, describing each painting and sculpture by way of an anecdote about the home's bygone inhabitants: gloved women in satin and pearls; overdressed men in dinner jackets, high collars, and cravats. She took pains to show us the "miserable living conditions in the servants' quarters", which weren't much different from the living conditions in my last parish.

By the time we entered the drawing room—which was not for drawing, Dina informed us, but for withdrawing—Andrew was fully engaged, soaking up every aesthetic detail. But my attention was waning. I wondered whether Dina might think it rude of me to break from the group and slip over to the powder room. Something made me hesitate, probably deep-seated childhood conditioning, the fruit of many a middle-school field trip. Did I need permission? Would it be suspicious if I were just to walk out of the room? I'd hate to be rude.

My go-to problem-solving method, WWPMD, wouldn't work in this case. When was Philip Marlowe ever bored stiff by a droning tour guide? No, this was the domain of Emily Post, the "patron saint" of etiquette and decorum. Here the question was, What would Emily do? *Discreetly make your way to the back of the room, nod genteelly to anyone standing by the door, and step out,* she'd say. So I did, and as I stood next to the door, about to make my discreet exit, the *click clack, click clack* of sandals slapping against the marble floor echoed from the corridor.

I stepped into the hallway and saw the feet in the sandals and followed the legs all the way up. *Stunning.* That's the word that popped into my mind. Until that point we had been gawking at sumptuous specimens of man's creative power—paintings and sculptures and murals and architecture. In that corridor I was instantly reminded of another creative power. The Divine Artist, whom I had sought in the open sea as I sat on the edge of the Giordanos' master bed, I now found in the figure of a woman.

She wore a sundress, which is appropriate because she was like the sun, wrapped in a dress. And, as if she were the sun, I averted my eyes and walked past her, pretending she didn't exist. But she did exist. And her toenails were painted pink, complementing the blue in her dress. But I wasn't looking.

Ordination to the priesthood does not affect biology. Though one promises celibacy, the male's innate radar for potential mating partners does not shut off. As a seminarian, a young man develops habits—tactics, really—on how to react when a new blip appears on the screen: thank the Lord for beauty in the world, remember she is God's daughter, wonder whether this child of God is as beautiful on the inside as she is on the outside. By the time he is ordained, these reactions no longer require much conscious effort; they have become second nature. Yet that day, and in that state of gloom and despair, my virtue flagged.

When I rejoined the group, she was there, apparently just a late arrival. I positioned myself away from her, toward the front, with only an elderly couple and Dina in my line of sight. But as we moved through the house, our positions shifted; I drifted to the back, where I could have had an unobstructed view of her, but I resisted. Instead, I took an intense interest in the craftsmanship of the floor, then the chandelier, and then the wallpaper. Yet I could not ignore the flashes of chestnut and blue in my peripheral vision—and in my imagination a full mock-up of her angelic figure continued to form.

This was stupid. *What, never seen a beautiful woman before? Snap out of it.* The self-chastisement worked, for a while. I regained my senses, found my interior footing, and shook off the temptation. But that effort, while valiant, lasted only until we moved into another room. I caught her scent and felt her warm presence a foot or two behind me, and my imaginary mock-up returned to my mind's eye.

The imagination, I know, is a bit of a used-car salesman. That fabulous humdinger of a vehicle with brand-spanking-new tires, when one gets close enough to examine it, has a rusted undercarriage or the passenger window doesn't quite go down all the way. I just had to look to discover the bowed legs, the eyes too close together, the ears too small, or the nose too big. Then I would see, not some otherworldly goddess, but a normal human being, a person, infinitely valuable in God's eyes, a sister, a daughter, maybe even a future platonic friend.

Nonchalantly taking up a new position, I slipped a furtive glance and found, there by the window, illuminated by the late morning sun, not pyrite but pure twenty-four-karat gold: skin the color of honey, head perfectly balanced on a delicate neck, fine jawline framing an unassuming face. She was like a still life painting, pretty and with unadorned elegance, a single luscious rose in a plain vase. She was the girl next door—if you lived next to Mount Olympus.

My sly glimpse had unconsciously turned into a full-on stare. She caught me and smiled. Heat rose to my cheeks, and I sheepishly looked away. Andrew was next to me. "I think we should go," I said.

"She won't bite." He walked over to examine an ornate sideboard.

"Was it that obvious?" I whispered, trailing after him.

He chuckled. "Your sudden interest in that gaudy chandelier a few minutes ago gave you away." He looked back toward the woman, who had moved on to get a closer look at the grand piano. "Besides, I think she was hoping you'd look at her. She wasn't exactly playing coy."

"What do you mean?"

"Oh, Christopher. So naïve. Have you never been out of the rectory without your collar on? You know, you're not so hard to look at yourself."

"Can we just go?"

"Fine. Little Miss Sunshine doesn't know what she's talking about anyway. She said this was a Louis XV. It is not. It was probably made in Orlando for a *Beauty and the Beast* interactive display. And I swear, that painting over there came from Walmart."

❧ ❧ ❧

We lunched at another overpriced restaurant and afterward tried renting a sea kayak and were laughed at by the person behind the counter. "You joking? There's a storm coming." We ended up coming home, where I took a long nap and tried unsuccessfully to finish *Crime and Punishment*—not exactly a beach read.

When sunset came, there was no show. A proper sunset needs some clouds, but not too many, to reflect its gorgeous colors. The first night we had perched up on the balcony of the west-facing guest room. The view had been spectacular: the wispy clouds blazed as if they were flammable and someone had struck a match. But not tonight. The overcast skies only gave us ever-darkening shades of gray.

The wind had picked up, and pieces of dead palm branches were strewn over the veranda, which was on the opposite side, facing the ocean. Andrew insisted we have dinner outside despite the breeze, since it might be the last night the weather would allow it.

"Tonight we graze," he said. Grazing was his term for picking at tapas plates he had spent several hours preparing. He had me sit out on the veranda with an Old Fashioned in hand while he put on the finishing touches, nursing a bourbon of his own. A Wynton Marsalis and Miles Davis mix played on the outdoor speakers.

My thoughts alternated between my situation, the girl I saw at the museum, my situation, Allison, and the girl I saw at the museum. This had to stop. *Think holy thoughts. Think holy thoughts.*

The veranda was off the kitchen, and I could see Andrew at the island hovering over a few plates, dripping this, dabbing that, dolloping the other. I was sick of this distraction regimen he had me on. I needed a purpose, something my mind could sink its teeth into.

Fighting for my priesthood was useless. The best I could do was make phone calls or send emails to the chancery, which I had already done too often; now my calls were sent directly to voicemail and my emails were filtered as spam, or so I imagined since I didn't get any responses. If I couldn't do anything on that front, I'd have to find something else. Maybe I would volunteer at a homeless shelter or a hospital or something.

Andrew tucked a bottle of wine under his arm, put the tapas plates on a tray, and, backing through the screen door, stepped onto the veranda.

Andrew. Maybe he was my purpose. He'd been trying to help me, but maybe I should've been helping him. This business about the money laundering was troubling, for sure. But more troubling was the state of his soul. Since we'd been in Palm Beach I never saw him open his breviary, pull out a rosary, or sit in quiet contemplation. It's recommended priests celebrate Mass every day, even if we're alone. Despite my restrictions, I was still allowed to say Mass in private, and I did so in my room on an empty dresser. I made overtures for him to join me, but he always needed to run out and grab some groceries, or prepare breakfast, or make an urgent phone call. All excuses.

A coffee table sat in front of a love seat flanked by two white wicker chairs with pink floral cushions. Andrew set the tray on the coffee table and handed me the bottle of wine, dusty and old, and a corkscrew. "Open her up. I'll just grab some glasses." He returned with the glasses in one hand and a bottle of Four Roses Single Barrel bourbon in the other. "Top you off?"

"No thanks. I'm good. I'll have some wine." I started to pour, and he held out a hand to stop me.

"Oh no, that needs a good hour before it'll be ready to drink." He paused a moment, face scrunched in thought. "Go ahead, down that bit."

I did. My lips puckered and my tongue shriveled as if I had just licked a tailpipe. He laughed.

"Sorry, I forgot to open it ahead of time. I looked all over for a decanter. Can you believe a place like this doesn't have a decanter?"

After grabbing a piece of rolled prosciutto, he sank into the chair opposite me and sighed a big relaxing sigh as if he'd just spent the last ten hours hauling bricks at a construction site. He looked out at the ocean, nibbling the end of the prosciutto roll. "Now, this is the most civilized moment I've had all day," he said. "You know, the great houses were never meant to be museums. They were meant to be lived in, like this one. Yes, of course, the lords ought to open their estates to the hoi polloi occasionally—maybe once a year—but not like that. Tour guides and maintenance people running around. Did you see that oaf in the billiard room working on the outlet? I was tempted to grab him by the tool belt and yank his pants up. I mean, there were ladies in there. Oh, but you know that." He winked and sipped his bourbon.

I was only half listening. My brain focused on formulating my line of questioning. Maybe I'd tackle the money laundering first, then suggest prayer as a way to re-center himself. This was the moment: he'd finished all the dinner prep, the soothing clarion of Wynton Marsalis' trumpet wafted through the air, he was surely on his second bourbon by now, and he was in a nostalgic mood.

"Penny for your thoughts," he said.

"Do you launder money for the mob?" It wasn't supposed to come out like that. Not that it came out accusingly. It came out flat, almost as if I had asked, *Do you ever shop at Whole Foods?* I wanted to end with that question, not lead with it. I was thinking what angle I should take, and I had arrived at that question as my goal when he said, "Penny for your thoughts." And now it was out.

"Well, where is this coming from? What an accusation." His look of consternation faded. "Oh, wait, I know.

Is this about that enchantress at the museum? Trying to think about something else, is that it? Shake it off, old man. Besides, you'd make Allison jealous." He giggled.

"Stop, not funny. I don't care about the museum girl, and I haven't thought about Allison since you had her text me." I lied. And he knew it. But how he connected my asking about money laundering to those wayward thoughts, I still don't know. "Look, I appreciate all you've been doing for me. I really do. It's just that it's not working. I know your intention is to get me to drown my sorrows and all. But honestly, this isn't me." That's also not what I wanted to say. "Well, what I'm getting at is, all these sensual delights, they're weakening me. I should be in a monastery somewhere, praying. I should go to the garden like Jesus did. When he was in his trial, he went to be alone and prayed. And I'm here sipping bourbon and eating truffles." *No, stop. Not like this.* This was supposed to be about him, not me. *Focus.*

"You don't like it? I'm not making this enjoyable for you?"

"It's not that. I mean, I like it, I like it all. I like it too much. Here's the thing. We're priests. We're supposed to live like Jesus. Not like this." There, that was better. *We. We're* priests. Not personal yet. *We're* going down the wrong path, *together.* That's the angle. I'm just as guilty as you, except I'm not.

He reached for the wine and poured an ounce into my glass. "Smell that."

I was supposed to say it smelled like black currant or raspberries or leather or something, but it just smelled like wine.

"Swirl it around and take a big whiff. Stick your nose in the glass. Good. Now sip it and let it swish in your mouth; make sure it gets under the tongue. Go on. Okay, now, without swallowing, breathe in over the wine. Good. Now swallow."

The wine was different. Smoother, less metallic. I still couldn't tell whether it had overtones of plum or blackberry, but it was a world different from the first sip.

"You see," Andrew said, "it takes time to open up. And that was only fifteen minutes. It needs to breathe deep, stretch out its legs, and unwind. Like you. Sure, you could have gone to some monastery, but be honest: you would have been climbing the walls. You'd finish more wound up than when you started. You're not a monk; you can't sit still that long. Your stay at the rectory in Newark proved that. Why do you think I wanted to remove you from that situation?" My body tensed as I recalled the steady drip of the rectory's AC unit.

Andrew droned on. "Now, it's true, I could have taken you to Rome or Paris, or Boston for that matter, and we could have gone church hopping. But this was available, offered on a platter. If Gina G. found out we paid beaucoup bucks to jaunt over to Rome while passing up her offer for all this, I'd never hear the end of it. I know you're not really going to escape your thoughts, but if your insides have to be tortured, why not pamper your outsides?"

"No, Andrew. I'm not thinking about *me* anymore. It's *you* I'm thinking about. You don't pray. You don't celebrate Mass. And this money stuff. Jack told me why you left the parish six years ago. He told me everything: about his big blunder, about the donations to cover it, about the IRS investigation. And if I hadn't seen the same patterns since you arrived, I wouldn't have believed him. I mean, Andrew, the Montalcino Foundation? Really? Couldn't you be more creative? Brunello is your favorite wine. It comes from Montalcino, Italy." That all came out too fast. This was not going right.

"So Jack told you. Very naughty of him. Did he tell you everything? Did he tell you about what he did when—"

"I don't care what he did or didn't do. This isn't about him. It's about you. What's going on, Andrew? Level with me."

He downed the rest of his bourbon and poured another. He was stalling for sure, trying to think of an answer. Then it came. "Why should I? You've already made up your mind about me. You listen to everyone else. You let it simmer in your mind. You watch me, and everything I do reinforces this image you've concocted. 'There he goes again, buying something. Must be using dirty money because Jack says he's a crook. Oh, that generous donation from the Giordanos' foundation—don't touch that because you know it's Mafia money. Jack told me.' You know, Christopher, you could have asked me about this instead of letting your mind work up all sorts of conspiracy theories."

No, he was not going to turn this on me. "I'm giving you a chance now," I said. "That's what this is. We just needed a quiet moment, when we're both calm, and I thought this was it."

"Really? 'Do you launder money for the mob?' That's how you start this crucial conversation? Not, 'Hey, Andrew, I heard some stories about you. I really couldn't believe them because I know you. You're my friend. So what's the real deal?' No, you ask me if I launder money. Is it because you see me prodigally throwing money around? I've already told you where I get my money."

"Yeah, you told me some elderly lady left you an inheritance and you've been smart with your investments. But Jack said you told him about some real estate—"

"Screw Jack. I don't care what that fat old blowhard who never got his purple hat says. Who are you going to believe? Me—your friend—or Jack Leahy? Really, Christopher. I can't believe we're even having this conversation." He was red in the face. Andrew never got red in the face. He never blushed, squirmed, or so much as bit his nails. He was always above the fray, like a kid sitting up on a tree branch taunting the bully below because he knows the bully can't climb. Now he was hurt and flustered.

"I'm sorry. That was unfair. You're right. We could have talked about it before. I didn't mean to accuse you."

He sat, looking out at the ocean awhile. The wind rustled in the palms, and the crashing waves were getting louder. After several minutes, he poured some wine into my glass, popped a stuffed mushroom into his mouth, and said, "I think I'm going to call it a night. Enjoy the wine. Shut the lights off when you go up, if you don't mind."

22

The Girl from Ipanema

I awoke to whirring drills and slamming hammers. Every morning my alarm had been the gentle light of the rising sun; today all was dark. My head was pounding from the wine the night before. I had finished the bottle. I'd never drunk like that before. Sure, I'd gotten drunk plenty of times in college, but never as a priest, and never to kill my pain. The sides of my tongue felt bloated, my body felt a strange combination of tingly on the surface and numb underneath, and my conscience felt prickly. Why did I drink all that wine, and why did I look at that girl in the museum? My inner therapist had the answer: *You're trying to escape.*

My mind was foggy, but I had one thing clear: Andrew was right. I had jumped to conclusions. I was right to be suspicious, but of whom? Andrew and I were outsiders. We came into Monsignor's world, populated by his people. We were seen as extraterrestrials. The natural reaction was to fight us off, like in *War of the Worlds*. How was I so sure everything Monsignor had confided to me was true?

It didn't matter now. I was alone. My best friend, my only friend at this point, thought I was suspicious of him.

I slid off the bed, landing on creaky feet, and held my hands over my ears, attempting to block out the drilling and hammering. The alarm clock read 7:36.

I donned a robe and slippers and descended to the ground floor. The whole house was dark. A light emanated from the kitchen along with the gurgle of percolating coffee. Andrew was already dressed, in clericals, and had just set two plates on the table. If he was in clericals, it meant he was leaving—not just to get eggs, but leaving, leaving.

"What's going on?" My voice was hoarse.

"They're putting up the hurricane shutters. They arrived early. Said they've got a lot of houses to do today. The storm is coming in faster than anticipated."

"And you?"

"I'm off, old man. They will collect me at eight."

"Where are you going?"

"New York, of course. Or have you forgotten the deal?" He poured a cup of coffee and sat at the kitchen table, where he had already laid out two place settings, cut fruit, fresh-squeezed orange juice, and toast.

"Right. You need to go back for the weekend Masses. I just thought you'd stay till tomorrow morning. The vigil isn't till five. Can't you take a morning flight and then come back here after the noon Mass on Sunday? You wouldn't be gone more than thirty-six hours." I was desperately trying to convey that I was sorry, that I didn't suspect him anymore. That I wanted him around, I needed him.

"Take my advice and don't become a travel agent. There's a hurricane coming. It might hit tonight. All the flights tomorrow are already canceled. They automatically rebooked me on the nine thirty this morning. I actually tried to get you a seat so I didn't have to leave you here. There's no way. I mean, you could go to the airport and try standby, but it's more likely the Mets will win the World Series than you will get a flight."

"Hey, they've got a decent team this year," I said, expecting him to smile. He didn't.

"My point, friend, is that you ought to make yourself comfortable. You're stuck here. And there are worse places to be stuck." He forked a slice of kiwi. "I've ordered groceries. They'll be here at two. The generator is on the side of the house. If the power goes out, the generator turns on automatically, so you don't have to do anything. Oh, and I've left a prepaid card for your needs on the counter. Don't say I never did anything for you." Just before sliding the kiwi into his mouth, he said, "Sit down. Eat." I sat but didn't touch the food. "If you have any trouble, you have my cell and Gina's. But don't bother Gina, please. I told her we weren't going to be here this weekend so she wouldn't worry."

"What happens if something does happen? I mean, what do I do if some branch comes flying through the window or something?"

"Christopher. Did you see the windows?"

"Sorry, right. It's early."

"Listen, relax. The storm hits this afternoon, and it'll be over by tomorrow afternoon, guaranteed. It's not that big, and it's moving quickly. You'll be fine. The Bath and Tennis will still be open for brunch this morning. I checked. Go, eat, enjoy, then come back and hunker down. There's a stack of books in the den—those self-help books you like. Play whatever music you want. Dance as if no one is watching, and all that."

"How about I pray?"

"Yes, that too. Wonderful idea. Make this a little retreat weekend." He looked at the glass in front of me. "The orange juice is fresh squeezed."

"Of course it is. Thank you."

"Don't look so glum. This is an adventure. Enjoy it. Once I leave, you can go back to your brooding with no distractions. But I hope I've taught you something this past week. There is a world out there, and you can live in it if you choose to. If you want to sulk on the couch the rest of your life, you can do that too. It's your choice. But I hope you choose life."

I rolled my eyes.

"I must be going. It's almost eight, and I need to brush my teeth."

"Safe trip, Andrew."

"Bath and Tennis for brunch. Go. You must."

I nodded.

❦ ❦ ❦

The Bath and Tennis Club. Sure, why not. Last hurrah before a hurricane wipes me out. A natural disaster is kind of a good way to go, actually. Should be quick and easy. Yes, Mom and my siblings will miss me, but they'll get over it. My life's purpose is finished. I've done a lot of good things in my now thirty-nine years of life. I would like to have done more. Maybe I should write a letter or something. I could clear the air about the accusation, if anyone would believe it. I could say good-bye in a meaningful way. I would have time to write exactly how I feel about all those people who have had such an important impact on my life. Many probably don't even realize the effect they've had. Wouldn't that be a nice thing for them to hear? It would surely soften the blow of my untimely death. They could frame the letter or put it in a drawer and pull it out when they're feeling low and need a pick-me-up.

And I would write a special one for Allison. I would tell her how I never stopped loving her, how beautiful she is both inside and out, and how painful it was for me to leave her but that I needed to follow my call, even if it turned out the way it did. And as I lay dying, about to be swept away by a storm surge, I'd declare, *I love you.*

Those were my silly, ludicrous thoughts as I sat at a table by myself in the club's dimly lit dining room. I knew they were ludicrous, but I found pleasure in indulging them. There is a kind of warmth in dark fatalistic melancholy, like a hot toddy when you've got the flu. I sipped my coffee and let the melodramatic scenes unfold. The setting—a country club ballroom turned bunker—wasn't perfect, but it worked.

Ordinarily the dining room would have been bright and cheerful at that hour. Sunlight would pour in through the floor-to-ceiling windows, and sparkly reflections off the pool would dance on the ceiling. Old money would sip mint juleps while new money would nurse Aperol spritzes. A dripping man in swim trunks towel-drying his hair would wander in through the open French doors, realizing quickly he was underdressed and, embarrassed, make his escape.

Now the windows were shuttered. The Spanish Mediterranean décor and dim chandelier lighting gave the room an oddly medieval castle feel, perfect for brooding. The only natural light filtered in from the hall through the entryway. A long buffet table lined with silver chafing dishes, flickering Sternos underneath, divided the room. I sat in a dark corner on the far end, like a derelict ne'er-do-well in some noir detective movie. If only I had a martini and a cigarette.

The room was empty except for two flocks of snowbirds on either side of the entrance pecking at their eggs Benedict. I was amazed there were any people at all. Everything else on the island had closed the afternoon before, and all nonessential employees were supposedly off the island. Then it dawned on me: this was the soup kitchen for the wealthy. These folks—all elderly—surely didn't cook for themselves. Their usual food sources—the quaint Italian bistros, the haute cuisine restaurants, even the little diner-drugstore on South County Road—were all closed. These people had no option but to come to the club, and it was probably the only decent meal they would get till the storm passed. A sudden feeling of pity came over me.

As I sipped, not a martini but my third cup of coffee, my eyes lazily followed a waiter rushing between the two tables and the kitchen. As he passed the club's main entrance, a silhouette appeared in the doorway. It was her. The girl from the museum. It was her hips and her head and her height, and it was especially her hair. Then, as she crossed the threshold and stepped toward one of the tables, it was her walk and her legs. As the soft glow of a wall sconce lit her features, it was her honey-colored skin and her hair again, those silky waves of chestnut now swaying as she glided to one of the snowbirds' tables.

She sat softly in an empty chair, just on the edge, leaning forward, smiling, nodding. *I know, it's so good to see you too*, she seemed to say. *Yes, it's been forever.* I could read the over-pronounced *forever* on her lips. *Oh, I can imagine how hard it is with this storm coming*, her concerned face said. Now settling in, she rested her purse against the leg of the chair. She slipped her heels off, tucking her bare feet under her seat.

Oh, the bare feet killed me. I shouldn't look. But why not? I wasn't lusting after her. To lust is to turn her into an object, something I seek for my own pleasure. I was merely admiring her beauty, like I admire the *Mona Lisa* or the *Girl with a Pearl Earring*, which in turn allows me to admire da Vinci or Vermeer. I admire her beauty and thus admire her Creator. It's perfectly fine. What's more, I had been looking for a sign of God's presence, and maybe this was it—the angel he had sent to console me in my agony.

Or so I deluded myself. A delusion that was instantly dispelled when she caught me staring, again. I instinctively turned to the window, which was shuttered.

It was too late, though; I was sure she saw me. But maybe she didn't. The room was dark (did I mention that?), and someone had crossed our line of sight heading to the buffet the moment she looked up. If she did catch me, it was for less than a second. Then I did what any self-respecting man would do: I pulled out my cell phone and started to scroll through text messages. I kept scrolling even though I saw her approaching out of the corner of my eye.

"Hi. Excuse me. Sorry. Didn't I see you at the museum yesterday?" She had a slight accent. Exotic. European? Maybe French?

I acted as if she had woken me from deep thought. "Uh. Yes. Yes, I was there." I stood up.

"Are you following me?" she asked with a smile.

"No. No, no. Not at all," I said, knowing she was just joking but really answering the question, *Were you just staring at me?*

She put out her hand. "I'm Sofi."

"Hi. I'm ... Chris, Chris Hart," I said, taking her hand. "Nice to meet you."

"I didn't mean to disturb you. Are you waiting for someone?"

"I'm here alone, actually. A friend of mine is a member. I'm not. He said I could put brunch on his tab," I said, feeling I needed to justify myself. "Just getting a decent meal before I hunker down for the storm, you know?"

"So no one's sitting here?" She looked at me with an expectant smile.

"Nope, no one. Just me." I smiled back.

"May I join you?"

"Oh, yes. Of course. I'm sorry. Please, have a seat." I had blushed so many times at this point she probably thought it was my natural color. "Can I get you something to eat? I'll try to get the waiter's attention."

"Um, well, it's a buffet, so maybe I'll just grab something in a bit."

"Yes, right. How about coffee?"

"Okay. Sure."

I signaled the waiter with a pouring motion. He nodded and eventually came with a carafe of coffee, filling the cup in front of her.

"Are those relatives you're with or just friends?" I asked.

"So you *were* watching me," she said with a sly smile.

Blood rushed to my face again. "No, no. Not really. I just looked over and happened to notice ... I mean, well ... let's face it, besides me, you're the only one here under eighty. You stand out." Yeah, that was it. That worked.

"Okay. Fair enough. I guess that's why I noticed you too."

"So, you come here often?" *Lame question.*

"No, not really. I don't live down here. But who does, right?"

"Right. Just snowbirds, I guess. You don't look like a snowbird to me," I said with a grin. *Oh, this is getting worse.* "So you're visiting someone?"

"Kind of. My aunt lives in West Palm. My father has a house here on the island. That's where I'm staying. That was my aunt's friend over there. She wanted to take me to brunch here. 'Oh, you must come to the club,'" she said, feigning a highborn accent. "'You must try the crab cakes. They're to die for!'" She gave a cute smirk. "And since I had no one my own age to play with, I agreed. But then I had second thoughts, and I kept putting her off. We finally settled on today. I thought the storm would have been my out, but I guess not." She put her hand on the table palm down, leaned in, and whispered, "Actually, I have to tell you the truth. I'm using you. She thinks you and I are friends." My eyes widened. She smiled. "I mean, I can talk about garden clubs and art gallery exhibits for only so long ... I needed to escape. I hope you don't mind."

"Of course not. I'm glad you stopped by." What? No I wasn't. What did I say that for? She was dangerous. She was stunning, her voice was sweet and silky and delicious like French yogurt, and my heart was pounding as if a hummingbird were trapped inside and desperately trying to escape.

I would really have preferred that she had just stayed with her aunt's friend. I couldn't say that, of course. I wouldn't want to be impolite, now would I? Andrew always said I was too nice. He was right. I should have said, *Lady, it was nice meeting you. Now be off with you.* But at this point I was desperate for someone to talk to, so in need of a friend. Besides, even if she left, I would keep thinking about her. *I should get to know her as a real person. Better to find the flaws and imperfections that I couldn't find the first time in the museum.* Surely she had a flaw I could grab hold of to crack my infatuation.

"So you're staying with your father?" I asked.

"Oh no. I'm all alone in that big place. I don't remember the last time he came down here. He bought the house as an investment and lets friends use it, and, every so often, his daughter. I come down when I need to get away. And this time, I really needed to get away. So here I am." She shrugged. "How about you? What brings a good-looking guy like you here?"

I hesitated. The inner dialogue now became heated.

I am not going to tell her the truth. No way. Not yet.

And why not?

I don't know. I just don't think I should right now. We just met.

Why? Because admitting you're a celibate priest is going to ruin your chances with her?

That's ridiculous. I'm not interested in her. This is going nowhere.

Oh really? So why don't you go ahead and tell her you're a priest?

And what am I going to say? I'm a suspended priest being accused of molesting a kid?

No. Just that you're a priest.

Be quiet. Can't I have a conversation with her? She's a human being. She deserves to be treated like any other human being. She just insinuated she's going through a tough time. I can't do ministry, but I can still be a listening ear. I'm just going let her talk.

"What am I doing here?" I finally said. "Sort of the same as you, I guess. I needed to get away. So here I am."

"All by your lonesome?"

"Yeah. I came down with my friend, but he had to go back north for the weekend. I've been going through some stuff, and he convinced me to come down. We're staying at some friends' house not far from here on South Ocean Boulevard."

"Oh, he must have really twisted your arm to get you to a house on South Ocean."

"Well, he kind of did. I actually don't like the beach. I'm not a big fan of Florida, in fact. I'm kind of a mountain guy. I like woods and lakes, things like that."

"Cheers to that!" she said, lifting her coffee cup. I lifted my own, clinking it against hers.

"You don't like the beach either?"

"Heck no," she said, rolling her eyes. "I like the quiet solitude of a spring valley or, better, a cabin on a snowy mountainside. You know, when the snow falls silently in the soft light of dusk, but you're inside the warm cabin looking out, wrapped in some comfy afghan in front of a crackling fireplace, reading a book, sipping hot chocolate ... or something a little harder." She lifted an eyebrow.

I sighed interiorly. How I wished I could be transported to that place she just described. And as she described it, I could see her there, and me with her, in front of that fireplace. *Stop. No. I can't be thinking this way.*

"So, where are you from?" I asked, changing the subject.

"Brazil, believe it or not. Land of beaches." She shrugged: *What can I say?* "My family moved up to New York when I was fifteen. Now I live in Brooklyn. I found a job in Manhattan, but it's too expensive to live there, so I got a place in Brooklyn—like everybody else. But that's expensive now too. So I'm not sure what I'm going to do."

"You live with anyone?"

"No. I used to. Long story. Let's not go there, shall we?"

"Right. I didn't mean to pry."

A symphony erupted from her purse. "Oh, sorry. That's my phone," she said as she fished for it. "It's just the alarm. I have to go. I'm sorry. This was really pleasant."

"Yes, it was for me too." *Phew. I'm safe.*

"Listen, maybe we can get together sometime," she said as she stood up. "I'm not sure how long you're staying here, but I'd love to see you again."

"Yeah, that would be nice. I'd like that." *Idiot, what are you saying?*

"Do you have a card or something?"

"No, unfortunately. I don't even have a pen and paper." I started rummaging through my pockets with a faux regretful look on my face. "Oh, I found a pen," I said, pulling a Bic out of my pocket. "But no paper. Darn." That was a lie. I had a piece of paper, but my wits were returning to me. There was no way in hell I was going to give her my number. This had to end here.

"Hmm, let me see that." She leaned over the table. With one hand she took the pen, and with the other she grasped my hand and turned it palm up. Then she wrote her phone number in big, round, feminine numbers, and then "Sofi" with a little heart over the *i*. "There," she said. "Call me sometime."

She pulled her purse over her shoulder, winked, and walked away in that same fashion-show-runway walk I saw in the museum, hips swaying, long legs floating her across the room. I closed my eyes and sighed. What was happening to me?

Stormy Weather

The wind whipped, and debris flew through the air. Fringes on the awning over the club's entrance flapped furiously; rain pelted my face even though I was under cover. There was no way I was riding my bike home in this. I tried Uber, but of course, no cars were available. The club's receptionist only laughed when I asked her to call a taxi.

"What can I do?" I asked.

"I don't know, sir," she said with a sympathetic smile. "But we're closing in ten minutes. The staff still have to cross the bridge."

"Right. I guess it's not that bad. I'm staying just down the street. I'll tough it out."

🙟 🙟 🙟

It took thirty miserable minutes to reach the Giordanos' gate. I stared at the keypad trying to remember the code, straddling the bike, my feet submerged in a three-inch-deep puddle. Two wrong attempts, and I wondered whether I'd be locked out if I failed on the third. A waterfall poured down my face. Then, with the gate finally open, I slogged to the garage, which had another keypad. *Couldn't they have used the same code?* Finally in the garage,

I propped the bike up against the wall, entered the house, grabbed a towel from the laundry room, and, dropping my wet clothes in a pile, went to shower. Oh, the sublimity of simple pleasures: a hot shower after a clammy ride in the rain.

I wiped the steamy mirror, and a haggard face stared back at me. Pale bags made it look as if I were perpetually squinting. I pressed beneath my eyes and down my cheeks, then noticed Sofi's name and phone number hadn't completely washed off. The writing faded a bit more when I rubbed my hands under the faucet, but it was still legible. The indelible mark of my lust. Yes, I was willing to call it that now. Indelible, except a part of me knew if I scrubbed just a bit more, it would come off. But I didn't.

The food delivery was supposed to arrive at two. The appointed hour came and went. So did the hour after that, and at three thirty I texted Andrew: *Food delivery never made it. Who did you order from?*

Response: *Genovese's 561-555-4141.*

I called. Recording. "I'm sorry. Due to inclement weather, we are temporarily closed. Please try back later."

I foraged the pantry and the fridge and turned up exactly one can of tuna, a quarter bottle of red wine, a single slice of *soppressata*, and three olives. What happened to last night's leftovers?

Pizza places weren't delivering. If I could get to a hotel on the mainland (island hotels were way too expensive), I could wait it out there—room service and all. But taxis, Uber, and Lyft were all off the table, and I was not about to bike over to the mainland. What now? Maybe call the police and ask them to give me a ride over? I could tell them I'm stranded with no food, in my ten-thousand-square-foot mansion.

The police. Hmm. No, I wouldn't call the police.

Then came a reluctant thought. I could always call Sofi. She had a car. It was probably a nice car. Just a quick ride over to a hotel on the mainland, nothing more.

Sofi. Hmm. No, I wouldn't call Sofi. Besides, could I even get a hotel this late?

Okay, so I would stretch my meager fare as long as I could. Tomorrow could be a day of fasting. No problem. I've done that before. It'll be good for me. With Andrew gone, no pressure.

It was decided, and I was at peace until five o'clock, when my stomach grumbled. This was going to be a long weekend.

The wind and rain got fiercer. Pebbles and stray branches rapped against the storm shutters. The projections on my weather app had the storm only nipping us, but the winds were still over fifty miles per hour.

It was now six o'clock. I poured the last of the wine in a glass, plopped onto the living room couch, still savoring the feel of dry clothes, and pulled out my breviary. I went through the required readings for that hour, eyes scanning the words but none sinking in until I read this:

> Lord, make haste and answer;
> for my spirit fails within me.
> Do not hide your face
> lest I become like those in the grave.

How well those words described what my heart felt. *Do not hide your face lest I become like those in the grave.* As I sat under the dim light of an ornate end table lamp, I felt on the verge of becoming like those in the grave, that is, lifeless and alone.

If Andrew had been there, he'd have told me, *You're overreacting. You know you didn't do anything wrong. You'll beat this.* But would I? Maybe in the ecclesiastical courts, but in public opinion? Would I ever get my name back? Would anyone ever trust me again?

I caught the downward spiral of my thoughts and grabbed a novel off the coffee table. *Irresistible Billionaire* by L. N. Darling. The glistening hunk of hairless muscle on the cover and the voluptuous tart clinging to him suggested it wasn't my kind of book. I fished around in a basket of magazines and beach reads and pulled out *Eat, Pray, Love.* Okay. This might work. Let's see what perennial wisdom Ms. Gilbert has to offer.

I had made it to chapter 6, the part where Liz breaks up with her adulterous paramour, David, and asks herself what *she* wants (spoiler: not David), when the power went out. Wasn't it inevitable? I stumbled to the wall, groped for the switch, flipping it on and off several times, as if that might actually do something, then tried a few other switches. Nothing. I shrugged in the darkness, felt my way back to the couch, and plopped down, waiting for the generator to kick in. It didn't. Of course it didn't. Nothing else was going as planned; why stop while I was on a roll?

A deep breath, a sigh, another deep breath, and a lunge upward and onto my feet. Guess I'd have to try to figure out what was wrong with the generator, which was outside being battered by the storm—or maybe I could just go to bed early and look at it in the morning. My father's voice echoed in my subconscious: "*What would be the responsible thing to do?*"

I tapped my phone's flashlight icon and made my way to the front door only to notice the battery on my phone was down to 20 percent. *Whatever.* I slipped on my still-soggy shoes and plunged into the storm, pulling myself along by porch railings, bushes, and house siding, bracing myself against the headwinds.

Andrew said the generator was on the side of the house. Now, which side?

I guessed right. Chalk up at least one victory. The generator sat against the side of the garage not far from the HVAC units. I figured it was the generator; I had never actually seen one before. I didn't even know how one worked. I supposed it ran on gas or propane. Was it empty? Was there a reset switch I needed to hit? Spark plugs to replace or a fuse, maybe?

As I peered over the mystery box, a gust came up, slamming me against the house, forcing the phone out of my hand. Its flashlight lit up the horizontal rain making it look like snow. I plucked it from the ground and wiped the mud from the screen. The battery was down to 10 percent. *This is ridiculous.*

I tried to throw a switch or two on the generator, looked into a tube I thought might be where the gas goes, read a gauge distorted by the rain, kicked the box, pounded it with my fist (which hurt), and succumbed to the evidence: I was not going to fix the generator.

So I devised a new plan. I worked my way back to the front door. In the safety and shelter of the foyer I would use the remaining power on my phone to watch YouTube videos on how to troubleshoot a generator. My plan was immediately foiled when I tried to open the front door. It occurred to me then—not before, when it would have mattered—that in the five days we'd been there we had never used the front door. We'd always gone in and out through the garage, using the code, which was now useless because ... no power. And it was no use trying to lift the garage door manually; I couldn't even get my pinky under it. No key was hidden under the mat or in the bushes or under a rock. All the doors and windows were locked. Back at the front door I tried the ol' slide-a-credit-card-under-the-lock trick, and the card got stuck. When I got it unstuck, the wind ripped it out of my hand and into the darkness. I felt like Gene Kelly but from some alternate evil universe. Tonight's feature film: *Swearing in the Rain*. (Mental note: Add cursing to the list for my next confession.)

Now friendless, homeless, and credit-card-less, I wedged myself into a protected corner between the garage and the front of the house and sank to the ground, head in hands. I thought I might cry. I was just so sick of it. I was so done. And I was so soaked. My feet squished in my shoes; my shirt stuck to me like plastic wrap.

I lifted my head from my hands and saw Sofi's number. With 6 percent battery left, I called.

But she didn't answer. I tried again. Again no answer. Not even voicemail. *Seriously? How is this even possible?*

Then I got a text.

Sofi: *Who is this?*

Me: *Chris Hart. We met at the club this morning.*

Sofi: *Oh, hi!* A smiley face emoji beamed back at me.

Me: *Hey, listen. I'm in a jam. Power's out where I'm staying. Generator doesn't work. No car. Can you help?*

Sofi: *Oh no! Address?*

Me: *1234 South Ocean Boulevard.*

Sofi: *Be right there.* And, of course, she had to insert a heart emoji.

Out of the frying pan, into the fire.

🙂 🙂 🙂

She pulled up in a white Mercedes SL-Class ragtop. I scaled the fence, splashed down in my favorite puddle, which was now a small pond, and squish-ran to the passenger side.

When we arrived at her house and pulled into the garage, I realized I'd left her leather interior dripping wet and felt bad. "Should I get a towel or something for this?" I asked.

"I'll take care of it. Let's just get you out of those clothes."

"What?"

"My dad leaves clothes in the master bedroom. He's bigger than you, but maybe you can make something work. There are fresh towels in the bathroom. By the way, do you like salmon?"

"Sure," I said as she led me through the kitchen to the master bedroom. The house was boxy, not quite as large as the Giordanos' but still impressive. Instead of the typical Mediterranean revival style, it was contemporary: clean lines, spartan walls, the occasional unframed canvas with splotches of primary colors. "Well, I was thinking, maybe you could take me to a hotel somewhere in West Palm?"

She stopped and looked back at me. "You're kidding, right?"

"Well, I mean—"

"I could barely keep the car on the road as it is. I'm not driving over that bridge." Her furrowed brow lightened. "Anyway, the bridges are closed in weather like this. Sorry, *meu amigo*, you're staying here tonight."

❧ ❧ ❧

None of her father's clothes fit me. Oversized, gaudy beachwear filled the closets and drawers: light-colored floral shirts the size of parachutes, and Bermudas of every color Crayola ever came up with, minus burnt umber. I managed to find one plain Lacoste golf shirt, XXL, and a pair of sweatpants with a sufficiently sturdy drawstring to reduce the forty-two-inch waist to my thirty-four. The only footwear that fit was a pair of pink-and-blue flip-flops. At first dismayed, I was heartened by the thought that maybe the white-trash look would protect me from any unwanted advances.

Skittishly I ventured out to the kitchen, where I found Sofi, her back to me, chopping the ends off asparagus spears, a sweaty glass of white wine next to her. If I was dazzled by her elegant glamour at the museum and the club, now I was bewitched by her adorable simplicity. No stunning dress; no million-dollar hairstyling; no high-heeled shoes—no shoes at all, in fact. Just a snug gray pullover—sleeves pushed up just below the elbows—and a pair of cutoff jean shorts, her hair up in a clip. Bossa nova played low over the ceiling speakers, and as she chopped, she shifted foot to foot to the rhythm of the music.

"Want a glass of wine?" She didn't look back at me.

"That's okay. I'm fine."

"All right. Make yourself comfortable. Dinner will be ready in a few." She was humming to the tune.

The kitchen, living room, and dining room were all open concept, defined more by the furniture and slight changes in color tone than anything structural. The décor was minimalist, all sharp edges and angles. I sat on a low contemporary white couch that formed a broken square around a matching low contemporary white coffee table. Knickknacks were all abstract geometrical shapes mostly in subdued earth tones. Several translucent blue-and-yellow glass bowls were affixed above the fireplace, lit by halogen spotlights that cast green shadows on the beige wall. A few magazines fanned across the coffee table, mostly architectural and fashion rags. I picked one up and crossed my legs.

"Hey, is this you?" I asked.

She came closer, wine glass in hand. "Oh, yeah. That's me. A few years ago. Like five or six. It was the only time I made a cover." She went back to dinner prep.

"So you're a model?" I raised my voice enough so she could hear me.

"Yup."

"Do you like it? Modeling?"

"Nope. I always wake up unemployed. I do a job, and then I never know if they're going to hire me back. You have to be really good or really famous to get contracted. You know, like Keira Knightley? She's the Chanel girl. I've got some regular clients, but it's not like I'm on staff. I'm not even on retainer." She was now chopping lettuce. "It's also a job that has a time limit. I mean, I'm not going to look like this forever, you know."

Right. (Mental note #2: She won't look like that forever.)

She continued on. "And what do you do?"

"Me? Well ..." Here we go. The inevitable question. Now what? Tell her? *Yes. Now's the time.* "Um, it's kind of hard to explain ..." *No it's not. It's one word. You can say it. P-r-i-e-s-t.* "I'm in service."

"Oh really," she said, obviously distracted. The ting of a fork hitting the floor rang out; I looked over just as she bent over to pick it up. "Do you like it?" she asked, throwing the fork in the sink and digging in a drawer for another one.

"Yeah, a lot. I mean, I did. I'm kind of on leave right now. Maybe fired. I'm not sure."

"That doesn't sound good."

"No. It's not."

"Does that have something to do with why you're down here?"

"Yeah, kind of."

She put two plates on the table, gave the setting a last once-over, hands on hips, and said, "Okay, I think everything's ready. Do you mind eating in the kitchen? I hope not. I thought the dining room might be too formal. What do you think?"

"Sure, whatever, that's fine."

The kitchen table was a square high-top, with four bar-height chairs around it, illuminated by a single halogen light set in the ceiling above. "Nice outfit, by the way," she said, giving me a smirk.

The salad was perfectly arranged: colorful, balanced, laced with crisscrossing oil and balsamic vinegar drizzles; the salmon, a dark pink sprinkled with capers and some type of herb.

"Are you a chef too?" I asked.

"I like to putter." She lowered the lighting, lit a candle, and adjusted the music. The song was "Desafinado". I had heard it performed by Sinatra in English, but this version was in Portuguese and had a slower tempo; the voice was female and sultry.

After a few shallow comments about Brazilian jazz and how hot it must be in the Amazon, I started to clam up, resisting the connection I felt forming, and which I didn't want. Several times she started to say something and then checked herself, waiting for me to make the next move.

The raging storm outside broke the silence: a large branch bashed against a shutter, a gust of wind howled, and hard rain splashed in waves on the side of the house. We looked at each other wide-eyed, then laughed nervously.

I felt it was time. I needed to come clean. It wasn't fair otherwise.

"Listen, I need to tell you something," I said.

"You're married."

"No. I mean ... yes ... well, not exactly. I'm not married per se. I'm ... I'm a Catholic priest."

She fell limp against the chair, a wave of relief washing over her face. "Now it makes sense. Oh, what a relief. I was like, what the heck?" She spoke rapidly. "I mean, I didn't see a ring, but you also weren't making any moves. At first I thought you might be gay. I mean, you were with that guy at the museum, so I thought maybe. But then I knew you were into me. So I was like, what's up with this dude? Is he just chicken or what?"

I smiled and chuckled a bit. Now I, too, was relieved. Finally, it was out in the open. The tension dissipated. My muscles relaxed. "Yeah. So that's it. I mean, I'll be honest, I find you remarkably attractive. But, you know, I'm committed."

"I get it. I get it. So, 'service'. Code for 'priest'."

"That's right."

"But you said you might be fired. Can a priest be fired?"

"Well, sort of. I mean, I'm on what's called administrative leave. I can't act as a priest. I can't dress like one. I can't celebrate Mass, except by myself, or hear confessions or baptize or any of that. I can't even read at Mass."

"What'd you do?"

"Nothing."

She gave me an incredulous look.

"No, really. I was set up." I took a gulp of water. "Look, it's a long story. I don't think you want to hear about it."

"Well, if you prefer, we could talk about the weather all night." She arched a coy eyebrow.

I wanted to tell her. I wanted to spill it all, every last grimy detail, but there was so much she wouldn't understand, so much I couldn't explain. Where would I start, and would it even be right?

She noticed my hesitation.

"Are you sure you don't want any wine?" she asked.

"You know, I think I'll have some after all."

"Good." She got up and brought back the half-empty bottle of California chardonnay. "And now we can toast."

"Toast? To what?"

"To my anniversary."

"It's your anniversary?"

"Uh-huh. That's why *I'm* here. To celebrate my anniversary."

"Wedding anniversary?"

"Yup."

"Oh, I'm sorry, I didn't know you were married." She wasn't wearing a ring either. "Is your husband away on business or something?"

"No. I guess it's more accurate to say I *was* married. Till death do us part, right?"

"Now I'm really sorry. How long has it been?"

"Two years. Today. So it's actually a double anniversary." She pointed at my plate. "Hey, dig in. I'll talk while you eat. Then you can talk while I eat. Sound good?"

"Um, yeah."

She took a sip of wine and a deep breath. "I don't know where to start. Um ... we had a fight. A big fight. You know, one of those fights when you say horrible things you don't really mean, but you do ... sorta ... I mean, the stuff you always wanted to say but never did. Everything you held back, every little annoying thing about him that grates on you but you look past because you love him? All that suddenly came spewing out. The stupid things, like the pee splattered on the toilet rim, the empty milk carton left in the fridge, the way he ate, like a cow, spitting food everywhere. Those things.

"And then, of course, the bigger stuff, like, 'Why the hell don't you get off your butt and help me?' and 'Can you ever come home on time or at least tell me *when* you're coming home, or *if* you're coming home?' And those things you secretly suspect but aren't quite sure about? In a fight they become facts—totally, unquestionably factual. Like when *Who is that woman he's texting?* becomes 'You're having an affair with that woman you keep texting.' I mean, nine years of crap came vomiting out."

"You were together nine years?" I asked.

"More than that. We were married nine years, but we were high school sweethearts. I was fifteen when we met; he was sixteen. I had just arrived from Brazil. New school, new culture, new language. It was hard, but he was there for me. He was the only one who would have the patience to let me try to say complete sentences and not finish them for me. And at first he was really respectful. I mean, he wasn't trying to run the bases with me, right?"

I nodded.

"He was so sweet and kind, but tough too. He could be a real jerk when he wanted to be. Actually, he was a jerk pretty much all the time, but not to me. He was gentle with me. Kind of old school. He'd open doors for me and stand up when I walked in the room. I think his dad had a big influence on him. The way his father treated his mother was exceptional. I saw it. His father was a cigar-chomping wholesaler, had his own business. Used to being the boss. He was a big guy who swore a lot. Really gruff. But his wife had this way of calming him, and he'd treat her like a queen. Apple doesn't fall too far from the tree.

"We married young. I was only eighteen." She picked up her napkin and dabbed the corner of her eyes. "Then after nine years of marriage, we had that stupid fight. Like I said, it was our anniversary, and we were fighting really bad. I don't even remember what started it. It was just the accumulation of a lot of frustration building up for months, maybe even years. We were screaming at each other. He put his fist through the wall. He had never raised his voice at me all the time we were together, but that day it was as if he had taken all the really bad words in the dictionary, strung them together, and choked me with them.

"He threw this brass duck we had on the mantelpiece across the room. I got scared. Then—I'll never forget, and this is what really stuck with me—he opened the front door, looked at me, and said, 'You know, you're a prissy little self-absorbed witch who can't stand not getting what she wants. Well, guess what—tonight you have no choice 'cause I'm doing what *I* want. I'm gone.' Then he slammed the door behind him. And you know, it's not the words so much. It's the way he said it. The way his lips were quivering. The little vein that popped in his neck. I'll never forget that. He meant it. He really did. At least at that moment."

"I'm sorry," I said.

"The next part's the important part. After he left, I was on the floor crying. I just lay there in the fetal position bawling my eyes out for hours. Then I got a call. It was the police. He was dead. Just like that. Dead. Had a brain aneurysm. He was a marked man, could have gone at any time, and it was right then after our fight that it blew. But you know what? Do you know where it happened? Outside a florist's shop. The police officer described it to me. He was flat on his face, probably just walked out the door. The dozen red roses he had bought were lying right next to him, and there was a little card. It said, 'Sofi, I'm sorry. I love you more than life. Please forgive me.'"

I sat speechless, staring at her. She wiped tears from her eyes and started to eat. I was almost finished but couldn't pick my fork back up.

"May I ask his name?"

She took a swig of wine and smiled. "Well, that's just it. That's what makes this night worth toasting."

I looked at her, perplexed.

"His name was Chris."

Had I been drinking something, I would have sprayed it all over the room. "You're kidding me," I said.

She shook her head. "What are the chances, Chris? That you and I would be here together, tonight? That I wouldn't be all alone on the two-year anniversary of my husband's death? That I would be with Chris tonight?"

I fell back in my chair. "I'm not that Chris. I'm not your Chris," I said weakly.

She responded with an equally soft tone, "I know. But for some reason we're together, aren't we?"

It would seem so. For some reason—for some mysterious, but obviously orchestrated, reason—we were together. Who can make the storms swell and the power go out? Who can make two lives come together with such uncanny timing? Was it coincidence? Impossible. This had all the marks of an intelligence. I was supposed to be there, and so was she. The candle lit up her face. Her gentle smile, her full, plush lips, her green eyes like wet emeralds looking at me imploringly were a gateway to a deeper being, a someone, a soul in need of connection and love. Was all this, all my past troubles, meant to bring us to this moment? So I could find her? What reason could there be for her own loss? Robbed of her love at such a young age. And there I was, two years later, when she had sufficiently mourned that loss and was ready to be filled again. I who had also lost—lost my purpose, my mission. I who was also in need of connection and love. Maybe this was meant to be.

I shook my head, as if to rouse myself from a trance. No, no. There's another explanation. I cleared my throat, put on my Tom Brokaw voice. "Well, you do have a point there. Wow. Amazing how things work out like this." I paused. "Hey, I know this is kind of a mood killer, but, um, do you mind if I use the restroom?"

🕊 🕊 🕊

When I returned, Sofi was at the kitchen counter preparing the next course.

"I thought we could have dessert in the living room," she said. "Good with you?"

"Yeah, okay, sure."

"Can you bring the wine glasses? I'll bring the plates. I'm almost done."

We had just opened our second bottle of chardonnay. It required every bit of concentration for me to get from the table to the living room. I placed the bottle and glasses on the coffee table with the delicate attention of a Jenga player and sat as if one wrong move would make the couch collapse.

I recognized the song piping through the sound system: "Dança da Solidão". It was part of an international jazz mix my brother had given me for Christmas one year. I loved it. The same sultry female voice had been singing all night. The tempo was soothing.

Soon she joined me, two plates of angel food cake in hand, topped with syrupy strawberries and pillows of whipped cream. She sat in the corner of the couch, propped up on her elbow, slender legs stacked to one side, plate on the cushion in front of her. She pulled the clip from her hair, letting it fall over her shoulders.

"Your turn," she said.

"My turn?"

"Your story. The fired priest hanging out in South Florida. What's that all about?"

"Yeah, well, I guess I owe it to you. All right, let me think." A strong gust of wind came up, rattling a shutter, then settled again. "Have you ever heard of the White Death?" I asked.

She shook her head.

"Have you ever read *Hamlet*?"

"In high school. I didn't really read it. Shakespeare's English was too hard for me at the time. I got the *CliffsNotes*."

"Well, I don't know if you remember, but there's this scene where Hamlet wants to kill his uncle Claudius to avenge his father's murder. But he sees him praying. Hamlet won't kill him because he might go to heaven. He needs to catch him in a sinful act so he'll go straight to hell. That's the difference between the White Death and the Black Death. Now let me tell you how that applies to me."

A glass and a half of wine later, I had told her everything. Well, almost everything. I didn't give away any names, and I didn't give away any sins either—just the facts. It was the first time I had ever been able to tell anyone about it, except for Andrew, who had listened only distractedly. She was so attentive. She hung on every word. Eventually she set her dessert aside and slid over to me.

"I was almost at peace with it, you know," I said. "Until one day they took out this girl, Ashley. She was a waitress at this Italian dive in East Springdale. She was so innocent. I mean, she had her issues, but she wasn't a gangster. Not like these other thugs ... What? Why the look?"

"Nothing, it's just so sad. Please go on," she said.

"So anyway, I tried to save her. And I failed. So I got mad, and I tried to do something about it. And the next thing I know, I'm accused of abusing a minor. They must've had it all planned out, ready to pull the trigger when they needed to. They knew that would shut me down, totally blow any credibility I had."

"Can't you defend yourself somehow?"

"Oh, that's the beauty of it. They leaked it to the press, so it doesn't matter. 'Priest Accused of Abuse' makes the front page; 'Priest Exonerated' makes page C23, bottom corner. Maybe I can prove my innocence—ha! Prove my innocence. Did you hear that? That's the way it is for us. Guilty until proven innocent. But even if I do, even if this person's claims never materialize, I'll always be getting these sidelong glances wherever I go. People whispering behind my back, 'Did you hear?' 'No, is it true? He denies it, but ... you know.'" My blood was boiling now. "And the guys downtown don't care. It's all protocol. One of 'em went on vacation in the middle of this. 'We'll look into it when I get back.' Seriously, I don't think anyone really cares. They just go about their lives. What is it to them? It's all self-interest, about protecting the coffers."

And it wasn't just the guys downtown who didn't care. I didn't say it to Sofi. I don't think I could have even said it to myself. But I felt it. In the recesses of my soul a conviction secreted and hardened: God didn't care. I had given him my whole life. I had given up everything for him. I had given up Allison for him—twice. I was smart; I could have been successful in business or whatever. And I gave it all up for him. And now what? I ended up with nothing. I even lost my reputation.

"What about your museum friend?" Sofi asked.

"Andrew? Yeah, he's been great. But he never once asked me how I'm feeling. Not once. If I ever tried to bring it up, he just handed me another glass of something or said, 'What about parasailing tomorrow?'"

My hand was shaking. I hadn't noticed until she reached over and touched it. I had been staring at the coffee table.

Now I turned to her. She looked into my eyes and said, "I understand."

"You do." It was a statement. She did. I could tell. It was on her face, in her eyes. She understood. She understood *me*. She knew pain and could understand my pain. She didn't try to make it go away; she let me feel it, but she felt it with me. She moved in closer. Her hand went to my cheek. I put my hand to hers. I looked deep into her caring eyes, the only eyes in the universe that understood. A force, like an invisible string, pulled us closer. I knew what was going to happen; I wanted it to happen. Just to spite it all I wanted it. What did I owe anyone anymore? Who was I supposed to be faithful to now? There was a moment, a flash of lucidity, when I could choose. And I chose her.

❧ ❧ ❧

I can't remember how we got to the bedroom. Once I gave in, it was a headlong hurtle down into the throes of passion. All inhibitions gone, I gave myself over to her completely.

My memory of the episode is a blur. Maybe it was the wine, or maybe my mind wants to block it out as if it were some traumatic event.

That's the paradox of sex. In the right context it's one of the most sublime of human acts, quasi-sacramental, life-giving. And in the wrong context it can be one of the most traumatic experiences, marking a person for a lifetime. Any activity so powerful it can create a human being or gouge a person to the depths of his soul is anything but a fun triviality. It can be the expression of total self-gift or a selfish act of rapacity. It can also be routine, much like the most sacred rites of religion.

I fell. The passion drove me, the need for connection, feeling her need for me, wanting to give myself to her and fill her. Yet the moment I finished, the passion broke like a fever. As if a switch had been flipped, the rich film-like texture of the experience, the soft lighting, the warm hues, suddenly clicked to stark, grainy VHS, like a cheap eighties porn video. In an instant I was drawn back to myself. *Where am I? How did I get here? What have I done? Dear Lord, what have I done?*

Ingratitude. As I lay on my back, Sofi's warm body cuddled up to me, ingratitude was the main charge I brought against myself. Not impurity, not lust, not even the covetous grasping for what wasn't mine, what couldn't be mine, what mustn't be mine. Ingratitude despite everything I had received.

Over the past six weeks I had slipped deeper and deeper into darkness, a darkness so thick even the memory of sunny days was a faint impression, hard to recall. I had forgotten how the world works, that as black and cold as the night can get, the sun still burns with consistent heat—our star, immovable, burning hot, unquenchable. It is we who rotate and change and turn away. But long as the night may be, the sun always rises in the morning. That is what I forgot.

Even if the sun had risen, I wouldn't have seen it, my face smothered in my own selfishness. And instead of lifting my head, looking to the horizon, patiently waiting for day to come, I had looked for a new source of light and warmth.

I don't know what most people do after a moment of passion like that. Do they whisper tender words to each other, or do they just lie together in silence, savoring each delicate feeling like you would after tasting a rich dessert, letting the tang and sweetness linger on the tongue?

As we lay there, her head resting peacefully on that soft spot where my shoulder meets my chest, her hand on my heart, her leg over my leg, I felt her heart beating, but out of sync with mine: two drummers from two different bands, drumming on their own, for their own reasons. How many men at this moment would swell with pride, like a cheetah having conquered its gazelle? Yet I felt like a rat in a trap. I wanted to throw off the hand and the leg, push her away, off me, out of my life. How could she do this to me? Take advantage of my weakness like this? How dare she?

Suddenly she stiffened. Could she feel the change in my heart? Had my body turned as cold as my soul had? I looked down at her, trying not to move my head. Her eyes were open wide, as if she had just remembered something important. She didn't look up at me; she just stared into the dimly lit room. Then she slid her body off mine and rolled over to the other side of the bed, her back to me now, bringing her knees to her chest, the sheet pulled tight around her.

What did I do? No, she didn't take advantage of me. I took advantage of *her*—this poor woman on the rebound, having lost her husband only two years ago. Two years isn't long enough to get over something like that. Of course she fell for me. It's her anniversary, and here I am, her new hero come to save the day. And I liked that. I wanted that. I wanted to be her hero. I wanted to save this damsel in distress. But now, look at her, curled up in a ball on the other side of the bed. She's come to realize it too. She knows she doesn't love me. She just loved the idea of me. The idea of her husband come back from the dead. I took advantage of her emptiness to fill my own. And I didn't even know her last name.

24

House of the Rising Sun

When I woke, everything was silent. No more howling wind or battering torrents. The morning was still and quiet. A sliver of sunlight peeked through a shutter that had separated during the night. The light hit my face. I squinted, propping myself up on my elbows, my eyes adjusting. A form, a silhouette at the foot of the bed. It was Sofi. She came into focus: a silk bathrobe tied tight, her hair draped over her shoulders, her delicate fingers wrapped around a Glock nine-millimeter pistol with a silencer, which was aimed at my head.

I tried to assess the situation. Was the woman I fell for last night really pointing a gun at my head? There must be some other explanation. This is all normal, somehow. Andrew's lesson about normalcy bias came to mind, but I couldn't remember what I was supposed to do.

Tears slid in lines down her cheeks and around her mouth, partially hidden by the gun.

"Sofi." I spoke slowly, deliberately. "What are you doing?"

Her arms trembled; she must have been holding the gun a while. But she held it like a pro. My uncle Alex was NYPD for twenty years and a Marine for five years before that. He taught me how to hold a gun, much to my mother's chagrin. Sofi would make him proud. To my relief, her finger was along the barrel, not on the trigger, which meant she wasn't ready to fire.

"Sofi, please put the gun down."

"I can't . . ."

"You can. You definitely can."

"I can't do it. I can't shoot," she said, as if to herself. She was staring past me now, eyes glazed over, but the gun was still trained on my head.

"It's okay, Sofi. It's all okay." I tried to sound reassuring, peaceful, like the host of a classical music station. My heart, meanwhile, was doing its best to crack my sternum.

The tip of the gun trembled more now. She dropped her shoulders, loosened her stance, and let her arms fall to her sides, the gun dangling from her right hand. She turned without a word and walked toward the dresser. She had lost that seductive runway-model stride. Now it was a slow, dejected plod.

Though her feet and legs were still bare, there was nothing provocative about her. The mirror above the dresser reflected a tear-stained face, long and empty. Her glamorous glow had faded; the angelic halo had evaporated. She was ordinary and pitiable.

Should I have felt pity? Shouldn't I have been angry? If someone points a gun at you and then walks away, isn't anger the appropriate response? But I wasn't angry. Whether by adrenaline or grace, I kept calm. Maybe it was the shock that hadn't worn off. Maybe it was a still-enamored heart—no, that wasn't it; my infatuation had vanished the night before when my conscience had slapped me in the face.

I heard her unscrew the silencer and place the gun in a case, clicking it shut. She leaned on the dresser, her back to me still, hands spread out, head hung low, like she was going to be frisked. Then straightening, she turned around and slid down along the dresser to the floor. Folding her arms over her bent knees, she laid her forehead onto her forearms, her light brown hair falling around her like a monk's cowl.

Pity was the right sentiment. It defied logic, I'll admit. But as I overcame my normalcy bias and began to work the Rubik's Cube again, the situation started to make sense.

She had seduced me, true enough. Ours was not the casual encounter of two lonely souls but a deliberate plan. She must have arranged everything, as improbable as it seemed—after all, she couldn't control the weather. She lured me to this bed, where she had planned to kill me. Why? Only one explanation made sense: the Black Death. Cardelli's final play. I was a liability, a witness to a murder, and he had to get rid of me. It wasn't enough to frame me since all that did was kill my credibility for a while. He had to go all the way, and he was using this poor girl to do it. And something stopped her; some semblance of conscience stayed her hand. As the colors on the cube aligned, it was pity I felt for Sofi, and anger at Cardelli.

I leaned out of bed and grabbed my pants from the floor. After sliding them on, I padded across the room and sank down beside her.

Her breaths were long and quivering. I leaned back against the dresser and waited. We were motionless a good while. Soon her breathing calmed, but she still sat with her face buried in her forearms.

"It wouldn't have worked, you know," I said, my head back, arms crossed, legs outstretched. "You needed to do it in the middle of the act."

"What are you talking about?" she said into her lap.

"You see, the way I understand it, the Black Death is when you catch someone in the middle of a mortal sin so he goes straight to hell. Isn't that it?"

"Yeah, I guess."

"So you would have had to kill me before I asked God to forgive me. Once you ask for forgiveness, assuming you're sincere, you get it, priest or no priest."

She looked up at me through strands of hair, her blood-shot eyes squinting a bit, then put her head back down. "This is so messed up."

"Yeah, I'd say so. It's actually a superstitious farce, to be honest. God can't be manipulated like that. Don't get me wrong, confession is important and when available, necessary. I mean, to hear a voice say 'I absolve you' and know he's speaking for God is powerful. But in a pinch, it's not required. You just have to say you're sorry and mean it."

"It's crap. Fourteen years of this BS." This was not the elegant dame with the slight Brazilian accent I had met at the club. The cute spark in her voice was gone, and so was the accent.

"What's that?"

She moaned. "Never mind."

"Fourteen years?" It wasn't hard to guess what she meant. "Fourteen years of seducing men? That's a long time. Even before you met Chris, I guess." I was ready to wager my retirement there was no Chris.

She shook her head, then lifted it. "Terry. His real name is Terry."

"Terry. Okay. So, not Chris." At least there was someone. "Is the story true? About him dying two years ago?"

"Sort of. He died. But not of an aneurysm. He was shot outside a liquor store. It was payback for some bad stuff he did. And it wasn't two years ago. More like four."

"What else?"

"What do you mean?"

"His name was Terry, not Chris. He was shot, didn't die of an aneurysm. You're not from Brazil. What else?"

"My name isn't Sofi. It's Julie." She took a deep inhale. "And Terry, well, we weren't high school sweethearts. I was in high school; he wasn't. He was my dad's bodyguard for a while. That's how we met. I was sixteen. He was twenty-eight. And we never married. That's why I took a liking to Ashley." She faced the bed now, but she must have sensed me look at her in surprise. "Yes, that's right, I know her. Knew her. She was me. Older guy taking her down the wrong path." She turned to me, eyes intense. "I had no idea they killed her till you said it. I seriously thought Brian did it."

"I believe you." I pulled my knees up and hugged them, mirroring Julie's posture. "And it's not your anniversary either, huh?"

She ran both hands through her hair. "You know, I trained as an actress. That's what I really wanted to be. I *am* a model. That part's true. But I really wanted to be an actress."

"Where are you really from?"

"New Rochelle. My mom was from Brazil. I grew up listening to that accent. I can imitate it no problem."

"Ashley wanted to go into theater."

"I know. She wanted to do set design. She was really good too. The bastards. I can't believe they killed her."

"So where'd you meet her?"

"Stefano's. My brother's place. Half brother. I was there a lot. That's where I always got my next job."

"Wait, your brother owns Stefano's? So that makes you a Cardelli."

"You're quick."

I had to let that one settle. I was sitting next to Paul Cardelli's daughter. This was important information, but it wasn't computing.

"Your dad got you into the family business?" I asked.

She scoffed. "Yeah, at fifteen. Soon as I started turning heads." She began rubbing her shins slowly, like she was cold. "You know, it's not that hard to seduce these guys. Just go to the bar they always go to. Smile, wink once. Then they're all over you like flies on crap."

"So that's your job? You seduce guys, get them to sleep with you, and then ... *pop*?"

"Not *pop*. The gun is a backup, just in case things go wrong. Normally I'd slip something in the guy's drink. He says, 'Buy you a drink?' I say, 'No, allow me.' I'd slip him a Mickey. By the time we were done, or even before, he'd be out. Then I'd text the guys to come get him, and I'd go home. That easy.

"Imagine, I started at fifteen," she said. "I didn't want to. I never wanted to. I had to. I had no choice. And it took a toll. I did drugs to cope. I should be dead. I should have died at eighteen. I didn't 'cause of Terry. He saved me, really. At least from the drugs. He got me into other things, though. He wasn't the gentleman I painted Chris to be, but I'll give him credit for getting me off drugs."

"So you didn't actually kill them?"

She shook her head. "No, I knocked 'em out. I had no idea what happened after that. I did my job and went home."

"You didn't suspect—"

"I didn't care. Whatever happened to them, they deserved it. I mean, I didn't know exactly what they did, but I knew they were all slimeballs."

"Like you?"

"What?"

"Sorry, but a girl who seduces guys and leaves them to die ... kind of slimeballish to me."

"Yeah, but I didn't have a choice."

"Right. Did they?"

"Yeah, they did. Absolutely they did. All those guys were the same. They were in it for the money, the power, the influence. They were all moving up the ranks till they got greedy, went too far, and had to pay the price."

"Really? I thought you didn't know what they did exactly."

"I knew enough. I grew up in that garbage. I swam in it." She looked down at her knees. "I'm drowning in it."

"But you did have a choice. You could have stopped. You could have gotten out."

"No. No, I didn't. There was no way out."

"Because of your father?"

"Yeah."

"But *I'm* not dead. You chose not to kill me."

"Yeah, but that's different."

"Why? Because you learned about my past? You got to know me? As a person?"

"Yeah. And you listened to me. You weren't after me like the other guys."

"So there were no other cases where you thought, *Maybe he doesn't deserve it?*"

She shrugged.

"Never a moment when you thought, *I can't do this?*"

She clutched her knees, fingers pressing into them. The contour of her arm muscles deepened.

"And why didn't you listen to that voice? Why did you go through with it?"

She put her head back and breathed out long and slow.

"Julie, why did you stay in this life? Why didn't you get out?"

She released her grip on her knees, pulling her hands back into her lap. "You know, for me last night was real," she said. "I was lying through my teeth about a lot of stuff, sure. But something was honest about it. I was enjoying the part. I was into it. I stepped into another life for a while. I think that's what I like so much about acting. It's a chance to get out of who I am and be someone else, the me I want to be. Last night I was who I wanted to be. I was Sofi and lived in Brooklyn. My dead husband was a good guy, and he loved me and wanted me for me, not just my body. While we talked, it was like I had escaped into Sofi's life, and her life was my life. And ..."

"Yes?"

Her lips tightened. She looked down, then chuckled. "You see, I'm trapped. I can't tell you the truth because you won't believe it. You're going to think I'm just being my manipulative little self. So forget it. Look, just call the cops or whatever you need to do."

"Julie, keep going."

"Forget it. Call the cops. I won't put up a fight."

"And say what, you didn't kill me? Besides, you did me a favor. I'm supposed to be dead, but I'm still alive. It's a nice feeling." I smiled. "I was taking the whole life thing for granted."

"Ha ... ha."

"If you want to be Sofi, what's stopping you? Why don't you be her?"

She pulled her knees in tighter, hugging them. "Last night, you loved me."

"I used you."

"No, before, when I told my story, Sofi's story. You listened to me; you cared. I could see it in your eyes. You weren't playing the game, trying to get me in bed. And I thought, if only it were true. And I wanted it to be true, and I felt it was true, kind of. Even if the words were a lie, I was expressing myself, and I felt like you were listening, and ... I felt loved, for real. That's why I couldn't slip anything in your wine. And when, you know ...

after, when I was with you, I had escaped from my reality. I had believed I could be loved. And then it hit me:
I couldn't be loved. I can't be. I'm not."

"You are."

"For a moment, I thought I was doing something good.
As Sofi from Brooklyn, I could comfort someone, love
him, the only way I knew how. But I even messed that
up. Instead of helping, I became the other woman. You're
married, sort of. And I became the other woman. Who
could love someone like that?"

"I know someone who could." I pointed up.

She stared out across the room toward the bed, her
face agitated, as if it sealed off a raging storm. "Chris"—
her voice was restrained—"don't try to save me. I'm not
worth it, trust me. Do what you know you need to do.
Call the cops. I've gotten away with this long enough."

"You are loved, Julie Cardelli. You are lovable."

"Stop. Call the police or I'll do it." Her voice was even,
but her body was tense.

"It doesn't matter what you did. None of it changes the
fact. You are loved."

"Shut the hell up." The words came out with a bit of
spit. Her bloodshot eyes welled with tears.

"Whether you want to be or not, you are infinitely
loved and can't escape it."

Her faced had turned a purple-red, as if it would burst
from the pressure.

"Accept that you are loved."

She gritted her teeth, the tension rising to a tremor.

I leaned over to her and whispered, "You are loved
immeasurably, totally. No matter what you did, it is no
match for his love."

Suddenly, she let out a guttural scream and shot up. I
pulled back, shocked. She charged across the room, ripped

the linens from the bed, and pummeled the mattress, fists pounding more and more furiously, desperate wails ringing out with each hit. She then crouched, dug a shoulder into the side of the mattress, and shoved it halfway off the box spring, collapsing, exasperated and sobbing.

Approaching on tiptoes, I knelt beside her and placed the palm of my hand on her back. It was warm and heaving. Her breaths escaped in quiet whimpers. She turned, sliding off the box spring, and embraced me. I held her, rocking back and forth, gently stroking her head. "It's going to be all right. It's going to be all right," I said softly, as if to a child. "God loves you, Julie Cardelli. Accept that, and you can be free. Do you want that? To be free?"

She nodded against my shoulder and said through her sobs, "Yes. Yes, I do."

25

Can't We Be Friends?

We both went to shower, in different bathrooms. I washed, but still felt dirty. Steam billowed out as I opened the shower door, fogging the mirror and leaving my reflection headless. What a great image: a man without a face. No identity. Despite escaping death and coaxing my would-be assassin back from the dark side—a very priestly thing to do—my priesthood was now in deeper jeopardy. Before last night, I was innocent, wrongly accused. Now I was guilty, not necessarily of a crime, but of breaking my vows. The steam slowly covered the rest of my reflection until I faded from existence.

I wiped a spot at eye level; my worn face blinked back at me. I had told Julie confessing to a priest wasn't required to avoid hell, which, strictly speaking, was true. But it's not enough just to escape hell. I had committed adultery, of a sort. She said it. She was the "other woman". Never mind I was seduced. Never mind I was drunk. I cheated on my spouse, and my spouse knew it. Yeah, I said sorry. Was that enough? What if my spouse wasn't God but a woman, and she knew?

What if my wife, knowing I had cheated on her, found me at the scene of an accident, sprawled out on the pavement, both of us thinking I was going to die, and I said to her, *I am so sorry for what I did*? Would she forgive me? A decent woman probably would, out of compassion.

But what if the paramedics came, stabilized me, and got me to the emergency room? What if I recovered and life went on? At some point, wouldn't my wife say, *So are we going to talk about this?* Adultery is not an offense forgiven with a wink. Nor would a deathbed apology be enough. If I didn't show my contrition in a real, tangible way—get down on my knees with two dozen roses and a box of chocolates in my arms, bring her breakfast in bed every day for the rest of my life, surprise her with a diamond necklace I had mortgaged the house for, stuff love notes in random places like her shoes and her purse and the cup holder in her car—every little offense after that would act as an X-Acto knife, slicing our relationship until we were irremediably cut off from each other. But even if I did all that, the best it might do is stop the tear from getting worse. I couldn't sew it back up; I couldn't undo my betrayal. Regaining trust could take the rest of our lives.

With God it'd be different. Sure, I still needed to reconcile with him in a real, tangible way. I still needed to kneel down before him, say I was sorry, and let the priest, his representative, tell me what to do—probably not give God roses, but something more significant than praying three Hail Marys. But once I did all that, the tear would close and we'd be as tight as ever.

I watched water bead on the ends of my bangs. The gash was fresh and stung as if it were in my own flesh. I needed reconciliation.

A drop of water rolled from my hair down to the tip of my nose and splashed into the sink. My head was swollen with sorrow and a desire to heal the wound I had inflicted, but that wasn't all. I had been driven to my lowest point, not by hapless circumstance, but by an individual: a person who had enslaved Julie, killed Ashley, and ruined my future.

I gave my reflection a headbutt, then slammed my fist on the counter. I needed confession, but I wanted revenge.

#~ #~ #~

Shaved, dressed, and motivated, I was in the kitchen frying up eggs and hatching my plot when Julie appeared—now in jeans, a loose white T-shirt, an unbuttoned cardigan, and Keds.

"You look ... modest," I said.

She gave me a smirk as she sat at the kitchen table. I returned a warm grin as I laid a plate of eggs before her.

I knew Julie would be key to any attempt to get back at Paul Cardelli. But could I trust her? Was this morning's deluge of tears just a flash flood, or had the tide finally come in? Can someone do a one-eighty that fast? The Samaritan woman did. Saint Paul did. Was Julie another one of those miracle stories? Maybe God had been working on her for a while, and I was just the final tipping point. Either way, trusting her was the only option I could see.

"Sooo ... I was thinking," I said. I poured coffee into her cup, then into mine, and sat in front of her. "You ever see the movie *The Count of Monte Cristo*?"

"Isn't that a book?"

"Movie too—1934, Robert Donat and Elissa Landi. Great adaptation, except for the ending. The protagonist, Edmond Dantès, gets wrongly accused and tossed into prison. He escapes by faking his death, then takes revenge on the people who put him there."

"Hmm, nope. Doesn't really sound like my kind of movie."

"The point is, I've been thinking about next steps. I'm supposed to be dead, right?" Julie nodded. "So, let's fake my death."

She gave me an expectant look: *This'll be good.* "And how are we going to do that?" She slid a slice of egg into her mouth.

"You take a picture of me lying on the bed. No, better: video. You'll tape your phone to your chest. While it's recording, you'll wrap my apparently dead body in the bedsheet, then drag me out the sliding glass doors onto the dock and into the Intracoastal Waterway. Just like in the movie. We'll do it at dusk so it's light enough to film but dark enough so anybody watching won't know what's going on. Then you show the video to your boss or whoever it is you have to convince. We're both free, because I'm dead, and you, well, mission accomplished." I smiled, satisfied with my brilliant plan.

"Seriously?" She squinted at me as if I had suggested we move to a vegan commune in Greenland. "Here's a better idea. See this phone? I snap a pic of your dead body, send it to a preprogrammed number, then destroy the phone. The maids come, take the body, and remove every shred of evidence you were ever here. Yes, the maids. The inconspicuous maid squad with questionable migratory status that no one pays attention to. How does that sound? 'Cause that's how it's done." She shook her head. "*Count of Monte Cristo.* Really?"

I stood and paced, slightly dejected but persisting. "When are they expecting the picture?"

"I have another forty-eight hours to make contact. Normally it's twenty-four from the time I get the phone to the time it's destroyed. They gave me a long leash this time. Guess they knew I'd need time to cuddle up to you." She gave me a sly smile.

"Right. Anyway, we have to move fast. We'll take your car, head back to New York, get information. It's a long shot, but I know this guy in the IRS. Been a long time, but—"

"Chris, stop. What are you trying to do?"

"We have to end this."

"This isn't a movie, *meu amigo*. You can't just show the IRS some accounting irregularities, like my dad is Al Capone or something."

"IRS or FBI. The FBI must want your dad. Your brother Paul alluded to that. They need information, stuff they can pin on him so they can prosecute. What if we get them that information?"

"You want me to rat out my dad?"

"Your father is hurting a lot of people, and he's got you trapped. And me too, for that matter. If he goes to prison, he won't be able to hurt people anymore."

She lifted an eyebrow and gave me that smirk again: *You've got to be kidding.*

"I mean, that's what prison's for, to take the bad guys off the streets," I said.

She rolled her eyes like a too-cool teenager. "Even if you could pin something on my dad, which would be practically impossible, he's got a whole empire he'd continue to control from his prison cell. He's got people in the system."

"So we topple the empire. Expose it all."

Another eye roll as she sipped her coffee.

"There's no other way," I said. "This won't stop unless we stop it."

"What movie are you quoting now?"

"I'm serious."

"You are, and it's adorable."

"Julie, please."

"You don't understand. He's shielded. The organization's segregated; no one knows what the other guys do. There's like three people in the whole world who know how it all works, and they keep it ... complicated. Just to untangle it all, to follow the strings to their ends, is impossible. The FBI tried. They couldn't do it. You think you can do better?"

"No, *I* can't. But *we* can."

She scoffed.

"Seriously. Why are you and I together? Why didn't you kill me last night? You chose to keep me alive. Why? Come on, you know there's a reason. Someone has to do this eventually. You're an insider. You have information the FBI can't get. We can start there."

She shook her head and looked toward the living room, then back at me. "Not enough. I don't have enough information."

"But you can get it. You have access."

"Once they figure out you're still alive, I'm out. All access cut off. Maybe even more than out."

"One strike? That's it?"

"If they think I'm compromised, yeah."

"Daddy's little girl has no pull?"

Another arched eyebrow, this time with a side of pressed lips: *Please.*

I continued pacing. "Any other loose pegs? Someone you know in the organization that we can use as an entry point? Maybe a guy that's got the hots for you. Maybe between the two of you, you could gather enough intel?"

"Loyalty is everything. Betrayal is a death sentence. My dad's been at this a long time. You don't stay at the top that long without knowing everything going on in your organization. He even keeps a psychologist on retainer, if you can believe it. Monitors the ones he thinks are loose pegs, as you call them, to see if they'll fall out. Even I had to see the guy once. What a—"

"That's it," I said. "Psychologist. Connie. I completely forgot about her."

Julie looked confused. "No. Frank. The psychologist's name is Frank. He's so stereotypical: black turtleneck, tweed jacket, disheveled hair. Just needs a goatee and——"

"No, I mean, Connie is this psychologist I know. Sister of a guy your dad knocked off. She's got dirt. Before her brother died, he told me *she knows*. I don't know what she knows, but it's gotta be serious. And more important, she's still alive."

"So that's your in?" she said. "You're going to see what she knows?"

"Nope. *You're* going to do that. I already tried. She hates priests. I think she hates men in general, but priests for sure."

"No. I'm not getting involved. We need to split up."

"Julie, it's too late. You *are* involved. In fact, you've put together a pretty airtight case for your involvement." I sat again and took a swig of coffee. "Exhibit A: There's a time limit on that phone, and unless you send them a picture of a dead body in forty-eight hours, they're coming after you. Exhibit B: You don't have a dead body, so you can't send them a picture. Exhibit C: These people are some-how omniscient, according to you, so there's nowhere for you to hide. Exhibit D: You can't trust anyone else but me right now, per exhibit C. So, unless you want to recon-sider killing me, you're involved up to your eyeballs."

It was Julie's turn to stand. She walked over to the island, picked up her keys, and started to play with them. "Where does she live?"

"Her office is in Peekskill. I don't know where she lives, but I could find out, maybe, through her mom."

"You really want me to go back to New York?"

"Well, that's the idea."

She stared pensively. "I can't fly. They'd see the charge on the card." She was thinking things through; this was good. "Can't take the Mercedes. They can track it."

"They can?"

"LoJack. Pretty common in luxury vehicles."

"Right. Well, there's a car at the house where I was staying. Porsche. It doesn't work, though."

"Yes it does. Just needs spark plugs." She gave me a knowing smile. "I pulled them. Couldn't have you running away."

"I suppose you did something to the generator too?"

"Um, yeah."

"Didn't think that was an accident."

"None of this was."

"Right. I was set up. I know. It's still just hard for me to believe. I mean, can you really control the weather?"

She dropped the keys on the island and walked back to the table but didn't sit. "We'll take the Porsche. It's not theirs. That'll work."

"Well, *you'll* take the Porsche. I'll stay here and wait for Andrew to come back. Then I'll come up with some excuse and get him to buy me a ticket north. Besides, after last night I really need to get to confession, and he's the only priest I can—"

"No!" It came out almost as a shriek. "You can't do that."

"Why not?"

She turned away.

"Julie, what are you saying?"

She circled the island, tapping the granite countertop with her nails. Then she stood behind the chair opposite me. "He arranged everything. I helped, but it was all his idea. Even the hurricane. I mean, we didn't expect it to work. Well, he did; I didn't. I wanted to do it in New York. He said he needed to get you out of your element, loosen you up. Then we heard the forecast, and he was like, I've got an idea. We had a backup plan, but ... Crazy, I know."

The eggs were still on my plate, untouched, cold. I looked at them and wanted to vomit. I put my head in my hands and moaned a little.

"Yeah, sorry," she said. "Not sure how close you guys were, but ... sorry. Normally I get my jobs from Sal. This time Sal had me talk to Andrew. He never told me you were a priest. He didn't tell me he was either. He just told me you'd be difficult to seduce, but he gave me tips."

Everything suddenly fell into place. All the little red flags I was oblivious to now waved at me as if I were in the grandstand at a Communist Party demonstration. "The snowy mountainside cabin, the fireplace?" I said. "I should have been surprised a perfectly tanned Brazilian would prefer a snowed-in cabin over a beachside bungalow. He told you to say that, right?"

"Did I get the bare feet thing right?"

I sighed. "Spot on."

A slight smile of satisfaction crossed her lips.

"How deep is Andrew into the mob?" I asked, still trying to fathom that my best friend set me up to be murdered.

"Don't know. That was the first time I met him."

"It doesn't make sense. What's motivating him?"

She shrugged.

I stood up and walked across the room, then back again. I sat down and got up again. "Julie, he was my best friend," I said, still trying to convince myself. "Do you understand that?"

She flashed sympathetic eyes at me.

In my head I ran through all that we had experienced together, all the things I could have done to offend him, all the reasons he could want me dead. Nothing clicked. I thought of our conversation at dinner in Rome. I had divulged that episode with Timmy Cook. I should have kept my mouth shut. Was he the kid I supposedly abused? Did Andrew bribe some eyewitness to rat on me anonymously?

Julie was patient, letting me soak it all in. She had started collecting the breakfast plates when I said, "Fernand."

"Who?"

"Fernand Mondego. *Count of Monte Cristo.* He was Dantès' best friend, who betrayed him to get his girl."

She sighed and carried the dishes to the sink.

"Well then," I said, "he gets what Fernand got."

"What's that?" she said over her shoulder.

"Never mind. Do you agree we have to get out of here?"

"Definitely. Like I said, we've got maybe forty-eight hours before they're onto us. Maybe less."

"So we go to the other house, get my stuff, fix the Porsche, and take off."

She looked back at me. Leaving the dishes in the sink, she approached, getting uncomfortably close, her eyes meeting mine. "Another question first."

"What?"

"Why do you trust me?"

I didn't, not entirely. But I couldn't tell her that. Instead, I put my hands on her shoulders and bent my head down to hers. "Because I believe in second chances."

26

Fifty Ways to Leave Your Lover

We merged onto Florida's Turnpike in West Palm, and Julie was quiet, aloof. I worried she was reevaluating things. Would her resolve crumble before we reached New York? Then she said, "R&B."

"What?"

"You asked what kind of music I like. R&B. I like R&B."

That started it. A simple question, only slightly more interesting than "What's your favorite color?", was all it took to pull the finger from the dike. By the time we reached Jacksonville, she was downright chatty. She liked cooking, *Pride and Prejudice* was her favorite movie (the 2005 version with Keira Knightley and Matthew Macfadyen), and she had a Chinese crested dog named Fluffy. (She had to explain the irony: Chinese crested dogs are hairless.) I was wary she might be manipulating me again, but then she dropped a personal detail you'd tell someone only if you felt sure he wouldn't use it against you: she did goat yoga. She showed me a picture of herself planking with a goat balanced on her back. I almost swerved off the road.

Sometime in the evening, north of Savannah, she talked about her mom and Christmases spent on the beach in Brazil. She reminisced about long chats with her sister, Lily, and the plans they used to make to run away together. Lily actually did run away, but it didn't go well for her. She died of a drug overdose in a Las Vegas hotel room.

Julie finally opened up more about her father and their complicated relationship. If that morning, in her dejected anger, she could see him only as a power-hungry mob boss who had enslaved her for his own ends, now in a calmer, more dispassionate moment she admitted he had treated her well as a little girl.

She didn't know exactly what he did back then. She knew only that he was rarely around. She remembered when things began to change. The family moved from a one-bedroom apartment in Hoboken to a mansion in Scarsdale when she was eight. She woke up early to the slamming of a car door and from the top of the stairs watched her father stumble in, his shirt bloodstained. Later she found out he had come close to death that night. A business partner had double-crossed him. He had to make a choice: leave it all and start a new life in some other country or seize control and eliminate his rivals. He chose the latter.

He still had a conscience then, albeit warped. He rationalized that if he had to execute people, the least he could do was send them to their eternal reward. And for those who betrayed him, to hell with them, literally. It was something he had heard the old Sicilian Mafia used to do, so he adopted the methodology. He wasn't even Italian. He was Polish. Cardelli was the name of a San Francisco barber he went to once.

He brought Julie into his schemes when he discovered his main rival had a thing for underage girls, and he wasn't blind to his own daughter's beauty.

When she told me this, my mind returned to my sin. Her conversation had distracted me from it all day. But with that last comment, it was back in plain view, as if it sat on the hood of the car. And my heart ached.

🙽 🙽 🙽

We were making good time, and I considered driving straight through to New York. We were both tired from all the expended emotions, so Julie convinced me to stop for the night. "Sleep is a weapon," she said. "That's from *The Bourne Identity*, the book." She jabbed me with her elbow.

We checked into a budget motel in a small town outside Raleigh—separate rooms. I didn't expect much, and my expectations were met: stained comforter, stench of mold, cigarette hole in the shower curtain, and a wall-mounted AC unit that gurgled all night.

I had handed her the car keys the night before so she could take the first shift in the morning. Not smart, I know. We became buddies on our eleven-hour jaunt up the East Coast, but I shouldn't have forgotten she was an assassin. When I knocked on her door early the next morning, she didn't answer. I scanned the parking lot; the Porsche was gone. I found something else instead: two men in suits getting out of a shiny car with New York plates. They walked into the motel office. I had a sense they weren't looking for vacancies.

I shot back to my room, grabbed my bags, and dashed down the emergency staircase and out a fire exit, leaving the door buzzing behind me.

Out on the street, I hoped to see a taxi, or anyone, pull around a corner. But this was a one-stoplight rural town, and it was Sunday morning. No taxis. No cars that weren't parked.

I schlepped about a quarter mile before I heard the sharp twitter of a loose hubcap behind me. Could this be my ticket? I turned, ready to stick my thumb out, and saw Julie driving a green Pontiac station wagon with faux-wood paneling, a relic from the early 1980s.

"Where are *you* going?" she asked as she pulled up beside me.

"Me? What about you? What the heck?" I threw my bags in the back and jumped into the passenger seat.

"Did you lose your phone or what?" she asked.

"No, why?" I pulled my phone from my pocket. Dead.

"I had to switch out the car."

"Just go."

"What?" She picked up on my paranoia and looked around.

"I saw two guys go into the motel office. They're onto us."

"No. Impossible. It's too soon." She pulled away from the curb.

"I don't know. Two dudes in dark suits. New York plates. Sound like your guys?"

"What were they driving?"

"Chevy Malibu. Looked pretty new."

"Could be them. Or could be a rental."

"But how would they find us?"

"What card did you put our rooms on?"

"A prepaid one Andrew left me. I mean, if we're on the run because of him, I'm going to milk him for it. Besides, mine blew away in the storm."

Julie let out an exasperated sigh. "They can track that card."

She ground the accelerator into the floor and checked the rearview mirror. "We gotta lay low. No stops except for gas. We'll take secondary roads, go along the coast. An unexpected route. I've got some cash. We'll pay every-thing in cash."

I looked back to see whether the Malibu was behind us. The grimy rear window made it impossible to see. The side mirror wasn't much better. I examined the car interior: sticky dashboard, evergreen air freshener dangling from the rearview mirror, collection of mariachi CDs on the visor.

"Where did you get this car?" I asked.

"We were too conspicuous in the Porsche."

"I understand that. What did you do with it?"

"I traded it. I gave it to some guy, and he gave me this."

"But that Porsche wasn't ours to trade."

"It wasn't ours to take either, but I don't recall you getting all worked up over that."

"Because I know the owners, and I thought I could explain when it's all over."

"You mean when we're dead?"

"No, when we've provided the FBI with all the information to put these jerks behind bars."

She grunted in frustration. "Don't you see, if we don't play this smart, we won't live to tell a single soul what we find out, if we find anything out in the first place."

I was flipping the ashtray lid. "Well, you could've at least traded it for something a little faster."

※ ※ ※

Four hours later, somewhere outside Norfolk, I said, "Pull off. This exit coming up."

"What? No way. We still have enough gas."

"Pull off, please."

"What's up?"

"I'll explain. Just trust me." She cautiously took the exit.

"Left here." I kept my eye on the structure, towering above the little houses. "Now a right ... at the light, take a left."

"You wanna tell me where we're going?"

Cars lined the street. A father feverishly unmoored his baby daughter from her car seat in the back of a minivan; the mom, with a boy tethered to each hand, charged down the sidewalk. An elderly couple, finely dressed, walked as briskly as their old bones would allow. Coming to the end of the street, we passed the entrance to St. Clarence Catholic Church.

"Church?" Julie said.

"It's Sunday."

"We're running for our lives, and you want to go to church?"

"Precisely."

"Forget it." She clenched the steering wheel with both hands, knuckles white, and accelerated.

I laid my hand gently on hers.

"Just pull into the parking lot so I can show you something. Then we can leave if you want."

She pulled around the block and into the parking lot. It was packed. Last-minute stragglers were darting between parked cars toward the entrance.

"Do you see? Isn't it incredible?"

"A bunch of people going to church. It's Sunday, and we're in southern Virginia. What else would you expect?"

"It's eleven thirteen. Mass starts in two minutes. That's why they're all rushing."

"So?"

"So, we weren't going to go through Norfolk. We weren't going to stop here. I just saw the steeple. I didn't know it was a Catholic church. But it is. What are the chances they have an eleven-fifteen Mass? Not eleven, not eleven thirty. And we arrive just two minutes before it starts? All that is a coincidence? Park the car."

Her face was blank. "All right. But we're leaving early."

❧ ❧ ❧

The interior was traditional, country, newly renovated: mahogany-stained pews sat on dark hardwood flooring; white ribbing held up a peach vaulted ceiling; white wainscoting ran along light blue walls under classical stained glass windows; an ornate reredos crowned a glassy marble sanctuary.

What stood out, because it clashed with the otherwise delicate and tasteful interior, was the crucifix. Oversized and gory, it hung directly above the main altar, suspended by four cables. Christ's knees were gaping black holes, and his skin was lacerated on every inch. Blood on the crown of thorns looked as if it were about to drip onto the altar below.

We stood in the back, next to the door, so we could make a quick getaway in case we were followed. I dipped my fingers in the holy water font and flicked them at Julie. She gave me a look as if to say, *What's that all about?* "Just wanted to see if you'd sizzle," I whispered. She rolled her eyes.

Julie fidgeted through the first part of Mass, constantly looking around, scanning the crowd, checking the glass doors leading to the vestibule.

The priest began his homily. And as all priests do when they hear another priest preach, I was internally critiquing his style. He was good—eloquent, yet not esoteric. His stories were interesting and on point. At one clever turn of phrase I smiled and looked over at Julie. She stared at the priest, mesmerized, tears rolling down her cheeks.

Then it was time for Communion. Everyone lined up, and Julie was going too. I held her back. "We can't."

Her expression, like a little girl about to open her first Christmas gift, now changed to confusion. "Why not?"

"We're not in the state of grace."

"What does that mean?"

"Our souls are too dirty right now. We have to get them cleaned."

And as if I had just ripped the Christmas present from her hands and jumped on it, she said in too loud a voice, "This is a bunch of bull," and stormed out.

I went after her and couldn't get her to stop until we reached the car.

"Julie, please. Just give me a chance to explain."

"This is such crap. Did you hear the priest? He said that line of people in there is made up of sinners. That Jesus is ready to receive us just as we are, that God is a Father who loves his daughter just as filthy as she is. And you're telling me I'm not clean enough?" Tears flowed in torrents.

"Julie, yes, that's all true, but we need to make one step first. We need to confess our sins. That's all."

She got in the car and started the engine.

I opened the passenger door and looked in. "Please. Give it a little more time. Come back in."

She had one hand on the wheel and the other on the gear stick.

"If you're not coming back in, then please wait for me here. I need to go back. Just wait for me, okay?"

"We gotta get out of here," she said without looking at me, her voice cracking.

"Please. Just wait."

🕆 🕆 🕆

Mass was almost over. Another five minutes, and the priest would be out front saying good-bye to parishioners. Another fifteen minutes, and he'd be back in the sacristy changing and chatting with the sacristan. That was twenty minutes before he'd be free. Too long. *Will she wait for me that long?* Then I saw him: an older priest stepped in through a side entrance and slipped into the sacristy. I was a fish in the desert, and he was a bowl of water. I needed confession. It wasn't a desire or a nice-to-have; it was a need. I made a beeline for him.

The old priest was rummaging through a closet muttering to himself.

"Excuse me, Father?" He didn't hear me. "Um, excuse me," I said, louder.

He turned, a look of mild interest on his face.

"Sorry, Father, could you ... could you hear my confession?"

He eyed me up and down as if trying to figure out whether I was human.

"You're not from here, are you?" he said in a slow, genteel drawl. "Where you from?"

"New York."

"Thought you might be. We don't get many tourists round here. You visiting family or something?" The words dripped from his lips slower than Heinz ketchup from a bottle.

"Just passing through. In a hurry, actually."

"Oh. Gotta get going, huh?"

"Yep, that's right."

"This your first time to Virginia?" he asked, pulling a shoe box from the closet and setting it on the counter. A muffled organ blast told me Mass was ending.

"No, I've been here before. Closer to D.C., though. Say, if you want, we could do confession right here. I won't take long."

"I don't get up that way much anymore myself. Took the altar boys a few times, back when we used to do that sort of thing. D.C.'s a nice town, though. Especially in the spring, with the cherry blossoms. Course, the politicians tend to muck it up, if you know what I mean." He pulled some batteries out of a drawer and put them in a wireless microphone, checking to see if they were still good.

I tapped my fingers on my pant leg. "So, should I just go out to the confessional, then?"

"What's that? Oh yes, do that. Make yourself comfortable. I'll be out in a minute or two."

I immediately said a prayer: *Oh, dear Lord, please send the fire of the Spirit and light it under his bum ... or at least grant Julie patience.*

People were streaming out of church. Two small groups loitered near the sanctuary, chatting. I made my way to the confessional: two closets side by side with curtains instead of doors. As I was stepping in, I turned to the back of the church, hoping to see Julie. Instead, the figures of the two men from the motel swam against the current. I yanked the curtain closed and prayed they didn't see me. *They couldn't have seen me. Their eyes were still adjusting to inside lighting. Too many people around; they would have looked at the people closest to them first.* I couldn't convince myself; I knew they must have seen me.

I hugged the wall, hoping my legs weren't visible under the curtain. The next few minutes seemed eternal. The chatter in the church died down. Then I heard voices approaching. Two people, women, discussed songs for an upcoming funeral: the organist and the cantor, I guessed. They stopped right in front of the confessional, unaware of my presence. *Good. Just stay there.* They didn't. They kept moving toward the front of the church.

Suddenly, a hand ripped the curtain open, the light from the church bursting into the dark confessional.

"Oh, you. Wrong side, son." It was the priest, chuckling.

"Right, sorry, I'm used to this side." I took a deep breath and emerged into the church, keeping my head down and scooting around to the other side, as if exposure to the light would burn me alive.

I drew the curtain and knelt down, my face an inch from the metal screen in the wall separating the two sides. The priest flipped a light on. Now, through the screen, I saw his blurry profile. "In the name of the Father, and of the Son, and of the Holy Spirit." He continued in the slow drawl as if he were trying to kill time before a dentist appointment, sometime next week. But now his pace comforted me: I wanted to delay my departure from this space as long as I could. Worrying about Julie taking off on me now was useless. If she hadn't left before those guys arrived, then she was probably dead. If by some miracle they hadn't seen her, she was either figuring out a way to rescue me or had escaped; either way would be fine by me. And if they saw me, then they were being awfully respectful letting me go to confession.

I tried to recollect myself and remember why I had risked so much to be in that confessional. "Bless me, Father, for I have sinned. It's been a month since my last confession."

"You a priest?"

"I'm sorry?" I asked, flustered.

"Are you a priest?"

"Um, yes." Evidently he had understood what I meant when I said I was used to being on his side of the confessional. "But I'm not a good priest. That's why I'm here."

"Must be really bad if you had to come all the way to Virginia to go to confession," he said, and laughed.

I chuckled. "No, that's not the reason I'm here. I was in Florida, and I'm heading back to New York and stopped off here. Anyway, what I want to confess is that I was unfaithful. I slept with a woman. I guess I was ungrateful too, which led to me being unfaithful."

"Pretty girl?"

"Very."

"Seen that before. David. Samson. Heck, Adam, the man himself. A man's downfall is always a woman."

"Well, I don't know. I've been helped by some too."

"Oh sure. The Blessed Mother. She's a woman. A priest can't survive a day without her."

"Yes, but regular women too."

"I know. I know. I'm just tryin' to make light. Take the edge off a bit. What else you got?"

"That's it, really. I mean, I drank too much, which was also part of the problem. I suppose if I hadn't drunk so much, I wouldn't have given in so easily." My knees were getting sore. "Well, I guess I should also confess the desire to kill a friend of mine. Although I never really decided to kill him. I kind of toyed with it. It's a long story."

"Hmm."

"And I swore up a storm the other night. Oh, and now that I think of it, I did seriously think of going on a rampage and killing a bunch of Mafia thugs. They were hurting a lot of innocent people. Not that it would justify a rampage. And it was only a fleeting thought. Well, it lasted a day. I did a little planning about how I'd do it, but then I came to my senses."

"Uh-huh."

"And I think I took the Lord's name in vain too. Once."

"That all?"

"Yeah. I think so."

"Hmm ... well ..." He shifted in his chair, groaned a little. I could hear the clacking of rosary beads behind the metal screen. "Let me ask you something. What did you think of that crucifix out there?"

"Pretty graphic."

"Yessir. It's Spanish, from Spain. I like 'em gory like that, and Spanish people are the best at it. I got it at auction a few years ago through a friend of mine in Seville. Man oh man, it was a bear to put up there." He coughed. "Let me guess: you got yourself into a mess because you're a good fella. You wanted to help somebody, and it went wrong. That it?"

"Pretty much."

"Mm-hmm. And that pretty girl you slept with. You were tryin' to help her too, weren't ya?"

"Yep."

"Yeah, that's right. Still are too, but now you're like Superman with kryptonite around his neck."

"That's exactly how I feel."

"So that crucifix ... you and I see something different from what most people see, don't we? I mean, everybody sees a bloody corpse, a tortured, mangled body. Most people, though, say it's a work of art. They say, 'What a beautiful crucifix.' It ain't beautiful. Nah, nothin' pretty about it. It's disgusting, really.

"Now, you and I know it's supposed to be ugly. Supposed to remind us of what sin looks like. That's what a sinner's soul looks like. That's what *your* soul looks like, Father." He piled his rosary in one hand, then the other, as if it were a Slinky. "Now, you think because you're a priest, you shouldn't look like that. You're supposed to be Jesus Christ himself. You're supposed to be clean and tidy so you can save people.

"You're the doctor of the soul. The doc can't be sick. Am I right?" He didn't give me time to answer. "Well, let me tell ya, as an older brother in the priesthood, you got it all mixed up. Your job is to be Christ for others, all right. But unlike Jesus Christ, you're just human. You ain't divine. Every effort you make to be just like him is doomed to fail, 'cause you can't give what you ain't got. You can't turn yourself into Jesus. He's got to do that.

"But that doesn't mean we don't contribute. Sure, we play our part. Know how we do that? With our sin and failure. That's right. The doc's sick. Now the doc can heal others. Don't look confounded, son. It's Theology 101.

"Jesus became man so that, as a man, he could save mankind. How did he save mankind? By taking on himself the sins of all the world. Like a big sponge, he just sopped it all up. And that's what you see there in that bloody crucifix—a grimy sponge. And you, Father, you became that too. Just like Jesus went into the depths of sin to rescue us, without sinning himself, you fell into the depths of sin to save somebody else. Except, like I said, you're human so you messed it up. You sinned. What Jesus looked like on the cross, you are. All grimy in your soul. But I tell you, in your very sin you latched on to another sinner, and just as Jesus sticks his hand into the grime to pull you out, he pulls her out too.

"Now you gotta finish the job. But not by your puny efforts, son. You got to do it through him, with him, and in him, by the power of Almighty God. You just gotta let him work. Through you. You follow his lead. Don't resist. Do what he tells you.

"There'll be consequences for your sin, that's for sure. Don't shy away from that. Embrace it. You deserve it. Better to suffer the consequences here than in the next life, know what I mean? So yes, don't sin no more. Stay on your game, son.

"That's it. That's my sermon. Remember it. Say three Hail Marys when you get out of here. Now say your act of contrition ... Go on. Say it."

Startled, I began reciting the act of contrition out of habit, then composed myself and said it deliberately, from my heart, trying to squeeze the meaning out of each word: "Oh my God (*my God, mine, the One who created me, nurtured me, sustains me*), I am sorry for my sins (*I am sorry, desperately sorry, for* my *sins, the ones* I *committed, not anyone else*) with all my heart (*and soul and mind and body and every fiber of my being*). In choosing to do wrong and failing to do good (*both choosing to have sex with Julie and failing to protect her*), I firmly intend, with your help (*please, God, help me*), to do penance, to sin no more, and to avoid whatever leads me to sin (*from now on, never again; my life is yours, and I will live it for you*). Our Savior, Jesus Christ, suffered and died for us; in his name, my God, have mercy. (*Amen.*)"

That felt good. Spiritual realities don't often carry physical effects. I pray but don't feel anything; I receive a sacrament, and no tingly sensation runs through me, no buzz like I just drank a shot of vodka. That shouldn't surprise me. This God I worship, I don't see or hear or smell or touch, so why should I expect to feel him some other way? But sometimes I do feel him. And in that moment, as the priest said the words, "I absolve you, in the name of the Father, and of the Son, and of the Holy Spirit," I felt him. My body became light, my vision sharp, my sinuses clear.

I also felt confident. I was ready. The priest left. I stayed. Still there on my knees I prayed three Hail Marys, which was good enough, it turned out. Then I stood, pulled my shoulders back, took a deep breath, and drew the curtain aside.

Stepping back into the church, I saw what I expected: the two men in suits were standing, one at the main entrance, the other at the side entrance. No way in or out except through them. *That's fine. I'm ready. They want to finish what Julie couldn't bring herself to do. I'm ready to go.*

27

With a Little Help from My Friends

"I'm ready," I said to the suit near the main entrance. His friend stood watch by the side door opposite the confessional. "I suppose you want to take me someplace less conspicuous?"

His eyes went wide, probably amazed I was so calm and nonchalant about the whole thing. "Um, we passed a Chick-fil-A two blocks down," he said. "It looked pretty deserted. Does that work?"

"Whatever. It's your show. I thought you'd take me into the woods somewhere. What are you planning? Stick my body in a dumpster or something?"

The other man approached. They exchanged glances. "I think there's been a misunderstanding," said the first. "Maybe we should introduce ourselves. I'm Special Agent McMillan. This is my partner, Special Agent Cress. We're with the FBI. You're Father Hart?"

Wait, what? "Yes ..."

"We've been looking for you for some time. We have a situation we thought you could help us with. Could we go somewhere and talk?"

"Uh ... yeah ... all right. I guess Chick fil-A will work, then."

Peering out at the parking lot from the church entrance, still at the top of the stairs, I surveyed the cars, not finding the green Pontiac.

"Looking for someone?" said McMillan.

"No. Not really. Nice day, isn't it?" It wasn't a nice day. It was overcast and humid. They led me to their car. "Say, can I see your ID? I mean, anyone can say he's with the FBI." As if we were outside a saloon at high noon, they both drew their wallets and flashed them at me. They looked official—gold shield with Lady Justice holding her scales, FEDERAL BUREAU OF INVESTIGATION, DEPARTMENT OF JUSTICE printed in big letters. But I had never seen FBI badges before. For all I knew, they bought them at the Dollar Store. The ID cards had their names: Stephen P. McMillan and Randall T. Cress.

We drove to the Chick-fil-A. It was deserted because it was closed. As New Yorkers, McMillan and Cress couldn't fathom why it'd be closed on a Sunday. I clued them in. We opted for the Golden Fortune Dragon, a Chinese restaurant across the street. It, too, was empty, but open.

We sat in a corner, far from the kitchen. The interior was dimly lit. A big-screen TV had the FedEx Cup play-offs on. A mute waiter left three waters, a takeout menu, and a pen. "Can I get some lemon for the water?" I called out after him.

Special Agent Cress pulled a folder from a briefcase and laid out six photos, all candid shots of men—getting out of a car, crossing the street, sitting in a diner. All were color photos, not black and white like I was used to seeing on cop shows.

"Do you recognize these men?"

I did recognize them. All of them. They were three of the men I had confessed in that room above Stefano's. "Should we be doing this here?" I asked.

He looked out at the empty restaurant, then sipped some water. "I think we're safe. So how 'bout it? Recognize them?"

I stripped the paper off a pair of chopsticks and pried them apart, trying to think of an appropriate response. "Can't say I do." That was clever of me.

"Right, that's what we expected. These photos"—he pulled out another three—"were all taken within a half hour of the other ones." The first set of photos were all different: different people, different angles, different locations. The second set were almost all the same—same angle, same location, same subject: me. The lighting varied a bit—some were taken at dusk, some at night—but all had been shot from a height, through a window, into a room where I sat, purple stole around my neck, hunched and listening. In each of them, only the knees of my penitents were visible, but my face was crystal clear.

"Can you tell me who is in these photos?" Cress asked.

"Do I need to?"

"All right. Here's another photo. Recognize her?"

"Yes. She was a waitress in East Springdale. Same restaurant where you took these photos of me."

"You know she was murdered?"

"Yes. By her boyfriend, right?"

"That's the story. CSI is convinced. We're not. Someone else was at her house that night."

I looked around. "Do I need a lawyer?"

McMillan interjected, "We're not here to get you in trouble. Don't worry." It looked like McMillan was going to be good cop and Cress bad cop. "We've been watching you for a while. At first we weren't sure if you were a willing participant or just being roped in. We understand you can't tell us what you heard these people say. We just need you to identify them as people you were with at Stefano's. That's all."

"Can't do that. Sorry. I know you've got photos of me there, but if I testify, I'd have to say why I was there. I can't do that."

McMillan gave Cress a facial shrug, as if to say, *I tried.*

Cress pulled out another photo. I stopped him. "How about you just pull them all out and stop teasing me like this?"

"Just two more after this." He slid the new photo across the table. "Recognize this guy?"

"Yeah, that's Sal Grisanti. He's kind of the operations manager for the organization from what I can tell."

"What was your interaction with him?"

"He threatened me. First time, it was a veiled threat— basically wanted me to know he knew I was getting curious and I needed to watch it or else something could happen. Second time, I was headed to see you guys, actually. I mean, the FBI. I took the train down to Manhattan, and he found me. Showed me photos of my family all taken unawares. He didn't say anything. It was obvious: I go through with what I had planned, and they're dead."

Cress pulled out another photo. "Second-to-last picture. I suppose you know this guy?"

"Andrew Reese. Reverend Andrew Reese. My associate. Let me guess, in league with Grisanti and the others."

The waiter came back. He nodded at the untouched menus: *Do you want to order?*

"Any preference?" McMillan said, glancing over the menu.

"None," I said. "Well, maybe some Mongolian beef and that breaded shrimp stuff?"

He circled a few items, looked at Cress, who only waved a hand, and then circled a couple more items and handed the menu to the waiter.

"Hey, don't forget the lemon," I said as he walked off, hoping he wasn't deaf as well as mute.

"So, you suspect Reese is involved with the mob?" Cress asked.

"Up until yesterday morning, I thought he was my friend. If anyone was involved with the mob, I thought it'd be Monsignor Leahy."

"No, he's clean," McMillan said. "He used to do your job. That's why we're not pressing you to tell us what the guys said. He explained. Confessional secrets. We get it."

"So what happened yesterday?" Cress interjected.

"What do you mean?"

"You said you thought Reese was your friend till yesterday morning. What happened?"

How could I answer that? I knew the truth about Andrew because Julie had told me. But so far Julie's name hadn't come up at all, not even an insinuation. I couldn't let it slip now. In retrospect it's kind of funny that the one name I was most careful not to let slip was of the one person whose confession I didn't hear. But the agents had one photo left. Was it hers? "Before I answer that, can I ask you how you found me?"

"Your brother," McMillan said. "We knew you were at his house for a while, and then you went to some parish in Jersey, but then you disappeared. We couldn't figure out where you went, so we approached the pastor, a Father Hugh something or other, who gave us nothing. So we went to your brother. He told us you were staying at a house in Palm Beach with Reese. The owner was a Robert Giordano. We found the location of the house, waited for the storm to pass."

"Lucky for us it was only a tropical storm," Cress said. "We got to the house yesterday, late morning. Garage door was wide open. We contacted the Giordanos. They told us about the Porsche, so we tracked it."

"How did you track it?" I asked.

"LoJack," McMillan said. "Pretty common in luxury vehicles these days."

"So I've heard."

"We had to work with Mr. Giordano's wife, Regina, to find it. It was registered stationary at the motel all night, but when we got there this morning, it was gone."

"Yeah, well, a car like that in rural Virginia stands out," I said. "Someone hankering for a joy ride might've helped himself." I didn't lie. I just pointed out possibilities.

"So that's why you were thumbing it?" McMillan asked. "We saw you jump in that old clunker. You almost lost us, but we caught the Pontiac at a gas station not far from here. Driver said she had dropped you off at the church." So they didn't know Julie. Thank God. But who was in the last photo?

Cress shifted in the booth and leaned in, serious. "Let's talk about Reese," he said. "You said he was your friend. What happened?"

"He arranged to have me murdered." I explained the White Death and Black Death rituals and the accusation against me, and then how Andrew had convinced me to go down to Florida, softened me up for the kill, and had this girl try to seduce me. That's when I lied: I said she failed, that I sniffed out the plot before they got me. *Aren't I smart.* I also explained about Andrew and Monsignor's run-in with the IRS six years ago and the irregularities I found just before I was accused. "So, what's the deal with Andrew?"

The waiter arrived with a large tray. He placed a stack of plates and chopsticks on the table, followed by little white boxes of rice, bags of egg rolls, and disposable aluminum trays covered in clear plastic with assorted dumplings and beef strips. You would think if we were dining in, they'd at least put the food on platters.

Cress dumped an entire box of rice and a container of General Tso's chicken onto his plate and began to shovel it in as if he had just been released from a concentration camp. McMillan was more refined: he dished a little bit of everything onto his plate, keeping each item isolated, and used chopsticks like a native. In between bites, they took turns explaining.

"Andrew's father, Harry," McMillan said. "That's the connection. He was a UPS driver in the Bronx. At this one warehouse on his route, he took a liking to a pretty receptionist. Apparently her boss noticed. And her boss, who worked for Cardelli, got her to ask Harry to make some deliveries, you know, off the clock and off the record. After a while, Harry ended up quitting the UPS job and working full-time for Cardelli making deliveries."

"But he moved on from delivering packages," Cress said, a strand from a pea pod stuck in his teeth.

"Human trafficking," McMillan said. "We'll leave it at that. And he got caught. Looks like he's got another ten years still."

"So that's who Andrew visits every Monday, his dad," I said. "And let me guess: he's like Holly Golightly visiting Sally Tomato."

"Who?" Cress asked.

McMillan chimed in. "*Breakfast at Tiffany's*. Sally Tomato was a guy in prison. Holly used to pretend she was his niece and slip him information. Truman Capote. Man, he's good."

"Blake Edwards, you mean," I corrected.

"No, Edwards directed the movie. I'm talking about the book."

"Can we continue?" Cress said. A simultaneous nod from McMillan and me. "The mob's always looking for places to wash their dough, right? They use cash-based businesses mostly—laundromats, bars, things like that. But the volume these guys bring in needs a lot of different venues. Now, charities aren't scrutinized as much. Donations come and go; Uncle Sam doesn't pay as much attention. You set up a foundation with a nice website. It all looks legit, maybe an account in the Cayman Islands or something, and eventually they get their money. Harry introduced his son, the priest, to Sal Grisanti."

"So Reese becomes a new venue for laundering cash," McMillan said. "Except he got greedy. Started taking some for himself."

"Lucky for him," Cress said, "the IRS started catching on. Too much heat for Cardelli's guys to do anything to Reese. Guess they decided to let it all go, and Andy went to Italy. Hey, are you going to eat that egg roll?"

"What? No, here. Take it," I said. "I can't believe Andrew would just start laundering money like that."

"No, they had something on him," McMillan said. "Not sure what. But he was being blackmailed for sure."

"Yeah," Cress said, "could be a relative they were threatening or something."

"What we can't figure out is why he came back and started it all up again," McMillan said.

"That's what we thought you could help us with," Cress added.

I shifted in my seat and gulped what was left of my ice water, crunching on the cubes. "Maybe he thought enough time had passed?" I said.

"Maybe."

Things were starting to come together for me. Once I accepted Andrew had a dark side, I reinterpreted a lot of what I knew about him. Little bits of information I had gathered over the years and stored in mental boxes, which sat on shelves way in the back of my brain, now took on new significance. Slowly I pulled them out and spread them on a table, but the puzzle wasn't quite coming together. Pieces were still missing.

"So, the last photo?" I asked.

"Right, here it is," Cress said. It was Richie O'Brien. "He was our inside guy. He was dishing us tons of information. He'd give it to his sister, Connie, who would pass it on to us. That way he wouldn't get pegged as an informant. If he had met with one of us or tried to mail or email something, he was bound to get caught. But there's nothing unusual about seeing a sister every week."

"Randall Cress," I muttered. "You're Randy?"

"Yes, that's right. Why?"

"I just overheard Connie talking to a Randy. Now it makes sense."

"Yeah, Richie was the accountant," McMillan said. "He had his hands on all the financials. That's how we found out about Reese, or at least it's what gave us the lead. We were really making progress with Richie, just needed a little more, but then they—" He drew his finger along his neck.

"Right. I know. I said the funeral. Okay, so what now?"

"Well, we thought you could help us put something together. We were hoping you could give us something or someone. We need a new in. You're in."

"No, you're mistaken. I *was* in. I'm not *in* anymore. I'm out. Way out. In fact, they're trying to kill me right now."

The agents looked at each other.

"That's right. Actually, now that I think of it, I'm glad you're here, because that's the one thing I can tell you. I'm on the run, and I need protection. Isn't it providential that I should meet you two just when all my options have run out? Oh, and I'll need some clothes because that Good Samaritan drove off with my suitcase."

28

Sinnerman

Cress, McMillan, and I made friends that day. That's what happens when three public servants take a nine-hour road trip together. We started talking sports, then swapped war stories. I told them about roadside anointings, deathbed conversions, and exorcisms. They were most interested in the exorcisms. I ended up telling true ghost stories for over an hour.

Then they told me what I wanted to hear about: stakeouts, counterterrorism operations, undercover drug cartel infiltrations. I figured they were making half of it up, but I still hung on every word.

Somehow we got on the topic of evil people. I maintained that people were basically good but make bad decisions. Evil creeps into their lives, and they get trapped by it, but there's always a chance to escape, always a possibility for redemption. They disagreed.

"Father, that's because the evil people you see all come and confess their sins. They're actually sorry for what they did," McMillan said.

"Yeah," Cress said. "The people we see deny, deny, deny. They lie and manipulate. After one conversation with a perp, you're convinced he's a reincarnation of Honest Abe. Then you see the selfie video of the same guy carving up his five-year-old like a turkey."

McMillan again: "Like that Emma Swenson. She killed her husband and three kids in cold blood. I had that case. I interviewed her. She was a real hottie, even in that orange jumper they gave her in prison. Her voice was sweet as cotton candy, and she had me wrapped around her little finger. And don't think I was a rookie. My partner at the time, a female, she kept me straight."

"Yeah, I remember that case," Cress said. "She had this whole story about how a guy broke into the house, held everybody at gunpoint for hours, and then slaughtered them while she watched, as if he were trying to torture her. Said she didn't know why someone would do that to her. Sounds ludicrous, but when she told the story—I mean, she could cry on demand, it was amazing—you actually felt sorry for her, like you wanted to go find the bastard and take him out. When they finally showed her all the evidence, she was cool as a cucumber. Her whole story fell apart, she was totally exposed, and her reaction was to smile. That's it. She just smiled."

As they went back and forth explaining anecdotally what in technical language might be called malignant narcissism, sociopathic narcissism, or psychopathic narcissism, I kept thinking of Julie. Could that be her? Is that what she was, a narcissistic sociopath?

I was in the back seat, my phone plugged into a charger in the central console. I grabbed it and began googling terms like *narcissism, narcissistic personality disorder, sociopathy,* and *psychopathy,* as well as other forms of antisocial personality disorders. (Interesting fact: *Antisocial,* in the psychological sense, doesn't refer to a person who hides in his basement playing video games, turning down every party invitation that comes his way; it refers to a person who doesn't care about others' rights or feelings, like someone who scams the elderly out of house and home.)

As with most of my own medical issues, after twenty minutes of intense Google research I felt totally competent to diagnose Julie. I read through the descriptions, and they just didn't fit her. For one, she admitted her guilt with specificity. Narcissists apparently don't do that; they can't accept they're wrong. Even if they may make vague apologies for "not being up to par" or "missing the mark", they'll never say "I forgot to pay the bill," or "I cheated on you," or "I'm sorry for what I said because it hurt you." And while her ruse was brilliantly manipulative, her facade dropped too easily in the face of goodness. Sure, she probably had traits of narcissism, but not the type those articles described and especially not what Cress and McMillan were still talking about forty-five minutes later.

As I scrolled through pages of characteristics and descriptions, Julie was little by little being exonerated while someone else was being incriminated: Andrew.

🙜 🙜 🙜

It was Monday. Andrew visited his father in Sing Sing on Mondays. I had to hope Andrew thought I was already dead. I also had to hope he wasn't lying about his post-prison-visit tradition: a gourmet burger and bourbon at Black's Tavern.

I got there early, chose a table in the corner, and sat facing the door. It was a small place, with a brick-and-hardwood interior—much closer to blue-collar than I thought Andrew would ever stoop, which says a lot for the burger. I asked the waitress for two bourbons, neat, and two glasses of water, one with lemon. A burly man, thirty-ish, was parked at the bar, his back to me, an unsightly swath of white flesh where his Iron Maiden T-shirt separated from his jeans. At the far end of the restaurant, an

Asian woman in a dark pantsuit pointed at paperwork, speaking slowly and deliberately, while a young Hispanic man in work boots, jeans, and a maroon hoodie tried to follow what she was saying. It was as close to the O.K. Corral as one could get in Westchester County.

Through the window I caught Andrew's Mini Cooper drive up. I pretended not to see him enter and hang his black fedora on the coatrack and salute the bartender. I scrolled on my phone. Andrew marched straight to my table and sat opposite me as if we had planned to meet at that very spot, at that very hour.

Slowly I lifted my eyes from my cell phone, laid it on the table face down, and stared at him, his countenance as blank as a Degas ballerina's. A fire raged inside me, but I forced myself to breathe evenly and relax every muscle. I was still and appeared calm.

"Christopher," he said with a nod.

"Andrew."

I wanted to stare into his eyes, search them deep—peer past the facade down into his soul, if he had one. And if I couldn't actually read anything in them, I wanted at least to make him feel that I could. It turns out, staring into both eyes at the same time is impossible. I had to pick one. And as I was figuring that out, I ended up switching back and forth from one eye to the other, which ruined the effect. Still, I kept a straight face, lips tight, and waited.

He lifted the bourbon and wafted his hand over it. "Maker's Mark. Decent choice." He set the glass down. "Thank you kindly, but I will not partake. I have given up drinking for the time being. I feel I need a tad more austerity in my life."

"Is that so."

"Yes. I am making changes. I've been through a few things recently that have made me rethink my priorities."

"Have you really."

"I'm thinking of going back to Rome, perhaps. Or elsewhere in Italy. I haven't decided."

"Oh, that close?"

"I thought Rome would be sufficiently far. Have you a better place in mind?"

"Not better. More appropriate. A little hotter, actually. Someone tried to send me there recently. You may know her." My jaw clenched as I said it, unwilled.

He took a sip of water. "Yes. I think I do. Nice girl. Brave."

"Brave? Is that what you call it?" My pulse rose, beating loud in my ears. I wanted to come across as cool and collected, but my jaw trembled slightly.

"She didn't go through with it, did she?"

That smirk. I hated that smirk. I wanted to reach up and rip it off his face.

"I'm sitting here, so I guess not," I said.

"Indeed you are. As you should be. Call me traditional, but I like a happy ending. I think that's why I never liked *Gone with the Wind*. Rhett Butler walking out the door leaving poor Scarlett crying on the stairs. So sad."

"What makes a happy ending, Andrew?"

"You know, the boy gets the girl, the stolen jewels are returned, the good guy lives."

"And the bad guy?"

"To prison, I suppose."

"Or dies."

"Yes, something definitive. Getting his just deserts and all that. But it must be cathartic, hopeful. Something that leaves you with a sense that all's right with the world."

"How's our story going to end?"

"I'm not sure yet. I haven't decided."

"That's right. You always did decide how the story would go."

"I did, yes. It's a gift. Not everyone can be writer *and* director, you know. But I must say, I wouldn't want any leading man but you. I suspect any director would give his gallbladder to have someone like you."

"How long have you been writing your screenplay? Since Rome?"

"You know, it's a delicate decision when to start a story. You start too early, and people get bored. The modern audience wants action. Start in medias res, in the middle of things, they say. Too much scene setting—those long sequences with the opening titles scrolling past—and you lose them." He shook his head, lips pursed. "You know, I recently rewatched *To Catch a Thief.* You remember, Cary Grant and Grace Kelly? Fabulous film, but there must have been ten minutes of opening credits scrolling over a still shot of travel posters. Today Hitchcock would have to cut straight to the woman in curlers screaming about her stolen jewels.

"So, how about me being blackmailed by the mob? That's a good place to start," he said. "The dilemma: What's Father Reese to do? He's been at St. Philomena's less than a year. He reluctantly complies at first. Receives a few donations, makes them look as legitimate as he can. But they want more and more, and one can only do so much, prudently. But the blackmail, this sword of Damocles they hang over him, makes it impossible to say no. Nice setup, right?

"So Father Reese makes a little error, on purpose. They thought it was Monsignor, but it was I. The plot thickens ... The IRS gets involved ... Father Reese gets a full ride to Rome and much more." He flashed his TAG Heuer watch, then pulled out his car keys, twirled them on his finger, and put them back. "But you know, they just wouldn't leave well enough alone. Fast-forward a few years. Scene: Interior. Rome. Dark, musty cellar of a restaurant. The blackmailers present a new scheme. Father Reese wants nothing to do with it, but what can he do? Enter Father Christopher Hart."

"So it was in Rome," I said.

"Yes, but I knew I'd have to change the script as we went along. Did you know that's how *Casablanca* was made? They changed the screenplay daily during filming, and now that movie is considered one of the best of all time.

"My original screenplay had me back at St. Dominic's pretending to be the best money launderer in town. Cardelli's highest rate of return—" He stopped suddenly. "You know his name's not really Cardelli? It's some Hungarian or Polish name. Cardelli was his tailor or something when he lived on the West Coast."

"Yes, Polish. And it was his barber."

"Good. Anyway, where was I?"

"Highest rate of return."

"Right. So how would I get them such a great return? By supplementing from what I was taking from the other crime families, who would watch their money go to Cardelli and suspect the larceny was his doing. But I never got that far.

"You see, I found out my roomie was involved. I couldn't believe it. My own dear Saint Christopher involved with the mob? Oh, I know, I know. You weren't actually doing anything illegal; you were just the priest on the payroll to ease their consciences. You know Sal Grisanti asked me to keep tabs on you? But you were a good boy, so it was easy, until you decided to go to the FBI. You really shouldn't have done that. I had to tip off Sal and his boys. What could I do? No harm done, though. Just a little scare from Sally.

"But you wouldn't give up. You had to go see young Paul at his restaurant. That was a hoot. I knew he'd surely send you packing once he discovered the mix-up, and then, embarrassed and discouraged, you'd throw in the towel. But you told him you witnessed a murder." He put his face in his hands, shaking his head, then popped it up again. "Well, that did it. That brought the wrath of old Paul Senior down on you. You weren't going to last twenty-four hours. Do you realize you could have died?

"So I interceded. I said, 'Pauly, you cannot kill a priest. You'll go beyond hell for that one. My boy Christopher won't say a word, I promise. Sal scared him half to death; how is he going to rat out old Pauly? No, just leave him alone and he'll be fine.'

"But of course he couldn't. He set up that abuse accusation. He thought they'd send you to some convent where you'd be locked up the rest of your life. Shows how much he knows about the Church. Then, when he found out you had been put on administrative leave and couldn't perform your priestly duties, he thought you were fair game. So he ordered the Black Death.

"I interceded again. I wasn't going to let my dear friend perish. I said, 'Pauly, let me take care of this.' Cardelli's idea was to get someone to seduce you. I knew that was a nonstarter. I told him, 'Christopher doesn't have a sensual bone in his body. He's all cold showers, hair shirts, and self-flagellation.'"

"I slept with her, Andrew," I said.

"You did. Yes, I was wrong on that point. But she didn't kill you, and that's the important thing. Brave girl. I knew she wouldn't go through with it once she got to know you. I was right about that. And that's the point. You see, it had to look convincing. Otherwise I couldn't save you.

"You know," he continued, "she wanted to do it in New York? Meet you in a bar somewhere. Come on to you, rub up against your leg like a cat, purr a little, get you to pet her, and then go for the proverbial jugular. I said to her, 'No, not my Christopher. He would never fall for that. You can't even get him into a bar. We need something more elaborate. Need to break him down, get him to lower his guard, but slow and easy. It won't be enough to get him liquored up one night. We need to turn up the heat gradually. Then maybe, just maybe.'" His eyes drifted; he was no longer speaking to me. "'Why, it would take an act of God to get him to fall,' I said. And when I saw the hurricane building, it was carpe diem. That became plan A. We had a plan B and C, but plan A worked. The timing was impeccable, wasn't it?

"And talk about an A-list leading man, you! You made it, when you accused me. It was that night on the veranda, just before I was to depart for New York. I felt you still weren't malleable enough. Still a little stiff. I needed something. And then you came out with that accusation, and I had a fabulous opportunity to feign indignation. Yes, that did it. You would feel you had offended me and now your last friend in the world had left you. You would be alone, alone, alone."

"You make me sick," I said.

"Now, that's gratitude. You should be dead, but you're not."

"So let me get this straight. You connived with this 'brave girl' to wear down my defenses, capitalize on my darkest moment, and get me to sleep with her, knowing her plan was to kill me, and I should be grateful?"

"When you put it like that—"

"Was that your plan?"

"As I said, it was all intended to save you."

"That doesn't even make sense, Andrew. How does that even make the littlest bit of sense?"

The smirk returned to his face, and he reached for his once-forsaken bourbon. He raised the glass to his lips and drained it. *He's flustered.* This was my chance.

"That's an impressive screenplay you put together," I said. "But it's missing something. The big reveal in the third act. Something to make the audience say, 'Wow.' So I've got one for you. It took me from Florida to New York to come up with it.

"I figured you had somehow used my little confession back in Rome about Timmy Cook against me. Maybe got the kid to accuse me, and maybe got someone who knew about that relationship to corroborate. But it didn't make sense. Why would you do that? And just as we came over the Hudson, the sight of the Upper West Side inspired me. So I pulled off on 225th Street. Do you remember who lives in an apartment on West 225th Street?"

The smirk disappeared, and the muscles in Andrew's neck tightened. His breathing wavered as if he was trying hard to keep it even.

"Come on, Andrew. You can say the name."

"The Raffertys."

"That's right. The Raffertys. You remember we didn't just talk about Tim Cook at dinner in Rome. We also talked about Mikey Rafferty. You remember that conversation? You were so remonstrative about my getting close to adolescent boys. Hypocrite.

"So when I saw that exit off the parkway, I couldn't help it. I had to pull off. I had my new friends, Special Agents Cress and McMillan, go in while I waited in the car. They asked dear Mrs. Rafferty if a Father Chris Hart had done some unspeakable things to her boy. She said yes. She said only a couple months ago her son had pointed to a picture of me and said, 'He abused me.' She was so happy law enforcement was finally taking her seriously. Fortunately, the FBI agents believed me when I said I didn't abuse anyone but I thought I knew who might have.

"To make sure, they went to find Michael at his apartment across town. You know he's nineteen now? Just celebrated his birthday. Of course you knew that because you bought him the watch he was wearing. A TAG Heuer, a lot like yours. So you bought him stuff and told him you'd pay for his college. That's the price to cover for your abuse?"

"I wouldn't call it abuse. We were friends—"

My fist came down hard on the table. "He was twelve!" The entire conversation had been too loud. The waitress slipped into the kitchen; the bartender washed clean glasses in the sink behind the bar; the Asian lady focused more intently on the paperwork on the table. I was worried about the big guy at the bar. His tattooed triceps tightened, and he was poised to push off. Andrew and I went silent, staring at our bourbon glasses, mine untouched, his empty, and soon the guy relaxed again.

Andrew whispered, "It was a stressful time. Everyone looked up to me as if I were the next Fulton Sheen. I received offers from CNN to be a commentator, for Pete's sake. The pressure to perform, to live up to everyone's expectations—it was all too much. I mean, I had just been ordained. What did I know? Then I found out my father was a criminal. Imagine, the man you admired your whole life turns out to be a mafioso. The pressure was enormous. And Mike—he was clingy, and we'd have fun together. We'd horse around, that's all."

"Horse around? You ruined his life. Ruined. As in destroyed. Do you know he almost committed suicide a year ago?"

Andrew tapped a knife on the table, breathed on it, and polished it with a napkin.

"Is that what gave you the idea?" I asked. "Oh, you didn't think I knew? At first I couldn't figure it out. I could see you paying him to keep quiet, but why pay him to blame me? Then the FBI finished telling me what happened when they visited Michael. Get ready for this one. Michael wasn't alone in the apartment. When they arrived, the door was slightly ajar. Something wasn't right. The agents found two of Cardelli's thugs about to throw Michael out the window. The suicide note, written on his own laptop, had just been emailed to his dad. Something about how he just couldn't live knowing I was at large. Man, what timing. Beats your hurricane."

Andrew shifted in his chair, looking away and tapping his fingers on the table as if he were patiently waiting for me to finish.

"So that's the big reveal for your screenplay," I said. "Cardelli had been holding the fact that you abused Michael Rafferty over your head. You came back to get out from under the sword, as you say, but your little scheme to pit the other families against Cardelli wasn't working. So you figured out another way. When I witness the murder, you see the opportunity. Carpe diem." I grinned. "You know I'm as good as dead. All you have to do is figure out how to make that work in your favor. You come up with the plan. You get Michael to accuse me. But then you see that the cops won't get involved and Michael is wavering—turns out he has a conscience. So phase two of your plan kicks in: you take me to Florida, then fly back for the weekend Masses so you're conveniently absent while I'm killed. You were supposed to fly back down tonight, pretend to realize I'm nowhere to be found, and then report I'd gone missing. A fugitive from justice. Meanwhile, poor Michael Rafferty, abused Michael Rafferty, conveniently commits suicide. The abused is dead, and the abuser is missing. Cardelli no longer has anything on you. All the loose ends are tied up. Was that how the story was supposed to end?"

Andrew licked his teeth under closed lips, a brief sign of life on an otherwise stone face.

I pushed him further: "Was that what happened? Did I nail it?"

He was looking toward me but not at me, his eyes unfocused.

I continued my barrage. "Tell me, did you molest Michael Rafferty? Did you orchestrate to have it pinned on me? Did you arrange for both of us to die?"

"Touché. I like your script better. More marketable."

"Andrew, this is serious. I need you to say it because it's the only way I'm going to believe it. Did you abuse Michael Rafferty and arrange for us to die?"

"Yes." It came out like a slow hiss.

"Thank you." I finally picked up my bourbon and drank it in one slug. Then I flipped my cell phone over. It was recording. For the first time I saw his face go white. "A little trick I learned from Paul Junior: cell phones make great recording devices. But don't worry. You won't get nailed for murder. Just two counts of attempted murder and sexual abuse of a minor."

His body stiffened. He looked down at the empty bourbon glass, then over to the shelves of bottles behind the bar. "I suppose you have law enforcement lined up outside to arrest me, is that it?"

"Something like that. But take your time. You want another drink?"

Andrew stood and dropped the keys to his Mini Cooper on the table. "Take care of her for me," he said as he started for the door. Then he stopped and approached the bar. He laid a fifty-dollar bill on the counter. "That's for the bourbons, Jimmy. And this is for you." He placed his watch on the bar and slid it toward the bartender.

The Asian lady and the Hispanic man stood in front of the door. As he approached, they both flashed badges. The woman read him his Miranda rights, and the man put handcuffs on him. Andrew looked back at me and winked.

29

As Time Goes By

I had hoped my story would have a happy ending. In real life, endings are usually bittersweet, filled with nostalgia and remorse and gratitude and pain for what was lived, and hope and fear and uncertainty about what is to come. Rarely is the line between ending and beginning sharply drawn, and often one doesn't appreciate the ending's significance until it's time to celebrate its anniversary. I was always intrigued by the way the heartwarming story of the prodigal son ends: unresolved. The merciful father forgave his prodigal son, but would the older brother do the same? We're not told. Some stories are better left unresolved.

I was pondering how my story would be resolved as I reinstalled myself at St. Dominic's. The FBI had cleared things up with the archdiocese, allowing me to return. I had the majority of my belongings packed in boxes in the basement and another few trifles in my brother's garage. The packing exercise had been a nice chance to purge, but now, as I rehung picture frames and replaced books on shelves, things looked sparse.

"Something missing, Reverend Pastor?" Monsignor said.

"Oh, hi, Jack. No, I think it's all here. I just have less than I remember. Guess that's a good thing."

"You doing okay?"

"Yeah, I'm okay. You want to come in?" Monsignor was standing in the doorway. This was a new Monsignor; he never waited to be invited in.

"Mind if I sit?" he asked.

"It's called a sitting room for a reason." My banter was lost on him; he wasn't in the mood.

I sat across from him in the recliner my last pastor had bequeathed to me. "I suppose you're going to tell me I told you so," I said.

He pushed up his bottom lip and shook his head. "I'm sorry about Reese. I should have come clean from the beginning."

"No, no. I wouldn't have listened. You think you know someone, right? I still can't get over it, kind of like I'm in denial. Maybe some alternate explanation will come out in court or something."

"Not much chance of that. He's crooked."

"I know it's naïve of me, but I just don't understand. A priest. A man who's submerged in grace, surrounded by all that's holy—how can he do something like that?"

Monsignor pursed his lips. "Yeah, well. That's the Church, filled with saints and sinners, and most people are neither all that saintly nor all that sinnerly—that a word? But I know what you mean. Priests should be better than that."

"I used to think just hearing confessions was enough to keep me on the straight and narrow. It's like a vaccine. Listening to how other people screw up their lives. When the consequences are laid out so clearly, it's easier to spot the temptation and not fall into it," I said. "And miracles. We witness miracles too, all the time. Minor ones, at least."

"So did Judas."

"True, that."

"Betrayed him for only thirty pieces of silver," Monsignor said. "Reese got a whole lot more than that."

"Still, I hope Andrew won't end up like Judas."

"Suicide's not his style. Besides, I don't think they'll get much on him in the end. I heard the victim isn't willing to cooperate. I can't figure that one out. Guess he's scared."

"I heard that too. And on the attempted murder charges, he'll probably get a plea bargain for giving information about Cardelli."

Monsignor patted the arms of the chair and glanced around. His face was more basset hound than bulldog now. "Cardinal's coming. He's speaking at all the Sunday Masses. Wants to clear your name."

"I heard. That's good of him. Joe Palin contacted me; they want to do a front-page story for *Catholic New York*."

"You going to do it?"

"I don't know. I mean, I appreciate the effort to clear my name, but there are parts of the story I'd rather not talk about, you know?"

"I do know. Pray about it. You won't get another chance."

"How's everything else? Rita still giving everyone a hard time?"

I had been away only seven weeks, but it felt longer. Monsignor gave me his report, and nothing had changed at the parish. Rita was still sassy Rita. Gretchen was as controlling as ever. Bea Dunne was left out in the cold regularly because Jerry never arrived on time to open the church. Maria still prayed for everyone.

It could have been seven years, and nothing would have changed. That's the thing about old Catholic parishes in old Catholic cities: New York, Boston, Philadelphia, Baltimore, Chicago, and so many more. They don't change.

There's something homey about that, like my parents' house on Staten Island (before they moved to the condo in Pennsylvania). The same sand-colored couch with the hot cocoa stain on the underside of the left cushion (my brother did it, honest), the same discount Rocky Mountain oil painting in the den, the same apricot Saxony carpet in my sister's room, and the same royal-blue carpet in the room my brother and I shared. Home was home. It was stable. It didn't change.

I had wanted to change St. Dominic's. I had wanted to make it contemporary and inviting to a new type of parishioner. It was a good idea, but one can go too far. I'd be all for pulling the stodginess out of it, replacing the outdated carpets and the pastoral paintings, but at the same time I had a new appreciation for hominess.

How good it was to return to the stability of a home, and how important it is for people to know that no matter what happens in their lives, no matter how much they change, no matter the decisions they make, they have a home in the Church.

"Did they tell you," Monsignor asked, "about that Mrs. O'Brien you used to visit? She passed away two days ago from a stroke."

"You're kidding."

"Two deaths in the same year." He shook his head, then coughed. "That's tough. Funeral's on Thursday. You want me to take it?"

"No, I'll do it. Thanks. I think it's important I be with the family. Besides, I've got some unfinished business with one of them."

That was the bitter part of the ending, which was ripening into a beginning. I had wanted to visit the O'Briens again but had hoped the investigation would gain steam and I could tell Lupita her son was a hero. As it was, she still thought he was just a good accountant who died of a heart attack.

The wake was on Thursday night, the eve of the feast of Saints Simon and Jude. Saint Jude is the patron of lost causes. I knew I would see Connie there, and I said a little prayer to the saint for her. I had no expectations that the death of her mother would bring on some religious awakening, but I hoped she'd soften a bit and maybe explain why she was so evasive with me. Maybe all that I went through could have been avoided if she had just trusted me enough to share what she knew.

"What did you expect, Father?" she said with her customary curtness. We sat in a damask-wallpapered side room at the funeral home, the stifling perfume of roses and lilies hanging in the air. "They knocked off Richie because he knew too much. I was afraid I'd be next. How was I supposed to know you weren't working for them?"

It made sense. She already didn't trust me, and she couldn't be too careful in that cloak-and-dagger game. I didn't fault her. "I just wished we could have worked together," I said.

She straightened her back and adjusted the little pillow she sat against. "I suppose you're right. But I thought if I didn't give you anything, you'd drop it. I didn't expect you to be so relentless. And I do feel a bit of remorse in how I treated you. You're a good man, Father. I saw how you were with my mother. I have been rude to you, and I apologize. It was all to keep you out of things. Perhaps unconsciously, I suspected something like what happened to you, well, might just happen."

"How do you know what happened to me?"

"Randy Cress. I thought he and I were done, but something happened and I needed to call him. That reminds me. I have your suitcase in my trunk. Some man gave it to me. A shifty fellow. Bug eyes, slick hair. Didn't say his name. He caught me coming out of the office. Gave me a scare. He was fidgety, like we were about to do a drug deal. He told me this convoluted story about some woman who had given a ride to a man who was headed to see me. Said the man had left his suitcase in this woman's car. She said I would know what to do with it. I didn't buy his story one minute. I left the suitcase in an empty office till I could get Randy to come and take a look at it. Thought it might be a bomb or something. Anyway, Randy figured out it was yours and filled me in on everything."

"Not everything."

"You mean there's more?"

"I don't suppose the man said where the woman is?"

"No. He was in a hurry. He rather forced the suitcase on me. I wasn't happy about that."

❧ ❧ ❧

I spent some time with Maggie at the wake too. She was in hostess mode, but when I pulled her aside to see how she was doing, the waterworks started. "I just can't get over it. First poor Richie's heart attack, then Mom." Maggie obviously didn't know the true cause of her brother's death. "Why did God do this?" It wasn't the time for theology, not when the feelings were raw like that. I took her hand and told her God loves her mother and her brother more than she does. "I know, you're right. It's just the timing. I guess we were blessed to have Mom around as long as we did. But I mean, having to get that house ready to sell ... it's going to be a job, and I've got three estate sales this month and two townhouses I'm in the middle of flipping."

❦ ❦ ❦

When the last of the mourners trickled out, I walked Connie to her car and got my suitcase. Back at the rectory I just dropped it next to my dresser and got ready for bed. Then my father's voice in my head piped up: *"Do you think the maid is going to unpack that?"* I told the voice I'd do it in the morning, to which he replied, *"Why do tomorrow what you can do today?" Right, Dad, thanks.*

Whoever handed off the suitcase to Connie must not have opened it, or if he had, he wasn't the curious type. Lying on top was a padded five-by-nine-inch envelope with *Meu Amigo* written in round, feminine handwriting. I slid the contents out: a postcard from Rio de Janeiro, blank, with two pieces of notepad paper folded and Scotch-taped to it, and a ring box with a little statuette of a goat. Julie's handwriting filled the pages, front and back:

My dearest Father Chris,

Sorry to bail on you like that. I'm not sure you'll believe me, but I felt bad about leaving you, so I turned around. I thought I'd get gas while you were doing whatever you had to do. Then the FBI surprised me. I knew at that point it was better I just let you go with them.

There was a lot I wanted to tell you in the car, but I couldn't. I didn't know how to put it into words, and I was second-guessing myself a ton. In that church, listening to that priest, it all became a lot clearer, but then I bolted.

You asked me why I didn't escape the life earlier. I wasn't lying when I said I felt I didn't have a choice. I wanted out. I so wanted out. But I felt as if Dad's people were everywhere. No matter where I went, they knew. Whatever I said, they heard. I really felt I couldn't escape.

So I had to rationalize it. I convinced myself I was ridding the world of bad people. That worked for a while, but then I started justifying it differently. I didn't blame myself for what I was doing. I was forced to do it, by my dad. And I felt like every time I sent one of those jerks to hell, I was sending my father there too. So my feelings went from reluctance to desire. I relished the opportunity. Then someone I loved was shot outside a liquor store. Death changed for me. The guys I was sent after were a lot like Terry. And then I stopped seeing my father and started seeing Terry. Sort of like my conscience started speaking again, but I still felt trapped.

Then there was this guy. The last one. A nice guy. He didn't fit the mold. He didn't look at me as if I was something he wanted to chew on. He was sweet and kind and listened to me. Really listened. And I was lying to him. I felt so bad. I was surprised at how bad I felt, because I was so used to pushing through. And then he told me his story. And seeing my life from the outside, I understood how horrible it all was. How twisted. I saw my lies for what they were.

I heard the love in his voice as he spoke about the men he was trying to save, the struggle to do the right thing, to live up to his calling despite the utter loneliness he felt. And when he said he felt abandoned by God, I wanted to grab him and tell him that God was right on top of him, so close he couldn't see him. I could see him, and I could hear him speaking. When you told me about Ashley, it was all I could do not to break down and cry.

And well, you know the rest.

I want you to know I'm free now. I'm completely free. I was a slave and now I'm free. Your friend Andrew helped with that. Who else would they let me confess to?

Death comes for us all, sooner or later. I'd rather live, of course, even if I had to call myself Sofi. But I'm now happy to give my life if it means others may live.

So, here I go again. I have to confess another lie: I told you I didn't have enough proof to get my father and his cohorts convicted of their crimes. In fact, I do have information. A lot. I've been collecting it for years. It was going to be my insurance policy, my Get Out of Jail Free card, if I could ever work up the courage to use it.

The goat thingy in the box is actually a pen drive. Everything the Feds need is on there: payroll, info on shell companies, lists of connected parties, photos. It's all there.

Please know I'm happy. Finally happy. And free. Know that you will have someone in heaven praying for you. May you have many long years saving souls like mine.

Love,
~~Julie~~ Sofi

ACKNOWLEDGMENTS

The first person I should thank is actually three Persons: the Father, Son, and Holy Spirit. People have told me I have a gift for writing; the reader can be the judge. But if it's true, then I must thank the Gift-Giver first and foremost. And while I'm at it, I ought to thank Our Lady, whose gentle presence was felt constantly through the writing process.

Next I would like to thank Father Erik Burckel, my faithful critique partner. His frank criticism and honest feedback saved me from much embarrassment. I admire his patience and persistence as he read through so much early material, some of which, thankfully, never saw the light of day.

Katie Warner has a special place in my heart for her tireless encouragement and the insider's perspective she gave me on Catholic publishing. But more so for the example that she and her husband, Raymond, set for faithful Catholic families. You are truly witnesses of what it means to be evangelizing Catholic parents.

My dear sis, Michele, and her husband, David, have been important supporters of my efforts to write ever since those horrid short stories I produced as an adolescent. Michele and David have been with me from beginning to end, cheering me on, supplying perceptive criticism where needed, and giving me a comfy chair to sit in and a glass of French wine to sip while I finished my final edits.

I am indebted to Amy Harmon for offering to read my manuscript, for spending a couple of hours with me on the phone giving me pointers to improve the story, and for brainstorming titles with me. I think we landed on a good one.

I am also grateful to Katherine Reay for her encouragement, for helping me navigate the publishing world, and for setting the example of a determined author getting her message into the world.

To all my beta readers—Matt and Heidi Brisson, Tom Clements, Joan Kingsland, Nancy Nohrden, Emily Roman, Bernie and Rachel Towne, Meg Whalen, Mary Wolff, and Cathie Zentner, as well as Fathers John Bartunek, John Connor, Patrick O'Loughlin, John Pietropaoli, Paul Waddell, and Bruce Wren—thank you, thank you, thank you! Your sincere feedback improved the book tremendously.

I must also thank my religious congregation, the Legionaries of Christ, and especially my superior, Father John Connor, L.C., for encouraging me to develop my skills as a writer and giving me the time to do so.

I am grateful to the wonderful people at Ignatius Press, particularly Laura Shoemaker, Kathy Mosier, and Father Fessio. It is always a risk publishing a debut novel. Thank you for your willingness to take that risk. In the same line, I'd like to thank Gail Gavin for her thorough copyediting. Sorry for subjecting you to countless comma splices, misplaced modifiers, and pronouns without clear antecedents. What a torture it must have been. Your sacrifice has prevented so much suffering for so many readers.

Finally, I'd like to thank my mother. It was enough that she brought me into the world, but her constant optimism and deep faith have been a light that has kept me going even in the midst of darkness. Thanks, Mom! I hope you enjoy the book.